J.D. STANTON MYSTERIES

A SHIP POSSESSED

Also by Alton Gansky:
J. D. Stanton Mysteries
Vanished
Out of Time

The Prodigy
Dark Moon

J.D. STANTON MYSTERIES

A SHIP POSSESSED

ALTON GANSKY

ZONDERVAN™

GRAND RAPIDS, MICHIGAN 49530 USA

WWW.ZONDERVAN.COM

ZONDERVAN™

A Ship Possessed
Copyright © 1999 by Alton Gansky

Requests for information should be addressed to:
Zondervan, *Grand Rapids, Michigan 49530*

Library of Congress Cataloging-in-Publication Data

Gansky, Alton.-
    A ship possessed / Alton Gansky.
       p. cm.
    ISBN 0-310-21944-2
    I. Title.   II. Series: Gansky, Alton.   J. D. Stanton mysteries ; bk. 1.
PS3557.A5195S55 1999
813'.54—dc21

                                             98-45221
                                              CIP

Interior design by Melissa M. Elenbaas

Printed in the United States of America

03 04 05 06 07 08 09 /❖ DC/ 14 13 12 11 10 9 8 7 6 5

Leaping off cliffs was exhilarating—at least for Jeffrey Thompson. Which was good since he was about to exchange perfectly solid ground for clear, open air.

He checked his rigging, adjusted his harness, and repositioned his helmet. Then Jeffrey took hold of the tubular aluminum frame of his delta wing hang glider, made several quick steps toward the 110-foot precipice, and charged headlong over its edge.

Tipping the nose of the glider slightly, Jeffrey dropped a dozen feet before pushing the metal control arm forward, allowing the large kite to billow with air. Dipping the wing slightly to the right, he rose easily in the cool morning and sailed north.

He was flying too early in the day and he knew it. Hang gliding was best done in the warmer hours when thermals caused by sun-heated air rose from the surrounding ground. Cool air was heavier and had fewer thermals. But he was experienced, having made hundreds of such flights. As long as the early morning skies remained uncluttered, the ocean blue, and heaven bluer still, he would launch himself off cliffs to enjoy the oxymoronic combination of thrill and peace.

The wind gently flowed past the ear holes in his helmet creating a low, consistent whisper which Jeffrey considered his personal mantra. It was an easy sound, like the respiration of a sleeping child. To him the tone was more beautiful than any music. The wind spoke to him, called him, loved him.

His wife couldn't understand this truth. She still viewed him as a child trapped in a mind that refused to mature, or as a male who felt the need to validate his masculinity. But he knew it was nothing of the sort. This was not about machismo. It was an act of simple addiction, the behavior of one who was possessed by the need for unadulterated solitude. In the air, he was as free as the white and gray gulls that shared the currents with him. They were brothers in the air and when he flew, he could see the world as they did. It was this bird's-eye perspective that kept him coming back to the Torrey Pines glider port. Sky above, ocean and sand below, and nothing but openness around him. For Jeffrey Thompson, being airborne was always preferable to being earthbound.

Shifting his weight to one side, Jeffrey began a slow, easy turn that reversed his northerly course south. Now the ocean was on his right and the cliffs of La Jolla and Torrey Pines to his left. Below him, the beach was deserted, but he knew that soon hearty sunbathers, ready to enjoy the unseasonably warm March sun, would make their way down the narrow dirt path that linked the top of the cliffs with the shore.

Jeffrey knew every inch of this beach, at least from the air. It was his knowledge of the area that first made him notice that something was out of place. It was difficult to make out at first, but Jeffrey could see a large, dark object in the ocean just at the invisible line where the saltwater waves crashed in upon themselves. At first he assumed he was seeing a stranded whale. Such things happened from time to time, although not often in San

Diego. But he soon noticed the gray color of the object and its long, straight lines. It was no whale.

Expertly, Jeffrey guided his hang glider over the waterline and waited patiently until he was close enough to take a better look. What he saw made him gasp. He circled the area several times. Each time he passed over the object he uttered, "Unbelievable. Unbelievable!"

He was looking at a submarine beached in the sand—a very old submarine.

Chapter 1

A hushed voice: "Stanton has to be happy with this. After slicing his drive into the rough, then two stroking onto the green, he now lacks a fifteen-foot putt to be one over par. Of course, fifteen feet is a long way, especially over mixed grass with a diverse cross grain that . . ."

"Do you mind?" J. D. Stanton snapped. "I'm trying to play a little golf here."

Jim Walsh cleared his throat and grinned sheepishly. "Sorry, just trying to create a little atmosphere."

"I know what you're trying to do. You're a stroke behind. If I miss this putt we'll be even and you'll have your first and best chance of beating me."

"I . . . I'm hurt," Walsh said, his voice oozing with insincerity.

"Sure you are." Stanton lowered his head, eyed the cup, then the ball. Slowly he drew back the putter and gently swung it forward. The club head made a soft "clack" as it struck the ball. Starting off straight, the ball began a slow curve toward the hole. A moment later it dropped in.

"You are the luckiest man in the world, Captain Stanton," Walsh said loudly. "That ball should have stopped short by two feet, but no, it just kept rolling. And do you know why?"

"Because the universe is centered around me?" Stanton replied with false arrogance.

"There are plenty of people who would debate that with you—including my sister."

"I remind you," Stanton said as he placed his putter back in his golf bag, "that your sister has been my wife for twenty-five years. She's still happy about that, you know."

"That's because she doesn't play golf with you." Both men laughed as they stepped into the golf cart.

"True, she is a wise woman."

"I still think you're the luckiest man on earth."

Stanton looked around the verdant golf course. He agreed. He *was* fortunate, indeed. His whole life seemed blessed, a fact that was not wasted on him. Of his thirty years in military life, four had been spent as a student at Annapolis, fourteen in service aboard or around submarines, and six years as captain of his own Ohio class nuclear sub. The final six years, he had taught naval history at Annapolis. Forty-eight years old and six months into retirement, he spent his days writing history books, reading, and playing golf.

"Well," Stanton said finally, "are we going to talk until it's dark, or are we going to play the final two holes?"

Jim Walsh did not answer right away. He was looking toward the frontage road that ran by the golf course. "That may depend on those two." Jim nodded toward a man and woman, each dressed in standard khaki naval uniforms. They had emerged from a dark blue sedan and were walking toward them.

"What do you suppose they want?" Stanton asked. "They look serious."

"Don't ask me, I'm just a chaplain, remember?"

"Yeah, well, I've been retired for six months. They can't be here for me."

"I bet the fine print on your discharge papers says different."

Stanton sighed heavily. Jim was right; he could be recalled back to duty on a moment's notice, but that was unlikely. Only something extremely urgent could trigger such a recall.

"Well, if they're here for either one of us, it can't be good. When they come looking for the chaplain it means something bad has happened."

"Amen to that," Jim exclaimed.

Neither man moved from the golf cart to meet the two officers, preferring to wait until the last second to find out why the navy had dispatched two of its people to a golf course.

"Excuse me, gentlemen," the woman said. She had a pleasant round face graced by intelligent brown eyes and short auburn hair. Stanton judged her to be no older than twenty-five. Her lieutenant bars looked as if they had just been taken out of the box that morning. With her was a stocky ensign with a ruddy complexion. He looked even younger. "I'm sorry to bother you. We are looking for Captain Julius D. Stanton."

Stanton cringed. He hated the name Julius. "That would be me," Stanton said without humor. "That's Captain J. D. Stanton, *retired*."

"Yes, sir," the lieutenant replied. "I'm Lieutenant Donna Wilcox and this is Ensign Harold McGlidden."

Stanton nodded slightly, but said nothing.

"Sir, I've been asked to escort you to—"

"Perhaps you didn't hear me, Lieutenant," Stanton interrupted. "I'm retired. I'm no longer in the navy. Now I play golf three days a week. This is one of those days, and you're burning my daylight."

"Yes, sir. I understand." Donna stiffened. "Nonetheless, sir, my orders are to present you with this." She held out an envelope. "I am to escort you to the location specified in that document."

Stanton snatched the envelope from the woman's outstretched hand and quickly opened it, barely noticing the bold words *Eyes Only* printed on it. It took only a moment for Stanton to examine the paper.

"Is the admiral inviting you to tea?" Walsh asked with a wry smirk.

"Hardly," Stanton replied solemnly. "It's an invitation, sure enough. I'm being recalled to active duty."

"Does it say why?" Walsh inquired sympathetically.

"Not specifically, no."

Donna cleared her throat. "Excuse me, Captain, but those orders are secret and for your eyes only."

"I'm aware of that, Lieutenant," Stanton retorted sharply. He was angry and frustrated by the recall. "This is Lieutenant Commander Jim Walsh. Please don't insult the chaplain to his face."

"Yes, sir," Donna responded. "No insult was intended. It's just that—"

"It's just that you're doing your duty." Stanton softened his tone. "I can't fault you for that." Turning to his brother-in-law, Stanton continued, "It looks like the game's over, Jim. They're pulling in my leash."

"I understand. Just as well, I was going to beat you anyway."

"Not in this lifetime," Stanton snorted. Addressing Wilcox and McGlidden, Stanton said, "Very well. Meet me at my home. I'll change into my uniform—"

"Begging the captain's pardon, but we've taken care of that," Donna said. "We first went to your home looking for you. Your wife was good enough to provide us with a uniform."

"My wife gave you one of my uniforms?" Stanton said with surprise. "You actually had the audacity to tell her that I've been recalled and then to ask for a uniform?"

"Yes, sir."

Stanton looked the lieutenant over. "I don't see any bruises. You seem to have come through that unscathed."

"Yes, sir. She was very gracious to us." Donna smiled. "But if I may, sir, I would suggest taking flowers with you when you return home."

"Saving it all for me, is that it?"

"I can't be sure, sir, but flowers never hurt."

Stanton laughed. "I'll take that under advisement. Take me to the clubhouse; I'll change there."

"Very good, sir." Donna and McGlidden stepped aside to allow Stanton to walk to the car.

Turning to his brother-in-law, Stanton said, "Why is it I feel that this is going to be a very long day?"

"Instinct," Walsh said. "I'll take care of the clubs and the cart; you take care of yourself."

N
⋏

Stanton stood looking at himself in the mirror. Despite not having worn the khaki uniform in half a year, it still fit. He would never admit it to the two naval officers who waited in the hall outside, but he enjoyed the feel of the uniform. Despite his protestations about being called back to duty, he missed the daily routine of the navy. He missed giving and receiving salutes, he missed the missions, but most of all he missed the sea.

While many sailors complained about the required WES-PACS that bound them to six-month excursions at sea, Stanton relished it. He did not miss land, did not miss the city. All that he ever missed was his wife whom he loved dearly. He knew the months he spent at sea were lonely and difficult days for Peggy, but she was resilient and never complained.

The very weight and feel of the uniform made Stanton feel good. He had always liked the way the cut, the emblems, and the color made him look. At middle age, he was still trim and fit. The gray in his short, dark brown hair was just enough to make him look refined and experienced without appearing old. His hazel eyes still sparkled, still beamed intelligence and confidence.

A knock on the door jarred Stanton's mind back to the moment.

"How are we doing, sir?" It was Donna's voice.

Instead of answering, Stanton stepped briskly from the men's room. His two escorts immediately came to stiff attention.

"As you were," Stanton said. "Let's get this over with." He walked down the aisle to the country club dining room and out the entry doors, Wilcox and McGlidden close on his heels.

N
Λ

August 1, 1943
150 nautical miles northeast of the Azores

Richard Morrison was angry.

Concussion.
Rocking.
Lurching.

An ear-ringing noise reverberated down the metal cylinder in which Morrison stood.

It shouldn't have happened, Morrison thought. *It was a bonehead mistake—my bonehead mistake.* Looking up from the fingernail

14

he pretended to nonchalantly clean, he looked at the men who surrounded him. Each gazed at him with anxious eyes, awaiting any words that came out of his mouth. He said nothing, returning his gaze to the chosen fingernail.

He wanted desperately to reach up and pinch the bridge of his nose, or to rub his eyes, but that could be interpreted as nervousness or even fear. Although such an interpretation would be correct, it would send the wrong signal to his crew, something he did not want to do. He had to appear unflappable.

Concussion. Once again, Morrison was rocked back and forth. The sharp sound pierced his ears and made his head pulse with pain. The deep underlying rumble that accompanied the concussion vibrated through him, threatening to liquefy the very marrow of his bones. He and his crew were in hell.

"Depth?" he asked quietly.

"Passing one-five-zero," came the loud reply. Answering was a sailor in the control room who Morrison knew could not be over nineteen years old. The lad was scared stiff; fear oozed through his words.

"Very well," Morrison said calmly. "Water temperature?"

"Five-three degrees and dropping steadily."

"Maintain crash dive until two-two-five feet, then ease the bubble to zero. They should have lost sonar by then."

"Aye, Captain, maintain dive to two-two-five feet."

Creaks and groans echoed off the metal bulkheads as the water pressure compressed the submarine's skin.

"Two more splashes, Captain." The words came from a sweaty sailor who monitored the hydrophones.

Morrison could feel his crew tense. Each one knew that more depth charges were on their way, and if they exploded close enough to the USS *Triggerfish* they could cause severe damage, maybe even send her to the bottom with her crew encased in the hull of a massive metal coffin. An explosion just fifty feet away could cripple the boat; twenty-five away the blast would be lethal. Their remains would never be recovered.

It had happened to many others before. Already the United States had lost over twenty submarines. In each case an epitaph was written in the record books: "Overdue and presumed lost."

The words appeared in Morrison's mind like the credits at the end of a Betty Grable movie: "USS *Triggerfish*, overdue and presumed lost." Sixty-five brave men overdue and presumed lost; six officers, overdue and presumed lost; scores of wives, children, parents, and sweethearts left to wonder at the final fate of those whom they loved.

It was that last thought that most bothered Morrison. He had been in tough situations before. He had even had to endure depth charges before, but in those times he had endured knowing that his life was right and that he had taken care of matters that would arise in his death.

This time was different. He had left something undone, words unspoken. Morrison had always been a family man. He loved his role of husband and father and had taken great care to protect his family from disruption and anxiety, at least the best he could during a world war. But the day he shipped out, he and his wife had a rare argument. Morrison was tense about the upcoming mission; he hadn't slept well and was feeling slightly ill. His wife Sandi, a normally quiet and reserved woman, had been pressing him on some matter that he considered unimportant in light of his departure. Now for the life of him, he couldn't remember what it was she wanted. All he remembered was snapping at her and she returning words of like kind. Soon they were shouting, their hot words permeating the small navy house with anger.

Morrison had stormed out of the house, his duffel bag over his shoulder. As he looked back he saw his wife in tears and their four-year-old son standing at the door. He turned his back and walked away.

That image haunted him every hour he had been at sea. Once his anger had settled, he realized the foolishness of the argument and recognized its source as simple fear. He was afraid he would never hold his wife in his arms and never see his boy grow. She had been fearful that her husband might lay entombed in a submarine at the bottom of the Atlantic Ocean. Instead of facing those fears they had argued.

Morrison felt the perfect fool. He wished with all his might that he could have those moments to live over again. There would be no argument, only embraces, hugs, and kisses.

Concussion.

The lights flickered, blinked out for a moment, then returned. A second later another explosion. The submarine rocked harshly, causing the crew to frantically grab for any support possible to keep themselves from falling headlong into a bulkhead.

Morrison heard his executive officer swear in the control room one deck below him. "This guy really knows what he's doing."

"Splashes."

The exec swore again.

Not only had Morrison left home under the worst possible conditions, he was also responsible for their present danger. It had been a mistake, the kind of mistake that a junior officer would make, not something a seasoned captain on his third patrol would do. They had been bearing down on a German supply convoy and, in keeping with their general orders to sink any and all enemy ships, had taken a depth of fifty-five feet. Through the periscope, Morrison had counted the number of ships in the convoy. It was a small one with a troopship, a tanker, and a supply ship, as well as two smaller craft. All of this was led by a warship fore and aft.

Plotting torpedo solutions based on the bearings given by Morrison, the crew targeted the trailing warship. The idea was simple: kill the aft warship, then take a new bearing on the lead ship which would attempt to circle back on the sub. Two torpedoes for each would leave two more in the bow tubes for one of the supply ships. Once those "fish" were in the water, Morrison would call for a crash dive, level off deep allowing his crew to reload the bow tubes, and then they would again assume periscope depth. If possible they would begin a pursuit of the remaining ships.

It was a good tactic and would have worked well had not Morrison's mistake and bad luck short-circuited the plan. Morrison's blunder had been an elementary one. Normally when the periscope broke the surface, Morrison would check for ships by making a 360-degree search. But when he had looked through the periscope, he immediately saw the convoy, and forgoing normal procedures he began issuing attack commands. Had he searched the entire horizon he would have seen yet another ship, a German destroyer, bearing down on them from close range.

Still the plan might have worked if the MK–14 torpedoes fired had exploded instead of impacting the side of the target with an impotent thud. He wished his boat had been equipped with the more reliable MK–18 torpedoes. Too many men had died because of faulty magnetic detonators.

A third of the *Triggerfish*'s crew was new, including the radar operator who took a few minutes too long to note that the smudgy blip on his screen was a ship closing on their location. When he did realize the significance of what he was seeing he shouted a warning:

"Conn, sonar, target bearing one-eight-five and closing fast."

Morrison immediately spun the periscope around. What he saw made his stomach turn: the bow of the destroyer making thirty knots right at them.

"Down scope," Morrison shouted. "Crash dive."

The exec relayed the command and added: "Take her deep. Fifteen degree down bubble. All ahead full. Dive! Dive! Dive!"

The Klaxon belched its dive call. Immediately the ship, directed by its bow planes digging into the water, dipped sharply down.

Issuing more commands, Morrison barked, "Rig for collision!"

Throughout the Gato class submarine, men scrambled to shut hatches and to take positions. In the maneuvering room seamen pulled levers that would crank the electric motors to full speed. On the surface the *Triggerfish* could make twenty-one knots with all four of its diesel engines churning. Submerged, however, her top speed was limited to nine knots.

Five minutes later the word came that splashes were heard on the surface. The sensitive hydrophones were picking up the sound of explosive depth charges hitting the surface and beginning their deadly descent.

"Hard right rudder!" Morrison commanded.

"Aye, hard right rudder," came the reply from the control room.

The first explosions were too far away to cause physical damage, but the sound alone shook the crew. Fortunately, the destroyer did not yet know the *Triggerfish*'s depth or bearing. Morrison's hope was to dive deep enough to lose the surface ship. The water became colder the deeper the sub traveled. If the submarine could drop below a cold thermal layer, then the destroyer's sonar would be reflected back without revealing the *Triggerfish*'s position. The density of the cold water would surround the sub in a blanket of protection.

Ping!

Ping! Piiiiing!

Sonar from the surface had found them. A crewman began to swear unrelentingly. The executive officer, Steve Sapolsky, shot him an angry glance that carried more meaning than any words could. The sailor immediately fell silent.

Although Morrison and his crew were well below periscope depth, he could still see in his mind the activity on the surface. One of the battleships would circle back to help the destroyer track and sink their prey. That meant that many more depth charges would soon be on their way. It was a cat and mouse game, and the *Triggerfish* was the mouse.

In review, some would call this a comedy of errors: torpedoes that would not detonate, a captain who made a fundamental mistake, and a radar man who failed to see a target. Except there was nothing comedic about the situation. Each underwater explosion rocked the submarine violently and each concussion was felt with teeth-jarring intensity.

There was only one goal at this point: survive. If they were lucky their craft would remain functional and they would not have to return to port for repair. If they were unlucky, then there would be nothing to repair and they would all be dead—buried in a grave of cold, dark seawater, the surface with its warmth and air eight hundred feet above.

Morrison's mind raced back to that recurrent image of his wife, eyes red from crying, and his son standing in the doorway, thumb resolutely stuck in his mouth, as Morrison walked away in a huff. That was no way to part. As far as he was concerned, he had to survive if only to make amends.

"Depth?" Morrison asked firmly.

"Passing two-double-zero."

"Very well," Morrison replied with a nod, then to his executive officer he said, "Secure for silent running."

"Aye," the exec repeated then barked the related orders. "Secure for silent running. Bring us level at two-two-five feet, ahead slow. Rudder amidships."

The *Triggerfish* slowed as it leveled in the dark, cold waters. Throughout the boat crewmen began shutting down all machinery that might make noise that could be radiated through the hull and heard by the enemy "on the roof" 225 feet above them. Even the circulation system was shut down so that its fans would not give away their position. Then every man stood silently in place. When essential words were uttered they were done in the quietest possible whisper.

"Splashes." The words were spoken breathlessly. "Sound distant."

Moments later the sound of two depth charges, conducted by the thick seawater, rattled through the sub. This time, however, there was no rocking. The explosions were too far away.

"All stop," Morrison ordered.

"All stop, aye!"

The exec leaned forward toward his captain and whispered, "You don't want to take her deeper? We're capable of greater depth."

"I know that," Morrison said quietly. "I'm betting they know it too. They'll assume that we'll level off just above our crush depth. If they do, the depth charges will drop below us."

Sapolsky nodded. "Now what?" he asked.

"We wait," Morrison replied softly. "Now we wait."

N
Λ

Stanton spent several moments taking in the sight before him. He blinked repeatedly, unwilling to believe his own eyes. "This is a joke, isn't it?" he asked no one in particular.

"No, sir," Lieutenant Donna Wilcox said evenly. "It's not a joke. It's not a drill. It's not a test. It is the real thing."

Stanton continued staring.

"It's a submarine, sir," Donna offered.

"I know it's a submarine, Lieutenant. I write books about naval history; I skippered a submarine for a lot of years. I know a submarine when I see one."

"Yes, sir. Sorry, sir."

"Of course," Stanton said, softening his tone, "I never served on anything like that. It's a museum piece."

There were a few moments of silence as Stanton took in the long straight lines before him. The tide was moving out, revealing more of the sleek shape that peered through the waves. Its bow was sharp and angular, unlike the modern teardrop shape that was standard on nuclear submarines. Its conning tower, which leaned slightly to one side, was boxy and cluttered with periscopes, antennae, radar dish, and lookout stations.

"Incredible," Stanton offered.

"It's a little before my time, sir," Donna replied.

"It's a lot before both our times," Stanton said, walking closer to the shoreline. "She's magnificent, but her kind went out of service over four decades ago."

"Yes, sir."

"Look at her, Lieutenant," Stanton said like an auto collector eyeing an antique car. "Improved Gato class. They were the workhorse of World War II. They were a masterpiece of nautical engineering for the time. Quick on the surface and deadly underwater. Long range too. If you had to be on a submarine during the war that was the type to be on." Stanton chuckled. "They even had air-conditioning."

"I wouldn't know, sir," Donna replied. "I never understood the wisdom of getting on a boat that sinks on purpose."

Stanton glanced at the lieutenant next to him. He knew that she was not a submariner from the moment he met her. Not only because she was a woman and women didn't serve on submarines. That observation was obvious. But there was something that went beyond gender. An officer who earned the submarine logo of two dolphins bracketing a submarine always wore them proudly.

"Fill me in, Lieutenant," Stanton said firmly.

"At 0645 this morning a Mr. Jeffrey Thompson was hang gliding when he spied the sub aground here on Torrey Pines beach. He called SUBCOMPAC and made a report. The Coast Guard was notified as were the local lifeguards. Between them and the San Diego Police Department the area was secured before the beach crowd arrived. This being March the crowds are minimal, especially here."

Stanton nodded. He had been driven to the top of the cliffs overlooking the beach and then began the slow and slippery trek to the shoreline, leaving Ensign McGlidden with the car. His highly polished shoes were now covered in dirt and sand. This was not an easy place to reach, and for that he was thankful.

"After the area was secured, my commander sent Ensign McGlidden and me in search of you. He felt that with your experience and understanding of naval history, you would be the best one to oversee the investigation."

"I'm honored," Stanton said with a slight touch of sarcasm. He was, however, glad he had been called. Just seeing the old submarine was a thrill.

"Has anyone been aboard yet?" he asked.

"No, sir," Donna replied. "We were awaiting your orders."

"Do we have an identification?"

"We're working on that. All we have is the designation SS–210."

"The *Triggerfish*," Stanton said, bewildered.

"Excuse me, sir?" Donna said with amazement. "You know the name of the sub?"

"I know more than that," Stanton explained. "The *Trigger-fish* was Captain Morrison's boat. He was her skipper when she went down in 1943. Exceptional man."

"Went down?"

"Well, she was believed to have been lost in August of 1943. Her last position was a couple of hundred miles north or northeast of the Azores. She never came back."

"It looks like she just has."

"Yeah, over fifty years late."

A tall, imposing man in a Coast Guard uniform trudged through the sand toward Stanton and Donna. He held his head high as if attempting to ignore the little plumes of fine powdery sand that were kicked airborne with each step. It was difficult, Stanton decided, to look dignified when walking through sand.

Upon reaching the two, the Coast Guard officer offered a sharp salute to Stanton, who returned an equally crisp response. Although the Coast Guard was assigned to the Department of Transportation during times of peace, military courtesies still held across service lines.

"I'm Commander Ira Stewart, U.S. Coast Guard," the man said in words delivered as sharply as his salute. "I take it that you're Captain Stanton."

"Correct."

"I'm your liaison with the Coast Guard," Stewart said. "I've been ordered to support you in any way possible."

Stanton looked the man over briefly. He was taller than Stanton by three inches, stately, and possessed a self-confidence and dignified intelligence that made him look as if he should be smoking a pipe. There was a hint of gray in his hair that augmented his warm gray eyes. His quick smile and easy delivery contrasted with his sharp, angular features. Stanton judged him to be a man that was quick to laugh, but who took his work seriously. He felt an instant rapport with him.

"Pleased to meet you, Commander," Stanton offered. "This is Lieutenant Wilcox. She is . . ." Stanton paused for a moment and looked at Donna, perplexed. "What exactly is your function here, Lieutenant?"

"Personal aide, sir," the young officer answered. "I'm your personal aide."

"She's my personal aide," Stanton said with a wry smile. Stewart reflected the grin and nodded at Donna. "You were the first on the scene?"

"Correct," Stewart replied, turning to face the bulky metal enigma stuck in the mire. "We immediately set up an ocean perimeter with one cutter and several smaller craft patrolling just beyond the breakers. We also stationed some men along the beach to make sure no one approached the sub. As you can see, the navy sent a few marines to secure the shoreline."

"Has anyone actually been on the sub?" Stanton asked.

"No. We have orders not to approach. Besides, most of the deck was still underwater at the time. If we had opened one of the hatches we would have flooded the interior."

"Good," Stanton uttered, walking toward the shore.

"Good?" Donna asked. "Shouldn't we get on the boat as soon as possible? I mean, what about the crew?"

Stanton shook his head. "Too much is at stake. The only people I know who use ancient subs like these are third world countries. For all we know, some terrorist could have planted explosives or worse on that boat and is just waiting for us to open a hatch."

"What could be worse than explosives?" Donna asked.

"Chemicals. Biologicals. Many things really," Stanton said.

"As far as the crew is concerned," Stewart joined in, "they're most likely not in there. If there was anyone on board, they have either left under the cover of darkness before she beached, or they are all dead."

"But it doesn't make sense," Donna continued. "How would a terrorist get hold of a World War II submarine?"

"There are any number of countries that would sell a surplus sub for the right price. Although that's not likely in this case."

"So what do we do now?" Donna inquired. "I mean, we have to do something, don't we?"

"Yes," Stanton answered patiently. "But we are going to do it step-by-step and with the greatest care."

N
↑

Without the benefit of forward motion the *Triggerfish* slowly rose through the ocean depths. The easiest solution to the problem would be to order all ahead slow. The bow planes would then force the nose of the craft down into the depths. But starting the engines meant the sub ran the risk of detection, and that could be the end of its crew. Morrison had convinced himself that he was through making mistakes.

"Depth?" he asked quietly.

"One-three-five feet and rising slowly," came the whispered reply.

"Time?"

"One hour ten since the crash dive, sir."

"Very well," Morrison replied, then turned his attention to the sailor monitoring the hydrophone. "Anything?"

"Nothing, sir."

Thirty minutes ago the same sailor had informed Morrison that he could hear the propellers of both surface ships moving away.

The air was becoming heavy with the smell of men. With the circulation system shut down, the filters could not properly convert carbon dioxide into oxygen. Nearly eighty pairs of lungs struggled to seize their share of the diminishing breathable air.

Enough was enough, Morrison decided. There was a chance that a mistake had been made and that one or more of the attack ships still hovered above them like deadly, steel blimps ready to send the *Triggerfish* to the bottom the moment she broke silent running. Still, the odds were low that such was the case. Most likely the hydrophone had correctly relayed the truth of the matter: the destroyer and warship were gone.

There was only one way to find out.

"Take us up, Mr. Sapolsky," Morrison said aloud. His voice sounded strange in the silent sub. "Make it periscope depth."

"Aye, sir." Turning, he commanded, "Secure from silent running. Three degree up bubble; ahead slow. Let's stay alert. This may not be over."

Men who had held their silence for what seemed an eternity began to chat idly. The sound of the prattle was a welcome relief to the suffocating blanket of reticence they had all been forced to wear.

A wave of relief washed over Morrison as he realized that the danger was past. He and his crew had survived, overcoming mistakes and bad luck. His thoughts ran to his family. He wished he could pick up a phone and hear their voices. That was impossible. Later, he could take time to write them, but it could be weeks before he could send or receive a letter.

Part of him hoped that the *Triggerfish* had sustained sufficient damage to require a return to port; another part of him felt stabbing pangs of guilt at just the thought. He had a job to do; he had been commissioned to fight for his country. But he was human, and no captain's insignia could remove his emotions. In battle he could be as cold and firm as the steel hull that surrounded him, but even that hull could fold beyond its crush depth.

"Periscope depth, sir," Sapolsky said.

"Very well, Mr. Sapolsky. Up periscope." A crewman pushed a lever that activated the hydraulic lifts that would raise the sighting device through fifty-five feet of murky Atlantic.

Pulling down the control handles, Morrison draped his right arm over one and held the other tightly in his left. Spinning quickly around the axis of the periscope, he made a quick survey of the surrounding sea. Not wanting to repeat his previous mistake, Morrison took another sighting, this time more deliberate.

"Seas are calm, two-foot swells at most. No targets visible." Morrison's words were calm and professional, but his heart was racing. They had really made it. "Sonar?"

"Sonar clear, sir."

"Very well. Surface. Mr. Sapolsky, please make sure that we're clear on the SJ and SD radar. I don't want some plane or ship unloading on us now."

"Aye, sir."

"Once we're on the surface, have the chief-of-the-boat compile a complete damage report."

"Aye, sir."

"Once we're clear on the radar, then let the men take turns topside. I think they might like some fresh air."

"Yes, sir, I'm sure they would appreciate it."

"You have the conn, Mr. Sapolsky," Morrison said soberly. "I'll be in my quarters . . . writing a letter."

Morrison's quarters consisted of a small desk, a single bunk, and a sink all crammed into a space only slightly larger than the walk-in closet of his home. On the walls were a rack for books, an intercom box, and a picture of his family.

Spartan and cramped as it was, it still had its advantages. Unlike the enlisted men who slept in a bunk that a crewmate had just vacated ("sharing the stink," they called it), he had a bunk to himself. He also had a small degree of privacy. There was no door to separate his quarters from the activity in the corridor, only a curtain hung across the doorway. In a submarine, however, a curtain provided some seclusion, an item coveted by any submariner.

Penning the last words of his log entry, Morrison closed the book and placed it in the wall rack. The chief-of-the-boat had brought a better than expected report. The *Triggerfish* had sustained only minor damage, most of it electrical. Estimated repair time was less than two days. That was the good news; the bad news was that any thought of pursuing the German convoy had to be dismissed.

Taking a lined piece of paper from the tiny desk he laid it out and began to write:

> *Dear Sandi,*
>
> *It's near midday here in the Atlantic and we are staying busy with some minor repairs. I have much to write, but only two words come to mind: I'm sorry. I should never have left the way I did, and now each moment that passes is filled with regret. I should have left with words about my undying love for you and little Ronnie. I am proud of you both. Being married to a navy man is no easy task—especially in war. I only wish . . .*

"Captain to the bridge!" The tinny voice of Steve Sapolsky poured from the intercom, invading Morrison's thoughts. Quickly he folded the letter and placed it in the desk. Walking briskly, Morrison made his way from the cabin down the narrow gray passageway, up a slender metal ladder, and through the hatch that led to the open-air bridge.

The air was cool and heavy with the smell of salt. A gust of wind blew through Morrison's dark hair. The sun was high in the sky, and its bright light forced the captain to squint and his eyes to momentarily tear. Sunlight was vastly different than the dim artificial light in the boat.

Standing on the wet metal deck, he took a quick survey of the sea around him. Gentle ocean swells caressed the hull of the sleek submarine as it moved slowly in its northeasterly direction.

"What is it, Mr. Sapolsky?" Morrison asked wearily.

"Lookouts have spotted something fifteen degrees off our starboard bow," Sapolsky replied, pointing out the direction.

Morrison took his exec's binoculars and held them to his eyes. He scanned the sea in the direction that Sapolsky had indicated. At first he saw nothing, but then a small, dark object bobbed into view.

"I have it," he said, "but I can't make it out."

"I think it's a raft," a voice above him said. Morrison turned to see one of the two lookouts perched on the conning tower. "It looks like there may be someone aboard, sir."

"Mr. Sapolsky, bring us to bear on the raft. Let's also get some men with side arms up here just in case our unknown doesn't want visitors."

"Aye, Captain."

Orders were barked out by Sapolsky, and soon the *Triggerfish* had turned to its new bearing. No one spoke on the crowded bridge. There was nothing to do but wait until the sub had closed the distance of rolling sea between it and the raft.

Men on deck, who were enjoying the few moments of sun allowed them, watched intently as the raft grew from a mere speck on the water to a recognizable shape. Every eye above-board, except the lookouts who maintained a constant vigil of both sea and air, was fixed on the mysterious float.

"Whoever he is, he is a long way from home," Sapolsky offered.

The captain was peering through his binoculars. "Judging by the uniform he wears, home is somewhere in Germany." Turning to the lookouts, Morrison asked, "Do you see any other rafts or any sign of debris?"

"No, sir," both lookouts answered in near unison.

"Odd," Morrison said. "Why would there be only one survivor if a ship went down? Why don't we see debris? There should be an oil slick at least."

"I don't know, sir. Maybe our guest can tell us—assuming he's alive. He's not moving."

"All stop," Morrison ordered. There was still better than thirty yards between the raft and the *Triggerfish* but Morrison knew the momentum of the sub would continue to propel it forward.

A crewman with a long pole equipped with a hook on the end leaned forward, pressing his stomach against the metal cable that served as a balustrade along the edge of the deck. He stretched until he had snared the small raft, then took a step back, pulling the float to the hull.

Several other crewmen, two armed with military issue .45 caliber pistols, helped pull the raft to the edge of the deck. Together they pulled the mysterious occupant over the steel cable barrier and laid him down on the wood slats that covered the top of the metal hull. The pharmacist's mate pushed his way through the crowd of sailors and knelt next to the man.

"His uniform is German navy, sir," the corpsman called out.

"I can see that, Mr. Armstrong," Morrison shouted in reply. "Is he alive?"

"Yes, sir, he seems to be breathing regularly." Armstrong paused as he looked down at the unconscious German. "He looks dehydrated and has a heck of a sunburn. He's been out here a long time."

Morrison and Sapolsky looked at each other with surprise.

"That means that he's not from that last convoy," Sapolsky said. "They've been gone only a few hours."

"True enough," Morrison agreed. "But where did he come from?"

Sapolsky shook his head and looked down from the conning tower to the deck. "What's that in the raft?" he said to Morrison.

It had escaped Morrison's notice at first, but the raft, which at first appeared empty, contained a satchel or some kind of bag. "Mr. Armstrong," Morrison called out. "What's that in the raft?"

Armstrong walked over to the raft which, like its former occupant, lay on the deck. He reached over the rubber floats, pulled out the bag, and set it on the deck.

"It's a leather bag, like what a doctor carries," Armstrong noted. "Shall I open it, sir?"

"Unless you know another way of seeing what's inside," Morrison said strongly.

The sailor bent over the satchel once again, fumbled with the latch, then opened the mouth of the bag wide. He peered in. He gazed at the contents for a moment, then stuck his hand into the bag and moved it around.

"Well?" Morrison asked.

Armstrong turned to face his captain. Morrison could easily see his puzzled expression.

"Dolls, sir! It ain't got nothin' but dolls."

Captain Morrison stepped from his cabin and started down the narrow corridor. At barely over thirty inches wide, the passageway was too tight to allow two men to pass each other without one of them turning sideways. The submarine was designed for war, not comfort. Every inch of the boat's interior was utilized with priority being given to mechanical, electrical, and weapons systems. Everything else was squeezed into what little space remained. There were not even enough bunks for the crew. Instead, they "hot bunked," with one crewman waking up another for his shift, then crawling into the still warm rack for his turn at sleep. Those not lucky enough to be assigned a berth in the crew's quarters slept in the forward or aft torpedo rooms with the twenty-one-foot-long, 3000-pound torpedoes as bunk mates.

Morrison's destination was less than six steps down the passageway. A stout, black sailor stood guarding the door to one of the officer's wardrooms. The *Triggerfish* was capable of sustaining seventy crew and ten officers. On this patrol, however, the complement was smaller with just sixty-five crew and six officers. That left one corner of an officer's stateroom free for their guest.

The black crewman came to attention as Morrison approached. "Captain," he said.

"As you were, Benton," Morrison replied. "Any change in our friend?"

"Not that I know of, sir. Armstrong is in there with him now."

Morrison nodded and stepped into the wardroom. Armstrong, a willowy, red-haired young man from upstate New York, was seated in a padded metal chair. He started to stand, but Morrison waved him off.

"How's he doing?"

Armstrong shook his head. "I can't find much wrong with him. He's dehydrated and sunburned real bad. I can't get him to come to for more than a minute or so. He's been able to drink some water, but then he passes out again. There's not much more that I can do for him."

Morrison took in the still form that lay on the thin mattress. The skin of his face, neck, and hands were a deep red. Small white blisters dotted his forehead and checks.

"We searched his uniform," Armstrong offered. "Found nothin'. Chief Hill was with me when I went through it. He noticed some loose threads on the shoulders and sleeves. It looks like all his insignias were ripped off. He sure must have made somebody mad."

"The chief filled me in. He also brought me the statues."

"Those little dolls? Beats me why he would hang on to those things. And why would they put them in the raft with him? It just don't make sense."

"I think they're more statues than dolls, Armstrong. They mean something to him." Morrison nodded at the unconscious German.

"I guess so."

"When do you think I can ask him some questions?"

Armstrong shrugged. "No idea, Skipper. But I'll let you know as soon as he comes to for more than a minute."

"Very well." Morrison turned and walked from the room.

N
⋏

Americans, Karl Kunzig thought behind closed eyes. He had been conscious for more than two hours by his estimation, but he did not want his rescuers to know that. He wasn't ready to answer questions, and he needed time to think, time to formulate a plan.

His throat was raw, his face hot and tender. Every part of him ached. It hurt to breathe, but he had to lie still. He had to listen, had to think of a story—a believable lie. All he knew at the moment was that he was on an American submarine. That could be bad, but it was better than dying of exposure in a raft on open sea. Still his next step must be carefully considered and executed or all could be ruined and he would spend his days in an Allied prisoner of war camp.

That will not do, Kunzig thought to himself. *That will not do at all.*

Chapter 2

S he's a picture, isn't she?" Stanton said softly.

"Excuse me, sir?" Donna Wilcox asked.

"The sub, Lieutenant, the sub. She's beautiful, isn't she?" Stanton had been standing on the beach staring at what still seemed like an apparition to him, a ghost that had left a cold grave to rise again and seek human contact.

"If you say so, sir."

Stanton took his eyes from the *Triggerfish* and looked at the young woman standing next to him. She stood ramrod straight, hands clasped behind her back. He and his wife had never had children but if they had, they might be the age of this young lieutenant.

"If I say so?" Stanton made no attempt to hide his amusement. "You know, most officers in the navy develop a love for the sea and the ships that sail her. Even old ones like the *Triggerfish*."

"Yes, sir, I know. My father was career navy. It seems that was all he ever talked about."

"I take it you don't share his feelings for the sea."

"On the contrary, sir, I love the sea very much and have applied for sea duty. Being an aide to an admiral has many advantages, but I didn't sign up to sail a desk."

Stanton nodded. It was hard enough being a man in the navy. Being a woman was far more difficult.

"I just prefer ... newer craft, sir."

"I see," Stanton replied easily. "The *Triggerfish* is too old for you to appreciate, is that it?"

"I haven't given it any thought, sir."

"Well, Lieutenant, you're looking at a piece of history. It was boats like her that won the war in the Pacific. Take a moment to take in her lines, Lieutenant. Rake bow, 311 feet and nine inches in length, and carrying a complement of seventy enlisted and up to ten officers. That boat is a testimony to creative engineering. Only analog computers—nothing like what we know as computers—diesel engines, electric motors for undersea propulsion. Vastly different from our nuclear subs today. You have to admire what they were able to do back then. They made it work. Sometimes by spit and guts, but they made it work all the same."

"I imagine it was a difficult life, sir."

"They used to call it the 'coffin service.' When you signed aboard the likes of her you had a one in three chance of dying at sea."

"One in three, sir?"

"The United States lost about a third of the submarines that left base on patrol. Still, they brought Japan to its knees."

"I'm confused, sir," Donna said. "Didn't I understand you to say that the *Triggerfish* went down in the Atlantic?"

"That's right. Submarine warfare wasn't as successful in the Atlantic. Most of the submarine activity was conducted by European allies. We had a few subs there, mostly doing lifeguard duty or intelligence work, but not many. The *Triggerfish* was one of the few."

"She looks well taken care of."

"Now that is a mystery, isn't it? Clearly she hasn't been floating at sea for fifty years. She's been maintained. But by whom?"

"If I didn't know better, I'd say she slipped away from some nautical museum."

"She didn't, Lieutenant. She's the real article all right. The questions are: How did she get here? And where has she been?"

"Looks like they're done."

Stanton turned his attention to a man in a black wet suit walking toward them.

"Inspection is complete, Captain," the man said. Water dripped from his close-cropped hair and down his face. "She's tight as a drum under the waterline, sir. All water intakes are closed. She should float easy enough. Once you get her off the sand, that is."

"I figured as much," Stanton said. "But I wanted to be sure before we take her in tow."

"May I ask where you're taking the old girl, sir?"

"Now that we're sure she's not leaking diesel fuel, battery acid, or something worse, we'll have her towed to Coronado."

"I take it that the search for hazardous materials and explosives was negative," the diver said.

"You wouldn't be in the water if it wasn't," Stanton said firmly. "I had a UDT unit here within thirty minutes of my arrival. All that was left was an underwater survey of the hull."

"She's clean, Captain. Real clean. With the tide coming in she's starting to float clear at the stern. That gave me a chance to eyeball the rudder. It looks good. No damage from the grounding that I could see. Propellers show some use, but not fifty years' worth."

"Marine growth?" Stanton asked.

"No, sir. Clean of all barnacles and such. If you ask me, she's been holed up somewhere."

"But where? And why appear now?" Donna asked.

"I don't know, ma'am, but I envy you two."

"Envy?" Donna said.

"Sure," the diver replied. "How many mysteries like this do you get to see in a lifetime? A real-life ghost ship."

Stanton stared at the gray hulk beached on the sand. "A ghost ship? I hadn't thought of her that way."

"This is going to sound crazy, Captain." The diver hesitated.

"You can talk freely. What's on your mind?"

"Well, sir," he scratched his chin. "I heard something when I was inspecting the stern, near the aft torpedo doors."

"What did you hear?" Donna asked with renewed concern. "Crew noises?"

"No, ma'am. It wasn't crew noises. Didn't sound human at all."

Stanton studied the man. "Mechanical noises, then?"

"No, sir, not that either. I've been under the hull of a lot of ships, sir, that's my job. But I've never heard anything like this. I can't describe it, but it was eerie, like something out of a horror movie. The best I can do is say that it sounded like a basketball in a dryer—*thump, thump, thump.*"

Turning back to the helpless *Triggerfish*, Stanton watched as three-foot waves broke over her metal hull, tossing up ghostly white spray into the air. He had had every inch of her surface examined for leaks, biological agents, signs of bombs, everything, and she came back clean.

What he hadn't inspected, and what filled him with uncertainty, was the inside of the submarine. That was still a mystery. For some reason, he didn't feel good about it, not good at all. He knew that the gnawing inside him was an irrational emotion, but it was nonetheless there.

"We had a full acoustical survey done," Stanton said firmly. "A team of the navy's best listened from stem to stern and heard nothing. There's nothing in that submarine."

"Nothing alive," Donna commented softly.

"Submarines make noise," Stanton said. "Especially old ones."

"I'm sure you're right, sir," the diver said. "I just thought you should know."

"I've noted it, son. You've done good work." The uneasiness in Stanton's stomach grew.

N
⋏

Morrison and Sapolsky walked briskly from the control room forward to Wardroom Two. Crewmen ducked out of the way or flattened themselves against walls and bulkheads to clear a path for the two senior officers.

Without hesitation both men plunged into the wardroom. Armstrong stood to his feet. Seated at the small metal table was the man they had fished from the sea. His face was drawn, and his dark blond hair was matted to his scalp. He sat slump shouldered and held a cup of water in his hand which he sipped gently. He didn't look up when Morrison and Sapolsky entered.

"Captain," Armstrong said, acknowledging his skipper's presence. He then turned his attention to the passenger. "He's been conscious less than five minutes, sir. I called you as soon as he sat up. He's still pretty weak."

"Has he said anything?" Sapolsky asked sharply as if the German were not in the room.

"No, sir," Armstrong replied. "Not a word."

Morrison took a seat on the bench opposite the man and studied him. He was thin and wore only his underwear. He sat stone still. The captain watched as the man took another sip and then shivered. His burned face, swollen lips, and blistered skin made him look pitiful. "Benton!" Morrison said loudly.

The sailor who had been watching the door for the last four hours poked his head in. "Yes, sir?"

"Get this man some clean clothes and skivvies."

"Aye, sir."

The man looked up from his cup of water. "Thank you," he said hoarsely.

"You speak English?" Morrison asked.

"Quite well, actually," the man said. "I'm Karl Kunzig, of the . . . formerly of the German Gestapo. Since you have my uniform, I assume you have surmised that." The man had no accent.

"We had guessed as much," Morrison said. "Of course, there were no insignias to help us out."

Kunzig chortled weakly. "Trust me, Captain, the uniform is much better for it."

Sapolsky spoke: "You don't sound German to me. Why?"

Morrison watched as Kunzig slowly turned his head to face the standing Sapolsky, but he did not speak. His gaze was hard.

"My executive officer, Mr. Sapolsky, has asked you a question," Morrison said firmly. "I think he would appreciate the courtesy of a reply."

Kunzig pursed his lips. "Yes, of course. I am sorry, Captain. I am not used to being questioned."

"I'm afraid I have a lot of questions for you."

"As would I, if I were in your place. I am not your typical German, Captain. My father was German, my mother British. My father taught math in Berlin and made many useful friends in various universities. That afforded me the opportunity to study in London. Middle Eastern archaeology is my field. My accent made me stand out with my peers at school. I prefer to blend in so I made every effort to strip it away."

"Archaeology?" Morrison said. "Is that why you have the bag of little statues?"

"Yes. They are very important to me and priceless in the academic world. I tried to carry some of my work with me when I was about my duties. I am studying ancient Canaanite and Hebrew cultures."

"Hebrew?" Sapolsky said with a start. "Why would a good German want to study Jews?"

Again, Kunzig turned to face the executive officer. "Mr. Slapsky—"

"Sapolsky," he corrected tersely.

"My apologies, Mr. Sapolsky." Kunzig offered a small nod. "I am not a *good* German—not by current standards. You are right when you think that the Jews are persecuted in my land. It is a horrible thing of which you know only a little. Perhaps when this is all over, you will know more than you care to. But not every German approves of the official policy. Many of us oppose the way the Jews are treated. Especially me."

"Why especially you?" Morrison asked suspiciously.

Kunzig, looking like a man who was about to bare his soul, stared at Morrison. "I have Jewish blood."

"A member of the Gestapo has Jewish blood," Sapolsky said with disbelief. "Not likely."

Morrison raised a hand to silence the officer. "Go on."

"As I said, my mother was English. Her mother was Jewish. And to answer your next question, no one knew about it. My mother even kept it from my father."

"How is that possible?" Morrison asked.

"My grandmother and grandfather died when my mother was young. She was reared by adoptive parents. She took their name."

"Is that why you were set adrift in a raft?" Morrison asked. He was uncertain about the thin man in front of him. He was unhesitating in his answers and his remarks seemed planned, rehearsed. Morrison had expected resistance. Name, rank, serial number, and nothing more.

"No, Captain. As I said, no one knew. I was cast off for other reasons."

"Such as?"

"I am not a supporter of the war. The whole thing is ludicrous and is being led by an insane man. Hitler will ruin my great country."

"Then why join up with the military?" Sapolsky asked.

Kunzig guffawed loudly, his voice echoing in the tiny room. Morrison, surprised, cut his eyes to his exec and saw him stiffen.

"What's so funny?" Sapolsky demanded.

"You think I had a choice?" Kunzig said, replacing the laughter with bitterness. "You think I chose this? Military service is not voluntary, Mr. Sapolsky. They have ways of finding you and insisting that you serve. No one asked my opinion, Commander; no one sought my permission. I had to think of my mother and father. Both are elderly now and neither is in good health. That's how they do it. They don't just threaten you, they threaten your family."

"But still, you are Gestapo—"

"Because of my education, my knowledge of English, and my father's connections," Kunzig interrupted.

"What did you do for the Gestapo?" Morrison asked pointedly.

"Intelligence. Mostly naval issues."

"Such as?"

Kunzig shrugged. "My office monitored Allied ship locations and activities. I passed the information on to my superiors, who passed it on to their superiors."

"You tracked ship movements?" Sapolsky asked.

"Yes."

Morrison and Sapolsky exchanged glances. Turning back to Kunzig, Morrison asked, "How good was your information?"

"Quite good. It may surprise you that some of your citizens are more than willing to provide us with information—for a price. There are more such people than you may think."

"U.S. citizens selling information to the likes of you?" Sapolsky spat. "I doubt it."

A small smile crossed Kunzig's face. "I have only seen this room and the one with the bed. But I can prove my point. I know I'm on a submarine. That much is obvious. What I don't know is which submarine. What craft is this?"

No one spoke.

"Please, gentlemen. It's going to be very difficult for me to walk away, isn't it? Where am I going to go? Telling me the name of your ship cannot hurt."

Still no one spoke.

A sigh escaped the swollen lips of the German. "Captain, may I have your name?"

"Morrison."

"Would that be Richard Morrison?"

Morrison was dumbfounded. "Yes," he answered cautiously.

Kunzig closed his eyes and thought for a moment. He then began to recite: "That would make this the USS *Triggerfish*, Gato class submarine, commissioned April 15, 1943, launched by the Electric Boat Company of Groton, Connecticut. Shakedown cruise took place during the first two weeks of

May off the Bahamas. The *Triggerfish* is 311 feet, nine inches in length, twenty-seven feet, three inches across the beam. She displaces 1,525 tons surfaced and over 2,400 submerged—"

"Kunzig—" Morrison said but the man kept his eyes closed and continued his recitation.

"—seven-eighths-inch-high tensile steel hull, test depth of 400 feet—"

"Kunzig—" Morrison said again.

"—but that's a ruse. Your actual test depth is closer to 600 feet."

"What—"

Kunzig continued as if he were lecturing a group of young sailors. "Originally meant for duty in the Pacific out of Pearl Harbor but reassigned to Squadron 50 in Scotland to patrol off Iceland and Norway. You sailed July 18th. Which brings me to a question." Kunzig opened his eyes and stared at Morrison with a penetrating gaze that made him feel as if his soul were being examined. "What are you doing so far south, Captain? Iceland is a long way from here."

The muscles in Morrison's jaw tightened like compressed steel springs. He clenched his teeth. Hearing his boat described in such detail by the enemy had enraged him. "How do you know this?" he demanded.

"As I've already told you, we have sources in your country."

"Who?" Sapolsky spat loudly. "I want names."

Kunzig shook his head. "I can't tell you that. I have never dealt with them directly. There are other people who do that. I just digest the information and pass it along."

"But how can you know all those details?" Morrison asked.

"I have a photographic memory, Captain. I never forget what I see, hear, or read."

Morrison was stunned. Part of him wanted to reach across the table and slap Kunzig, but another part wanted to know more.

"If it's helpful to you," Kunzig said smoothly, "I can tell you about any German warship."

"You're willing to sell out your country?" Sapolsky asked with disgust. "Not much of a patriot are you, Kunzig?"

"That's enough," Morrison blurted at Sapolsky. "We'll take whatever information he's willing to give."

"Mr. Sapolsky," Kunzig said evenly, "I am a patriot, but to my country, not to Hitler. I am no more a traitor to my land than your George Washington was to his when he fought the British in your war of independence."

"Captain?" a voice said from the doorway. Morrison turned to see Benton with his hands full. "Here's the clothing you requested, sir."

"Very well," Morrison answered. "Set them in the stateroom and resume your post. I'll have someone relieve you soon—" A tiny, fuzzy voice from a speaker interrupted him.

"Captain, we have contact on SJ radar." It was the voice of the junior officer of the deck.

Morrison was on his feet in an instant. "Get dressed, Mr. Kunzig. I'll have more questions for you later—a lot of questions."

Kunzig gave a nod.

"Stay with him, Armstrong. I want you on him like white on rice. He is to be confined to this ward and the head. Is that clear?"

"Aye, Captain. Crystal clear."

"Good. Get him something to eat and let him shower if he wants. Benton's here if you need him."

Morrison walked from the room, carrying with him a suffocating sense of uneasiness.

With determined steps, Morrison quickly moved from the officer's quarters into the control room and stood behind a young, red-haired, freckle-faced man who looked barely old enough to shave. He had his eyes fixed on a round, green display. A yellow band radiating from the center of the screen swept clockwise around the display.

"What have you got, son?" Morrison asked.

"At three-one-zero degrees relative, sir." The young man pointed at the screen. "Eighteen thousand yards."

Morrison watched as the sweeping yellow band "painted" four small dots. He knew that there were at least four ships and maybe more. Since radar could not see through ships, small vessels could be concealed behind the larger craft. This was especially true at the limits of the radar. It was not unusual for a single blip to become three as the submarine closed the distance between it and the other craft.

"Stay sharp," Morrison commanded as he turned and climbed the steel ladder that would take him from the control room in the heart of the boat through the conning tower and onto the open-air bridge.

The air was scented with salt and a stiff breeze blew from the north. The submarine rocked in the swells of the open ocean. The gold medallion sun was descending slowly toward the horizon. Above them, strips of high clouds formed a patchwork canopy under a graying sky.

On the bridge was Commander Sapolsky and the junior officer of the deck. Perched above the bridge deck were two lookouts who assiduously scanned the sky and sea with binoculars.

"Smoke," Sapolsky said, pointing into the ever-darkening distance. "Off the port bow. Can't make out much." He handed his binoculars to Morrison, who raised them to his eyes.

"Radar shows multiple contacts making twelve knots," Morrison offered calmly.

"Chief Hill reports all repairs complete," Sapolsky said, his voice tinged with adrenaline. "We're ready to go hunting, Skipper."

"Very well," Morrison said. "We'll have to do this in the dark. We've got less than an hour of sunlight. Let's get close enough to identify the targets, then we'll go from there."

"Yes, sir."

"Bring us about to three-five-zero, all ahead flank. Let's see who is coming to dinner."

"Aye, Captain." Sapolsky stepped to the bridge intercom and repeated the order.

The metal hull of the submarine began to vibrate as the four powerful diesel engines came to their full 5,400 horsepower. A spray of seawater cascaded over the raked bow as it plowed through the dark green ocean and ran along the flat deck caressing it in a foamy embrace. Like a porpoise playing in the surf, the bow of the *Triggerfish* rose and fell with the swells. The thick smell of diesel fuel filled the air.

The submarine accelerated as the twin propellers dug into the ocean. In less than ten minutes the *Triggerfish* was clipping through the ocean at twenty-one knots.

A powerful sense of pride permeated Morrison as he watched his submarine plow through the water. The sea, the sub, the men. He loved it all. But he also knew that this was no Sunday outing. If the convoy of ships they were now pursuing were indeed Axis, then people would die tonight. He was determined that it would not be his men.

This was going to be a long night. Morrison knew what every submarine commander knew: Success and survival depended on patience and planning. The pursuit they had just begun would take hours. He had to maintain a sufficient distance not to be seen, yet draw close enough to identify the targets, judge their strength, and fire torpedoes. Anything could go wrong, and it often did. Very few submarine crews got an opportunity to undo a mistake. They had been lucky earlier, escaping as they did with only little damage. If the *Triggerfish* were a cat, it had used up all its nine lives. This time there could be no mistakes.

"Let me know when we have visual contact," Morrison said to Sapolsky. "I'm going to take a look at the charts."

"Yes, sir," Sapolsky immediately replied.

Chapter 3

Hermann loaded his fork with pork piccate and brought it to his mouth. He chewed slowly, his mind more on the television than on his meal. A man in a blue blazer that sported a patch which read "News 12—The Eyes and Ears of San Diego" in yellow letters was speaking into a handheld microphone. A brisk breeze ran its invisible fingers through his lacquered coal black hair.

"... the source of the mystery ship is still unknown. What is known, however, is that it is a World War II vintage submarine which ran aground sometime last night. As you can see..." The camera began a wide pan along the beach. "... a crowd has gathered to take in this unusual sight. Military police with the help of the San Diego P. D. have cordoned off the area around the submarine. Coast Guard boats patrol the area just beyond the shoreline. No one is being allowed near the vessel. With me is Captain J. D. Stanton of the navy. He is the man in charge." The reporter turned to the tall, middle-aged man in a uniform. "Captain Stanton, there seems to be a great deal of security around the submarine. Can you tell us if there is some danger?"

"It's purely a precaution," Stanton said. "This is clearly an unusual event. We wanted to make sure that no one injured themselves by climbing on the submarine or by being exposed to hazardous materials like battery acid or diesel fuel."

"Have any leaks been detected?" the reporter asked. "Any pollution?"

"None at all."

"What about the crew?"

"There is no crew." Stanton's voice was flat, unemotional.

Hermann chuckled. This Stanton wasn't making it easy on the reporter. He wasn't giving anything away.

"How can that be?" the reporter asked.

"That's what we're investigating," Stanton commented easily.

"So what happens next, Captain Stanton?"

"I am ordering that the ship be moved from here and towed to a place where she can be examined more closely."

"Why not conduct your investigation right here?" the reporter pressed.

"This is a public beach. Our work will progress more smoothly at a naval institution."

"Where exactly will she be taken?"

"I have a couple of options on that."

"How do you explain the sudden appearance of a World War II submarine on a San Diego beach?"

"I don't. Not yet. I think it's better that we wait for the facts before we come to any conclusions. Don't you?" Hermann watched as Stanton offered a small smile. Most people would have missed it, but Hermann missed nothing. He hadn't achieved as much as he had by being inattentive. Stanton was clearly in charge of the interview, not the reporter.

"Of course," the reporter stammered. "It's just that—"

"It's just that you are curious," Stanton interrupted. "I understand that. I'm a little curious myself, but things must be done in their proper order. First we investigate, then we have answers."

"Will you keep the citizens of San Diego posted on all future developments?"

"That decision is not up to me. My senior officers will decide such things."

"What will happen to the submarine after the investigation?" the reporter inquired.

"Technically, she has never been decommissioned."

"What's that mean?"

"It means that the USS *Triggerfish* is still property of the navy. The navy will have to decide what to do with her. Now," Stanton said firmly, "I must get back to work."

Hermann watched as the navy captain turned on his heels and walked out of view of the camera.

"Well, there you have it," the reporter went on. "A real ghost ship on a San Diego beach. This is Barry Ludlow, Channel 12 news at Torrey Pines State Beach."

Hermann put down his fork and leaned back in his chair. He swallowed hard then dabbed at his lips with a linen napkin. The USS *Triggerfish?* It was a name he had not thought about in years, not since he was a child. Standing, he began to slowly pace around the private dining room that adjoined his plush and popular German restaurant. Normally he reveled in the opulence of the room, its fine furnishings, leather chairs, chandelier, teak tables, matching paneling, and thick pile carpet—he was a man accustomed to the best of everything—but his thoughts were elsewhere.

The *Triggerfish*. Like an ancient, mysterious sea creature, the name rose from the dark depths of his memory. Disbelief swirled around him. He could hear his father's voice; he could recall the story.

Was it true? Yes. Perhaps. Perhaps it could happen.

Returning to the table, Hermann sat down and took a deep swallow of dark beer, draining the glass. The cool fluid flowed easily down his throat. A good feeling welled up in him.

The door to the private dining area opened and a red-haired man in a white shirt and dark pants stepped in. "Can I get you anything else, Mr. Kunzig?" His voice was weighted with accent.

"Another beer, Victor. I have some thinking to do."

N
ʌ

"You enjoyed that, didn't you, sir?" Donna said with a smile. She handed him a portable radio.

"I don't have much patience with the commercial news media," Stanton replied. "It used to be an honorable profession, but it's been reduced to a ratings driven entertainment business. Nothing but sound bites preceded by exaggerated hyperbole."

"But how do you really feel, sir?" Her smile broadened.

"I'll feel better when we have the *Triggerfish* in Coronado."

"It will make security a lot easier. Not to mention our investigation."

"That's why we're doing it, Lieutenant," Stanton said. He was watching the crew of a large tugboat tie off two-inch-thick towlines to the submarine. A sense of urgency filled him. While he would have preferred to do this after dark and away from prying news cameras, it was neither feasible nor safe. The sun was setting quickly, leaving no more than two hours of sunlight. Once the *Triggerfish* was beyond the breakers, she could be easily guided south along the coast, around the Point Loma peninsula, and into the protected waters of San Diego Bay. From there the *Triggerfish* would be guided to the U.S. Naval Amphibious Base and moored. The tricky part was pulling the sub free of the sand.

Sand, Stanton knew, especially wet sand, has unique qualities. When a ship of substantial size runs aground, the weight of its hull compresses the underlying sand, forming a powerful vacuum. This vacuum is made all the worse by the action of surf. Beachgoers experience the phenomenon when they stand at the tide line as incoming water floods around their feet, then is drawn back out to sea again. It takes only seconds for the sand to cover the bather's feet, creating a natural suction beneath them. Stanton was facing more than the weight of a person; he was attempting to move hundreds of tons of steel. The tugboats had their work cut out for them.

"You're worried about her, aren't you, sir?" Donna asked.

"I'm confident in the tugboat crews," Stanton answered quickly. A second later, he admitted, "Yes, I'm worried about her. I'd hate to see anything bad happen."

"In some ways, I feel that something bad has already happened. We just don't know what it is. I can't help wondering what happened to her crew."

"Me too, Lieutenant," Stanton agreed softly.

"Sir, you don't suppose—" Donna stopped abruptly and stared at the submarine.

"Don't suppose what?" Stanton prompted, drawing her attention back.

"All this talk about a ghost ship. You don't suppose—"

"That she's haunted?" Stanton laughed. "No, I don't think we'll find any ghosts walking around on the *Triggerfish*."

"That's not what I mean, sir. It's not the immaterial that concerns me, it's the material." She took a deep breath. "What about the bodies, sir? When we finally open her up, will we find a boatload of corpses?"

The image of rattling skeletons and decaying bodies strewn about the insides of the submarine filled Stanton's head. He had read his share of ghost stories and had dismissed them all. Still he was a man with an active imagination. That's why he loved history as much as he did. It was not a dry subject to him. Each account of a naval battle or historical event was played out in full color and active pictures in his mind. No movie could be clearer or more real.

Macabre images of skeletons dressed in uniforms standing post at the control wheel, the chart table, the galley, the radio, and the radar flashed on the movie screen of his mind. He struggled to suppress a shudder.

"I have no idea what we'll find when we open her up, but I'm sure there won't be any ghosts."

"I hope you're right, sir."

The radio in Stanton's hand crackled to life. "We're ready, Captain Stanton." It was the skipper of the lead towboat.

Holding the walkie-talkie to his mouth, Stanton said: "Very well. Tide is as high as it's going to get. Take her out slow."

The sound of the tugboat's powerful diesel engines echoed off the towering cliffs behind them and rolled like thunder down the beach. Spectators began to cheer and applaud. Stanton watched as the hawsers drew taut. Once all slack had been removed, the tugboat captains applied more power. White foam began to bubble behind the powerful craft as they struggled to pull the *Triggerfish* free.

"Come on, come on," Stanton said under his breath, attempting to will the sub into open water. The sound of the tugboat engines crescendoed as their propellers dug deep into the ocean. "Let go of the shore, baby. You can do it."

"I don't think she can hear you," Donna said.

Stanton frowned. "That's the problem with women in the navy, Lieutenant. They just don't know how to talk to ships."

"Just so long as they don't talk back, sir."

"Oh, they talk back all right, Wilcox. They talk back real loud."

As if on cue a low groan like the guttural growl of a bear filled the air.

"She's breaking free," Donna said loudly. "She's moving."

The groaning grew in intensity as if the submarine were in pain from some unseen torment.

"She sure sounds like a ghost ship," Donna observed.

"That's just the hull scraping on the sand. You have to expect some noise. Submarines aren't supposed to drag bottom."

Reluctantly the shore released its sandy grip on the body of the antiquated submarine. Seconds later she bobbed in the water like a thousand-ton toy seeking a giant child to play with it. The tugs pulled the submarine against the tide and surf. Water crested over the hull, spraying the air with white, gossamer foam. On shore, the crowd broke into a frenzy of cheers, hoots, and laughter.

Turning his attention to Donna, he noticed that she was biting her lip. "You're not getting attached to the old girl, are you, Lieutenant?"

"Just concerned about the mission, sir. That's all."

"That's all, huh? If you say so, Lieutenant. Just be careful that you don't fall in love. They don't make them like that anymore."

"I'll be careful. It looks like we have company."

Stanton turned his attention in the direction of Donna's gaze. Commander Ira Stewart was walking through the sand toward them. He was wearing a thick red jumpsuit.

"Captain," Stewart said with a smile. "Are you ready?"

"I didn't expect you to escort me, Commander. That's what junior officers are for."

Stewart looked at Wilcox and grinned. "I couldn't agree more, but I have my reasons. Your chariot awaits." With a flourish, he waved his arm in the direction of a white Zodiac Yachtline 600 inflatable boat that rested where the sea met the shore.

Turning to Donna, Stanton asked, "Care to join us?"

Donna gazed at the three-foot breakers then at the Zodiac.

"Yes, Lieutenant," Stewart said, "you will get wet."

"No problem," Donna said. "What good is a sailor if she doesn't get her feet wet once in a while?"

"That's the spirit," Stewart said, clapping his hands together. "Shall we go?" Without waiting for an answer the tall Coast Guard officer turned and started toward the Zodiac.

"He seems excited, doesn't he?" Donna said.

"Why shouldn't he be? Look at the *Triggerfish* out there. It's like she's begging to go to sea. Commander Stewart knows a noble craft when he sees one." He started toward the boat. "Let's not keep the commander waiting."

Two young seamen stood by the boat that had been run up on the shore. Like their commander, they wore red waterproof jumpsuits. Stewart stepped lithely into the boat and turned to face Stanton and Wilcox.

"Here," he said with a laugh. "Better put these on." He tossed jumpsuits to them. Stanton and Donna quickly slipped them on over their uniforms. "Not only will they keep you dry as we make our way through the surf, but they have the advantage of making you navy swabs look like real Coast Guard."

"I don't think our eyes are beady enough," Stanton joked. A minute later he and Donna had joined Stewart in the Zodiac, and the two young sailors pushed the boat back until it floated free. Stanton and Donna donned life jackets. The sailors jumped into the boat and one of them took the helm. The large outboard motor came to life, and bathed in ocean spray, the boat charged forward through the surf.

With each small breaker, the craft would become airborne and then land roughly on the water again. Stanton could feel the pit of his stomach drop like a free-falling elevator. Donna looked tense and held tightly to the rope guide that ran along the top of the float.

Stanton turned to Stewart. "You're having fun bouncing us around, aren't you?" Stanton yelled above the roar of the motor.

"Oh, yes, Captain. Enormously."

Six wave hurdles later, the Zodiac was beyond the surf line and in smooth water. The helmsman steered a course for the submarine, which was slowly rocking in the water like a napping behemoth. In the dimming red sunlight the gray hull darkened and looked ominous.

"She doesn't belong, does she?" Stewart asked. "She's out of her time. An anachronism."

"She's *our* anachronism," Stanton said with admiration. "She was one of the beauties of her day." The crew fell into silence as they approached the floating steel hulk. The tugboats continued their tow, but at a slow speed, just enough to keep the towlines taut. Once Stanton and Donna were aboard, the tugs would slowly accelerate.

As soon as the rubber hull of the Zodiac bumped against the high tensile steel hull of the *Triggerfish*, one of the sailors scrambled from the boat and onto the submarine's flat deck. Stewart threw a nylon rope to the man, who quickly tied it off on one of the sub's starboard stern bollards. Then, holding tightly to the metal cable guardrail, he leaned forward and extended a hand. Stanton put a foot on the hull, took the man's hand, and allowed himself to be pulled up to the rail, which he easily stepped over.

"It's your turn, Lieutenant," Stanton said.

Donna licked her lips nervously, stood in the Zodiac, and took the sailor's hand, which pulled her effortlessly onto the hull and helped her clear the rail as if she were little more than a rag doll. The sailor had started for the inflatable craft when Stewart stopped him with an upraised hand.

Drawing himself to attention, Stewart snapped a sharp salute and said loudly, "Permission to come aboard, sir."

Stanton grinned broadly. "So this is why we had the pleasure of your company. Very well, Commander." Stanton returned the salute. "Permission granted."

Stewart beamed. "Thank you, sir. Thank you very much."

As Stewart boarded the craft, Donna leaned toward Stanton and said, "It seems you have competition for the affections of the *Triggerfish*."

"I would have done the same thing in his place."

The three passengers fell into silence as the blanket of night covered them. The Zodiac with the two Coast Guardsmen was gone. A stiff offshore breeze rose and pushed against their bodies. The submarine moved smoothly through the sea. Overhead, a helicopter from a local news station circled lazily.

"I wish we could go inside," Stewart said.

"Not yet," Stanton countered. "I'm as eager as you, but we must wait."

"I understand." Stewart was quiet for a minute then said, "Did I tell you that my father was in the silent service?"

"No," Stanton said with surprise.

"Served in the Pacific, Gato class sub just like this one. He died a few years back."

"I'm sorry."

"Thanks. He used to tell me about the war and his sub. He was on the *Skate*. Served as a radioman. He loved the service, especially sub life. He would tell me about it, but I could never understand what the appeal was. Cramped quarters, stale air, dangerous duty."

Stanton laughed. "I think it's an affliction you're born with."

"Perhaps. I'm beginning to understand now. He would love to have seen this." He paused. "Being on board reminds me of him."

Stanton patted Stewart on the shoulder. "Those men are worth remembering."

"Begging the captain's pardon," Donna broke in, "but why are we here? On board, I mean."

"Because we can be, Lieutenant. Because we can be. Now you can say you've sailed a World War II sub."

"I'm sure it will be the highlight of my career, sir. So what do we do now?"

"I don't know about you and Commander Stewart, but I'm going up on the bridge. I've been aching to do that since I first laid eyes on her."

"I'm with you," Stewart said eagerly.

"What about you, Wilcox? Want to check out the view from the bridge? If you're good, I'll let you climb up to the lookout perch."

"I think I'll pass on the lookout offer, but I'll join you two on the bridge."

"I'd offer you some coffee, but—"

A sharp, pointed, piercing noise shook the night. It was the compilation of every human and animal cry; of bending, tearing metal; the vibration of a dying universe.

Instinctively, the three each grabbed for support, fully expecting the sub to roll over on its side, or to suddenly break apart.

"What was that?" Donna cried. "Did we hit something?"

"I don't know," Stanton said with confusion. "I don't think so. There was no shudder, no change in momentum."

"But it sounded like it came from the sub," Stewart said.

"I'm going to check the bow, you check the stern," Stanton commanded. Both men moved quickly in opposite directions, leaving Donna standing by herself.

The radio Stanton carried erupted with static, then a voice. "Captain, are you all right? We heard a noise." It was the skipper of the lead tugboat.

"We heard it too," Stanton replied into the handheld radio. "No idea what it was. Hold course and speed. I'll get back to you in a moment."

The rubber heels of his shoes made a dull thud against the wood-planked deck. Ocean spray struck his face as he reached the bow. Leaning as far as he could over the still untested cable rail, Stanton stared over the side. Water flowed by easily as the tugboats pulled the sub at a mere three knots. He saw nothing but the simple passing of dark green water. Working his way along the port rail, he studied the hull the best he could. Still nothing. He continued his inspection until he had reached the stern. Stewart had mirrored his actions until he was at Stanton's starting point on the prow. The men and Donna met in the front of the bridge.

"Nothing," Stewart said without waiting to be asked.

"Same here," Stanton replied.

"What was it then?" Donna asked. Her face was pale and drawn. "Something had to make that noise."

Stanton shook his head. "I have no idea. We seem stable with no loss of buoyancy. Maybe the sound came from somewhere else."

"It sure sounded like it was right under our feet," Donna countered. "What now?"

"We continue on as planned, but we keep our eyes and ears open." Stanton raised the radio to his lips, keyed the microphone, and relayed his orders to the tugs. A man on each tug would be stationed to keep an eye on the *Triggerfish*. If it looked like she was listing the tugs would make for shallow water.

Every ten minutes, Stanton and Stewart repeated their inspection, and each time the results were negative.

"She seems stable enough," Stewart said. "We may have to chalk that sound up to one of the mysteries of the sea."

"I've never heard anything like that before," Stanton said. "It sure got my attention. I'll have her hull inspected again after we tie up in Coronado."

"Sounds wise," Stewart agreed. "She may be old, but she seems to have a life of her own. Is that offer to stand on the bridge still good?"

"Indeed it is, Commander. Indeed it is. What about you, Wilcox? You still up to standing watch on the conning tower?"

Donna was white as the moon. Her lips were drawn tight and her eyes darted about.

"Are you okay, Lieutenant?" Stanton asked with concern.

"Something's wrong, Captain. I can feel it. Something isn't right."

"What's not right?" Stewart asked.

She shook her head. "I don't know, but whatever it is, it's serious."

The two men looked at each other. Stanton wondered what his aide sensed that he did not. "We'll be fine. It's not that far to Coronado. We'll be there in a few hours."

Donna nodded silently but without conviction.

"I can have a patrol boat here in a matter of minutes," Stewart said sharply.

"Do it," Stanton said. "I hope we don't need it."

"It would be a shame to lose the sub, Captain," Stewart said.

"Not to mention what being rescued by the Coast Guard would do to my reputation. I'd have to turn in my uniform."

Stewart laughed and Donna surrendered a small smile.

"Now, everyone," Stanton said. "To the bridge. That's an order."

N
Λ

"Down scope!"

A mild, even hum accompanied the periscope as it descended into the conning tower well.

The *Triggerfish* was on the hunt.

Captain Morrison nodded at Sapolsky, who stepped forward in the crowded area and stood before the periscope. "Up scope," Sapolsky said. Immediately the scope began to rise again. Sapolsky bent over, pushed out the control handles, placed his eyes to the viewer, and followed the scope up until he was standing erect again. He did a quick turn around the axis of the scope, then slapped up the handles. "Down scope."

"The moon's a help," Morrison said. "I came up with four ships, two destroyers, a merchant vessel, and a troop carrier."

"Agreed. We should be in torpedo range in twenty minutes. How do you want to do this?"

"The destroyers are the problem. They have both speed and armament. We'll take out the rear warship first. The lead destroyer will have to come about to lay down depth charges. We'll turn on her, unleash a couple of fish, then dive deep. If all goes well, both targets will be sunk or immobilized. We can then track the other two ships. Agreed?"

"Yes, and—" Sapolsky was interrupted by a voice on the intercom.

"Captain, this is Armstrong. Mr. Kunzig wishes to speak to you."

Morrison frowned deeply, turned to the intercom box, and activated the switch. "I'm busy, Mr. Armstrong."

"He says it's real important."

Morrison made eye contact with Sapolsky, who shrugged.

"Very well. You and Benton bring him here."

"Yes, sir."

"Is that wise, Skipper?" Sapolsky asked.

"What's he going to do? Take over the sub all by himself? He's not going home again. He's a prisoner of war. Whatever he sees here will stay with him."

Two minutes later a voice came up the hatch from the control room below the conning tower. "Captain, I have Mr. Kunzig here."

"Send him up."

Karl Kunzig poked his head through the hatch that joined the conning tower with the control room. He finished his climb slowly until he was standing on the steel deck.

"This had better be important, Kunzig," Morrison said sharply. "I'm a busy man."

"You are beginning an attack run, are you not, Captain?"

"What makes you say that?" Morrison had no intention of offering information.

"I know we are underwater. The dive alarm was proof of that. You would not spend so much time underwater unless you were in the presence of the enemy. Why run your batteries down for any other reason? I also know that your speed underwater is half that of the surface."

"Maybe I'm conducting a drill." Morrison was incensed at Kunzig's knowledge of his boat.

"I doubt it," Kunzig said with a small smile.

"Get to the point," Sapolsky ordered. "Or stop wasting the captain's time."

"I wish to help," Kunzig offered.

"Help?" Morrison looked at Sapolsky, whose face showed the same puzzlement he himself felt. He turned back to his prisoner. "How can you help?"

"If you are planning on attacking a German ship, I can give you information."

"Why?" Morrison asked.

"As I told you earlier, I am not a supporter of the war. The sooner the war ends, the better off my country will be. I also want to prove my trustworthiness to you."

"I don't know, Skipper," Sapolsky said.

"How can you possibly help? You're no sub commander."

"That's correct, Captain. But I do know every German ship and every important detail about them. Including their captains. All I need is for you to let me see the ship or ships you are tracking."

Morrison stood in silence. There was no harm the German could do. Not with so many of the crew around. There was something about Kunzig, something ill defined, nebulous. Morrison made his decision. "Up scope."

Slowly the scope rose. Morrison stepped forward and aligned the sight with the small convoy. He then stepped back. "You have five seconds."

Kunzig pressed his eyes to the eyepiece, moved the scope slightly, and then stepped back.

"Down scope," Morrison snapped. He stared at Kunzig. "Well?"

Kunzig closed his eyes. He said nothing.

"The captain asked you a question," Sapolsky said.

Kunzig nodded. "Unless I miss my guess, Captain, you are planning to assault the rear destroyer, then turn on the lead one. Is that correct?"

It was as if Kunzig could read minds. "It is."

"Ill advised, Captain. There is a good chance that we will all die if you attempt that."

"He just doesn't want us to fire our fish at his ships," Sapolsky said pointedly. "We should have left him adrift."

"That is not it at all," Kunzig retorted. "I know the records of the captains of those two ships. The lead destroyer is under the command of a man named Hauser. He is one of the best. If you don't kill him first, he will kill you."

"And the rear destroyer?" Morrison inquired.

"A novice commander by the name Gabler. This is his first command. He is the nephew of a Nazi official, otherwise he would be little more than an electrician's mate."

"So you're suggesting that I take out the lead ship first, even though it means that Gabler's ship will be able to close on my position faster."

"Exactly, Captain. Hauser will find you and crush you. He has helped train our U-boat captains. He's unmerciful and possesses a killer's instinct. Some have said that he can smell an enemy ship."

"Well, he hasn't got a whiff of us yet," Sapolsky said confidently.

Morrison was thinking.

"Captain," Sapolsky said with disbelief. "You can't be seriously considering listening to this man."

Stepping to the hatchway between the conning tower and the control room, Morrison called down. "Chief, did you hear all that?"

"I did, sir," came a husky voice of Chief-of-the-Boat Bud Hill.

"What's your take on it?"

"Well, sir, from what you told me earlier, he did know everything about us. It makes sense he'd know about his own ships."

"Thank you, Chief." Morrison turned to Kunzig. "I'll take what you said under advisement, but know this: If I find out you're lying to me—no, if I even think you're lying to me, I'm going to let Commander Sapolsky fire you out of an aft torpedo tube. You got that, mister?"

"Yes, Captain, I understand," Kunzig replied calmly. "Should you decide not to take my advice and you fire on Gabler's ship, then you can expect Hauser's destroyer to break to port, not starboard. He will assume that you plan to follow behind the torpedoes. Oh, Captain, there is one other thing you need to know."

"What's that?"

"The troopship is carrying Allied prisoners of war, not German soldiers. I just thought you might like to know."

Chapter 4

Donna Wilcox stood on the bridge of the *Triggerfish* with her back to the steel tower. Her arms were crossed in front of her in a self-hug. There was coldness in the summer night, a chill that came from within her. It was a frosty fear that belied the warm breeze which blew across the hull of the ship and seemed to percolate up from the steel deck.

Before her, Captain Stanton and Commander Stewart leaned against the tubular metal rail of the bridge and chatted amiably, oblivious to the terror that was slowly consuming her. It was not the sea that churned up her anxiety, nor was it the fact that she was on a ship that was nearly sixty years old. It was the thought of what might lie beneath the deck of the bridge. It was the unknown that frightened her. The unknown always frightened her.

The sound they had heard had shaken her deeply. It was no mechanical sound. It was the cry of the ship—a wail that carried every negative human emotion. Why couldn't they sense it? Why did these men not know?

She bit her lip and closed her eyes. She was determined not to let the raging fear in her bubble to the top. It must be concealed. Concealed and controlled and pressed down. It must be kept in its place.

Fear was not a new emotion for Donna. It had been her constant companion since childhood when she had been afraid of the dark and the sounds that houses made in the cool of the evening. "It's just the house settling," her mother would say, shaking her head. "There's nothing to be afraid of." But there was. There was always something to fear.

Her mother could not hear it and her father was gone to sea much of the time, so Donna was left to wrestle with terrors only she could perceive. There were sounds under the bed and in the closet and in the attic and in the bathroom. Toilets did not flush, they roared; the wind did not blow, it moaned; and houses did not settle, they slowly crumbled under the weight of invisible monsters who sat upon the roof leaning down in the wee hours of the night to watch her . . . study her . . . lick their lips over her.

A shiver emanated from her spine and rolled through her body.

She had learned to hide her fears, to keep them to herself, sequestered under lock and key in the hidden places of her mind. Conquering her terrors had become her lifelong goal. Her fear of water was challenged with swim lessons, her fear of heights by climbing on the roof of her house when she was nine and her mother was at the store. She faced every irrational anxiety and conquered them, one by one. Although she was able to subdue her raging anxieties, she could never fully excise them.

The Naval Academy was another tool to face and conquer her terrors. It was also a way of proving her love for her father, a career navy man. She excelled in nearly every area of study and endeavor, but she never felt like she belonged. She continued on, hoping that life would someday become enjoyable.

At the moment, though, she wondered if she had any future at all.

The hull of the *Triggerfish* creaked and groaned.

Donna Wilcox shuddered again.

N
Λ

"Ready torpedo one," Morrison said firmly.

"Torpedo one ready, sir," came the reply.

"Solution is set," Sapolsky said.

"Fire one!"

"Firing number one!" The boat shuddered slightly as the 3000-pound, electrically driven Mark 14 torpedo was expelled from its bow tube. "Torpedo number one is away, sir. She's running hot and true."

"Ready torpedo two," Morrison ordered.

"Torpedo two ready, sir."

"Fire two!"

"Firing number two, sir. Torpedo two is away, running hot and true."

"Down scope," Morrison intoned as he stepped back. He was holding his breath.

"Twelve hundred yards and closing," Sapolsky said as he looked at his stopwatch. "We can't miss at this distance."

"We had better not," Morrison said. "Let's hope the fish explode when they're supposed to." Mark 14 torpedoes had been improved remarkably, but they were still prone to early detonation. At times they simply failed to explode.

"Nine hundred yards . . . eight hundred yards . . . seven hundred yards."

The countdown seemed insufferably long. Seconds seemingly stretched elastically into hours. Morrison closed his eyes. The image of his wife and son flashed into his mind. He missed them terribly, and he knew that he had to be at his best if he was ever to see them again. That was a sentiment that was shared by many of the crew. Everyone on a submarine had someone who was waiting for him. He wondered if he should not have taken Kunzig's advice. He had rejected it out of hand. There was no way he was going to let a former German officer tell him how to plan an attack. Despite his smooth words and apparent sincerity, the man was still a German officer. That could not be ignored.

"Two hundred yards ... one hundred yards ... impact."

Nothing. No concussion carried by the heavy seawater. Morrison waited. Then it happened. A rumble roared through the *Triggerfish*. A cheer went up from the crew. Another explosion and another cheer as the second torpedo found its mark.

"Up scope!" Morrison said sternly. He was peering through the periscope before the top of the device had pierced the surface. "We hit her amidships. She's going down." The crew in the conning tower and in the control room cheered again.

Quickly, Morrison turned his attention to the other warship. He set the crosshairs on its dark, moonlit hull. "Mark," he said.

Sapolsky looked at the degrees etched on the collar at the ceiling of the periscope. "Zero-two-five degrees."

"Make our course zero-four-five degrees—no. Belay that. She's turning port. I don't believe it, her captain's turning port." Morrison had expected that the lead warship, which was a good eight thousand yards ahead of them, would turn starboard to bear down on their position. But she was going the opposite direction—just like Kunzig said. "Down scope."

"He doesn't know where we are," Sapolsky said. "Our position is still concealed."

The captain shook his head. "He doesn't know where we are, but he should know our general area. The torpedo impact alone would show that we're starboard of the convoy. Why would he take a longer path to our area rather than the most direct approach?"

"Maybe he's afraid we'll fire on him," Sapolsky answered.

"When have you known that to stop a warship?" Morrison scratched his chin and thought. Kunzig had been right. "No, he's got something up his sleeve."

"Your orders, sir?"

Morrison raised a hand to silence his officer. His head was swimming with thoughts and permutations. In his mind he could see each ship on the surface and their relationship to the *Triggerfish*. The question was, what to do next? He could run. He could face the other warship which, unlike the one they had just fired on, knew the sub was in the area. Or he could fire on the troop and merchant ship.

He raised the scope again and took another bearing. The ship was still out of torpedo distance and gaining speed. With each minute that passed its increased speed made it a more difficult target to hit. The destroyer was a fast ship, far faster and more maneuverable than a submerged submarine.

There was no more time to think. "Make our course two-zero-five, flank speed." Morrison snapped.

"But that will take us away from the convoy, sir," Sapolsky objected. "We're not running, are we?"

"Do it, Commander. Do it now!"

Sapolsky called out the orders and the helm responded immediately.

"Prepare tube seven," Morrison ordered.

"An aft torpedo, sir?"

Morrison threw a piercing stare at his exec. He knew that Sapolsky was confused, but he would not tolerate his orders being questioned.

The unspoken message worked. "Aye, sir."

"Set the torpedo to slow and make its depth three feet."

"At that depth the destroyer is sure to see it, sir. It may be dark, but that full moon is giving off enough light for the fish to be seen."

"I hope so, Mr. Sapolsky. I hope so. Our friend on the ceiling wants to rewrite the rules of engagement. He wants to throw us off by doing the unexpected. Well, I can play that game too. All we have to do is keep our heads about us and follow orders. Got that?"

"Aye, sir."

"On new heading, sir," Chief Hill said.

"Very well. Up scope." The scope rose with agonizing slowness. Morrison picked his target—the merchant ship. "Mark. Down scope." It was a hopeless shot, but that didn't matter. Morrison had something else up his sleeve.

Seconds ticked by. Everyone in the tower looked at their skipper, and everyone in the control room below listened for the next order.

"Fire seven."

There was a rushing sound as the torpedo raced from its tube.

"Seven is away, sir, running hot and true."

"Hard to starboard," Morrison called out. This time there was no questioning of his orders.

"I get it," Sapolsky said with a small smile. "You're giving away our position by firing a shallow torpedo. The destroyer is going to assume the torpedo came out a forward tube, giving him a false course. Now you're coming about on him."

"Exactly, Mr. Sapolsky. Exactly. Let's just hope he buys it."

With its propellers churning at full speed, the *Triggerfish* began a stealthy ballet with the destroyer, which was rapidly bearing down on a position the sub had left minutes before. It was a deadly dance. The submarine needed to be within 1800 yards for good shot at a target, but if that target was a fast mover, then she needed to be even closer. But being 1500 yards from a warship put the submarine in dangerous waters. Depth charges would rock her unmercifully. Morrison was going to have to fire a pattern of torpedoes to kill the ship, but there was no guarantee that the destroyer would be hit or that the torpedoes would detonate. There was no room for error.

"Forward torpedo room reports tube one ready, sir," Chief Hill called up.

"That means we have tubes one, four, five, and six available in the bow and eight, nine, and ten in the aft," Sapolsky said aloud.

Morrison nodded. "All right," he said to the bridge crew. "Let's look alive now, gentlemen. It's time we bagged ourselves another destroyer. Up scope."

"Splashes," came the call from the sailor monitoring the hydrophones. "Sound distant."

Squinting into the scope, Morrison found his target. "Range, 1475 yards. Mark."

"Zero-eight-one."

"Ready tube one," Morrison snapped. "Fire."

"One away."

Morrison moved the periscope to set the next attack. "Mark."

"Zero-seven-eight."

"Fire four." Moments later torpedo four was in the water following a course a few degrees off from its predecessor. Soon torpedoes five and six were launched. The *Triggerfish*'s forward torpedo tubes were now empty, and it would be fifteen minutes before they were loaded again. Morrison began to pray for a successful run. If all went well, all four torpedoes would find their mark and detonate. If all went wrong, none of his crew would see the surface again.

"Ten seconds to first impact," Sapolsky said, looking at his stopwatch. Ten seconds passed. Nothing. The moments oozed by in thick slowness. Sapolsky shook his head. "Torpedo one is a miss. Eight seconds to impact of torpedo number four."

Like the rest of the crew, Morrison was holding his breath—again.

"I have impact, Captain," the sailor monitoring the hydrophone said. His voice was tinged with fear. "Sorry, sir, no detonation. The torpedo was a dud."

Morrison swore. Now everything rested on the last two torpedoes.

"Three seconds to impact," Sapolsky said.

The sub vibrated as concussive waves of water rolled over it. The crew cheered.

"Belay that!" Morrison ordered. There was one more fish in the water and he desperately wanted to hear the impact. It came eight seconds later. "Up scope."

The crew was silent as Morrison searched for the destroyer. It was there. Smoke, heavy with oil, poured from the stern of the ship. A moment later there was an explosion, followed by another.

"Well done, gentlemen," Morrison said with a laugh. "We hit her in the fanny. Two torpedoes in the engine room. The only place the ship is going is down."

The crew roared again, and this time Morrison allowed them the release.

"What now, Captain?" Sapolsky asked.

"Surface and pursue the merchant ship," Morrison answered. "That'll give us time to reload the tubes and charge the batteries."

"What about the troopship?"

"I don't know, Commander."

"You believe what Kunzig said about the POWs?"

Morrison shrugged. "I'm not sure. He was right about the lead destroyer. You get us topside. I'm going to have another talk with our guest."

"Yes, sir," Sapolsky answered immediately. "Oh, and sir?"

"Yes?"

"Good work, sir. Very good work."

Morrison answered with a smile and climbed down the metal ladder to the sound of applause from the crew in the conning tower and control room.

Stanton was exhilarated. Standing high on the submarine, the Coronado Bridge behind him, the warm August air caressing his face, the smell of salt water mingled with diesel from the tugs, the slapping of water against a metal hull reminded him of a truth he had spent months denying: He missed the sea.

The bridge upon which he stood was nothing like the one he was used to. He had skippered an Ohio class sub for COMSUBALT. That vessel had been larger, faster, and nuclear powered. It could do in a single patrol what the *Triggerfish* would require several to do, and it carried enough electronics to rival every ship in World War II.

There was a universe of difference between the two craft in every respect but one: the men. That never changed. The men who chose submarine duty were a special breed with hearts and minds unique in the navy. In that sense, nothing had changed since the advent of submarine warfare. Stanton may have captained one of the most technologically advanced machines the world had ever seen, but at heart he was no different than the former captain of the *Triggerfish*. There was a kinship that spanned the decades as if they were little more than minutes. Stanton wished he could have met the man who came to a mysterious end. No doubt that they would have been fast friends, but the passage of time made that impossible. The *Triggerfish* had gone missing a few years before Stanton was born.

Looking up, Stanton saw the news helicopter hovering in the distance. The airspace over the Naval Amphibious Base was controlled. They would have to videotape at a distance, which was just fine with Stanton.

"Tugs are coming about now," Stewart said easily. "They'll have us docked in short order."

"Too bad." Stanton looked at the wood dock that was thrust out into the bay.

"I know what you mean. That trip was entirely too fast." The tugs had towed the *Triggerfish* from Torrey Pines State Beach to Coronado in just under three hours. For some that would seem a long time, but to Stanton and Stewart it was an inadequate duration to spend on the bridge of the classic sub. "You don't suppose that they'll let us gas her up and take her for a little spin, do you?"

Stanton laughed. "I doubt it."

"I'm sure I could shanghai enough men to make it possible."

"Coast Guardsmen operating a sub? I didn't know that was part of your training."

"It's not, but we could make it work."

"I bet you could, Commander," Stanton said. "You'd probably have to fight off quite a few sailors first."

"We could do that too."

Again Stanton laughed and then turned to Donna. "What about it, Lieutenant? Would you fight for the honor of the navy and the right to be the first to take the *Triggerfish* out?"

She looked pale. "Sorry, Captain, that's just too much machismo for me."

A concern, like that of a father for his daughter, swelled within him. "Are you all right, Lieutenant? You've hardly said a word for the last three hours, and you look a little pale. Not seasick, are you?"

Donna shook her head. "No sir, just a little off, that's all. I'll be fine. Just a twenty-four-hour bug or something."

For reasons he could not articulate, Stanton didn't believe her. Something was haunting the woman. "Once we're docked and secure, you can go home. Get some rest."

"Thank you, sir, but I need to show you to your quarters. You did request a place to stay on the island."

"Just point the way, Wilcox. I'll find it."

Stewart chimed in. "We could sleep in the sub's berthing area. I've always wanted to do that."

"We?" Stanton said with mock surprise. "As I said earlier, I'm playing this one by the book."

"The navy has a book on dealing with mysterious appearances of six-decade-old ghost ships?"

"Sure," Stanton answered glibly. "I'm writing it right now."

"I want a copy," Stewart said.

"Autographed no doubt," Stanton replied.

"Sure. That way I can get an extra twenty-five cents for it at a garage sale."

"Cute," Stanton answered quickly. "You know, I could make you walk the rest of the way." Both men looked at the quarter mile of bay that separated the boat from the dock.

"I'm good, Captain Stanton, but I'm not that good."

Stanton guffawed then turned to see if Donna was laughing too. She wasn't. She stood motionless with her back to the tower and her eyes on the deck as if it were about to open up a dark hole and swallow her alive. Something was bothering her, something other than a twenty-four-hour bug. She was frightened. Stanton had seen fear many times before and knew it had its own look. Donna broadcast that look with every inch of her body. It was as though she sensed something. Stanton and Stewart exchanged glances, and he knew the commander had sensed her disquiet too. He needed to change her focus.

"Lieutenant Wilcox," he said firmly.

"Sir," she answered immediately, snapping her head up.

"Before you go home tonight, I would like you to arrange a pass for Commander Stewart. Can you do that?"

"Yes, sir, I can."

"Very well. I would like you to get on that as soon as we dock. Then call it a day. I want you fresh and here first thing in the morning."

"First thing, sir?" she questioned.

"0600 hours. I don't want to lose any daylight. That's not too early for you, is it, Lieutenant?"

"Uh, yes, sir—I mean, no, sir. I'll be here at 0600."

He turned to Stewart. "Assuming the Commander would like to be here tomorrow and can get the day off."

"I'll be here, Captain. I'll be here with bells on."

"Stow the bells, Commander. Just bring coffee. Real coffee." Stanton shook his head. "Most technologically advanced service in the world, and we still can't make a cup of coffee that wouldn't double for paint thinner."

"We have the same problem," Stewart said. "Maybe we should stop making it with water from the bay."

Stanton shuddered at the thought. "That would help."

"What's next, Captain?" Donna asked.

"I've already radioed ahead for a dive team. I want the hull searched one more time. I want to know what that sound was."

The expression on Donna's face said that she would just as soon not know.

Chapter 5

Bubbles raced up Dan Toller's faceplate in a frothy mass. Illuminated by the harsh white work lights mounted to the wooden pier, the seawater glowed an eerie moss green and the bubbles rose to the surface like an effervescent waterfall in reverse. He inhaled deeply, hearing the regulator on his yellow dive helmet release, surrendering a flow of sweet yet metallic air.

Weightless. Despite the heavy pair of tanks he wore on his back, the water and buoyancy compensator made Dan feel as if he were drifting in outer space, an image made all the more real by the dark sky above. Womblike the water supported him, caressed him, swallowed him whole.

Another noisy breath. Inhalation. Exhalation.

He looked at his watch: 2115 hours. He glanced at his gages: water temperature, sixty-two degrees; depth, ten feet; tanks, full. This was going to be an easy dive: warm water, minimum depth, minimum time in the water, easy work. Then he could go home.

Actually he should have already been home, sitting in his easy chair, his feet up, remote control in his hand, Dinky his cocker spaniel snoozing beside his chair. But if he couldn't do that, then he would just as soon be in the water.

He had always been a water rat, spending his summers at the beach, bodysurfing or skin diving. Not a week passed where he had not skipped at least one day of school to make his way down to the shore. Had he been more attentive to his studies, he might have chosen college over the navy. But such was not the case. He, like many of his generation, matured late. Now, at the still youthful age of twenty-two, he was seeing the value in education. Next semester, he would start classes at Mesa Junior College. *Who could say*, he would tell himself, *maybe there are officer stripes for me yet.*

In the meantime, he did his job and did it well. His comfort with the ocean made him the top diver in his class at the Naval Diving and Salvage Training Center in Panama City, Florida. After two years' service in Florida, he was transferred to San Diego. He excelled at his work, which meant two things: He was his chief's favorite diver, and he got all the difficult jobs.

This job, however, was a walk in the park. He had already done a free dive to inspect the hull of the submarine once today at Torrey Pines State Beach. Now he had been asked to do it again as it floated free in the bay waters of Coronado. Dan had anticipated this. Once the sub was free of the sand, he knew that another inspection would be called for. After meeting Captain Stanton, he knew this for a fact. Stanton was a no-nonsense, cautious officer, and it took less than ten seconds for Dan to realize that. Stanton would want a close inspection.

What Dan had not anticipated was Stanton's insistence that it be done right away. He had assumed that he would do a hull inspection the next morning. Chief Jerry Gerard had cornered Dan in a locker room just before he was about to leave for home.

"Sorry, Danny-boy," the chief had said, "but ya gotta hang for a while. They're bringing that sub in, and they want us to eyeball her hull one more time."

"Tonight?"

"Yup. Got a radio message and Captain Stanton wants the inspection done ASAP, if not sooner. I'm having work lights set up right now. You'll be in the water ten minutes after she arrives."

"Eager beaver, isn't he?" Dan said with a smile. "I suppose you could get a chopper to fly me out there and drop me in the water. Then I could swim alongside and inspect her as she's towed."

"Cute, Danny-boy, but don't act smart with the captain. He may not like your sense of humor."

"Got it, Chief. When is she due?"

"Another hour, maybe less. They're taking it real slow. You know, babying her along."

Dan chuckled. "They should. That boat is even older than you, Chief."

Chief Gerard raised an eyebrow. "Keep it up, smart mouth, and I'll find some really nasty work for you to do tomorrow."

Raising his hands in mock surrender, Dan said, "Take it easy, Chief. You know you're my favorite N.C.O. in the whole navy. We're buds."

"Well, buddy, just make sure you're ready in fifty minutes. And I want this inspection done fast. I was supposed to be at a poker game tonight."

"Just think of all the money you've saved by being here with me."

"Yeah, right. Just be on time. Be ready. And be quick. Got it?"

"Aye, Chief. I'll be there with a big smile."

"See that you are."

That conversation seemed ages away even though it happened just over an hour ago.

Dan bent his body at the waist, pushing his head down and then elevating his feet. His rubber swim fins broke the surface as he began kicking to gain forward momentum. Soon he was moving effortlessly through the water toward the steel leviathan that floated ten yards away. As he swam he flicked the switch on the DH-1, dual beam dive light. Instantly twin 100-watt beams pierced the water. The handheld light system was tethered by a long abrasion-resistant cable to a 500-watt generator on the dock. He had plenty of light, plenty of cable, and plenty of time.

The logical place to start was the bow of the submarine. Since the bow and two-thirds of the keel had been resting on sand at Torrey Pines, Dan had been unable to fully inspect the hull. The best he had been able to do was search for leaks and buckling. He had found none. But the boat had been towed off the sand, and that in itself may have caused damage.

Beams from the underwater light pushed back the green, inky water and fell on the gray steel hide of the *Triggerfish*. A few kicks later, he was able to run his gloved hand along the hull. Despite his thick nylon and neoprene gloves, the ship felt cold, icy, forbidding. Slowly, he ran his hands along the steel hull, taking note of every welded joint. The paint was deeply scratched as if a thousand tiny talons had clawed at it. That was to be expected. The unforgiving sand was sure to leave its imprint in the old paint. That didn't matter as long as there were no creases in the steel or buckling at the weld joints.

An unexpected chill ran down Dan's spine, surprising him. He felt warm. The wet suit he wore allowed ocean water in to form a thin layer of moisture between his skin and the suit. His body would then warm that water, creating a balanced and comfortable environment. It was not unusual to feel a chill when first entering the bay, but that lasted only moments. In fact, the bay was warm enough to dive in without a wet suit. But dive suits were worn as insulation against not only cold, but also unforeseen hazards such as sharp objects.

"How ya doing, Danny-boy?" The voice of Chief Gerard crackled loudly over the speaker in Dan's helmet. Communication was the reason that he was wearing a helmet instead of just a dive mask. Gerard wanted to maintain constant contact.

"Just peachy, Chief," Dan replied, knowing that the built-in microphone would relay his words topside. "How about joining me? The water's fine."

"It's better for you that I don't."

Dan chuckled. "How is that?"

"Just seeing me in the water would fill your little heart with envy. It would be hard on your ego."

"Thanks, Chief. I'm glad one of us is looking out for my self-esteem."

"How's she look?" Gerard asked, his voice turning serious.

"So far, so good. Her makeup is a little smeared from where she ran aground. So far there's no buckling or leaks."

"Those old coffins had sound equipment heads protruding from the hull. They shouldn't be too far back from the bow."

"Yeah, I see them." Dan turned on his back, swimming upside down, and moved along the bottom of the sub, patiently checking the hull as he did. He found the hydrophone heads. "I've never been under an old dog like this one, Chief, but these don't look right. They're pretty twisted and bent. You might be able to unload them at a garage sale, but that's about it."

"It's a wonder they weren't sheared right off when the tow began."

"It's a wonder," Dan echoed as he continued along the keel. "That seems to be all the damage."

His attention was directed to the steel in front of him, but from time to time Dan would look down the length of the submarine. Partly out of curiosity, partly to keep his bearings. When he had inspected the first half of the hull, he turned his light and shone it into the dark waters at the stern of the ship. He could barely make out the rudder between the twin propellers. It sat straight and true just like it did when he made his first inspection.

"How far back do you want me to go, Chief?"

"All of it, Danny-boy. Every inch."

Dan sighed noisily knowing that the sound would be carried to the surface. He saw no need to inspect the stern third of the sub. That part had not been aground and therefore should be unchanged from the last time he had inspected it. Still, orders were orders.

The problem with inspecting the hulls of ships was the monotony. There was very little to see. All he could do now was give it his best and concentrate. The work would go more quickly then and—

Thumpa, thumpa, thumpa, thumpa, thumpa.

Dan froze.

"What was that?" he asked with surprise.

"What was what?" the chief asked in return.

"I thought I heard something. It sounded like . . ." His voice trailed off.

"It sounded like what?" Gerard prompted. "What'd you hear?"

"A thumping sound. Like a basketball rolling down a staircase, or maybe . . . maybe a small animal running on a tin roof."

"I didn't hear anything up here. Are you sure you heard something?"

"Yeah, I am. Stand by." Dan leaned his head forward and rested his helmet on the skin of the submarine and waited. Any sound in the sub would be transmitted through the hull and into his helmet. His heart was pounding.

Nothing.

Nothing.

Thumpa, thumpa, thumpa, thumpa, thumpa.

"There it is again," Dan said excitedly. "I heard it as sure as I hear you. Is anyone walking on deck?"

There was a pause. Dan knew the chief was checking. "No. No one on deck at all."

"Odd," he said, wishing he could scratch his head. "I've never heard anything like it."

"Did it sound mechanical?"

"No. At least I don't think so." Dan's heart was still pounding and he didn't know why. Something inside him was screaming a warning he could barely hear but could not understand.

"Where are you?" Gerard asked firmly.

"About two hundred feet back from the bow, Chief," Dan said as he looked back over the hull he had just covered. Then he turned and looked astern. His heart skipped a beat. "This is crazy."

"What?" Gerard demanded. "What's crazy?"

Dan drew in a ragged breath. "The rudder. I was sure it was set amidships, but now it's cut starboard."

"Maybe the current moved it," Gerard offered.

"I'm in the same bay, Chief. If a current moved it, then it would have moved me too."

"Check that," the chief agreed. "Maybe it's busted loose from the helm or maybe—"

"Something doesn't feel right, Chief," Dan interrupted. "Something ain't right here."

"Take it easy, son," Gerard said firmly. "Ain't nothin' here that's gonna hurt anybody. Finish your inspection, then get up here. I'll buy you a drink when you're done."

"Aye, Chief," Dan said without conviction. He didn't think a drink would be much help.

Slowly, Dan moved along the hull, searching with his eyes, but now also listening with his ears. He had heard something. He was sure of it. Something in or on the sub had moved.

As he proceeded, he attempted to rationalize away his fear. So what if something moved inside the sub? It was an old vessel; something probably fell and rolled on the deck. The sub had, after all, taken a bit of a beating being run aground and then towed off the beach. Anything could come loose. Besides, whatever it was, was on the inside and he was on the outside. He looked astern again. This time the rudder was cranked full port. He started to report the change but decided against it. He felt foolish as it was, and he didn't want the chief to think that he was losing his edge.

Moments flowed slowly like cold molasses. In his chest, his heart thundered as if it were trying to break free. He could hear his breathing becoming more ragged. His mouth was cotton dry and his face soaked with perspiration.

Come on, he thought, *get a grip. A little noise and you freak. Stop being a baby. You should be ashamed of yourself.*

He felt no better, no calmer, no more assured.

Another ten feet of keel passed under his sight, followed by another ten. Dan touched the hull with his left hand as he held the bright light in his right. He paused, then willed himself to look ahead toward the rudder.

It had moved again. This time it was amidships—its original position.

"Rudder has moved again, Chief." He tried to sound calm but knew he was failing miserably.

"It must be broken loose, Dan. If so, there may be more damage. You'd better take a look."

Dan didn't want to take a look. His subconscious or something else was screaming like an air-raid siren. What he wanted to do was get out of the water as quickly as possible.

Knock it off! he shouted silently in his mind. *You've been in freezing water, fast currents, and deep diving with a 150 feet of water above you. Get a grip. Get a grip now!*

"Did you get that, sailor?" the Chief demanded.

"Aye, Chief. I got it. On my way."

Dan kicked, his flippers digging into the water pushing him forward. When he arrived at the rudder, he shifted to a vertical "heads up" orientation.

The rudder was fixed between the two, heavy, large props of the *Triggerfish*. A thick propeller shaft ran from the props themselves into the hull. A stern plane, used to raise or lower the stern of the boat when submerged, jutted out horizontally on the starboard and port sides.

Willing himself not to think, but to act, Dan reached out and seized the rudder and attempted to move it. It was locked in place. He examined the rudder support shaft that pierced the hull and provided the mechanical force necessary to move the large, flat piece of metal. Dan released the light so that he could use both hands. As he did, it slowly fell away, bound to him by a thirty-inch nylon tether. Darkness replaced the artificial illumination. With the rudder in both hands, Dan pushed and pulled. Nothing. He had hoped to find it swinging free, which would explain the movement. Instead he found it rigid, fixed.

"Rudder seems locked into place, Chief," Dan said. "She's rock solid. I can't budge her at all."

"Is it securely attached?" Gerard sounded puzzled.

"Best that I can tell," Dan replied. "Hang on. I dropped my light." He looked down into the darkness and saw the light right where it should be, less than three feet away. He reached for it.

Thumpa, thumpa, thumpa, thumpa, thumpa.

Dan snapped his head up toward the dark hulk above him. It was back. The undefined It. Quickly, he grabbed the light and shone it upward toward the hull.

There was a sound. A new sound. A terrible, frightening, deadly sound. Turning and pointing the light in the direction of the noise, Dan saw his nightmare. The propellers were turning.

"The props!" he shouted and attempted to kick his way back up the hull away from the spinning blades. At first he made headway, but just as he was about to turn over and swim for his life, he felt it—the current, artificially induced by the rapidly turning screws.

"What's happening?" Gerard's words echoed in Dan's helmet. "What about the props?"

Dan had no time to talk. He was being dragged into the churning shredder. "No, no, NO!" he screamed. Instinctively he reached up to grab for support, any support, something to help him pull himself away from the horrible death that drew him, clutched him. "No, no, no, no." It was a mistake. He grabbed the revolving propeller shaft which instantly tore his glove away and most of his hand.

Dan Toller screamed, his voice echoing in his helmet. As he did, he released the underwater light. The current sucked it back and into the props. The light was followed by its nylon tether, which was followed by Dan's arm.

His last sight was the white, churning, frothing water; his last sensation was the sound of a propeller blade striking his helmet.

Λ

"What the—" Chief Gerard said to himself. He was looking at the stern of the submarine. It took a second for him to realize what he was seeing. The submarine had come to life, its props spinning madly. "Dan!" he screamed.

Just then, the power cable that was attached to the handheld dive light began to tighten. Then it snapped taut, ripping it from the grip of Gerard's hands. The sub moved forward, straining at its moorings.

"Dan!" he bellowed again. Less than a second later the cable pulled the generator off the deck and into the water. "Dan!" The chief ran to the sub. He was screaming. "Help! Help!"

Twenty steps later he was on the deck of the sub racing to the stern. He slipped and fell, but was on his feet in a second. Leaning over the rail he saw the bubbling caldron of seawater.

"Dan!" Gerard threw a leg over the sub's cable railing. He had no idea what he was doing, but he had to do something. He had to try. He had to maintain hope.

One more look into the agitated water cruelly stripped away the last shreds of that hope. The white water was tinged with a growing cloud of red.

Then, as mysteriously as they began, the propellers stopped.

N
⋀

"Begging the captain's pardon," Chief Gerard said forcefully, "and with all due respect to his rank, I was here and you weren't. Your sub killed my diver."

"Chief—" Stanton began.

"And don't blame it on inexperience," Gerard shouted. "He was one of my best. Scratch that. He was my *best* diver. He knew what he was doing."

"I believe that, Chief, but—"

"It wasn't inexperience that put Dan Toller in a body bag. No, sir."

"As you were, Chief!" Stanton snapped.

"Yes, sir," Gerard answered, unable to disguise his anger.

"No one is blaming you or Toller," Stanton said firmly. "I can't imagine what it is like to see what you just saw, but I need to have you focused. Understood?"

"Understood, sir."

"Good. Now take a deep breath and start from the beginning."

"Yes, sir." Gerard related each event as it happened, but could offer very little information. His view was topside. All he could relate was the sudden churning of the ocean behind the sub and the power line snapping from his hands and the generator being jerked into the water.

Puzzled, Stanton could only shake his head.

"It's the truth, Skipper."

"I believe you, Chief. I believe you. I just don't see how it's possible." Stanton turned to Stewart. "I don't suppose you've heard of anything like this."

Stewart and Stanton had chosen to grab a bite to eat at a restaurant on base and swap career stories. One hour later a pair of military police officers found them, told them an accident had occurred, and that Stanton was to accompany them to the *Triggerfish*. Stewart tagged along.

"No, Captain," Stewart replied, bewildered. Over dinner it had been first names, but in the presence of an enlisted man proper titles were used. "Only ghost stories."

"I'm looking for something a little more substantial, Commander."

The three men walked to the edge of the pier. The area was bathed in blue and red lights from military police and an ambulance. There was little they could do but stare into the water and at the dark mass of the submarine.

"Something ain't right about that boat, sir," Gerard offered softly. "To tell you the truth, it scares me. It scares me a whole bunch."

Stanton looked at the squat man next to him. He didn't seem the kind to frighten easily. But seeing what he had seen was enough to intimidate anyone. "Did Toller have a family?"

"No wife or kids," Gerard replied, "but he's got a mom and dad who live up in Escondido."

"You want me to tell them?" Stanton asked softly.

"No, sir," Gerard replied immediately. "He was my man and he died on my watch. It's my job."

"Take a chaplain with you, Chief. Don't do this alone. It's not good for you and it's not good for his parents. A chaplain can help a lot."

"I haven't had much use for the chaplains," Gerard said. "I can't say that I could call one by name."

"Get in touch with Lieutenant Commander Jim Walsh. He's my brother-in-law. He's a good man. I'll vouch for him."

"Yes, sir."

"You're dismissed, Chief. There's nothing more you can do here."

"Aye, sir."

"Oh, and Chief. You might want to talk to the chaplain yourself. If I had just witnessed what you did, I know I would want to."

"Thank you, sir. I may just do that." Gerard paused. "May I ask a question, sir?"

"Feel free."

"What are you going to do next?"

Stanton thought for a moment. "The answers are still inside the sub. I think it's time we go in."

Gerard shuddered as he looked at the sub, its dull gray hull bathed in harsh artificial light. "Better you than me, Skipper. Better you than me."

From the air, Coronado Island looked like the arthritic thumb of an aged hitchhiker, stuck deep into the waters of San Diego Bay. There were only three ways to get to the island city: ferry over from the San Diego side of the bay; cross the Coronado Bridge; or drive up Silver Strand, the long, narrow, land bridge that connected Coronado with Imperial Beach to the south.

Only three ways to Coronado unless one had access to a helicopter, and Barry Ludlow had such access. The Channel 12 chopper hovered in position just outside the controlled airspace over the Naval Amphibious Base. Using the powerful zoom on the nose camera, he tightened the shot.

"Can't you get closer?" Barry asked with annoyance.

"Not and keep my license," the pilot snapped back. "This is as close as I'm going to get. Those navy types get pretty serious about their airspace."

"We wouldn't have to stay long. Just a quick flyover."

"Three chances, Barry: slim, fat, and none. Unless you want to get out and walk."

"Very funny." Barry turned his attention back to the video monitor. "There are sure a lot of red and blue lights down there. Something's happened. I just can't tell what."

The pilot looked over at the monitor at the feet of the reporter. "The ambulance is clear enough. Obviously someone is hurt."

"Obviously. Unfortunately, I can't do a story like that. I can hear it now: 'Sometime this evening, something happened to someone that required an ambulance. Thanks for tuning in.' I need more information."

"I guess you're gonna have to make some calls."

"I'll do that, you can bet on it, but it would be better if I had some ammunition. Something with which to press the issue. Pictures are good for that."

"You really think you can push the navy around? I spent eight years in the service myself. If they don't want you to know something, then you're not going to know it."

"I wouldn't be so sure. Where there's Barry, there's a way."

The pilot shook his head. "I'm getting low on fuel. I'm heading back."

"No. Give me a couple more minutes."

"You're welcome to stay, but me and the helicopter are leaving."

"I could have your job, you know," Barry snapped, hoping to intimidate the pilot.

"If the likes of you can take my job, then I don't want it. The truth is, you're hanging on at the station by a thread. Scuttlebutt has it that management hasn't offered you a renewal on your contract. That's got to be scary. Not knowing if you're going to have a job in a couple of months. I could go back to the producer and tell her that you were insisting that I do illegal and unsafe flying."

"All right, all right. You win. Let's go. But I will find out what's going on. We'll see how secure my job is then."

"Whatever you say, Barry. Whatever you say."

Barry swore under his breath as the helicopter banked to the right and flew toward the bejeweled skyline of San Diego. It was bad enough that his job was in jeopardy, but it was worse having the whole studio know about it. He would prove his worth to them. He was not sure how, but he would. He would get the story and that would bring him enough attention that they would not dare let his contract lapse.

Chapter 6

Silky smoothness. Embracing warmth. Air fragrant with lavender. A soft blanket of silence broken only by the occasional drop of water that fell from the brass faucet through the afghan of bubbles and into the hot bathwater.

Donna Wilcox let out a long, cleansing sigh. The moment was perfect and she wished that it could go on for days.

Leaving the NAB and that . . . that . . . submarine behind, she took a cab to her small house. If anything good had happened that day, it was that the powers that be had decided to moor the *Triggerfish* at the Naval Amphibious Base on Coronado. Since she lived in Coronado, it took her less than half an hour to call for a cab and arrive home. Tomorrow she would pick her car up from the Fleet Submarine Warfare Center where she left it. It would have to be in the afternoon since her presence was required at 6:00 A.M. Retrieving it tonight would require that she hire a cab, or bother a friend to drive her over the bridge around the city and into Point Loma and then make the drive back again. She was too tired and annoyed for that. Tired because of the length of her day, annoyed at her less-than-stellar performance before Captain Stanton. He had been understanding, but another captain might not have let her off so easy.

She sighed again, letting the hot water draw out the tension she felt in every muscle. Riding that old tub from Torrey Pines to Coronado should have been a thrill. It sure was for Stanton and Stewart. They maintained the proper officer comportment, but anyone with eyes could see that the men were having more fun than a ten-year-old at Disneyland.

Why hadn't it been fun for her? Was it because she was a woman? Was the love of the sea and the ships that sailed her gender-biased?

No. That wasn't it. Donna knew what the problem was. She was scared. Not of seasickness or even drowning. She had no fear that the vintage sub would sink in deep water. Her fear was ... impossible to define. It was irrational, insubstantial, devoid of reason. Yet it was there, covering her, burrowing into her heart and mind like worms in the soft, moist earth. And the longer she remained on the *Triggerfish*, the more apprehensive she became.

What terrified her? What oozed into her mind leaving her thoughts riddled with doubt? She had no idea, but she did know that the submarine filled her with dark foreboding.

It was time to put those thoughts aside, to force them from her mind. Slowly slipping further into the tub, she let the water rise up her body until it gently caressed her chin. She smiled, because the bubbles tickled her cheeks. Tilting her head, she plunged her tawny hair beneath the surface. The hot water made her skin and scalp tingle. A "champion" bubble bather since she was a child, she knew her healthy pink skin was turning red and wrinkled from its long exposure to water. That was just fine with her. The only other plans she had for the night included a Robin Cook novel and bed.

Nothing to do now but relax. Let tomorrow's troubles come with tomorrow. They had no place in the now. Not at this moment. She was treating herself, and she planned—

A harsh ringing filled the tiny bathroom. Donna sat straight up with a start. Water sloshed over the edge of tub and onto the pale yellow vinyl floor.

The ringing screamed for attention again.

"Why did I have to bring the remote in here?" she asked herself angrily. Quickly she grabbed a towel and dried her left hand. She then picked up the phone off the floor, pressed the answer button, and held it to her wet ear.

"Yeah," she said unceremoniously.

"Lieutenant Wilcox?" a male voice asked.

"Yes," she recognized the voice. It was Captain Stanton.

"Sorry to bother you at home, but I need you down here right away. There's been an accident."

"What kind of accident?"

"A death. I'll explain later."

She was nonplused. "I don't see what I can—"

"Lieutenant, I don't have time to talk. I think the press may get hold of this and if they do, then you're going to talk to them. I don't want to, so you get the privilege."

"Yes, sir. I'll be there in thirty minutes."

"Very well. Oh, and Lieutenant?"

"Yes?"

"We're opening up the sub tonight. Time to let the ghosts out of the ship."

Donna felt her heart seize in her chest. She sat in the hot tub feeling ice cold. A shiver ran down her spine.

"You still there, Lieutenant?"

"Uh, yes, sir. I'll be ready, sir."

"See you in thirty."

"In thirty, sir."

Donna turned off the phone and set it back on the floor.

N
Λ

The headlights of the silver Mercedes pushed back the blackness of the night-shrouded road as it weaved cautiously through the back streets of Riverside, ninety minutes north of San Diego. Turning from the paved road, Hermann directed his expensive sedan onto a narrow dirt path that jarred the car, challenging its suspension. Around him were countless trees whose leaves rustled in concert with each other. Opening the sunroof, Hermann took in a deep breath. Orange blossoms, rich and omnipresent, perfumed the air. The atmosphere was heavy with it, weighted with the aroma of sweet fruit.

He took his time not wanting to kick up clouds of dust that would settle on the leaves of the trees. He had too much respect for the orchard, and too much fear of the man he was about to meet. It was fear that he felt, but of a different kind than most: his was more closely akin to awe.

Hermann squinted through the windshield and into the darkness. He was being watched. No one came on this property without being seen. And no one made it this far without being stopped by serious young men dressed like farmers, equipped like soldiers. Fortunately, Hermann had had the forethought to call ahead.

Fifteen minutes after he had pulled off the road, the orchard gave way to an expanse of ground that surrounded a majestic Spanish ranchero house. The white stucco U-shaped building stood two stories tall with a balcony that ran the perimeter of the upper floor. Two men, each with AK–47 automatic rifles, kept watch from the balcony. Hermann pulled forward to the gate, parked, and exited his car. He made eye contact with the men, who nodded, acknowledging his right to be present.

Walking briskly through the night, Hermann made his way through the wrought iron gates that enclosed the courtyard at the front of the house. The gate swung easily, noiselessly. The courtyard was filled with plants and ornamental trees. A terra-cotta tile walkway ran through the verdant garden. As he approached, the massive, handmade, wood slab doors swung open on their heavy ornamental iron hinges. On the other side stood a short, stout woman with pale blond hair. She wore a maid's uniform.

"Good evening, Hilde," Hermann said, clipping his words. Hilde was a loyal employee, but she irritated Hermann with her chronic nervousness and her tendency to be melodramatic. Still, she was dependable and more importantly, safe.

"Good evening, Herr Kunzig," her voice was weighted with a thick German accent. "I hope your drive was pleasant."

"It was fine, Hilde." Hermann stepped into the lobby. "Is he well?"

"He is having a better day. Yesterday . . ." Her voice trailed off as she shook her head. She began to wring her hands and bite her lip. "I am worried about him."

"The doctors?"

"There is no more that they can do. Still, I hope. I pray."

Hermann sighed. "I see. Show me to my grandfather."

"He is on the back patio, sir. He is expecting you."

The elderly man was sitting straight up in a wheelchair sound asleep, a red wool blanket over legs made useless by a stroke. Hermann pulled up a white lacquered metal chair and sat opposite his grandfather. Hermann was a hard man but not without his sentimentalities. The sleeping man in front of him was all that he had in way of a family.

"Grandfather?"

The man before him had pale parchment skin, dotted with the dark blotches of age. His hair was a sparse thatch of gray that lay as limply on his head as his atrophied left arm lay next to his body. His breathing was shallow and irregular.

"Grandfather?" Hermann said more loudly. He feared he would startle his ancient relative. Hermann smiled to himself. Anyone else who saw the old crippled man could never conceive of the heat that resided in the wizened man's soul. He could wither most men by sheer will alone.

Instead of waking, eighty-six-year-old Gottshold Klaus Kunzig snorted loudly and shifted in his wheelchair. Hermann laughed to himself and stretched out a hand to touch Gottshold.

"Grandfather?" Hermann said, shaking him gently. "Wake up, Grandfather. It's me, Hermann."

"Huh?" Gottshold muttered in a heavy German accent. "Leave me alone, Hilde. Can't you let an old man sleep?"

"It's not Hilde, Grandfather. It's Hermann. I called to say I was coming. Do you remember?"

"Hermann?" The old man straightened in his chair and blinked in confusion. Hermann could see recollection slowly seep back into his grandfather's mind. "Of course I remember," he snapped in a voice like steel wool. "I'm old and crippled, but not stupid. Why does everyone think that because I'm old I have Alzheimer's?"

"No one thinks that you're stupid, Grandfather. I'm sorry to wake you."

"Nonsense." He waved a dismissing hand. "I sleep too much these days. Life has grown boring for me, Hermann. You, however, have nothing but bright days ahead. Schnitzel!" Gottshold bellowed suddenly. "Schnitzel! Where is that dog?"

The tiny clattering sound of dog toenails scampering along the tile entry echoed off the hard plaster walls. A chocolate brown dachshund scrambled into the room and came to a sliding stop at Gottshold's feet.

"Up, boy," Gottshold said. The dog complied, obediently jumping onto the old man's lap. "There's my boy. Have you been having supper while I sleep?" Gottshold turned to Hermann. "He eats, I sleep. It's about all we can do these days."

"Hilde tells me that you have been unwell."

"That woman worries too much. Besides, I am eighty-six years old. I'm entitled to my illness."

"We just want you to be well and comfortable," Hermann said.

"Those days are gone, Hermann." With his one good hand, he scratched the dog behind his ears. The dog responded by curling up on his lap. "You did not come here to speak of my health, Hermann. You said on the telephone you have questions?"

"Yes, I do."

"Well, before we speak of your questions, perhaps you will answer a few of mine. How are the restaurants?"

"Fine, Grandfather. Business is up in all four locations."

"Even Sacramento?"

"Yes," Hermann said. He and his grandfather owned upscale restaurants in Sacramento, San Francisco, Los Angeles, and San Diego. Hermann oversaw all the businesses. They had made him wealthy. "It has come along nicely."

"You replaced the cook?"

"Just as you ordered. He was gone the next day. The new man has real talent."

Gottshold nodded. "Good. Good. And the movement?"

"Growing too. We have twenty-five new members this month alone. We are moving slowly and cautiously. Just as you directed."

"Good. It is a mistake to grow too fast. Hitler learned that. Too fast is too much. Mistakes get made; details overlooked. The wise man is a cautious man."

"The training and indoctrination goes as planned. Already we have men in high places in the government. That glorious day is closer than ever."

"It's a shame that I shall not see it."

"Now, Grandfather . . ."

Again Gottshold waved a hand. "No, no. I know the truth of the matter. My day is gone. I have served the Reich well. I have poured my life, my blood, my wealth into rebuilding it. Not like those hotheaded skinheads. They are only interested in making a name for themselves. They do not understand our goals, our vision. They love violence for the sake of violence. We, Hermann, are the true believers. We will change the world again. Make it like it was meant to be. Free of the inferior races who pollute our world. We will bring in the new civilization, Hermann. We will bring in the Fourth Reich."

He had heard all of this before. Countless times since he was a boy, his grandfather had taken him aside to teach him the truth about the Aryan race. And Hermann had drunk it in like a thirsty man. He believed it, consumed it, preached it. It would not be long before he, Hermann Kunzig, would lead the new Reich into the future. It was a day he had prepared for, a day he longed for. A day not too far away.

Hermann watched as his grandfather's vision shifted to a place distant in time and place. He knew exactly what the aged man was seeing, for it had been described to him many times. He saw the densely massed people, their hands raised in the air. He visualized the dark-haired man in the brown uniform passionately speaking to the enraptured crowd. He recalled another man in uniform standing on the rostrum near the slight, mustachioed speaker as he shouted into the microphones. He saw himself, black SS uniform impeccably pressed and worn with superhuman pride.

Moments passed as Hermann let his grandfather replay the scene in his mind, seeing, feeling, hearing it all over again like Beethoven who could hear the music long after he had gone deaf.

Gottshold smiled then sighed. "They were days of glory, Hermann. Days of power and purpose. Days of . . ." His voice trailed off. "I miss them, Hermann. I wish to be young so that I can feel the strength of German idealism again. So that I can breath in the sweet air of conquest and feel in my heart the burning . . . the burning . . . the burning . . ." A tear, small and round, meandered down the old man's parchment cheeks.

Hermann said nothing. He sat in silence and in awe of a man who could still be so passionate about a philosophy now sixty years old. He wondered if he could ever be that passionate. He was consumed by the cause before him, but he doubted that the fire that burned in him would appear any greater than a candle compared to the heat that blazed from the heart and mind of his grandfather.

"You, Hermann," the old man said, recovering his composure. "You will lead the next century into greatness. I will be gone, but you will carry the torch."

"I will succeed, Grandfather. I will succeed for you and for the truth we hold. You will be the new patriarch, the father of a new nation."

Gottshold smiled proudly. "You make an old man proud. Your questions now, Hermann. What are they?"

"When I was a boy, you told me of your brother—"

"Karl," Gottshold interjected. A frown crawled across his face. "What about him?"

"The story has become vague in my mind. You said he disappeared during the war."

"Yes." The old man shook his head. "He was not one of us, Hermann. No, not at all. He could see no future in the Reich. He was too lost in his studies."

"Studies?"

"He was an archaeologist. He knew about old civilizations. That made him useful. That saved his life. Had he not known so much, he would have been killed as a traitor for some of the things he said."

"He did not believe in the cause."

"He believed only in himself," Gottshold said sharply. "He loved only himself and his work. Our great cause was an inconvenience to him. Still, he knew things, powerful things."

"What work did he do for the Führer?"

"He was Gestapo and worked in intelligence, but he was also used by Heinrich Himmler. Himmler believed that certain practices could help us win the war."

"Practices."

"Occult arts, Hermann. It is not talked about much. All SS officers were taught the meanings of ancient magical signs and astrology. Himmler loved all things pagan. It was in his blood and Hitler listened to him. My brother Karl was called upon to educate the officers about such things." The aged man shook his head.

"Did you believe in such things, Grandfather?"

"Yes," he replied softly. "Yes, indeed. Through the ages, great armies have turned to mystical powers to aid them in their causes." His eyes shifted focus to a distant, unseen place.

"The others believed in the occult too?"

"Many did. Some just pretended. Himmler, however, lived his life by it. He listened to anyone he thought might have a gift or special knowledge. Daily, he had his horoscope read and that of the Führer. Major decisions and actions would be launched or delayed, depending on how the stars were interpreted. Karl also searched for objects."

"What kind of objects?" Hermann shifted in his seat.

"The Holy Grail. Himmler even traveled to France to search an old monastery. He found nothing. There was another item … what was it?" Gottshold fell silent and closed his eyes. Hermann was afraid that the old man had dozed off again, but then his eyes opened suddenly. "The Spear of Destiny."

Hermann shook his head. "I don't understand."

"My brother Karl told me of it. He said that it had been found and brought to Germany. It was said to have great powers and assured victory to any army that possessed it."

"What is it?"

"The metal head of a spear, Hermann. The spear that pierced Christ's side while he hung on the cross."

The younger Kunzig studied his grandfather for a moment. Gottshold had reared Hermann from the time he was six. Since both his mother and father had been killed in a car crash, his grandfather was the only parent he had known. The discipline had been strict, but respectful and laced with love. His grandfather had taught him many things, but religion was not one of them. Gottshold Kunzig had no use for spiritual matters. Still, Hermann had grown up in a country that prided itself on the free expression of religion. Although he had never set foot in a church, he had heard the story of the Jewish Jesus and how he had died on the cross.

"Do you mean the spear the centurion used to stab Jesus?"

"Yes, yes. It was the only success that Himmler had. There were rumors that the cup of Christ had been found, but no one believed such stories. There had also been a search for the Ark of the Covenant, but that too was a waste of time."

"Ark of the Covenant. Like Indiana Jones?"

"Yes, but it was never found."

"I remember you saying that your brother disappeared."

The old man nodded. "We were to have a meal together but he never arrived. I checked with everyone I could, but he was gone. Later I learned that he was wanted by the Gestapo. Since I was his brother, I was questioned severely. Had I not been so useful to the cause and proven myself over the years, I might have been held accountable. Karl would have known that. His running away caused me great pain and eroded my position in the SS. But he did more than just run away: He stole things, things Hitler and Himmler held as invaluable. No effort was spared to find him; no cost was too great. But they failed."

Hermann's brain swirled. "You never heard from him again?"

"Not directly," Gottshold said wearily. Hermann could see that the conversation was wearing out the old man. "I learned that he had stowed away on a ship. Toward the end of the war I learned something else. Our navy picked up a signal from an Allied submarine. Karl's name was mentioned. That is all I know."

The old man drifted again, his eyes distant, his lips moving in silence. He took a deep breath and said wistfully, "We would have been victorious, Hermann. Our cause would have been realized, if Karl had not stolen the power."

"You really believe in the power of the objects?" Hermann asked.

"They all had it. All the great leaders. And we had it too. But Karl stole it, and with it went our victory."

Hermann remained respectfully silent, allowing his grandfather time to reflect. Then he asked, "Do you remember the name of the submarine, Grandfather?"

Gottshold shook his head. "Something to do with a gun."

"A gun?"

"Hammer, barrel, something like that."

"Trigger?"

"Yes." The old man smiled at hearing the word. "Trigger."

"The *Triggerfish*?" Hermann pressed. "Could it have been the *Triggerfish*?"

Gottshold thought for a moment. "Yes. The *Triggerfish*. Why do you ask? What is all this about?"

Amazed, Hermann leaned back in his chair. "I think your brother may have come back for a visit."

Gottshold's eyes grew wide. "Back? For a visit? You have heard from Karl?" The old man became excited and leaned forward in his chair. "Tell me, boy, have you heard from him? Does he have the objects?"

Hermann explained about the mysterious rising of the *Triggerfish*. As he did, his grandfather became all the more excited.

"Hilde!" Gottshold called loudly. "Hilde! Come here right now."

The woman scampered in, her eyes wide with fright. "What is it, Herr Kunzig? Is everything all right? Are you ill?"

"No, I'm not ill," the old man snapped. "Bring me the book. Bring it to me now."

"Grandfather," Hermann said, "you need to settle down. This is not good for you."

"Bring me the book!"

Hilde turned, ran from the room, and returned a minute later. In her hand was a large, old, leather-bound book. "Here it is, Herr Kunzig."

"Give it to me," he ordered, extending his hand. She complied. "Now leave. Leave now."

When they were alone again, Gottshold leaned forward, smiled, and said, "I have something for you, Hermann. Something very remarkable."

N
Λ

"You did not believe me, did you, Herr Captain?" Karl Kunzig was seated at the table in Wardroom Two.

Morrison just stared at the German. No, he had not believed him, not at first. Still, he had been right about the maneuvers of the destroyer. Had he listened, things might have gone more smoothly. Not that Morrison was complaining. The *Triggerfish* had sunk two battleships in a single encounter, then had chased down the supply ship and troopship, sinking the first and leaving the latter.

"I chose not to sink the troopship," Morrison said flatly. "That may have been a mistake."

"It was not a mistake. That ship carried prisoners of war, Captain. If you had sent her to the bottom, she would have dragged English and American soldiers with her." Kunzig smiled. "My guess is that you have used your radio to have the ship intercepted and the prisoners off-loaded. No?"

"Yes," Morrison admitted. The German seemed to know everything. "I don't have room on the submarine to take aboard that many people. Especially those needing medical help. I assume they will need medical help."

"Yes. Prisoners are not treated kindly. Better than the Jews, but not good at all."

Fury welled up in Morrison. He had heard stories about prisoners who had been tortured, starved, worked to death, and treated in unimaginable ways. It took every fiber of strength he had not to board the ship himself. In the early days of the war it was not unusual for Allied submarines to stop merchant vessels, board them to check their manifests, allow the crew to abandon ship, and then sink the vessel. The war was now too intense to allow that option any longer. Since the ship was unarmed, he

112

could force it to come to, but then what? He had to let it go, and let a surface ship deal with the matter. It galled him.

"Do not be angry at me, Captain. I did not put those prisoners on that ship. Indeed, I am the one who alerted you to their existence."

"I don't know what to make of you, Kunzig. You turned on your own people."

"With respect, Captain, I have done no such thing. I have turned my back on a dictator and the mindless lackeys who follow him. Anything I do to end this war will aid my people, not hurt them."

Morrison sat in silence. It was possible that Kunzig was truly fighting for his country, not against it. Morrison certainly had no love for Hitler. Why should Kunzig? Given the chance and in the absence of fear, anyone in Germany might turn their back on the madman that ruled their country. Kunzig presented a problem. What was Morrison going to do with him? How far should he trust him?

"Do you have paper and a pencil, Captain?"

"I do. Why?"

"It occurs to me that if I were in your place, I would be filled with confusion. You must be wondering what kind of man I am and what to do with me. I wish to prove my usefulness to you. May I have the paper?"

"Armstrong, get our guest some paper and a pencil."

Armstrong stepped from the small room and returned a moment later with a blank piece of paper and handed it to the German. Writing with impeccable strokes, Kunzig began to make a list. For fifteen minutes, he jotted down information in three columns. Then he handed it to Morrison. It took only a second for the captain to realize what he was reading.

"That should help both your cause and mine, Captain."

"This is a list of ships running blockades and . . ." He read a little more. "U-boat locations?"

"Patrol areas, actually. I can't know where the submarines are at any given moment, but I know the areas they patrol."

There was an uncomfortable silence.

"Go ahead, Captain. Test me. You will see that I have spoken nothing but the truth."

"And what do you want for all this information?"

"To live, to rest, to eat, and—if it's not too much trouble— to have my bag back. Those objects are very important to me and pose no threat to you or your ship."

Morrison stood. "Let's see how accurate this is first, shall we?" He waved the paper in front of him.

"And if it is accurate?"

"Then you can have your dolls back, Mr. Kunzig."

Chapter 7

The last fifty steps came with difficulty, but Donna Wilcox willed herself forward. After receiving Captain Stanton's call, she had phoned for a cab, been dropped off at the Guadal Street entrance to the Amphibious Base, and was escorted by a military guard to the moored *Triggerfish*. Stepping from the vehicle, she took in the macabre scene. Yellow high-pressure sodium lights did battle with the night. An ambulance, its red and blue lights flashing brightly, sat idle nearby. Military police stood on the pier and the road leading to it. In front of the submarine, standing ramrod straight, was J. D. Stanton. Next to him was Commander Ira Stewart.

She took in a deep breath, clenched her fists, and steeled herself for what the next few moments would bring. On the outside she was calm, her head held erect, her stride purposeful. Inside, she quivered with a fear she could not explain; an apprehension she could not qualify. It ate at her.

"Reporting as requested, sir," Donna said as she approached Stanton. He turned and faced her, gazing through those intelligent hazel eyes.

"Sorry to get you out of the rack, Lieutenant," Stanton said.

"I wasn't in bed, sir. Just relaxing."

"Nonetheless, I'm sorry to have to disturb you, but it couldn't be helped. This has turned bad real quick."

"You mentioned the press. Have they arrived?" Donna asked.

"Not yet, and with luck they won't. But if they do, then you get to talk to them. There will be no release of information about the dead sailor until I say so. We have his family to consider."

"May I ask what happened, sir?"

Stanton looked at Stewart for a moment, then answered. "A diver inspecting the hull was sucked into the propellers."

An image of the diver caught in the spinning blades of the submarine sent a cold shiver through her spine. "I don't understand, sir. Who was in the submarine?"

"No one," Stanton snapped back. "That's the confusing part. The dive chief said that no one had gone on board and the boat wasn't left unattended long enough for anyone to sneak inside. It makes no sense. No sense at all."

"Amen to that," Stewart said. "But someone must have cranked the diesels or the electric motors. I don't see how it could happen by itself."

"What's next, Captain?" Donna asked tentatively.

"It's time we go in, Lieutenant. Maybe we missed something. Maybe someone is on board, although I don't see how."

"We, sir?"

Stanton turned to face her again. She quickly read his expression. "Would you prefer to stay topside, Lieutenant?" he asked with no tone of accusation.

Yes! her mind screamed. "No, sir."

"Very well," Stanton answered. "Let's do it."

The hard rubber heels of their shoes made a thudding sound as Stanton, Wilcox, Stewart, and two military policemen stepped from the wood dock onto the deck of the *Triggerfish*. Not more than two hours ago, Stanton had been filled with childlike excitement, standing on the bridge of one of the great engineering feats of its time. Now that joy was gone, replaced by confusion, regret, and uncertainty. The *Triggerfish* had taken a life, and he didn't know how.

A breeze rolled off the bay, surrounding the small band in the smell of the sea. The medallion moon hung high in an obsidian sky. The submarine lay motionless in its bed of water, tiny waves licking at its sleek, steel skin.

Stanton forced his eyes to travel the slotted deck. Unlike modern submarines with their smooth cylindrical shape that was free of decks, the *Triggerfish*'s main surface was topped with long, narrow, wood planks separated to allow water to drain after surfacing. It was a good design for the 1940s, but a horrible one in the days of advanced underwater listening devices. The wood-covered deck alone would make enough underwater noise to render the craft little more than a target waiting to be shot.

"Odd," Stewart said.

"What's that?" Stanton asked.

"The planking. I didn't notice it before, but it's not right."

"You mean its condition?" Stanton inquired. "I noticed that too. After fifty-plus years the wood should be rotted. This looks fairly new."

"Someone took care of her," Stewart said thoughtfully.

"But who?" Donna asked.

"Let's see if we can't find out," Stanton responded. Again he glanced along the deck. There were several ways to enter the submarine. In addition to the deck hatch there was a forward and aft escape hatch. There were also two torpedo loading hatches and a companionway forward of the conning tower. He walked along the sub, studying each possible means of ingress. He then turned to the military police. "Hancock, Eastman, we'll make entry at the forward escape hatch," he ordered. "That will drop us down in the forward torpedo room. We can work our way aft from there."

He felt silly having two men, each armed with a Beretta M9 side arm, on the submarine, but the diver's death had elevated things—a big notch. Nothing would be taken for granted. Nothing would be assumed.

Stanton stepped to the hatch and reached for it.

"Better let me, Captain," Hancock said. Stanton scowled and started to object, but Hancock continued. "It's why I get paid the big bucks, sir."

It made sense. Stanton was letting his eagerness to see inside the sub get the best of him. "Very well, sailor," he said with a wry smile, "earn those bucks."

Hancock started toward the hatch and leaned over it.

Thumpa, thumpa, thumpa, thumpa, thumpa.

"What the . . ." Hancock jumped back.

Thumpa, thumpa, thumpa, thumpa, thumpa.

"What was that?" Stewart asked with a start.

"It sounded like a rat running through an air-conditioning duct," Stanton said with surprise.

Stewart said, "A rat the size of a dog."

Stanton was puzzled. He had had a trained crew with state-of-the-art listening devices check the sub out from stem to stern while it was still aground on the beach. They had heard nothing, nothing at all. But the sound was undeniable.

Thumpa, thumpa, thumpa, thumpa, thumpa.

Stanton cocked his head as he strained to make out the noise. "I've never heard anything like that aboard a ship."

"Or off a ship," Stewart agreed.

"Maybe someone is inside," Hancock offered as he reached for the hatch wheel again, his hand hovering inches from the metal wheel that would unlock the hatch.

"Belay that," Stanton snapped.

"Sir?" Hancock asked quizzically.

"Hold off, sailor," Stanton ordered.

"I don't understand, Captain," Hancock said. "Don't you want to go in?"

"I've already lost one man; I don't plan to lose another."

"Yes, sir." Hancock stepped back.

"Wilcox," Stanton said. There was no response. He turned to face her. She stood rigid, eyes wide, the color of her skin two shades paler than normal. The terror was obvious. "Lieutenant Wilcox."

"Huh?" she said softly.

"Are you with me, Lieutenant?"

She snapped her head around and faced Stanton. "Huh, yes, sir." She blinked hard. "Yes, sir. Sorry, sir. I was just lost in thought."

Stanton didn't believe her. Anyone with eyes could see the fear draped over her face like a black veil. "I want the acoustical team back here on the double," Stanton ordered. "And—"

"Captain?" Stewart interrupted. "A moment please."

Stewart had stepped from the still-secured hatch to the port side cable railing and was looking over the side.

"What is it, Commander?"

"Please, sir. A moment of your time."

Puzzled, Stanton took the three steps necessary to join the Coast Guard commander. "What have you got . . ." Stanton's voice trailed off as he tried to make sense of what he was seeing. A white substance was floating in the water, clinging to the hull of the sub. "What is that?"

The others joined him.

"Ice," Stewart said without emotion.

"Ice?" Stanton responded in disbelief. "Ice in San Diego Bay?"

"In my younger days," Stewart said, his eyes fixed on the water, "I served aboard an ice cutter in Alaska. It wasn't my favorite duty, but it did teach me what ice looks like, and I'd bet this month's check and my left arm that we're looking at ice."

Words failed Stanton. What he was seeing was impossible, beyond the rational. It was the gist of science fiction stories. Still, slabs of ice three feet long and two feet wide bobbed on the surface of the water.

"How is that possible?" Stanton demanded.

"It's not," Stewart said. "But there it is."

"Wilcox!" Stanton snapped.

"Sir?" The reply was immediate this time.

"In addition to the acoustics team I want a haz-mat team here too." Stanton wondered what the hazardous materials team would make of this.

"Yes, sir. Right away, sir." Donna spun on her heels and jogged to the gangplank and down the pier.

"Curious," Stewart said flatly. "What do you make of all this, Captain Stanton?"

"I have no idea, Commander. No idea at all."

"A mysterious and gruesome death, strange noises, and a breach in the laws of physics," Stewart offered. "Maybe you do have a ghost ship on your hands."

"I don't believe in ghosts," Stanton replied evenly.

"Well, sir, it sure looks like they believe in you."

N

Ʌ

The cellular phone chimed to life. Barry Ludlow swore and then snapped it up from its resting place on the passenger seat of the late model Volvo. The clock in his car read 11:50. Ten more minutes and it would be a new day.

"What?" he said tersely.

"Barry, this is Amy."

"I recognize your voice, Amy. What do you want?" Barry steered his car along the on-ramp from the 805 freeway to Interstate 8. "I've put in thirteen hours today. I'm tired and I want to go home."

"You told me to call if I heard anything about the submarine."

Barry's mood immediately brightened. Amy worked at the station and knew more about San Diego and its goings-on than the mayor. "You got something."

"Yes, something big. Real big."

"Well, don't hold out on me, girl. Tell me."

"You are going to owe me big time for this one, Barry."

"Come on, Amy. We're professionals." There was silence on the other end of the phone. "All right, all right. I owe you one, but this had better be good."

"It's good. There's been a death, and it's related to the submarine."

"Whoa! No kidding? Someone died? What happened? Someone fall off the edge and drown?"

"Better than that. A sailor got chewed up by the propellers."

"No way." Barry couldn't believe his ears. "How'd that happen?"

"I'm not sure, but somehow he got sucked in or dragged in or something."

"How do you know this?"

"I know someone who works at the Naval Amphibious Base. He called thinking I might be interested. Which, of course, I was."

"Of course," Barry repeated. "Did you get a name?"

"My source doesn't want his name used."

"Not the source, Amy. The man who was killed."

"Oh. Yeah, I got the name. Just a second." Barry could hear papers shuffling. "Here it is: Hull Technician Second Class Dan Toller."

"Dan Toller," Barry repeated aloud, committing the name to memory. "Do you know if he had family?"

"No."

"Can you call your source back and ask him?"

"I guess."

"Do it. In the meantime, get me the number of someone at the NAB. Maybe I can set up an interview."

"Okay, but my friend says that they're keeping a lid on this."

"Of course they are. That's their job. It's our job to blow the lid off, Amy. That's the structure and balance of the universe. Call me when you get the number, or if you find out anything else." Barry thought for a moment as he drove. He was oblivious to the other cars around him. "Next news show is not until 6 A.M. That gives me a little time. Do we have a camera crew available?"

"George Abbey is on the up board."

"Okay, call him. I want to do a shoot tonight while it's still dark. Better atmosphere that way."

"Shall I call Allison?"

Allison Tabor was the executive news producer. She was the one who assigned stories.

"No, she's home and probably asleep. Just put a note on her desk. That'll give me time to get a jump on this thing."

"Okay, but I'm not taking the heat if she gets angry."

"Don't worry. If a head rolls, it will be mine."

"I'm holding you to that."

Barry didn't reply. He simply hung up and began looking for the next off-ramp. His weariness was dispelled by the sudden turn of events. Instead of heading home and to a warm bed, he decided to take a drive to Coronado.

N

Donna Wilcox slowly walked back toward the moored submarine. Each step was an act of will over emotion, courage over fear. Her heart pounded, her mouth was dry, her palms were coated with a thin film of perspiration. But it was her stomach that caused her the greatest discomfort. It churned and bubbled like a caldron of acid set to boil. Terror and confusion stood stirring the bubbling mass like witches from a Shakespearean play.

She wanted to go home. She wanted to flee and leave behind the eerie ghost sub. Close and lock the door. Pull tight the shades. Push its image from her mind. But she couldn't. She had a job to do and her dignity to protect. Her image as a naval officer was at stake, as well as her self-esteem. So she walked, one deliberate step after another, back to a place she did not want to be.

I'm a rational person, she thought to herself. *I live by logic and discipline. I've been trained to face danger.* Her words were unconvincing. Questions filled her mind. What was the noise they had heard while the submarine was under tow? What was the thumping sound that had startled her and the others minutes before? And who could explain the sudden appearance of ice around the hull? But most of all—and this was the question she was afraid to ask aloud—did the others *see* what she saw?

Stopping abruptly, she slammed her eyelids closed and wished the image away, but it returned anyway. It came in full color and larger than life. The sight was unbelievable. No rational person could believe it. Her stomach tightened into a fist as she saw in her mind again what she had seen on the *Triggerfish*.

Maybe it really happened. Maybe the others had seen it too. Maybe, just maybe, she wasn't alone. But they had said nothing. How could they not say something if they had seen it? It was so remarkable that comments, even gasps, would surely have been made. They must have been blind to it. Not even Hancock who stood right over it had reacted.

No, Donna decided, she was alone with this and there was no one she could tell, no one from whom to seek advice, no one to come to her aid. She certainly couldn't tell Captain Stanton. His report would surely demand a mental exam for her and become part of her permanent record. *I can hear it now*, she thought. *Lieutenant Donna Wilcox claims to have seen an apparition.* No, that wouldn't do. She had no intention of spending her career being known as the crackpot from San Diego.

But the image had been real, or at least realistic. There on the deck, underneath Hancock's feet, the wood slats came to life. Changing, morphing into something that no designer could have intended or even imagined. A face. A brutal, leering, hateful, vengeful face appeared in wood. Its lips twisted into a snarling smile as it mouthed her name: "Donna." There had been no sound, no voice, but the message was unmistakable.

The face, the hideous, awful . . . unholy face had called her by name.

The change from dirt road to pavement was only slightly noticed by Hermann as he directed the big Mercedes down a side street toward Interstate 15. He had an hour and a half to think before he arrived home. He glanced at the red letters of the clock—1:00 A.M. He wasn't the least tired. Zum Deutschen Eck, his restaurant, would be closed. All except the bar, which had another hour of business before it locked its doors. There was no sense in going there. He would check the receipts tomorrow. That would be soon enough. Besides, his mind was on what his grandfather had told him. Everything else paled; every other thought seemed unimportant.

The conversation had lasted for an hour, then they shared a meal of liver dumplings prepared by Hilde. Afterwards, both men sat, Gottshold in his wheelchair and Hermann in a black leather recliner, and drank dark beer. Hermann wondered how healthy a heavy meal of red meat followed by beer was for his grandfather. Still, the man was old and ill and probably would not live many years longer. Perhaps not even many months. What use would a healthy diet be then? The old man deserved his treats.

Aged as Gottshold's body was, his mind was still sharp enough to surprise Hermann. He could remember things that Hermann, who was just over a third of the elderly man's age, had long forgotten. The conversation had a singular purpose: the book. In it were the notes of Himmler himself. Notes about the mystical powers he planned to use to win the war. At first it seemed like nonsense to Hermann, but the more his grandfather talked, the more he came to believe. Gottshold had been convinced that the items stolen by his brother Karl could have turned the tide in the war. The patriarch poured out stories of history, of how the giants of conquest had been dependent on sacred objects. And Hermann drank it in.

"You must find those artifacts. You must retrieve them at all costs. Our future will then be in our grasp." The old man's words were not formed as a request. They were an order that could not be refused.

A new Reich. What a glorious day that would be, when history was set right. When the truth and the might of the new Nazi Party would stand in full daylight, unhindered by the ignorant prejudices of historians. When the truth was known, when a glimpse of the glory could be seen, thousands would flock to the cause. And those who didn't . . . well, they could be handled easily enough.

Hermann was no fool. He knew that the cause would require more of himself than he could give. That an infusion of power must come from somewhere. Hitler had sought that in the occult. If it was good enough for the Führer, then it was something Hermann would pursue.

The conversation had continued on for several hours, but soon, driven by age and illness-induced fatigue, his grandfather tired. He had spent all his energy in instructing Hermann. Hilde wheeled the old man to bed. Hermann stayed a while longer thinking about what he had heard. On his lap was the book his grandfather had shown him. He had leafed through its dusty pages.

Turning onto Interstate 15, Hermann headed south toward San Diego. His mind, however, was nearly sixty years in the past.

Chapter 8

"Slow . . . slow; fast-fast. Slow . . . slow; fast-fast."
Captain Richard Morrison concentrated on the task,
counting under his breath. One, two—three, four—five,
six. One, two—three, four—five, six. It was working. He smiled
and looked at his wife, Sandi. She was gazing at him through
pure blue eyes, a broad grin across her face.

"Slow . . . slow; fast-fast," she said in a whisper. "Slow . . . slow;
fast-fast. You're doing great." Her fawn hair hung to the shoulders and bounced lightly with each step they took. She wore a
light perfume that covered her in a pleasing, aromatic aura. The
movement along the dance floor, the music from the band
onstage, and the firm, tender, loving feel of his wife in his arms
was intoxicating. It was one of those moments that he wished
could go on forever.

He turned sideways, leading her to do the same. What was it
she taught him? "In the promenade, noses follow toeses." That
was it. They were dancing the fox-trot, a dance she had taught
him only two weeks before. In the Officers' Club of the New
London Naval Base, Sandi had finally convinced him to step out
on the floor. He was a man of keen insight, great courage, and

naval expertise; he also had absolutely no rhythm. Dancing would never be his first choice, but if it meant spending time in close proximity to his wife, and if dancing brought her pleasure, he would navigate the dance floor the best he could.

He turned on his right foot and stepped into her with his left. She followed his lead deftly. "Very good, Richard. You're a natural." Her melodious voice put the music to shame.

"I have a great teacher and a gorgeous dance partner," Morrison had said, struggling to simultaneously keep time and talk.

"I bet you would say the same thing to any of the girls here."

"What girls?" he had said. "I see only you."

"Oh, you are a romantic, Captain Morrison. Don't ever change."

"The only thing I would change, Mrs. Morrison, is my departure date."

Her face clouded over. "Let's not talk about that now. That day will come soon enough. I don't want to think about it until then."

Leaning forward, he kissed her on the forehead. "I love you," he said softly and pulled her closer.

"I know," she replied. "I love you too. I just wish this night could go on until the war is over."

"Me too." A dark sadness filled him. It seemed heavy and thick like a wool blanket soaked with water. He gazed into his wife's eyes and saw tears brimming at the lids. "Hey, none of that now. Weeping in the middle of a fox-trot is considered bad form."

She surrendered a tiny laugh. "I worry, Richard. I worry about you constantly, but even more when you're at sea. I have this dream that you're never coming back. That you sail off on that stupid old submarine and the ocean steals you. I wait and wait, but you never come home." A tear broke free and trickled down her cheek.

"I'll come home, Sandi. I promise. I have you and Ronnie waiting for me. If I have to, I'll swim back. But I will be back. You can count on it."

She smiled weakly but said nothing.

The music ended and the other couples walked from the dance floor. Soon only Morrison and Sandi were left, oblivious to the rest of the world. They held each other. Comforted each other. Morrison wished that he could stay, but he had a job to do, and he would not shirk his duty. No matter how much he felt at the moment like doing so.

"Captain?"

Morrison knew of officers who refused to marry because they wanted to spare a wife the pain of being tied to a navy man in the middle of a world war. Women like his wife served their country in a way that would never be recorded in history books. There were no medals for bravery on the family front. The burden of child-rearing, finances, and more fell on their delicate shoulders, but most of all they felt the burden of waiting and not knowing.

"Captain?"

He wondered what it was like late at night for his Sandi. Did she sit on the sofa leafing through *Life* magazine, her eyes seeing neither picture nor word? Did she weep quietly, not wanting to wake their child? Did she pace the floor to pass the hours of a sleepless night? Did nightmares haunt her? He could see her curled fetal-like on their bed, staring blankly at the white walls of their small bedroom.

"Captain?"

Morrison felt empty, as if someone had pulled the stopper in his soul and all of his vitality, his life, his resolve drained away. He had known many brave men in his day, but none were braver than his wife and the thousands of other wives who watched the horizon for their one particular ship to sail home again.

A hand touched him on the shoulder. The Officers' Club dissolved away and was replaced by the green walls of his cramped stateroom; the music diminished to nothing and was exchanged by the dull roar of diesel engines; his wife—his lovely wife—melted into nothing, like frost on sun-warmed grass. He was alone and seated in the metal chair at his desk, the logbook in front of him.

"Are you all right, Captain?"

Morrison snapped his head around to see who had called him back from his memories. It was Sapolsky. His anger was subdued by the realities of life. He wasn't in New London, Connecticut; he was aboard the *Triggerfish*.

"I'm fine, just daydreaming."

"About home?"

"Yeah," he said sadly, "about home. For a moment I thought I was there. Really there."

"I understand, sir."

"Do you dream about home, Mr. Sapolsky?"

"Not if I can help it, sir. I try to put it out of my mind and live for the moment. Too much pain in memories."

"Are you successful? Putting it out of your mind, I mean."

Steve Sapolsky hesitated. "No, sir. Not at all."

Morrison nodded in sympathy. Part of him wished that he could put home on the "back burner." It could never be that way. Those longings demanded attention and would not be denied. Still, there were those moments like the one he had just experienced that were so undeniably real that he wished he could stay lost in those thoughts forever.

"I have a radio transmission, Captain. It seems that our guest gave us good information. There were ships everywhere he said there would be, at least close enough to count. He had the name of each ship right too. The Allied forces have been having a field day."

"We did pretty good ourselves," Morrison interjected.

"That we did, Captain. Two destroyers and a merchant ship in one day. That'll look good in the personnel folders."

"And our tour is not over yet."

Sapolsky frowned and held out a piece of paper. "That's the bad news, sir. It appears that they're pulling in our leash. We're not to engage the enemy. It seems that Herr Kunzig is too important to risk."

"What?" Morrison exclaimed as he snatched the message from Sapolsky's hand. He read quickly, then swore. "I don't believe it." Tension tightened around his head. For a moment, he regretted sending the message about Kunzig a week ago.

"We're to proceed to Scotland, be tendered there, and release Kunzig to MI6," Morrison read aloud. "Swell. Just swell." He swore again.

Sapolsky stood in silence. Morrison knew that his exec did not like the change in orders any more than he did.

"All right," Morrison began. "Plot the course. I'll be up after I enter this in the logbook."

"Yes, sir. Just one more thing, sir."

"What?"

"I stopped by to pay a visit on our guest. He has asked me about his things."

"Things? His statues?"

"Yes, sir."

Morrison sighed. "I promised him that he could have them back if the information he gave us was on the money. It appears that it was." He walked to the locker under his bed and opened it. He pulled out the small leather doctor's bag and handed it to the exec. "Here," he said, "it would be better if you gave it to him."

"Why is that, Cap?"

"Because right now, I don't know if I would pat him on the back for the good intelligence or punch him for getting our orders changed."

Sapolsky chuckled. "I may not do any better."

"Just give him the bag and then leave him alone. That's an order."

"Yes, sir." Sapolsky turned and walked away.

N
Λ

Kunzig was overjoyed but did his best to hide it. He wanted to embrace the bag that the arrogant Sapolsky had brought him, but refrained. Instead, he said simply, "Thank you," took the bag, and set it on the bed next to him. Sapolsky stood by for a few moments watching him. Kunzig knew that the officer wanted to see inside the bag again.

"Curious, Mr. Sapolsky?"

"I just don't know what a grown man wants with dolls." His words had a bite to them.

"Don't you recall our first conversation, Commander? These are not dolls, they are archaeological artifacts." *This man is an imbecile*, Kunzig thought.

"Artifacts, huh?"

"Yes. Let me show you." Kunzig rose and took the bag. "May we use the wardroom?"

Sapolsky looked in the adjoining room. "Yeah."

Kunzig stepped into the corridor and then through the opening into the wardroom. He sat at the metal table. Sapolsky followed. A sailor who was serving his turn at watching the German started to follow. Sapolsky waved him off. "Go get some coffee. I'll watch him for a bit."

"Thank you, sir," the peach-faced boy said.

"Just be back in fifteen."

"Yes, sir. Fifteen minutes."

Sapolsky joined Kunzig at the table.

"Since I have my bag back, I assume that the information I provided your captain was useful."

"It was," Sapolsky said.

Kunzig waited for more but quickly saw that nothing was forthcoming. He set the bag on the table and opened it. Tenderly he removed a small white figurine. He studied the object, admired it for a moment, then set it down on the table.

"That's one ugly doll, Kunzig."

The German laughed. The small statuette was made of ivory. Its head was elongated and bulbous. It had large circular eyes that covered half the face. Its nose ran from the middle of the head to the chin. There was no mouth. The body was stylized with the arms defined by round holes that separated the torso from the limbs. A similar hole split the legs. "It reminds me of a schoolteacher I had."

Sapolsky laughed, then caught himself.

"This is a Canaanite figurine from the Chalcolithic period, about four thousand years before Christ. It was used as a decorative garment pin."

"That thing is almost six thousand years old?"

"Yes. It's in remarkable condition for its age, don't you think? A colleague of mine found it last year. It's amazing. So beautiful."

"You think that's beautiful."

"As an artifact, yes. I think you'll like this one." He reached into the bag again and extracted a small thin metal figure.

"That one doesn't look much better. It looks like someone tried to make art out of a nail."

"Except this is no nail. It's a woman figurine from the middle Canaanite period II—bronze age. This one is not as old as the ivory figurine, only about 3,500 years. Oh, and it's made out of solid gold." Kunzig watched Sapolsky's reaction. All men responded the same to the presence of gold.

"Solid gold?"

"Yes, Commander. Very valuable for the gold itself, but even more so for its history. Let me show you another." He reached into the bag again and withdrew a flat stone with a relief etched into it. He set it on the table and turned it so that Sapolsky could see the image.

"What's that?"

"It's an image of the Canaanite god, Baal. He was the most worshiped god of the era. See here." Kunzig pointed at the image. "It's worn by age but you can see that he holds a spear in his hand. The spearhead is pointed toward the ground. That is because he was considered the god of fertility and the storm. Notice how the shaft of his spear divides at its end?"

"Yeah. It looks like a plant," Sapolsky said. "So this guy was the high-muckety-muck, huh?"

Kunzig shook his head. "No. There were many other gods. El, for example, was called the father of gods, the father of mankind, the creator of creatures. He also liked to drink heavily."

"Their gods got drunk?" Sapolsky laughed.

"Don't be so quick to judge, Commander," Kunzig said seriously. "Remember, their religion was vastly different than anything you encounter today. That's what makes them so fascinating."

"Weird is more like it."

"Weird? Let me tell you about Anat, a consort of Baal. She was known as the goddess of sensuality and war."

"Sensuality? Like Aphrodite?"

"Except Aphrodite didn't wear a necklace of human heads and a belt of human hands. Anat has a fierce temper."

"Has? You said, 'She *has* a fierce temper.'"

"I misspoke myself," Kunzig answered quickly. "Like many scientists, I tend to get lost in my work. I sometimes forget that thousands of years have passed between those days and now."

Suddenly the Klaxon sounded, its harsh horn reverberating through the ship. Kunzig tensed.

"Relax, Kunzig," Sapolsky said with a wicked grin. "It's just a trim dive."

"A what?"

"A trim dive. The officer of the deck is leveling the boat. Nothing to worry about."

"I see," Kunzig said. "Thank you."

"No sweat." Sapolsky stared down at the objects in front of him. "So what do you plan to do with all these things?"

"Study them, and put them in a museum for others to see. I would like to go back to my work as an archaeologist. That is, if I'm able to."

"We all have things we would rather be doing," Sapolsky said sternly. "Why should it be any different for you?"

"You do not like me, do you, Mr. Sapolsky?" Kunzig said abruptly.

"No, sir, I don't. If it had been up to me, you'd still be floating in that raft."

Slowly, Kunzig began to gather the ancient figurines and put them back in the leather bag. "You still see me as the enemy," he said softly. "I've done my best to help. That is why I gave your captain the list of German ships, locations, and courses. I wanted to prove to him and to the crew that I am just as opposed to the war as they."

"You are a German officer," Sapolsky rebutted.

"Was a German officer," Kunzig corrected. "As I have said all along, I had no choice."

"Maybe, but war is war, and war makes enemies. I didn't start this conflict, Kunzig—"

"Nor did I, Commander. Hitler started this war. I just happened to be living in the wrong place at the wrong time. The only thing that makes us different, Mr. Sapolsky, is the accident of our birth. It is only chance that had you born in your United States and I in Germany."

"You're still the enemy." Sapolsky's voice was flat.

"I am not!" Kunzig shouted. "Hitler is your enemy. Hess, and Himmler, and Goering, and the others, they are your enemies. I am a victim!" His voice rebounded off the steel walls.

"Take it easy, buddy," Sapolsky said firmly.

"What's going on in here?" It was Captain Morrison. Kunzig knew that his words had traveled the short distance to the captain's stateroom.

"Nothing, Cap," Sapolsky said. "Me and Mr. Kunzig were talking about his dolls."

What an idiot, Kunzig thought. *He still thinks of these as dolls.*

"Then what's all the noise about?" Morrison demanded.

"That is my fault, Captain," Kunzig said softly. "I have not been sleeping well. The sunburn bothers me night and day. I am afraid that I am a little sensitive. I assure you, Commander Sapolsky has said or done nothing wrong." *He is just an egomaniacal, self-absorbed cretin.*

There was a moment of silence, then Morrison said, "Very well. Just keep it down."

"Yes, sir," Kunzig said. "And Captain? Thank you for returning my things. It means a great deal to me."

Morrison nodded and then disappeared down the tight corridor. Sapolsky rose to his feet, gave a hard look at Kunzig, then left.

Kunzig took the bag and clutched it to his chest as a child would hug a teddy bear. He closed his eyes and began to rock slowly side to side. *Timing*, he said to himself. *Timing and patience. That's the key.* The right time would come and when it did, things would be different. Vastly different. It would not be he who was confined to the small room, waiting as each interminably long hour flowed by like a thick river of sludge. *My time is near*, he said to himself. *Very, very near.*

He placed the bag on the table again and opened it. Once more he removed the cult objects he had shown Sapolsky, and then, after a quick glance to make sure he was not being watched, he reached in the bag and removed the false bottom.

The bag itself was an ingenious design, crafted by the best in German intelligence. Used by agents to conceal documents or film, the bag looked normal in every respect. Even those trained to recognize such devices would have difficulty ferreting out the secret compartment. Captain Morrison stood no chance.

Peering in, he smiled, then let loose a quiet laugh. What he saw brought him great joy, and he and he alone knew why. On the bottom of the bag lay an object for which many countries would go to war. To him it was worth far more than the other objects, more than the entire collection of any museum. And the object was his, his to use.

Karl Kunzig felt like the most powerful man on earth.

N
⋏

Helen Muir stretched in bed, lifting her arms over her head and tightening each muscle from fingertip to pointed toe. The silk sheets rippled like water over her body. She groaned quietly and then rolled over. She realized she was alone.

She reached out in the darkness and gently touched the mattress where he usually lay. Nothing. Blinking back the sleep in her eyes, she looked out the window of the twenty-second floor of their Fredricks Building condominium in downtown San Diego. Daylight was easing back the darkness. She judged that it would be light in another half hour. He had not come home.

Throwing back the thick comforter and silk sheets, Helen sat up and draped her long willowy legs over the side of the bed and sighed. If there was anything she hated in life, it was waking up alone. Where was he? Should she be worried? He said he would be home late and that he might stay the night at his grandfather's, but he always said that and he always came home.

Why couldn't you hook up with a normal man? she asked herself. He was hard to live with. Late hours at the restaurant, frequent trips around the country, and of course his quick temper—his often violent temper. But most of the time he was good to her and he had money. That had to count for something, maybe everything. It was certainly better than what she grew up with: poor family, abusive father, tough neighborhood. If only the children who laughed at her in school and tormented her with words and jokes could see her, they would choke. And she would gladly watch them choke.

How their eyes would pop if they saw how much the painfully shy, ugly string-bean girl in high school had changed. She was not a scrawny little girl now. No, now she wore the best clothes, ate at the best restaurants, and had powerful friends. Her stringy, oily black hair was now a shiny, coal-colored mane that hung down to the middle of her back. Her former lackluster eyes now shone a brilliant Jacqueline Bisset blue. Men ogled her when she walked by. Helen smiled, glad that the past was past and that the future was now.

Her musing stopped abruptly. She had heard something, something outside the bedroom. It was a soft sound, muffled by the wall and door that separated it from the bedroom. *Hermann?* she wondered. Maybe he had come home after all. The alarm clock read 5:30.

Rising, she stepped to the end of the bed, slipped a silk robe over her body, and walked to the door. Placing her hand on the bronze doorknob, she paused and listened. First she heard the sound of the coffee pot, then papers rustling, then a cough—Hermann's cough. He *was* home. She did not know whether to be relieved, angry, or afraid. The truth was, she never knew what to expect from Hermann. Still, the very least he could do was wake her up and tell her he was all right. But that was a thought she would keep to herself. He hated to be corrected. Under that handsome skin of his was a deep well of anger.

The bedroom door opened into an expansive living area. Expensive wallpaper covered the walls. A series of tall, narrow windows looked out over the glistening bay. Just off the living area was an open kitchen and breakfast nook. Across from that was a raised, formal dining area set off from the rest of the apartment by a low teak rail. Art hung on the walls—"real art," she often reminded herself, not the kind bought in discount stores. Originals of the best contemporary artists. Her family could have lived for five years on the money spent on just one painting.

"I didn't hear you come in last night," Helen said quietly, not wanting to startle Hermann. He was seated at the dining-room table with a yellow legal pad in front of him. He was writing furiously.

"I just got in a few minutes ago. Maybe half an hour."

"You left Riverside that late?"

"No. I drove around a lot. I had some things to think about."
Hermann kept his attention on the papers in front of him.

Things, she thought. He used that term when he had secrets to keep. Best not to push it. "Can I fix you anything?"

"Eggs. Espresso first. Make it a double. I'm running without sleep."

"Perhaps you should lie down for awhile. You have a full day ahead of you." Helen, in addition to being his lover, was his personal assistant. She did the work he did not want to do.

"Cancel all that," he said bluntly. "Cancel the meetings and whatever else is on the calendar."

"You're kidding."

"No, I'm not," he snapped harshly. "Just do what I tell you. My time is short on this."

"Okay, okay. You don't have to bite my head off." She walked into the kitchen, pulled down a shiny bag of coffee beans, and scooped some into the grinder. The grinder roared to life. With skill born of practice, Helen made the espresso and carried it to the table.

"Anything else beside eggs?"

"Toast. Just eggs and toast. Then I want you to make some calls. Wait until seven. That will give me a little more time, then call the people on this list." He ripped a page off the pad and thrust it at Helen. The script was hastily written, but she was able to make out the names.

"Just these three? What about the others?"

"No, just those three. My time may be short, and I don't want to make mistakes. Too many people too soon will mess things up."

"Just what are you up to?" Helen asked.

"Fishing. I'm going fishing."

"Fishing?" Hermann was the least "outdoorsy" person Helen knew. "Since when are you interested in fishing?"

140

"Since I found out how to change the future."

Helen walked back to the kitchen. She knew better than to press the issue. Waiting was the only thing she could do at the moment. She pulled a carton of eggs from the refrigerator and wondered what new scheme Hermann had come up with. She had seen him carry out many plans, some of which were clearly illegal. This must be the same.

Hermann had been her hero, a man driven by a cause, a man of power and wealth. She had fallen in love with him eight years ago when she was a senior in college and a friend had introduced them. His good looks and smooth speech had made him irresistible. Over the months they had dated, she had listened to him as he offered his view of the world and the need for a strong central government. By the time she had learned of his belief that a single race could be superior to another, and that Nazism was his life, she was already hopelessly in love. She became his assistant and lover, and all seemed right with the world. But there was a darker side to Hermann Kunzig, an evil he had carefully kept from her. He was prone to fits of anger and violence. More than once, she had served as his punching bag, but he always made it up to her, with jewels and cars and promises to change. So she stayed, but the love had long since died, the victim of his cruelty.

Looking back to the dining table, Helen watched as Hermann worked feverishly. His head was down, his hair ruffled, and she had noticed earlier that his eyes were red from lack of sleep. Still he worked. She wanted to take him in her arms, to feel the firm muscles of his shoulders, but he wouldn't want that now. He was consumed by something she didn't understand. He would want her and want her soon, and when he did, she would be there for him. No project or plan could change that.

Chapter 9

Stanton was as frustrated as a man could be. He stood on the creosote-soaked dock next to the *Triggerfish*. The early morning sun had successfully pushed back the night, but had yet to penetrate the thick marine layer of clouds that hung in the sky like a shroud. The day was starting out gray and gloomy, which matched Stanton's mood perfectly.

All his life, he had been a man of action. Standing still was difficult for him. Activity was as much a part of him as breathing. At the Naval Academy his time was filled with studies, sports, or other endeavors. Most of his naval career had been associated with life on a submarine, and he had worked diligently to avoid any duty that required significant time at a desk. Even in retirement, he filled his days with golf, his wood shop, and travel. Waiting, with his arms across his chest as a small crew of experts reexamined the submarine from stem to stern, was wearing on his nerves.

The urge to step aboard and start dictating each action was almost overwhelming, but he knew it would be a mistake. Each crew had someone in charge who knew more than he did about their work. Stanton could navigate a submarine anywhere in the world, but he knew nothing about state-of-the-art acoustics. So he was left with the agonizing job of waiting.

At least his mind could work. Over the last few hours, Stanton rehearsed all that had happened, from his recall to active duty to the mysterious sounds he and the others had heard on the sub. Nothing new came to mind. His biggest fear was that someone was trapped on board, but that seemed unlikely—impossible. A submarine like the *Triggerfish* was little more than a two-hull cylinder. The external hull was less than an inch thick. If anyone wanted to gain the attention of those outside, all they had to do was bang on something, anything. Even a spoken word could be heard. But there had been no such noises except the hideous moan that came while the sub was being towed and the thumping sound they had just heard.

Stanton watched the men work. They gave no sign of discovery. Three times the chief in charge of the acoustics search had ordered everyone off deck and demanded quiet. Each time he had come up with nothing. They were making one last attempt.

"Doesn't look very hopeful, does it," Stewart said. He took a sip of coffee.

"No," Stanton agreed. "Sure you don't want to go home? You've been up all night."

"As have you, Captain. I wouldn't miss this for a week's worth of sleep. I'll stay as long as you'll have me."

A short-lived smile crossed Stanton's face. He was growing to admire this Coast Guard officer. He was sure that he had just made a new and lasting friend. "This part isn't very exciting," Stanton said.

"Are you looking for excitement?"

"Not really, just answers. I owe that and much more to the young man who died."

"It's not your fault, Stanton," Stewart said, setting aside the protocol of rank. "If this were my operation, I would have done exactly the same thing."

"How does a submarine come to life just long enough to kill a man?" Stanton asked angrily. His heart ached for the family of the diver that was killed. "It doesn't make sense."

"I don't know, but I'm sure you will find out. The answer lies inside that vessel." Stewart motioned with his coffee cup.

Stanton nodded. He wanted nothing more than to pop the escape hatch and drop into the belly of the sub, but he had to do things in the proper order. One man had already died; he was determined that would not happen again.

"Where's your young lieutenant?" Stewart asked.

"I sent her to find Hancock and Eastman. I gave them some time to grab coffee and a bite to eat."

"This has her shaken, doesn't it?" There was no condemnation in Stewart's voice.

"She'll be all right," Stanton answered quickly. "A good officer must learn to conquer his or her emotions. She'll grow through all of this."

"I think she senses something we don't."

Stanton turned to face his new friend. "Like what?"

"I have no idea, but her response, her reaction, tells me that she is feeling something she's not sharing."

"They teach psychology in the Coast Guard?"

Stewart laughed, then asked, "You're married, right?"

"Yes. Twenty-five good years. Why?"

"How many times has your wife been right about something when you've been wrong?"

"If you repeat this in public, I'll deny it, but more times than I care to mention."

"Women are intuitive, Captain. We men tend to work with step-by-step logic. Women have the same logic, but it's well-seasoned with intuition. As much as we may hate it, they often know things we don't. A younger man would deny it, but we old dogs have been around too long not to know it's true."

Stewart was right. Wilcox was far more apprehensive than he was. He had attributed that to her youth and lack of experience. Could there be more to it? Was she sensitive to something he was missing?

"Are you suggesting that I talk to her? Probe her psychic feelings?"

"No. I'm not saying this is a supernatural thing. I'm just saying that her view may be different than ours, and that it might be worth keeping an eye on her. Not because she's going to crack, but because of her natural intuitiveness."

"What is the National Organization of Women going to say to that?" Stanton asked with a grin.

"I don't care. I'm speaking from experience. I can't tell you how many times I wished I had listened to my wife."

"Your suggestion is noted, Commander." Stanton started to say something else when he noticed the chief of the acoustics team walking down the gangplank toward him. He was shaking his head.

"Sorry, Captain. Nothing. We've done this search four times now, and there is nothing making noise in that old bucket. If there were a frog in there and it burped, we'd hear. We ain't heard nothing. No biological sounds, no mechanical sounds. Just nothing and more nothing."

"We heard something, Chief."

"I don't doubt you, sir, but nothing is making noise now. I can't explain it."

Stanton pursed his lips in frustration. "All right, Chief. Clear your equipment and crew. I appreciate the effort."

"Aye, sir."

The frustration that had wrapped up Stanton's emotions so tightly took on another oppressive layer. The negative report was the second he had received that hour. The haz-mat team had tested the water again. They found nothing but ocean too warm to cause ice. Stanton knew he had seen it. Stewart and Wilcox backed him up, but now there was nothing. The ice disappeared as quickly as it had appeared. A disquiet bubbled up within him. He was missing something, and that angered him.

"Now what?" Stewart asked as he and Stanton watched the chief walk away.

"We go in."

"When?"

"As soon as the deck is clear and Wilcox gets back with Hancock and Eastman."

"And if we hear the sound again?"

"We go in anyway. At least the navy does."

"I'm with you all the way," Stewart said. "I'm not going to give you swabs the opportunity to say the Coast Guard backs out when the going gets tough."

"We'll probably say it anyway," Stanton joked. "I don't see any sense in destroying a good tradition."

N
Λ

"Why not use the helicopter?" George Abbey asked as he sat in the white van. "It's gotta be better than sitting here watching an old submarine through binoculars."

"Too noticeable," Barry Ludlow said. "I want to keep a low profile for the moment. Besides, the airspace over the base is restricted. I've learned firsthand that you can't get a pilot to fly into the area."

"We've had our profile low all night. I'm getting hungry."

"Don't blame me. I can't help it if we were turned away at the gate."

"Unfortunately, our press passes don't get us admission to secured military facilities." The cameraman stretched and let out a groan.

"We'll just have to watch in secret from here," Barry said seriously. Abbey laughed loudly. "What's so funny?"

"Secret? We're sitting not three hundred yards from the Naval Amphibious Base in a white van with large red letters that read '12 News' all over it. That and your Volvo parked behind it should make us almost invisible."

"What are you complaining about? Glorietta Bay Park is provided by the good citizens of Coronado. We have a right to be here."

"I didn't say we're doing anything illegal, just that we're not hidden from anyone. All you have to do is look at the military police truck parked at the fence over there to see what I mean."

Barry lifted a pair of binoculars to his eyes and fixed them on the white Ford truck that was parked a hundred yards away, separated from them by an eight-foot-high, chain-link fence topped with barbwire. Two marines sat in the cab. One was looking back through his own pair of binoculars. He found it funny. "It's like a Mexican standoff. They can't come out here and bug us, and we can't get inside."

"So what's the point? I've been up all night watching a bunch of sailors huddle around an old submarine."

"I told you. I got a tip that someone was killed there. That's still news in this town."

"Then let's run over to the coroner's office or something. I'm going crazy here. We're not going to see much anyway."

Abbey was right and Barry knew it. The best they had been able to do is shoot some footage of the submarine moored to a long dock that jutted out into the bay. While the shot was a good one of the dark hulk sitting silently in the water, illuminated by bright floodlights, it still lacked any real meat. There had to be another way to find out what was going on, and if there was, he was going to find it.

"Okay, here's what we're going to do. Let's set up in the park and tape sixty seconds of me with the sub in the distance. We'll frame the shot with the small children's play yard just to my right. That'll give it a little more emotional tug. You know, man killed a few yards from where children play. That sort of thing. Then we'll head back to the studio. I want to see if I can't force these guys into a press conference. Our story will break on the morning show, and the other stations will pick it up. I'll try to get the network to pick it up. That'll put more pressure on the navy. They gotta give us something."

"Maybe," Abbey said. "But I wouldn't bet on it. I gave the navy four years of my life and quickly learned that they pretty much do what they want."

"We'll see about that, George. We'll just see about that. Now get your camera, let's go."

$$\overset{\text{\tiny N}}{\Lambda}$$

The early morning air was starting to warm, and already it was heavy with the sounds of the slum street below—a baby crying; a husband shouting obscenities at his wife; an approaching siren; a television with an ancient sitcom playing—all of it oozed slowly, too slowly to constitute a genuine breeze, through the open window of the run-down apartment.

Max Rohl ignored all of it. His eyes were fixed on the smooth barrel of the gun before him. Slowly, tenderly, he caressed the

149

dark metal, stroking it lightly, lovingly, with a soft rag that he held in a beefy hand.

There were only two lights in the studio apartment: one came from the forty-watt bulb in the battered freestanding lamp next to his chair; the other from the end of his lit cigarette.

The air was permeated with the aroma of stale beer, spent cigarettes, and sweat. On the fold-out bed across the room slept eight-year-old Bobby, Max's nephew. Three more weeks and his sister would be out of jail and Max would be free of the useless rug-rat. It wasn't his job to raise the brat kid of his sister. He had another purpose. One he would fulfill someday. He didn't know when, he didn't know how, but he knew his destiny would come. He just had to wait for it, as all heroes had to wait for their moment in the sun.

Max was good at waiting. He was a man of as much patience as anger and deep churning bitterness. His freedom would come. It would come. He knew it. He believed it. That truth kept him alive; kept him out of jail; kept him alert.

It was all a matter of time.

Slowly, Max set the oily cloth down on the arm of his battered easy chair and then raised the AK–47 to his shoulder. He wished he had a different automatic weapon. It seemed wrong to be holding a Russian-made gun, but then there was a certain pleasing irony to it.

The gun stock felt good, normal, pressed into his shoulder socket, like it was a natural extension of his arm, of his soul. For a moment he closed his eyes and inhaled the beautiful fragrance of gun oil. To him it was as sweet as perfume, even if it was polluted with the odors of cigarette ash and beer. His imagination could filter all that out.

He opened his eyes and sighted down the barrel. Casually, evenly, he moved the gun, sighting on whatever came into his view: a stained pot on the hot plate in the corner, a rat as it ran along the baseboard disappearing through a crack in the wall, a broken chair next to the small dining table, the boy on the bed. He paused there for a long, protracted moment.

What would the boy think if he woke up and saw the barrel of a gun pointed at his head? Would he be frightened? Would he cry or scream?

Fear was good. Fear made a man strong and determined. At least it had for Max. Max knew fear and knew it intimately. It had been his companion, an unrelenting ghost that haunted his memory. And it never went away.

Max lowered the gun and set it crossways on his lap. He had not fired at another human being since April 17, 1971, and that had been a battle of utter failure. He was twenty then, full of himself and national pride, ready to charge ahead and die for his country. Instead of dying, he was captured along with fifteen of his comrades. He spent the next two years in a Vietcong prison waiting for rescue. When no rescue came, he made his own escape, killing a careless guard and fleeing into the jungle. It had taken him three weeks to work his way back to territory secured by Americans and South Vietnamese. Three weeks of fear, of hiding, of eating plants and bugs like some animal. Three weeks of waking at every sound. Three weeks of plucking leeches from his legs. Three weeks of agonizing hell in a foreign jungle.

Where were his friends? Where was his country when he needed them? They had left him to rot in a POW camp and that had left a deeper, more ragged scar than those given him by his torturers.

That was a long time ago—a lifetime ago—and everyone had forgotten it. But not Max. He still fought the battle in his mind. He was preparing to fight one more war, this time for a different cause and for people who would not abandon him no matter how bad things got. He had formed a new allegiance, one better suited to his worldview.

His time was growing short; he was not young anymore. Gray laced his wavy black hair and salted the stubble of his beard. Although he kept his mind and his six-foot-four-inch body sharp, he could not expect to live forever. Someday his reflexes would slow too much, his thinking become too clouded. If he was to do what he had been born to do, then he would have to act soon.

Max pulled another bottle of beer from the six-pack next to his chair, twisted off the lid, and sucked down a third of the warm fluid. He didn't drink beer for the taste, he drank it for its anesthetic qualities. That's why he sucked hard on the bottle even though it was still breakfast time. Hard work as a school janitor during the day; alcohol-induced numbness at night. It was pathetic, but it was his life.

Putting the bottle down, he lit another cigarette, inhaled deeply, and smiled. Of course this habit was unhealthy, but what did he care? He would never see retirement. He would be long dead by that time.

The phone call had come early, waking him from a sound sleep. The clock by his bed read 5:06, an hour and a half before he would normally rise. But Max did not mind, at least not after hearing the voice.

"Max," it had said in strong, even tones. "I need you."

"When? Where?" he had croaked through the phone.

"San Diego, this morning. Can you make it?"

San Diego was a two-hour drive away from his Los Angeles slum. "I can make it easy. Will I need my tools?"

"Maybe. Bring them just in case."

"Okay, Hermann. Eight o'clock. At the usual place?"

"Yes. And Max, this is it."

Max smiled broadly. "I'll be there."

Setting the AK–47 on the floor, Max reached over to the small battered end table next to his chair and picked up a 9mm HK pistol and began the process of cleaning again. In fifteen minutes he would wake the kid up, give him a bowl of cereal, and tell him to stay the night with some friend. Surely he could do that much. Someone would take care of him while Max was in San Diego. There was always someone to pick up a little boy. But just in case, he would leave the boy a key. There was enough cereal and frozen dinners to last him a few days. Surely an eight-year-old could handle that. And if he couldn't . . . Well, Max had too many other things on his mind to worry about that.

N
Λ

The Zum Deutschen Eck restaurant was empty as it always was at 8:30 A.M. Breakfast was not served here, just lunch and dinner. That was enough for Hermann who knew that the success of his restaurants lay in their uniqueness. People came here because it was different. Chinese, Mexican, and other ethnic food establishments abounded, but the number of good German restaurants were scarce. Soon, prep workers and cooks would be arriving to prepare for the onslaught of midday customers from the surrounding businesses. The present stillness would give way to laughter and serious business discussions. Attorneys would talk cases, salesmen would discuss products, secretaries would praise or vilify their bosses. All would eat. All would be complimentary, and all would be oblivious to the meeting that would be held in the basement below their feet.

Would they come to eat if they knew of Hermann's real purpose in life? Would they drink the dark beer and consume the hasenpfeffer, roast duckling, and the giant Thuringer sausage?

He doubted it. Only a few people could comprehend the dream or see its logic. His patrons were lost in their smaller worlds, occupied by smaller issues, distracted by lesser goals. That's what made it so easy. No one believed it could happen again. No one thought that anyone would try. They were wrong and soon they would know it.

He had made his call to Max early that morning. Since Max would have to drive in from LA he couldn't wait for Helen to crawl out of bed to make the call for him. She did make the other calls, just as she was told to. She was as efficient as she was beautiful. Still, he wondered about her. Was she as loyal as she appeared? When the time came, would she be strong enough to stand with him, or would she crumble?

Hermann would know soon. Fortune and the gods had dropped the golden opportunity into his lap. He knew they would. This was not just a dream, it was destiny. It was something that would come to pass because it must come to pass. That was the way with greatness; it always rose to the top no matter how hard the tiny-minded of the world struggled to keep it down.

True, it had failed fifty years ago, but mistakes had been made. This time there would be no mistakes, no madness to muddle the mind. This time it would be done right. Already people were in the right places, powerful places. Already there was sufficient money and adequate resources. There was not a branch of government that had not been infiltrated, no avenue of media that had not been touched. The funds were in place, the commitments, the weapons, the followers. Everything was ready; all that was needed was the right time—and that time was now.

Hermann walked through the dining room and down a narrow corridor that ran next to the kitchen. To the left of the hall were three doors, one marked MEN, one marked WOMEN. The last door had a plastic sign with the words PRIVATE. He inserted a key in the lock, turned it, and stepped through the doorway. Inside was a small room with a pair of elevator doors on the far wall. Making his way across the lobby, he approached the doors. There was no down button, just a flat plate of glass on the wall. Hermann placed the palm of his right hand against the glass and spoke his name. The biometric device scanned his palm, identifying a dozen reference points, then matched his voice pattern to the one it held in its computer memory. The doors parted. The press of a button started the cab down.

A thin smile slipped across his face. Over the next thirty minutes, the others would begin to arrive. Within the hour his key people would be with him, and everything would begin.

N
Λ

Donna sipped at her coffee. She felt simultaneously relieved and frustrated. They were supposed to go down in the sub soon after sunrise, but now there had been another change. Captain Stanton had been summoned by Admiral Robbins. Stanton's expression had said it all. He did not appreciate being pulled from his job to attend a meeting. It was, however, too much to expect the admiral to come to the pier. Captains went to admirals, not the other way around. So the descent was postponed once again.

That was how Donna thought of the inevitable entry into the submarine—descent. Like a spelunker dangling from a nylon rope over the open maw of some black, fearful cave. While the cave explorer might have to sink hundreds of feet, and Donna would only descend a few steps down a steel ladder, she found herself wishing it were the other way around. For some reason, the darkness in the submarine held more fear for her than anything else she could imagine. She couldn't explain it, but it was nonetheless true.

What was frightening her?

The face on the deck? That had been her imagination. It must have been. She was a rational person, an officer in the navy. She was trained and disciplined. There had been no face in the wood deck covering. There were no demons. She knew that intellectually. But she did not know it emotionally. No matter how hard her brain worked to dismiss the evil sound, the wicked face, the unusual death of the diver, her heart told her otherwise. Something was wrong . . . wrong . . . wrong.

She shook her head and set the white coffee cup on the desk. Her eyes burned from lack of sleep, her neck tensed into bands of rigid muscle. Donna rubbed her temples and wished that she was some place other than the small office with pale green walls.

In front of her was a computer monitor. Forcing herself to reread the words she had just written, Donna again began typing. Stanton had wanted to make use of the downtime. If they could not open the *Triggerfish* now, then they would use the time for other things such as reports. That job fell to her. The others were dismissed and ordered to return in ninety minutes. Stanton had told her to get some breakfast, then start a chronological report on all that had happened, from the initial sighting by the hang glider to the last inspection of the sub. "Leave nothing out," he had said crisply. "I want a full and detailed report."

He amazed her. She knew that he had not slept in at least thirty hours, yet he remained sharp and focused. Not bad for an old retired guy. Not that he was really that old. Upper middle age perhaps, but not much beyond. He was physically trim and his wits sharp as any man she had ever met. Here he was, called back to duty, snatched mid golf game, issuing clear orders and taking charge as if he were still doing so daily.

Stanton was the highlight of this nightmare. His firmness had never boiled over into anger. He was unwavering in his duty, but had not sacrificed his humanity. To her, he was everything an officer should be. Under any other circumstances, serving with him would be an education and honor. But these weren't other circumstances. The submarine, its dark gray bulk bobbing in the water, reminded her of that. It haunted her.

Focus, she told herself. *Focus on your work.*

But she could not concentrate. She tried to make the letters of the keyboard type out words, but her fingers would not move.

She closed her eyes, willing herself to relax, ordering her agitated mind to stand at ease. "Put it out of your mind," she said softly. "Think only of your work."

Her fingers began to move. The keyboard released near-silent clicks and clacks as each letter was typed. *Finally*, she thought, *finally*. A heavy sigh flowed from her lungs and she relaxed all the more. She just might survive this after all.

Donna opened her eyes and read the paragraph she had written.

Her heart seized in her chest. Her stomach tightened into a knot the size of a large man's fist. Bile pressed upward causing her to gag. These were not the words she expected. Instead there was a face—the same face she had seen on the deck of the submarine—composed of the letters she had just typed.

Her heart first thundered then fluttered like a leaf in a gale. Slowly she pushed away from the desk, but she could not tear her eyes away from the image. Raising a quivering hand to her mouth, she gasped for air as if she stood on the peak of Mount Everest. The sound of her heart pounded in her ears. The room began to spin. Darkness slowly crept in from the edge of her vision. She felt faint and nauseous. Slowly she began to slip down her chair toward the floor, her eyes still fixed on the computer monitor.

Consciousness slipped from Donna as she heard the door to the office open. "Lieutenant, the admiral cut me free and—Lieutenant, are you all right?"

Donna Wilcox slumped to the floor, her mind blank with the mist of unconsciousness.

Chapter 10

Mr. Sapolsky didn't tell you when he was in here?" Morrison asked.

"No, Captain," Kunzig replied. "This is the first I've heard of it."

"Well, there really was no reason for him to tell you. You're informed now. We will be making best speed to Scotland. You'll be handed over to authorities there."

The words were not welcome. Kunzig frowned.

"You don't like our new orders, Mr. Kunzig?" Morrison inquired.

"I cannot say that I do," Kunzig replied solemnly. "It is a little too close to Germany for my taste, Captain. I had hoped to stay aboard until you returned to the States."

"Afraid that some of your old buddies might come looking for you?"

That was exactly what he feared but for reasons he did not want to share. "It is possible that my life is in danger, Captain. If word ever got out that I was still alive . . ."

"Don't sweat it, Kunzig. I'm sure they'll bundle you up real tight and keep a lid on things."

A mixed metaphor, Kunzig thought. *Doesn't anyone have an education on this ship?* "I hope so, Captain. I hope so."

"That information you gave me proved useful. The powers that be want to know what else is in that head of yours."

If you only knew, Captain, Kunzig thought. *If you only knew.* "But couldn't that inquisition be done in the United States or even aboard this ship?"

"It's not my decision. You'll just have to live with it."

"I understand, Captain Morrison. Thank you for taking the time to tell me yourself. That was a very noble thing for you to do."

"Not really. I just thought you should know. I owe you that much."

Kunzig nodded. "If you show me the course you plan to take, I may be able to provide you with other information about German ship movement."

"No can do. Our duty has been restricted. For the moment, we are your cab ride to Scotland. I can't say that I'm pleased about that."

"I imagine not." Kunzig was feeling the anger grow within him. His plan had gone bad when he was thrown overboard, but he thought it had been resurrected when he was rescued. Now this turn of events made things all the worse. There had to be something he could do.

"Well, that's all I had," Morrison said and started to leave Kunzig's temporary quarters.

"Captain?"

Morrison turned. "Yes?"

"I have done my best to be of help to you. I think you see that. I was wondering if the guard is still needed outside my door. I really am harmless. Besides, there is very little I can do to cause you trouble. There are over seventy of your men against just me. I'd feel better if some trust were shown."

"Sorry, Kunzig. The guard stays. You're a foreign national on a military ship in a war zone. Regulations demand it. I plan to keep my rank and my boat."

"I understand, sir. I just wanted to ask."

Kunzig watched Morrison stare at him and thought for a moment that he might change his mind. Instead, the captain turned and walked away.

"This is not over yet, Captain," Kunzig said under his breath. "It is not nearly over."

"I'm fine. Really." Donna sat up straight in the leather desk chair. "I just fainted."

"Perhaps we should get you checked out, Lieutenant," Stanton said softly. "You hit your head on the floor."

"Not hard, sir. There's not even a bump. With respect, sir, I'd just as soon stay on duty."

"At the very least you should go home."

"Please, sir. I'd like to finish my job."

Stanton sighed heavily. The young officer was doing her best to prove her strength and dedication. That was commendable. He could order her to the hospital or home, but it might indicate a lack of trust.

"I really am fine, sir."

"Then explain yourself," he ordered with an even tone that carried no accusation or judgment.

"Yes, sir. I was starting the report as ordered when I became ..." She searched for the right word. "... woozy. I haven't eaten since yesterday morning, and I think my blood sugar may have dropped. That's all, sir. A bite to eat and I'll be fine. I should have had breakfast like you said."

Walking across the small office, Stanton took a wood chair that looked like it had been on the base since the forties, placed it in front of Donna, and then sat down. "All right, Lieutenant. It's time we cleared the air here. This whole submarine thing has you going, doesn't it?"

Donna folded her hands and looked down at them. Stanton could see her fear. Again she nodded but did not speak.

"I sensed it when the *Triggerfish* was being towed and we heard that noise. I picked up on it again, when we were getting ready to enter the boat. Do you know something that I should know?"

"No, sir. I mean, not really, sir."

"Not really?"

Closing her eyes, she sighed and then gently rubbed her temples. "It doesn't make much sense, sir. Not to me and it certainly won't to you."

"Perhaps I should be the judge of that, Lieutenant." Stanton tempered his voice. "Why don't you just tell me about it. From the beginning."

"I don't want to be booted out as unfit for duty, sir."

"Are you unfit for duty, Lieutenant?"

"No, sir!" she said emphatically.

"Then you have nothing to worry about. Tell me the story."

Donna took in a deep breath. "Something about the *Triggerfish* frightens me. It's an intangible thing. You were right when you noticed that I was ... uneasy during the tow. At first I just thought it was being on the deck of an old craft. I thought it might sink or something. At least that's what I told myself. But that wasn't really it at all."

"What was it then?" Stanton prompted as he leaned back in the chair.

"I can't say, sir. That is to say that I don't really know. It's a feeling. It's an irrational fear. I'm not afraid of the water. I love the sea, but the moment I stepped on that submarine I was consumed with apprehension. Something seemed terribly wrong, but I couldn't say what it was. Then there was . . ." Her voice trailed off.

"Then there was what?" Stanton prompted.

"Then when we were on the sub last night and we heard that thumping sound . . . I saw something."

"What did you see?"

"I'm sure I was just a little tired. We had been up most of the night and—"

"What did you see?" Stanton repeated firmly.

Donna looked around the room nervously and shifted in her seat. "A face," she blurted. "A horrible, monstrous face."

"Where?"

"On the deck. The wood seemed to change shape and it formed a face. It . . . it smiled at me."

"Smiled at you? The face smiled at you?" Stanton was having trouble believing his ears. He was tempted to relieve her of duty and to order her to the hospital for examination but something, an innate feeling, persuaded him to hold off.

"I know it sounds crazy and I wouldn't blame you if you had me committed, but I swear to you that that was exactly what I saw."

"What do you think all this means, Lieutenant? What conclusions do you draw from the sounds, the face, and your irrational fear?"

She pursed her lips and shook her head slowly. "I don't know, sir. But something is wrong with that submarine. Something evil, something horrible. It wants me, and I don't know why."

"You think it's a ghost ship, don't you?"

"I don't believe in ghosts, Captain. I'm not a religious person and never have been. That's what makes all this so confusing.

How do you explain it, Captain? What was that horrible noise we heard and that thumping? How can a trained diver be sucked into the propellers of a submarine when no one is on board to start the engines? How does that happen, sir? Even if I am crazy, it wouldn't explain those things." Tears welled in her eyes.

"At ease, Lieutenant," Stanton command with authority. "I never said you were crazy."

"I don't see how you can believe otherwise."

"Leave my thoughts to me, Lieutenant. Is that understood?"

"Yes, sir. Understood."

"Very well." Stanton stood to his feet. He should dismiss her without hesitation. She was fantasizing, hallucinating, or had experienced a psychotic break with reality. He could also see that she was tired and stressed from the near nonstop activity. She had been in the comfort of her home when the sailor's death necessitated her being called back. Perhaps he should just send her home. But that would be noticed by others. It would have to be entered into his report, and that might find its way into her personnel folder.

Of course, if he really felt that she was mentally incompetent, he would not hesitate to remove her from this assignment. But he did not feel that way. Instead, without knowing why, he believed her. He was a man of reason, of intellect, and of knowledge. Such "mystical" things had no place in his life. Still he felt that her words carried a ring of truth. If he were to be honest with himself, he would have to agree with her in some way. He too felt an uneasiness about the *Triggerfish*. Until now he had dismissed it as excitement and concern, but now he doubted those emotions. What if she were right and evil was associated with the sub?

All of his life, Stanton had been a churchgoer. Christian parents had provided him with deep spiritual roots, but a long career in the navy had made him a very practical man who worked out his life in logic and by regulations. Church had become a Sunday thing for him. When he retired from the service, he had promised his wife that he would once again become more involved in their local congregation. That had yet to happen.

It saddened him to think that his faith had atrophied over the years. He was still a believer and made no attempt to hide the fact. Still, he was not as active as he could be, nor did his faith occupy as much of his life as it once did. Now he wished he knew more.

"I suppose you'll relieve me of duty now, sir," Wilcox said sourly. "At least, I was honest with you."

"Are you wanting to be relieved of duty, Lieutenant?"

"No, sir. I wish to complete what I've started." Her voice was firm and determined.

"All right then, I expect you to keep me apprised of anything you feel or see that is ... out of the norm. Is that clear?"

"Aye, sir," she replied with a broad smile. "Thank you, sir."

There was a knock at the door. Stanton turned to see a young ensign standing in the open doorway. "Captain Stanton?" he asked.

"I'm Captain Stanton. What is it, Ensign?"

"Admiral Robbins wanted you to see this right away, sir." The young man held out a videocassette.

"What is it?" Stanton asked, taking it from the man's outstretched hand.

"The Admiral said that it's from this morning's news. Channel 12. He said you'd understand."

"Thank you, Ensign. Where can I find a video player?"

"There is one in the office next door. Do you want me to set it up, sir?"

"I think I can manage." Turning to Donna he said, "Shall we?" She stood immediately and walked toward the door.

N
Λ

"I wondered how long it would take before word got out," Stanton said with disgust. The image on the television was paused. He could see the *Triggerfish* moored to the dock.

"Me too," Donna replied. "I figured it would. Sooner or later the family or someone in the coroner's office would say something. I just didn't think it would happen this soon. Someone on base probably leaked it."

"Navy personnel?" Stanton was shocked. "Why would they do that?"

"Who knows, sir. Perhaps they're a fan of Barry Ludlow. Perhaps they're related to someone at the station."

"I guess how doesn't really matter anymore. The cat is out of the bag about young Mr. Toller. I suppose the public has a right to know, but I don't want this interrupting what we're doing."

"What's next?"

"You're the designated PR person for this detail, what do you suggest?"

"The way I see it, sir, is that we have two choices. One, we stonewall and not talk to anyone. You know, just clam up. But that has problems."

"Such as?"

"The media is a curious bunch. The more hidden the message, the more tenacious they become. They'll start pestering anyone and everyone they can. Since NAB is a secured facility, they can't come on base, but they sure can make a nuisance of themselves. They'll probably descend on Toller's parents."

"They don't need that right now, Lieutenant. Losing a son is horrible enough. They don't need some guy with a microphone and camera outside their door."

"I don't think it matters what we do, sir. The media will track down Toller's parents. Hopefully they won't be too insensitive."

Stanton frowned. "What's your second thought?"

"We feed the fish, Captain. Hold a press conference, tell them what we want them to know and nothing more. We can try to spin the information to our advantage. I might even be able to protect the Toller family some. You know, use guilt—the gift that keeps on giving."

"Perhaps," Stanton said. "But that decision is not mine to make. That will need to come from upstairs. Let's let the brass handle the press conference issue. If they decide to hold one, then you'll get the pleasure of leading it. I don't want to be any-where near it."

"Yes, sir."

"Are you sure you feel up to this?" Stanton asked.

"Yes, sir, I do. I won't let you down."

"Very well, Lieutenant. See that you don't."

N
Λ

Hermann pressed the button on the remote that turned off the power to the television. He paused, savoring the image of the submarine. His heart tripped with excitement. Only after he had let the picture percolate in his mind did he turn to face the others. They were waiting for him to speak. *As they should*, he thought.

"A death," he said to the three men and one woman who sat around a large oak table in the basement of the restaurant. "That will make things more difficult. Especially now that the media is more involved."

"But there is a good side to all of this," Victor said. He was the general manager of the Zum Deutschen Eck, a man of average build and appearance who was made noticeable by his bright red hair. He was also Hermann's closest confidant and he depended on him for his clear, almost psychic insights. "The video shows us exactly where the submarine is. It also shows that security is substandard."

"How so?" Hermann asked.

"Play the tape again, but without the audio. I'll show you."

Hermann used the remote control to rewind the videotape that he had made of the news report and played it back.

"If I may," Victor said reaching for the remote. Hermann yielded it. The image played across the large-screen television that sat in one corner of the room. The picture revealed a dark night pierced by the glow of high-pressure sodium lights that cast down a bright but soft yellow glow. Beneath the work lights was the *Triggerfish*. "First of all, I know this area. It is Glorietta Park and it is adjacent to the Amphibious Base. Also note the fence." Victor jumped up and stepped to the television. He pointed at a chain-link fence that separated the park from the Naval Base. "See how the fence runs out into the water and then stops. A swimmer could gain access to the base. Also the fence itself is only a little challenge. It has three strands of barbed wire along the top. Easy to cut."

"So you think access would be easy?" Hermann asked.

"Yes, as far as physical obstacles go. Armed guards are a different matter."

"How do we deal with them?"

"I don't know," Victor admitted. "We could get on base, but I don't think we would get very far. Perhaps with enough men we might overpower the security force."

"Not without a lot of bloodshed," Hermann stated. "And even if we made it to the sub safely, we would still have the problem of getting in, grabbing what we want, and getting out."

"We could have drivers ready nearby," Dennis Staub interjected. He was a thick man with heavy eyelids that made him look as if he were perpetually on the verge of a nap. His mind, however, was sharp and his loyalty unquestionable. He ran a hand over his bald head. "Or better yet, we could charge through the fence with a Humvee."

"The Humvee would have to be reinforced," Victor said, shaking his head. "And if we failed we would be sitting ducks."

"Our time is limited," Hermann said with frustration. "We don't know how long the sub will be there. The news report may force the navy to move it soon. We cannot lose this opportunity."

"What is on that boat that is so important?" Staub asked.

Hermann cut him a quick and hard look. "Something I want. That is enough." *They would not understand,* he said to himself. *They are loyal but they cannot comprehend the importance of what I seek.*

"I understand," Staub said quickly, bowing his head slightly.

"Our actions must be quick and flawless. This is the opportunity we have been waiting for. Our victory rests on the submarine. Our future is somewhere inside."

"Do we know where?" Victor inquired.

"No. Just somewhere inside," Hermann answered.

"For planning purposes, may I ask how many men will be required to carry the . . . items out."

"Just one. And I will be the one to retrieve it."

A thick silence filled the room. "Forgive me, Herr Kunzig, but is that wise?" Staub asked reluctantly. "You are far too valuable. If something should happen to you, then the new Reich will be doomed."

"I must go and I will go. What is on that ship must be in my hands and my hands alone." Hermann stared at the others with manic, piercing eyes. "And it must be soon. Twenty-four to thirty hours. No more."

Again silence. Hermann knew he was asking the impossible, but it didn't matter.

"You know of my dedication to you and to the cause," Victor said softly. "I am willing to lay down my life for you. You know that, Hermann. I have given my soul to this cause and will go to my grave supporting it, but I do not see how it is possible to do what you ask."

Hermann brought his hand down on the table with a loud slap and bolted to his feet. His chair flew backward. "You are here because you are the best in the movement. You, Victor," he said, pointing his finger at the man's face, "manage all our resources, and those resources are extensive. I have entrusted millions of dollars to your care because you are the best man for the job." He spun on his heels and pointed his finger at Staub. "You, Dennis, are responsible for all our recruitment. Every member of our party is known to you." Then he turned his attention to Max Rohl who sat quietly at the end of the table. "And you, Max, I depend on you to get things done. But you sit here in silence. Have you no opinion? Have you nothing to offer?"

"We walk in," Max said calmly.

Hermann was nonplused. "What? We walk in? How do we just walk in? Do you think they'll send us an invitation?"

"Yes, I do," Max said evenly.

"You're crazy," Staub spouted.

Max cut him a withering glance.

"Well, what I mean is . . ." Staub sputtered. Hermann cut him off with a wave of the hand.

"Tell me, Max. Tell me what you're thinking." Hermann picked up his chair and sat down again. "You have some scheme in mind, don't you?"

"That's why I'm here."

"Tell us," Hermann insisted eagerly. "Tell us all."

Max leaned forward and smiled. "I know the military. I know them very well. They will protect that submarine with everything they have. Not because it's important, but because it is their duty. But they will surrender it if something more important comes along. We will give them that something. And when we do, we will be able to walk on board the submarine, retrieve what you desire, and walk away at leisure."

"I don't see how," Victor said.

"You don't have to," Max replied harshly. "If you do what I tell you, then this will be a success."

"Can your plan be worked quickly?" Hermann asked.

"With the right men, yes."

"We have the best men," Staub said. "You tell me what you need, what skills they must possess, and I will provide them."

"You still haven't told me how this will work," Hermann said.

Max Rohl leaned over the table and let flow his idea. One hour later the four men were celebrating. The plan had been approved and set in motion.

The smell of dark German beer and cigarette smoke filled the basement conference room. It was early, too early to begin drinking, but an exception had to be made. The next few hours would be filled with feverish organization and planning. They would not sleep tonight and perhaps not tomorrow night, so time of day no longer mattered. *Let the beer flow for now*, Hermann thought.

Hermann Kunzig was the happiest man in the world.

Helen Muir had watched the transaction of ideas and with each decision reached, a chill ran through her. This day had to come; she had known that from the moment she learned of Hermann's connection to the underground Nazi movement. But by that time he was too much a part of her life. She had grown accustomed to the fine living he provided, the beautiful and expensive downtown condo and the other fineries of life. As his personal assistant and lover, she was privy to all his dealings, but she had always rationalized it away. How could any of this be more than an infatuation with greatness? A messiah complex? She told herself that it was a game with him, that it was not real, and that someday he would tire of it all. To believe otherwise would require that she make a stand, and that stand would cost her everything she had grown to love: the riches, the power, the man. Watching him now made her realize that it could even cost her life.

It had been a foolish self-construction, she realized. It was not Hermann who lived in a fantasy world, it was she. This was as real and as tangible as anything could be. And there was nothing she could do about it.

N
Λ

"You gotta sec?" Stanton asked into the phone.

"I always have time for my brother-in-law," Jim Walsh said. "Especially since he outranks me."

"I'm more in need of your spiritual advice than your military skills," Stanton remarked seriously.

"In my case they're the same thing. That's the way it is with chaplains. We give out both spiritual advice and salutes."

Stanton hesitated.

"You still there, buddy?" Walsh asked.

"Yes, I'm just not sure how to begin."

"Just start at the beginning and move on from there."

Leaning back in the desk chair in the small office he commandeered, Stanton let out a little sigh. "Okay, but this is going to sound weird. I'm warning you right up front that this is off the wall."

"I specialize in off the wall," Walsh said. "Go ahead, spit it out."

"It has to do with a young lieutenant I'm working with. You met her. She's the one that delivered the orders that pulled me off the golf course."

"I would have won that game, you know."

"Not in this lifetime," Stanton retorted. "I came out of a meeting with Admiral Robbins. I walked into an office she was using to see how she was coming on a report. I arrived just in time to see her pass out and hit the floor."

"Is she okay?"

"I think so, at least physically."

"You think there may be another problem?"

"I don't know. She said some weird things. The only way I can describe them is paranormal or supernatural and they're related to the submarine." Stanton reiterated the conversation, adding his own impressions.

"A face on the deck?" Walsh said with surprise. "You're right, that *is* odd."

"No, you didn't hear me right," Stanton corrected. "Not on the deck, *in* the deck. That is, the actual wood decking changed."

"I thought submarines were all metal."

"They are now," Stanton said. "World War II subs had about half of their metal decks covered with wood slats. It was a safer surface to walk on."

"That's not true now?"

"This is off the point, Jim, but let me clear this up. World War II subs were really surface craft that could submerge. They spent most of their time on the surface and dived only when needed. Today's nuclear subs are just the opposite. They perform better underwater than they do on the surface."

"Oh, I get it."

"Given what little information I've told you, what do you think? Is she unbalanced, or what?"

"Not necessarily. Is her jacket clean?" Walsh asked, referring to Lieutenant Wilcox's personnel and service folder.

"Yes. Actually all her reviews list her above average. Even so, these hallucinations are something to be concerned about."

"Has it occurred to you that she might be telling the truth?" Walsh asked.

"I'm sure she is from her perspective, but—"

"That's not what I mean," Walsh interrupted. "What if she really saw it? What if her premonitions and visions are true?"

"I wondered about that," Stanton said. "But how can such mumbo jumbo be real?"

"Is it mumbo jumbo? You're a churchgoer. More than that, you're a believer. True?"

"Of course."

"Then you know there is a spiritual world."

"I don't believe in ghosts, Jim. The *Triggerfish* is not a ghost ship." Stanton was emphatic.

"I don't believe in ghosts either, but the Bible is very clear about a spiritual realm. Surely you know that."

"I've never really thought about it," Stanton admitted. "Do you mean like angels and such?"

"Angels and demons. I'm not saying that's what's going on, but based on what little you've told me, I can't dismiss it just yet."

"Wouldn't it be easier to believe that the lieutenant is just . . . confused. That would be a lot simpler than demons."

"Is that what we're after, J. D.? Are we looking for the easiest answer to swallow, or are we looking for the truth?"

That took the wind from his sails. "The truth of course, but I believe that truth resides in the obvious, not in the bizarre."

Walsh chuckled. "That's true—normally. But what about this situation has been normal? How often does a sub that was listed missing nearly sixty years ago in the Atlantic suddenly surface on your doorstep in the Pacific? To my knowledge, nothing like that has ever happened."

This wasn't going the way Stanton had wanted. What he thought would happen was that Walsh would ask to see Lieutenant Wilcox and offer an opinion about her emotional state. If things were not as they should be, then he, as a navy chaplain, could refer her to a psychologist.

"Let me ask you this," Walsh said. "When you spoke with her, did you feel that she was unbalanced?"

"What difference does that make?" Stanton demanded.

"Go with me on this," Walsh insisted. "Did you feel like you were talking to someone who is psychotic?"

"I'm no expert—"

"But you know how to command a crew and that requires superior judgment. The navy has spent a fortune over the years to train you to be the best leader possible. You excel at that. You cannot command others without a feel, a second sense, for their stability. Now, I ask the question again: Did you feel that she was unstable, psychotic, or emotionally distraught?"

"No. She seemed stressed, but in control."

"And her file is clear. You know, there's a chance that she may be seeing what you can't."

"Okay," Stanton retorted, "let's say that she is. How can I tell?"

"Did you hear the unusual noises on the sub?"

"Yes. We all did."

"And you say that the sub's engines came to life by themselves. True?"

"I don't have an answer. I haven't been inside. But you're right. That seems to be the case. At least until I can get inside."

"I want to make a call and talk to someone. How can I get hold of you?"

"I have a cell phone with me," Stanton said. He gave the number. "Who are you going to call?"

"Let me hold off on that for now. I want to talk to him first before I start mentioning names."

"Okay. But you don't think I should refer Lieutenant Wilcox to you?"

"You can if you want," Walsh said. "But I'd wait. If you order her over to my office, she'll assume that you've lost confidence in her. Just keep an eye on her for now."

"Okay, Jim. Thanks. I'll think about what you've said, but I'm skeptical. There's a logical explanation for all this."

"Most likely you're right, but don't write off the spiritual side. There are times when it is better to listen to your spirit more than your head."

"That's not my way, Jim, but I'll keep it in mind."

The men said good-bye and Stanton hung up. Jim Walsh's words rattled around in his mind. The navy had not trained him to look at the world through spiritual eyes. The idea seemed ludicrous. Still, he had known Jim Walsh for more years than he cared to admit, and he had never known him to be irrational. In fact, Jim was the most "together" man he knew.

But angels? Demons? No, not possible.

Chapter 11

"You're sure of all this?" Barry Ludlow was standing behind his desk. After the early morning taping at Glorietta Park in Coronado, he had driven home, letting his cameraman deliver the videotape to the studio. The sun had been cresting the horizon in the east when he collapsed into bed fully clothed. Four hours later, he was up, showered, and back at the studio. The tape had played during the morning show and he wanted to see how his peers were responding; that and he had his regular assignments to fulfill. An hour later the phone on his desk rang.

"They actually backed off and called for more testing?" he said in the phone. The person on the other end was a young ensign in the base commander's office. She also had an infatuation with Barry Ludlow, something that was not wasted on the reporter. "This is great. I think I may owe you a night on the town."

He listened, then said. "That sounds fun. Maybe when all this is over we can do that." He listened again. "I love dancing," he lied. "Sure, sure. Let me get to work on this. Oh, and thanks. You've been a big help."

He hung up the phone and began to pace, rubbing his hands together with eagerness. The question was, what to do now? If he worked fast, he might have something for the evening news. What he needed was an interview. He snatched up the phone and called directory assistance. A moment later he was dialing the number to the Naval Amphibious Base on Coronado. He was greeted with a recorded message informing him of a new number to call. "Typical," he said to himself as he dialed once again.

A man, who identified himself as the public relations liaison for North Island Air Station, answered.

"Good morning, this is Barry Ludlow of Channel 12 News," Barry began in a professional tone. "I need some information about events at the Naval Amphibious Base, but I was given this number when I called over there. Does NAB not have a PR department?"

"Cutbacks, sir. That department was combined with ours." The man's voice was deep and resonant.

"I wonder if you might help me," Barry began.

"Is this regarding the submarine?" the man asked, his voice dripping with suspicion. Apparently he had seen the morning report.

"Yes. I was wondering—"

"I'm afraid that I have no information for you, Mr. Ludlow. That's not being handled through this office."

"What office is it being handled through, then?"

"The base commander, sir."

This was no good. His source was in the commander's office and she had already told him that the commander did not want to talk to the press. "Who is the liaison with the public on this?"

The man hesitated. "I don't have that information."

"Don't have it or won't share it?" Barry inquired pointedly.

"I don't have that information." The man's voice remained professional and unemotional.

"Who would have that information?"

"The base commander."

"Of course," Barry said. "I should have guessed."

He hung up without a further word. He began to pace behind his desk again. There was no doubt in his mind that he was being stonewalled. There had to be someone he could talk to. He ran over the events in his mind. He had done two reports so far. One from the Torrey Pines State Beach and the other last night . . . That was it. At the beach he had spoken to a Captain Stanton. "Maybe I could reach him directly," he said to himself as he snatched up the phone and called his contact at NAB. Maybe with a few sweet words and a couple of promises, he might be able to verify Stanton's continued involvement and even find a way to contact him.

N

λ

J. D. Stanton had just sat down at a table in the base restaurant with Commander Stewart and Lieutenant Wilcox when the cell phone he carried rang.

"Captain Stanton," he said answering the phone on the second ring. "Who?" Stanton shook his head in disgust. "Yes, I remember you. How did you get this number, Mr. Ludlow?" He saw Donna cringe at the mention of the reporter's name. "Actually, I think it does matter."

Stanton listened intently for a moment. The reporter's voice sounded confident, almost arrogant. "Yes, I am in charge of the investigation, but I don't handle media relations. Here." He handed the phone to Donna. He smiled and mouthed the word "Surprise."

Clearing her throat, Donna spoke, "Lieutenant Donna Wilcox. May I help you?"

As Stanton sipped his coffee, he kept a close eye on his aide. This would be a good test for her. While not a life-and-death situation, there was sufficient pressure having just had your commander thrust a phone in your face and say in effect, "Here, perform."

"It is too early, Mr. Ludlow, to release any information. I can tell you the submarine was towed here safely and without incident." Stanton caught Stewart's eye. Technically, she was right. No incident occurred, but there had been the noise on the trip, then the death (which the reporter already knew), and the thumping noise and bizarre appearance of ice (which the reporter didn't know).

Donna looked grim as she listened. Reporters could be tenacious and even rude. It was their job to get information, and even the slightest scent of a secret was like blood to sharks.

"I'm sorry you feel like you're getting the runaround, Mr. Ludlow. I can imagine how difficult your job is, but there is nothing to tell you right now." She listened some more. Stanton noticed her jaw tighten. Still, her voice remained the same. "I suppose I could make up some fantastic story for you to broadcast, sir. Of course it would soon be shown to be false and you'd be left holding the bag. But if it would help—"

A smile erupted on her face. "Yes, I imagine that would end your career. Honesty is demanded in your profession. But now you see my problem. I have nothing to tell you. That leaves only some fabricated report, but that's no good either. I guess you're out of luck for the moment."

She pulled the phone away from her ear. Ludlow was speaking loudly. For some reason, that made Stanton feel good. "Stonewalling? Of course not, sir. You're just running a little faster than we are. Are we going in? Yes, sir. At the appropriate time. And before you ask, I don't know when that is."

There was a pause. "Because I haven't been told. That decision is up to Captain Stanton and his superiors. A news conference. Well, sir, I really couldn't say. That would be up to the commander's office. Have you spoken to them?"

Donna looked startled. "Hello? Hello? He hung up on me."

Stanton and Stewart laughed deeply.

"Very well done, Lieutenant," Stanton said with a broad smile. "You handled him like a pro."

"Here, here!" Stewart said, holding up his coffee cup in a mock toast.

"He's not a happy camper," Donna said. "Can't say that I blame him. I almost felt sorry for the guy."

"Don't," Stanton said. "He'll have his story soon enough. Once we know what's going on."

"So when do we attempt to enter the *Triggerfish*?" Stewart asked.

"The admiral wants me to hold off until after sunset," Stanton answered. "That news report showed how easy it was to film across the narrow bay that separates the dock areas from the public park. Things are so close that we could sit at the yacht club on the other side of the park and watch everything that goes on. The admiral would like a little more secrecy, and since it is easier to wait for dark than it is to tow the sub somewhere else, we must wait a few hours."

"Fine with me," Stewart said. "After we eat, I'll run home and grab some sleep. I should change uniforms too. This one is getting a little on the wrinkled side. Assuming you'll let me back on the base."

"That can be arranged," Stanton assured him. He looked at Donna.

"I'll see to it, sir," she said.

"Very well. I think Commander Stewart has a good idea. Let's eat, grab a nap, and meet back here at . . ." He looked at his watch. ". . . 1500 hours. That'll give us time to get our ducks in order."

"Will do," Donna said.

"Bring a video camera too, Lieutenant," Stanton said. "If I see ice in the water again, I want proof."

"Yes, sir. I'll make sure it's fully equipped for audio too. That way we can wipe the smug grins off the faces of the boys in acoustics."

"Agreed," Stanton replied. Again his phone rang shrilly. "That had better not be that reporter again." He snapped up the phone. "Captain Stanton here." There was a pause. A grin crossed his face and he nodded. "Hi, Jim. What's up? I can do that. When? One o'clock it is. In your office? No, why don't you come out here. I'll get a conference room. Fine. I'll see you then."

He turned to Donna. "Lieutenant—"

"A conference room for 1300 hours, sir. I'll take care of it. I'll also see if I can't find out who gave your number to Ludlow."

"Thank you, Lieutenant. But then you'll go home and catch some z's. Understood?"

"Aye, sir. Understood."

Stanton smiled then gave a small nod. His aide seemed more confident, more self-possessed—at least outwardly. He hoped that the self-assurance had sunk to her core. Only time would tell that.

N
᛭

"The audacity!" Barry said loudly, glad that no one was in the room to hear him. "Of all the unmitigated gall! How dare they put me off like that. I can't believe that woman was fencing with me. I have a right to know."

He began pacing again. His mind bubbled like a witch's pot. It was no longer a matter of the news. It was more than a story. Now it was personal, and they had just crossed the wrong man. Somehow, some way, Barry Ludlow would get what he wanted, even if he had to take on the entire Pacific fleet to do it.

N
Λ

The late morning light filtered through the dirty skylights to mix with the harsh incandescent bulbs that hung from the high ceiling, giving the old warehouse an eerie, haunted feeling. The air was stale and dusty like the inside of an old crypt. The cavernous room was largely empty except for the special items that had been transported there from similar warehouses around San Diego. Hermann knew that this was just one of twenty-five such buildings scattered throughout the country. Plans called for the addition of twenty-five more such buildings over the next two years.

Hermann's black dress shoes thudded dully with each step. The noise echoed off the wood walls with their peeling white paint and the cracked concrete floor. Helen walked near his side, but one step back. Her refined beauty was a stark contrast to the aged, decaying structure.

Once a storage facility for San Diego's formally thriving tuna industry, the building was ancient in every respect except its alarms and locks. Outside, the sounds of traffic on Harbor Boulevard hummed through the air.

Before him stood two rows of men, each at attention and facing the row opposite them. Each wore military fatigues and a red armband. Between them stood Max Rohl. Max bowed slightly when he saw Hermann and Helen and marched toward them.

"Have they been briefed?" Hermann asked forcefully.

"Yes," Max said with his usual economy of words. "They understand everything they are to do. They are ready."

"And the equipment?"

"As you can see, it is all here."

"Everything?" Hermann asked.

"Everything," Max responded immediately. "Your forward thinking has made all this possible. We could never have gathered all that we need if you had not had the foresight to obtain them ahead of time."

"I have always known the right time would come. I just didn't know when or what shape it would take. We must be ready for anything, Max." Hermann glanced around the warehouse taking in the vehicles, weapons, and equipment. It was a tiny portion of what he had sequestered in various states.

"The time is the same?" Hermann inquired as he stared at the men.

"Yes. Early evening. When the traffic is heaviest."

"You're a genius, Max. A true genius."

"Thank you, sir, but you flatter me."

A warm wash of pride ran through Hermann. He loved this. He lived for this. Night after night he had dreamed of this moment. The details were different as was the timing. But that did not matter. This was the moment for which he had been born. This was the beginning. And there would be many such moments to follow. Hermann felt as if he were standing on the brink of destiny.

"Do you wish to speak to the men?" Max asked. "It would encourage them."

Hermann nodded, then walked slowly between the two ranks. He held his head high and spoke with authority. "A lesser man would stand here and see soldiers, men of war. But that man would be wrong. For you are more than mere soldiers, you are heroes. You are patriots. You do the gods proud. You men have been chosen for this wonderful task. You have been chosen because of your skills, training, and most of all, your loyalty to the cause for which we live, and for which we are willing to die." He took in the face of each man. Each was highly trained by the best in the world, the U.S. military structure. Former Green Berets, Army Rangers, and Navy SEALs comprised the men before him. It struck Hermann as ironic that these highly skilled, professional military men were trained by the very government they planned to overthrow. There was a certain poetic justice to it.

"But you have been picked for this glorious opportunity, not just because you're the best trained warriors in the world, but because you are men of purpose. You believe, as I do, that time for change has arrived. That a greater government is needed. Our society continues to decline. There are racial impurities that weaken us. It is time to return to a better plan, a greater purpose. What you do tonight will never be forgotten. You will be... No, you *are* heroes."

He need say no more. These men had proven themselves many times over. Their loyalty was as grand as his plan for a new Reich. Hermann turned toward the door he had entered a few minutes before. "Victor!" he called. "Bring us champagne. Today we celebrate! Soon we rule."

"Yes, mein Führer," Victor answered quickly.

A fine crystal glass was handed to each man. Victor then filled each glass with a generous measure of sparkling champagne poured from a magnum. When each soldier had received his drink, Victor filled Helen's glass, then Hermann's, who immediately raised it to his eyes, then out, extending his arm.

"To the future, to success, to the Reich," he said loudly. The men followed his lead, holding their glasses out in a formal toast. Hermann brought the glass to his lips and drank the entire contents. The men followed. When his glass was empty, he shouted, "Victory!" and threw it to the floor where it shattered into a shower of crystal shards.

"Victory!" the men repeated in unison and sent their glasses plummeting to the floor. "Heil Kunzig! Sieg heil!"

Hermann smiled broadly, came to attention, and raised his hand in the Nazi salute.

"Sieg heil!" the men responded.

Hermann faced Max. "They make me proud, Max. Only one thing remains."

Max was puzzled. "I believe everything is in order. We are ready to go at your command."

"I want you to find a role for Helen." Hermann placed an arm around her shoulder and felt her tense. "She wants to participate in our effort." Helen dropped her still full glass. Champagne splattered on her legs.

"I'm no soldier, Hermann," she stammered. "I'm afraid that I might ruin your great plan."

"You must participate," Hermann said, narrowing his eyes threateningly. "You must bear the honor and the responsibility. We must all show our commitment. We must share the risk. That includes you."

"But—"

He raised a finger with such speed that she thought that he was going to strike her as he had so many times in the past. Instead, he laid his index finger on her lips. "Hush," he said softly. "These men are risking everything, my dear. They do so because of their belief in the cause and their loyalty to me. We must all trust each other, and that trust must be sealed by participation. We all participate, we all contribute, we all bear the burden. All of us share in the risk. Do you understand?"

Helen lowered her head. "I understand."

"I knew you would," Hermann said. "So, Max, do you have something for my lovely Helen to do?"

"I will find a way to use her skills," Max said.

Chapter 12

The fresh uniform and three hours of sleep had reinvigorated Stanton. He would have liked to have spent more time in bed, blanketed in the sweetness of slumber, but he had promised to meet Jim Walsh and his mystery guest at 1:00. It was two minutes to the hour now as he briskly walked down the corridor that led to the conference room in the base administration building. Lieutenant Wilcox had been true to her word arranging for the room, and a pass for the civilian with Jim. Since the Naval Amphibious Base is a secured facility, getting on base could be difficult and often got bogged down in paperwork. Stanton could only assume that her connection to the admiral's office had been a help. As he turned the doorknob and entered the room, he saw that she had even arranged for coffee and Danishes. Walsh stood to his feet the moment Stanton entered the room.

"Gentlemen," Stanton said with a smile. "You beat me here."

"We haven't been up all night, sir," Walsh said.

"Can the 'sir' stuff for now, Jim," Stanton stated. "I'd like to keep this informal. Besides, we're family."

Seated next to where Walsh was standing was a thin balding man, with a large forehead and eyes that looked as if the blue had been bleached out of them. His hands, which were graced with long, pianist fingers, were folded in front of him. A small smile said that he was amused at the navy protocol.

"J. D., this is Hawking Striber. He's the man I told you about."

"Mr. Striber," Stanton said, extending his hand.

"It's good to meet you, Captain. Your brother-in-law speaks highly of you."

"That's only because I outrank him."

"Actually, my wife makes me do it," Walsh jested.

"Can I offer you some coffee, Mr. Striber?"

"Please call me Hawking, Captain, and no thanks. It's a little late in the day for coffee."

"Clearly you were never in the navy," Stanton said.

"No, sir. Never served in any branch of the military," Hawking replied, then added quickly, "not that I'm opposed to it, you understand. It just took me a long time to get through school."

"Hawking holds a Ph.D. in physics," Walsh added. "He's too modest to admit it, but he is one sharp cookie."

The comment seemed to embarrass the man.

"So where did you two meet?" Stanton asked as he poured hot coffee into a white cup emblazoned with the initials NAB.

"At a Bible conference, of all places," Walsh explained. "Hawking was one of the speakers."

"I'm impressed," Stanton said as he sat down. "Physics and the Bible. That must keep you pretty busy."

Hawking laughed nasally. "It does at that."

There was a moment of silence that signaled the end of the small talk.

"Well, Jim," Stanton began, "I believe you said you had something for me?"

"Yes. Well, I think so." Walsh took a sip of coffee. "After I talked to you on the phone about that personnel matter, Hawking's name came to mind. Some of the things you mentioned are up his alley."

"Physics alley or Bible alley?"

"I don't see a difference, Captain," Hawking interjected. "One explains the other. Jim tells me that you're a Christian. Is that true?"

"It is," Stanton said. The direct question startled him.

"Then you have some understanding of the Bible."

"I get around in it okay. Why?"

"Um, let me take that one," Walsh said. "Hawking specializes in the paranormal."

"The paranormal?" Stanton said with surprise. "I thought that would be the very antithesis of your belief."

"*Paranormal* is an unfortunate word," Hawking replied quickly. "The word carries more meaning in our society than it should. I study biblical paranormal phenomenon."

"I didn't know there was such a thing," Stanton offered flatly.

"Oh yes, very much so."

Stanton let slip a sigh. He was uncomfortable with this and it seemed a waste of time. His thoughts ran to the other hour of sleep he could have had, had he not accepted this meeting.

"You see, Captain," Hawking continued, "I study those things that are out of the ordinary, but still biblical."

"Such as?"

"The multidimensionality of God, biblical cosmology, non-human creations—"

"What kind of creations?" Stanton interrupted.

"Nonhuman. Angels, demons, the living creatures in Revelation, Daniel, Ezekiel, and the like. God did more than create us humans. He created other, shall we say, species."

"I understand the angel part," Stanton offered. "But I don't see what this has to do with me."

"If I understand everything Jim has told me, then it may have everything to do with you and the submarine you're investigating."

"Oh?" Stanton raised an eyebrow and directed his gaze to his brother-in-law. "And just what has he been telling you?"

"That there has been an unexplained death; that there have been unexpected sounds from the sub; and that one of your workers—"

"Officers," Walsh corrected.

"Officers," Hawking repeated. "One of your officers is acting strangely . . . as far as the sub is concerned."

Stanton was not sure whether to be angry with Walsh for telling this man everything or to feel comforted by his concern. Nothing of what he had shared was secret, at least not officially. The navy was simply trying to keep a low profile about Toller's death.

"All explainable in a logical fashion, I'm sure." Stanton took another sip of coffee. "I'm not one who sees demons around every corner and ghosts under every rock."

"Nor am I, Captain," Hawking rebutted firmly. "I'm not a kook or a psychic. I don't believe in ghosts, fairies, or leprechauns. But I do know that there are a great many things that cannot be explained by purely rationalistic platitudes."

"I still hold that everything will be explained once we have had time to study things at hand, especially once we've been in the sub itself."

"J. D.," Walsh said seriously. "I think you need to hear Hawking out."

"Is that what you think?" Stanton said more harshly than he intended.

"Yes, I do." Stanton could see the serious expression on his friend's face. "Not only do I think that, I feel it too."

"I'm sorry, Jim," Stanton said. "I'm still a little tired. All right, I'm listening. You think something paranormal is happening on my boat?"

"Again, I wouldn't use the word *paranormal*," Hawking answered. "And all I have to go on is Jim's assessment. I just think you need to be open to the idea."

"I don't see it, gentlemen," Stanton responded. "I appreciate your concern, but I know the sea and the ships that sail her. I will acknowledge that I am puzzled about a few things, but they will be answered in time."

"Perhaps you're right," Hawking said, "but couldn't we talk about this a little more? You don't have to reveal any secrets."

"What do you want to know?" Stanton asked.

"Tell me about the submarine. I already know that it appeared suddenly, and I want to talk about that in a moment. Maybe you could give me a little history. Just the high points."

Stanton shrugged. He had read the file on the submarine and had added his own information. The first book he had published was *Forgotten Heroes: U.S. Submarines in the Atlantic During WW II*. It had been published by Annapolis Press while he was still teaching at the Academy. The research he had done for that work had provided him with a wealth of details about the *Triggerfish* and other submarines overlooked in the Atlantic campaign.

"Very well," Stanton said. "Here are the highlights. The *Triggerfish* is an improved Gato class submarine. Her keel was laid in mid 1942 at Groton, Connecticut, and after a shakedown cruise she was assigned to several missions. Her first was shore patrol along the East Coast. During that time she also served as a training vessel for new submariners. Her second mission was a seek-and-destroy tour in the Atlantic. She received orders to join up with Sub Squadron 50 in Scotland. She never showed."

"Her captain was experienced?" Hawking asked.

"Very. Captain Morrison was one of the best. But you must remember that nearly one in three subs went down. It was dangerous duty."

"I can only imagine," Hawking said. "Was there anything unusual in their mission? Did they make any kind of radio report?"

"Nothing special. They did sink two warships in a skirmish and endured a depth charge attack."

"But nothing else?"

Stanton shrugged, then furrowed his brow. "Now that you mention it, there was a report about having picked up a German in a raft. Shortly after that they were ordered to Scotland."

"A German?" Walsh exclaimed. "Just floating in the ocean?"

"It would seem so. The change in orders came because the brass wanted to interrogate the man. I imagine it really frosted Captain Morrison. Skippers don't like to be pulled off duty like that."

"Then what happened?" Hawking prompted.

"No one knows. As I said, they failed to arrive in Scotland."

"Do you know who the German was?"

Stanton shook his head. "Not from memory."

"Could you find out?"

"I suppose, but why?" Stanton was becoming suspicious again.

"It could provide some information," Hawking said thoughtfully. "The more information we have, the better."

"Let me set the record straight." Stanton leaned over the conference table. "This is my investigation, not *our* investigation."

Hawking raised a hand. "I'm not trying to horn in on your work, Captain. I'm just trying to help. It just seems odd that a man is fished out of the ocean and sometime after that the sub goes missing. And we can't forget that it came back. Judging from what I saw on television, it looks like it's in pretty good shape. Is that true?"

"Yes, it is."

"Remarkably so?"

"Yes, remarkably so," Stanton confessed.

"I'm no sailor, Captain Stanton, but isn't that unusual?"

"Absolutely."

"How do you explain it?"

"Right now, I don't. But as we continue the investigation, the truth will be known." Stanton's words were more confident than he felt. "There's a good chance that someone has had possession of the boat. Someone like a third-world country."

A heavy pause stilled the conversation. Hawking broke the silence. "I saw the TV footage," he said. "If I'm not mistaken, there is a number on the submarine."

"Correct," Stanton said. "The number 237 is painted on the conning tower and on the hull forward of the bow planes." Suddenly Stanton saw where Hawking was headed.

"Captain, if you were a third-world country, or anyone else for that matter, and you came into possession of a submarine like the *Triggerfish*, would you leave the identification number on it?"

Stanton said nothing. Hawking had a point, one he had overlooked.

"My guess is," Hawking continued, "that the paint is what you'd expect from a submarine that had been at sea for a few months but not fifty-plus years. Am I wrong?"

A sigh escaped from Stanton. "No, actually you're dead on." Stanton felt sick. He should have noticed that. How had it gotten past him?

"How do we explain that, Captain?"

"I don't know," he admitted. "How would you explain it, Dr. Striber?"

"I can only suggest ideas, but such things have happened before."

"Happened before?" Stanton was surprised. "Submarines appearing from the past?"

"No," Hawking corrected. "Not submarines, but missing seacraft. Take, for example, the *Mary Celeste*. Are you familiar with it?"

"Yes," Stanton said. "All naval historians are."

"I'm not," Walsh admitted. "Bring me up to speed."

Hawking turned to Stanton and gave a questioning glance. "You go ahead," Stanton said. "I'm interested in your take on the matter."

"Okay." Hawking cleared his throat. "The *Mary Celeste* started off as the *Amazon* under a British flag. She was a brigantine—an old two-masted sailing ship. Eleven years after her construction, she had a new name and flag. She was called the *Mary Celeste* and registered as American. On December 4, 1872, she was found adrift six hundred miles off the Portuguese coast by Captain Morehouse of the *Dei Gratia*. Upon investigation it was discovered that the entire crew of the *Mary Celeste* was gone."

"They had abandoned ship?" Walsh asked.

"If they did, they did so in a big hurry. While it is true that a yawl was missing, it only serves to confuse the situation. The crew left so fast that personal belongings were left behind, including boots, tobacco, and pipes. Sailors usually do not leave such things behind. A medicine bottle was left open with the cork and a spoon next to it. In the captain's quarters was a piece of paper with incomplete calculations on it. In another area the boarding crew from the *Dei Gratia* found a small vial of sewing-machine oil standing on a table as well as an orderly array of reels of cotton. Apparently a crew member was planning on doing a little sewing, but left hurriedly."

"So they abandoned ship fast," Walsh said. "That happens."

"But the ship was sound and in good sailing condition," Hawking countered. "In fact, a skeleton crew from the *Dei Gratia* was able to sail her to Gibraltar, where Captain Morehouse claimed salvage. The question is: Why did the crew abandon ship? If that is what they indeed did. They left behind not only personal artifacts, but also the entire cargo of 1,700 casks of commercial alcohol. That's a lot of money to leave behind."

"And that may be the answer to the whole mystery," Stanton interjected. "At least that's what some historians have concluded."

"How so?" Walsh inquired.

"One of the casks was found open," Stanton said. "But—"

"Oh, I see," Walsh said. "The crew may have been dipping into the cargo a little too much. Is that it?"

"No," Hawking said. "The open container doesn't explain it. The alcohol was commercial grade. Entirely undrinkable. If the crew had been consuming it, it would have made them sick. The boarding crew would have found sick or dead crewmen, not an empty ship."

"I will agree that the *Mary Celeste* is a mystery," Stanton offered, "but that doesn't mean the crew simply disappeared. The yawl was gone. It seems clear that they did abandon ship. We just don't know why."

"True, but something scared them off, if they actually left. No crew member was ever found, dead or alive. But there are other cases. Consider the unexplained disappearance of three thousand Chinese soldiers just outside Nanking on December 10, 1939. No trace was ever found of them. Or the community of over a thousand on Lake Anjikuni in Canada that disappeared in 1930. They left dogs tethered to trees, food still on the stoves, and their guns in their places. A trapper by the name of Joe Labelle found the community deserted, kayaks still secured to the shore. The Royal Canadian Mounted Police investigated but found nothing. To make the scene even more macabre, the graveyard had been robbed, or maybe I should say emptied. Corpses were removed, leaving only the hollow graves."

"That's bizarre," Walsh said with a whistle. "I take it that the case remains unsolved."

"Correct," Hawking said. "There are many other cases."

"You're not going to bring up the Bermuda Triangle, are you?" Stanton said with disgust. "Those disappearances are probably due to bad weather and poor skills."

"I agree for the most part, Captain, but not entirely. While it is true that the most famous case of the Triangle can be explained away, not every such case can."

"What famous case?" Walsh asked.

"Five Grumman Avengers vanished on December 5, 1945, after leaving the Naval Air Station at Fort Lauderdale, Florida. Between them was a crew of fourteen. They never came back. Some cryptic messages were received. They seemed lost and were unable to see land. Despite a Coast Guard search, nothing was found. No wreckage, nothing. Over 260 U.S. planes scoured the ocean from above. Again, nothing. A quarter million miles was searched and nothing was found. The list of lost aircraft and ships is long: The *Cyclops*, a navy collier, lost in March of 1918; the Norwegian *Stavenger* went missing October 1931; the *Marine Sulfur Queen*, lost in February 1963. It goes on, but you get the idea. But Captain Stanton is right. Many of these may be nothing more than marine and air accidents. But they are, nonetheless, difficult to explain."

Stanton had to appreciate the strange man in front of him. He was sharp, articulate, and convincing. "So what am I supposed to get out of all this? A UFO full of Martians transported the *Triggerfish* through time?"

"No, not Martians, Captain Stanton," Hawking said. "I don't believe that we've had visitors from other planets."

"Well, that's a relief," Stanton offered. "I was starting to worry about you."

"I believe that we have been visited by beings from another dimension." Hawking's tone was emotionless and serious. He stared directly at Stanton.

For a moment, Stanton thought that Hawking was joking. He even let slip a little laugh. But it was soon clear that Hawking was not being humorous. Stanton leaned back in his chair and rubbed his eyes and wondered how he could politely exit the room.

"You think I'm a little over the top. Don't you, Captain Stanton?"

"Not to put too fine a point on it, Dr. Striber, yes. I'm afraid this sounds like nonsense to me."

"I understand," Hawking said. "I'm used to it. Actually, you believe the same thing."

"I'm afraid I don't believe anything of the sort," Stanton retorted.

"Did you not tell me you were a Christian?" Hawking offered smoothly. "I assumed that means that you hold the Bible to be the source of authority for life. Do you believe that about the Bible?"

"That it is the authority for my life? Yes. But I don't see—"

"Where is God?" Hawking interrupted.

"What do you mean?" Stanton was taken aback by the question.

"Where is God? Right now. Where is he?"

"Well . . . everywhere," Stanton answered, uncertain about the sudden change in direction. "He's omnipresent. Everywhere present at the same time."

"I agree, but how can he do that?" Hawking pressed.

"I don't know. He's God. He can do anything he wants."

"Again, I agree. But how?"

"I don't see where this is going," Stanton complained.

"You're familiar with the Christmas story. Who told the shepherds about the birth of Christ?"

"Is this a test?" Stanton objected. "I feel like I'm in Sunday school."

"Bear with me," Hawking insisted. "I'm leading up to my point."

"Angels," Stanton answered. "Angels told the shepherds of Christ's birth."

"Correct. At first it was one angel, then a multitude. Where did they come from?"

Stanton shrugged. "Heaven, I suppose."

"Where is heaven?"

"I don't know." Stanton was becoming exasperated. "You said you were leading to a point."

"I am and here it is. All through Scripture, angels appear. I mean that literally. They just appear. In fact, the two words most commonly associated with angels are *fear* and *suddenly*. The fear is often the result of the sudden appearance of the angel. Even a quick reading of the Bible verses that deal with angels show them to be intelligent nonhuman creatures. The question is: How can they suddenly appear and disappear?"

"Because God wants them to," Stanton suggested.

"I can't argue that. Where do you suppose angels are when they're not popping in on us humans? I think they're in a different dimension called heaven. In physics we have determined mathematically that there are ten or more dimensions. I believe all that is part of God's creation.

"In God's dimension," Hawking continued, "time is multi-directional. That is why 'a thousand years is as a day' to the Lord. If this is true of angels, could it not also be true for demons? After all, demons are fallen angels, are they not?"

"I suppose so," Stanton responded. "But I'm no theologian or physicist."

"I am," Hawking said quickly. "I can tell you that it works out on paper and is in keeping with the truth contained in the Bible."

Walsh spoke up. "But how does all this tie in to the submarine?"

"I need just another moment to lay the groundwork, if I may." Hawking cleared his throat and leaned over the table. "I want to talk about UFOs for just a moment, then I'll bundle it all up and tell you what I think.

"First, I think we can all agree that something is being seen in the skies. Most of it is misidentification, natural phenomena, and the like. But even if ninety-nine percent of such sightings can be explained away we are left with thousands of unexplained accounts. Many such sightings are made by trained people: police officers, pilots, military personnel, and others.

"Second, these sightings are unique in many ways. Objects suddenly appear and then disappear. Some travel at great speeds and then make rapid course changes that are impossible in the physical world. They change shapes while in flight. There are well-documented cases where UFOs have been tracked at impossible speeds, and even tracked straight into the ground, as if they had crashed, only to reappear again. Nothing in our dimension can do those things.

"What I propose is not new. Many theologians have suggested this. It is possible that what we are seeing are not beings from another planet, but from a different dimension. The observations indicate that we are not seeing a mechanical device moving through space, but one moving through space-time."

Stanton scratched the back of his neck. "You're saying that the *Triggerfish* is haunted."

"Possessed," Hawking corrected. "And before you ask, no, I don't know how or why. This is beyond the realm of traditional science. As a scientist, I can do the math to show multi-dimensions, but I can't move much beyond that. It fits, however, with both science and the Bible."

"You got all that from what little Jim has told you?" Stanton asked. "That's quite a leap, my friend. Quite a leap."

"That and your aide's ill-defined terror. From what I hear, something has her frightened."

"Again, you're making a huge leap," Stanton said.

"Am I?" Hawking raised an eyebrow. "Some people are more sensitive to spiritual things, Captain. There may be a reason for her fear. One you've not faced yet."

"Why her?" Stanton inquired. "Why not me or Commander Stewart or anyone else who has been around the sub?"

"I don't know anything about Commander Stewart," Hawking answered. "Your faith makes you undesirable to them. Is Lieutenant Wilcox a believer?"

"I can't really say," he began then stopped. "Wait a minute. When I was speaking to her after she fainted, she made a comment." Stanton thought for a second. He had been so concerned about her condition and health that words had not left an impression with him. "She said she wasn't a religious person."

"Unbelievers have no protection from the demonic," Hawking said. "That doesn't mean that every unbeliever is possessed or even oppressed by demons. To be quite frank about things, Captain, we don't really know why some people are subject to the demonic. There have been many people who link such activity to the occult and there is some reason to believe their arguments, but it doesn't explain everything. Consider the passage in Mark chapter seven. Toward the end of the chapter Mark recounts an encounter between Jesus and a Gentile woman. The woman has come to him asking that he cast out an unclean spirit from her girl. That same spirit is later referred to as a demon. Now here is the point I'm trying to make: The scriptural account describes the girl as 'little' meaning that she was young. Just how old we aren't told, but we are safe in assuming the child would be elementary school age. How is it a young girl like that becomes demon possessed?"

"I don't know," Stanton admitted.

"Exactly. And neither does anyone else. We can make grand conjectures such as, 'She was Gentile and many Gentiles worshiped pagan gods.' That's not a bad conjecture, but it wouldn't explain the possession of Jewish persons."

"So what are you getting at?" Stanton asked.

"Just this. When it comes to the world of angels and demons, we know much less than we think we do. The Bible has taught us many things, but it is silent about many things too. Why would demons be interested in Lieutenant Wilcox? I don't know. I'm not sure that we as humans can understand what motivates these other intelligent creatures. However, we do know that they interact with humans, that they can oppress humans, and that they can even possess humans. Why they would want to, we can't say. We can speculate, but we can't say with any certainty based on fact."

"She is handling things just fine, Dr. Striber." Stanton's words were quick. "I have no worries about her."

"I don't wish to be rude, but perhaps you should, Captain. I'm not an alarmist, but I know a little bit about these things. I can't guarantee that anything I've said applies to your situation, but from what you and Jim have told me, there is enough reason to be suspicious."

In truth, Stanton *was* suspicious. While unready to accept what he had just heard, he knew that he had several problems to overcome, several imponderables to answer. He looked at his watch. "I must go, gentlemen." He stood to his feet and extended his hand to Hawking Striber. "This has been interesting, Dr. Striber. I'm not sure what to make of it, but I will consider all you have said. That's all I can promise at the moment."

"It is what I hoped for," Hawking replied, shaking Stanton's hand. "If I can be of any service, please feel free to call." He reached in his shirt pocket and extracted a business card. He handed it Stanton.

"I'll keep you in mind." Stanton then shook hands with Walsh. "Jim will escort you off base. And please, Dr. Striber, let's keep this discussion between us."

"I understand, Captain," Hawking said.

Stanton's mind was filled with questions as he walked from the conference room. Emotionally and intellectually, he wanted to dismiss Hawking out of hand, but something in his soul would not let him.

Chapter 13

It came upon him as it always did. Without warning, without preamble. First, it was a slight sensation along the skin, then under the skin, then deep into his core. There were jolts of white-hot electricity that spread along the boundary where skull meets brain. His muscles tightened, cramped as the boiling heat of the event flowed down his spine like molten rock through a lava tube.

Voices. Light. Pain.

His fingers tightened on the artifact in his hand until it pressed the skin white and stretched it until the breaking point. Blood vessels constricted. His heart hammered like the piston in the engine of a great ship and his eyelids crashed shut. Acid boiled in his stomach as if it would eat through his flesh at any moment, spilling on the floor below.

Voices. Disorientation. Spinning. Spinning. Falling. Pain.

"No," he uttered barely above a whisper. "Not now. Please, not now."

The lungs in his chest heaved as they fought for air. Every nerve was aflame with fire and seemed to burn like lit fuses. The muscles in his jaw clenched shut.

The voices were in his ears and crawled over his mind like ants on a fallen piece of candy. Voices, unrelenting, unyielding, agonizingly persistent. Calling. Demanding. Ordering. Drawing. Consuming.

Intelligences, too numerous to count, too powerful to ignore, forced their way into his consciousness, seizing it like an army takes a town. Occupying. Filling. Controlling.

"No, please."

The voices called him. "Karl. Karl! KARL!"

He wanted to lift his hands to his ears to block out the words, but it was useless. Even if he could move, the voices were inside him. Not in the room with him. Inside him. Deep, deep, deep inside.

There was no running, no hiding. There was no hope, no help. Karl Kunzig would endure this again, like he had last time and the time before. He had no choice, no opportunity to do otherwise. Resistance was useless. They had him. They owned him. He had to give in; he had to surrender.

Alien. Foreign. Ancient. Evil.

He had been through this before. Too many times to count. He knew what would come next. He waited as apprehension settled on him like a heavy mist, like a thick fog. Then he felt it. He was drawn from himself, from his body, like a giant elastic cord had been attached to his spine and stretched until it could be stretched no more. With a snap, he was drawn through what only a few had ever seen, ever felt.

The Possession had come again.

Then, like a moment's thunder, the agony left. Karl Kunzig lay on the bed, his eyes shut, no longer aware of the rocking and pitching of the submarine. He could not move, could not respond. Despite where his body lay, he was the unwilling guest in another world. It was a world unseen; a world denied by rational men; a world as real as the one he had left a few moments before.

A sadness, profound in its depth, oozed up within him. He wondered what horrible mistake he had made in this allegiance, but it was too late. The die was cast. Nothing could be changed. It was as intractable as concrete.

He saw a world, white and misty, like frosted glass. He could discern no direction and had no idea if he was standing upright or hanging upside down. There was a hint of motion, a slow falling, but nothing more. No heat. No cold. No ambient sound.

He looked down at his hand and could see through it. Bone, muscle, tendon, veins, and arteries. He saw it with undiminished clarity. The first time he had experienced this he had screamed, as well as one could scream in the noiseless world. Now he was merely repulsed by it. That was the way of the Place and the Possession. The rules were not the same as his world.

Misty figures moved through the thick fog. Some were small and others large with unblinking tar-black eyes and tiny mouths. They carried about them an evil like an animal carries an odor. Yet they shone in a light brighter and whiter than the mist that surrounded them. On the outside they looked kind, benevolent, even loving, but Kunzig understood better than any man what lay beneath that veneer. The light that surrounded them seemed pure and inviting, but it could not hold back the stench of evil, of hatred that had steeped for centuries.

They came en masse, shoulder to shoulder. Ten next to ten, hundreds next to hundreds. As far as Kunzig's eyes could see there were the Beings. The Possession. Slowly at first, then faster than his mind could work, the Beings filled the space. Everywhere and at one time there were the Beings. Above and below, around and around, inside and out, Beings and more Beings.

Kunzig gagged on the suffocating mass. He closed his eyes, but the gesture was futile. Just as he could see through his hand, he could see through his eyelids.

There was no escape. Just surrender.

They spoke. Not one, but all simultaneously in a beehive-like chorus that made Kunzig's brain burn with scalding agony. Every synapse ignited, every nerve fired. He felt as if he had been dropped onto a woven nest of high power lines.

"We want the ship. We want the ship. Do not fail us again. We want the ship."

"But why?" Kunzig cried.

"The ship. THE SHIP!"

"The ship," Kunzig repeated, surrendering to a will stronger than his own. "But I can't do it alone."

"We will help."

The words were followed by a sound, strange yet hauntingly familiar. Laughter. Otherworldly in tone, but still laughter. Joyless mirth. Hollow hilarity. The sound was a wickedness borne on an evil wind.

It was hellish.

It was his own voice but not his emotion. The source lay elsewhere.

Karl Kunzig was suddenly alone again. For the moment.

N
⋏

Slowly, with each step an agonizing accomplishment of will, Donna walked along the long pier toward the *Triggerfish*. The sun had passed its zenith and had begun its slide toward the ocean. The afternoon light skipped off the bay and bathed the submarine in a yellowing incandescence. The green bay began to darken, reflecting Donna's mood.

Each step that brought her closer to the *Triggerfish* also raised her heart rate. It was silly, she told herself. It was irrational. After all, the submarine was just a machine, made by men for men. There was nothing more to it than that.

But her soul disagreed.

She was half an hour early. Every inclination she had was to stay away as long as possible, but she wanted to face this fear and face it alone. That was where the conquest was. She needed this victory for her personal esteem and to prove to Captain Stanton that she was a worthy sailor.

Her mouth was dry; her palms wet. She licked her lips and continued down the pier. Each step felt like a mile. Her heavy-soled shoes seemed to cause the pier to reverberate as if warning the sub that she was coming, coming just as it knew she would.

The face in the deck returned to her mind. The evil grin, the hideous look, all of it was still fresh in her mind. The noises returned too. She heard them all over again. The wail, the thumping, all of it. It haunted her, plagued her.

Donna shook her head. "Get with it, girl," she said softly. "How will you ever command others if you can't command your own emotions?"

After what seemed a journey of agonizing miles, she arrived at the gangplank that bridged the gap between the deck and the dock. Two marine guards stood nearby. They came to attention as she approached.

"As you were, gentlemen," she said firmly. She didn't recognize them. There must have been a shift change while she and the others were gone. "I'm Lieutenant Wilcox. I'm assigned to the *Triggerfish* with Captain Stanton. I'm due to meet him here soon."

"Yes, ma'am," the two men said in unison. Without further comment, she started up the ramp. She stopped abruptly. A chill, like the air from a freezer, washed over her. The skin on her arms and neck were covered with goose bumps. The cold seemed to seep into the marrow of her bones. She crossed her arms and shuddered.

"Is there a problem, ma'am?" one of the marines asked.

"Uh . . . no. No problem at all." She took a deep breath and forced herself up the gangplank and onto the deck of the submarine. At first, she refused to look down, fearing that another face might be staring back. Instead she put her hands behind her back, feigning a quiescence she did not feel, and slowly walked to the bow. She inhaled deeply, expecting the rich salt air to soothe her. Instead she detected a whiff of foul decay. She recoiled at the odor.

"Corporal, do you smell anything?" she asked loudly.

"No, ma'am. Like what, ma'am?"

"Like a dead cat or sun-ripened fish," she answered with disgust.

The young marine sniffed the air. "No, ma'am. Nothing like that."

"Very well," she said, not feeling well at all.

Donna took in her surroundings. The sun glinted off the water in countless sparkles. The bay was flat, unmoving, glasslike. Voices of happy children from the park that adjoined the base skipped along the water. The blue and white ribbon that was the Coronado Bridge stood high above the narrow bay, as cars leisurely traveled its spine. In the distance, across the bay, the gray hulks of navy ships floated idly at the moorings. Overhead, white and gray gulls called loudly to each other through a cloudless sky.

The day was perfect. The setting sun and clear skies would make a perfect postcard for the local chamber of commerce. There was no wonder why tourists traveled to San Diego by the millions. In many ways it was a paradise, a contemporary Garden of Eden.

The beauty of the day melted away. No matter how blue the sky, no matter how pleasing the setting sun, Donna could not shake the growing feeling of evil. Like the stench she had noticed as she stepped upon the deck of the *Triggerfish*, the sense of angry wickedness closed in around her. There was a serpent in her garden.

Something hot and putrid breathed down the back of her neck. She spun on her heels and saw—nothing. Before her was the long gray hull of the submarine, its conning tower standing erect like an ancient monument. But the breath had been real. She had felt it roll along her skin and ooze into her pores.

Easy girl, she whispered to herself. *Rein in that imagination.* She wished that Captain Stanton would arrive. The sooner he got here, the sooner they could end this investigation and the sooner she could go home, disconnect the phone, run a bath, crawl in, and forget that a world existed outside her home.

Directing her eyes to the forward hatch, Donna wondered what lay beyond it. Although reason told her otherwise, her senses said that death lay confined in the three-hundred-foot steel coffin called the *Triggerfish*. It was illogical to think it, to believe it, but deep in her heart she felt that the hatch had not been opened for over fifty years. The thought made her shudder.

Where was Captain Stanton?

Images began to boil up in her mind. Her imagination caused her to see young men with scraggly beards, walking the deck. It was the crew, long dead, no longer missed. Each tied by a supernatural umbilical to the submarine, a cord that bound them forever to its decks. They reached for her, stretching ghostly arms forward, beckoning, calling. Their lips mouthed her name in silence: *Donna, Donna, Donna.*

The sight pierced her heart, as if she had been run through with a lance of cold ice. The world was spinning. The ghosts approaching. She closed her eyes. "It's not real," she whispered to herself. "It's all in my mind. I don't believe this. I deny it. I repudiate it."

With an Atlas-like act of will, Donna forced her eyes open.

The specters were gone. She stood alone on the deck, drawing in ragged breath after ragged breath. A hot gorge of nausea welled up in her. Her mind spun. She felt ill. She was going to be sick. Quickly, she stepped to the cable rail and leaned over its edge. Again she closed her eyes and attempted to control her raging stomach. The last thing she wanted to do was vomit over the side of the sub, especially in front of the two marine guards. Their backs were turned at the moment, but the very recognizable noise of her illness would certainly draw their attention. *That would be good for the reputation,* she thought. *Lieutenant Donna Wilcox gets seasick on a moored submarine. It wouldn't take long for that little rumor to pass through every navy base in San Diego.*

Standing as still as possible, she waited. The fire in her stomach slowly eased. She took another deep breath. The pungent odor was gone. That was a plus. Donna blew out a long stream of air as she attempted to clear her lungs. The nausea had left as quickly as it had come. She opened her eyes—and froze.

It was impossible. It couldn't be. What she saw was irrational, illogical, beyond the realm of physics. But it was there, and Donna was staring right at it.

Leaning over the rail, Donna gasped loudly and let out a small cry. The ocean was gone, literally gone. The green waters of the bay had vanished, leaving behind a chasm utterly wide, abysmally deep. The submarine floated on a sea of nothing. It began to rock and pitch like a cork in a hurricane. Below her was not the bottom of the bay, but . . . but something different.

Something implausible. Instead of sand there was an orange glow that appeared many miles away, as if she were seeing to the very core of the earth.

The sub shook.

The glow grew.

She could not move. Her muscles were petrified by indescribable fear. Every nerve in her body seemed to fire at once, resulting in paralyzing tremors.

Orange turned red; red turned blue; blue turned white. It was flame. It was fire. It was the very heat of hell, and it was rising toward her. As it drew near, the glow became long and wicked flames, lapping upward at her, reaching for her. An overpowering smell of sulfur, thick and noxious, blasted upward like a wave of heat from a smelter. It struck her face and tossed her hair.

The flames did not come alone. A sound, mournful, heartbreaking, was borne on the heated air. It took only a second for Donna to realize that it was not the noise of wind she heard, but the tortured cry of countless lost souls.

The sub rocked again, lurching to the starboard side, Donna's side. She felt herself slipping toward the open maw of the flame-filled abyss.

"No!" she screamed. "Oh, God, no. Oh, Jesus, help!"

The fire was gone. In its place were the placid waters of the bay, lapping the hull of the *Triggerfish*. The cries were gone, the abyss closed.

"Ma'am, are you all right?"

Donna stared wide-eyed at what had been only a moment ago a portal to hell.

"Ma'am? Are you all right, ma'am?"

Blinking hard to push back the vision, Donna turned toward the voice. She was looking up at the two marines. "Wha . . . What?"

"Are you all right, ma'am? You screamed. Are you hurt?"

"Hurt?" The confusion that had been swirling like a tornado in her mind settled. "Hurt? Uh, no. I'm . . . I'm fine."

"Are you sure? You seemed real scared there for a moment."

Donna shook her head. "No, Corporal, I'm fine. Just got a little disoriented. Return to your post."

"But, ma'am—"

"I said, return to your post."

"Yes, ma'am. Call us if you need anything."

"Thank you, I will."

The marines walked down the gangplank and back onto the pier. Donna watched as they exchanged glances and then shrugged. She wondered how she would explain this. Or even if she should try.

Licking her lips, she wondered what she had seen, what she had experienced. Maybe she was losing her mind. Maybe she was ill—mentally ill.

Gently she rubbed the skin of her face. It felt dry and a little burned.

N
Λ

Hermann Kunzig sat in a rented blue Ford Explorer peering through a pair of binoculars. Max Rohl sat next to him.

"There it sits," Hermann said greedily, looking across the little park, past a swing set, and through a chain-link fence. "Right out in the open."

"Almost," Max agreed. "But it's still inside a secured area."

"For the moment, Max. For the moment."

The sharp ring of a cellular phone filled the cab of the truck. Max answered before it had a chance to ring again. "Yes," he said sharply. "Understood." He hung up and turned to Hermann. "Everyone is in place. We're set and ready to go."

A smile crossed Hermann's face. He lowered the binoculars and said, "Then it is time."

"I'd feel better if I knew what we were after," Max said.

"You will just have to trust me, my friend. But I can tell you that it is essential."

"That's all I need. Give the word and I'll start things in motion."

Hermann raised the glasses to his eyes again. "The woman has company. Two men. Officers I think. Good, we need an audience. Give the command."

Max dialed a number. A moment later he said, "Go," then immediately hung up. "Looks like we've got a good view from here."

"We do," Hermann said. "We shouldn't miss a thing." Slowly he redirected his binoculars to the Coronado Bridge. "Hand me the phone. It's time to place a little call to the base commander. He would never forgive me if he missed this."

N
Λ

"You look pale as a ghost," Stanton said as he crossed the gangplank with purposeful strides. Stewart was right behind him. "You feel okay?"

"I'm fine," Donna lied. "Lunch didn't agree with me."

Stanton studied the young woman. Her face was drawn and a shade lighter than normal.

"Do you need to call it a day, Lieutenant?" Stanton inquired. She hesitated. "No, sir. I prefer to stay on duty."

"You're sure?" Stanton probed.

"Yes, sir. Very sure."

Stanton had seen fear before and he recognized it in her. She was showing great courage by facing . . . facing what? "Very well," Stanton said. "It's time to put this thing to rest. Where are Hancock and Eastman?"

"They're on the way," Stewart said. "I see them now." He nodded down the dock.

Donna turned and called out, "On the double, gentlemen." Both men began to jog.

Stanton turned and made eye contact with Stewart. Both men smiled. Donna was taking charge.

N

Dennis Staub directed his large panel truck off Interstate 5 and toward the Coronado Bridge. He knew that an identical van was making its way from the Coronado side. Timing was everything. They had made several practice runs late yesterday and early this morning. Each pass had worked perfectly. That had not surprised him. He and his crew had spent hundreds of hours preparing for a day such as this. This was not, however, what he had imagined. When he first heard the plan, he had to suppress a burst of laughter. The fact that he was still alive testified to his successful restraint.

In the back of the van were two men dressed in military fatigues. They sat silently, heads down in thought. AK–47 rifles rested between their knees. In front of each man was a coil of rope and small bricks of white material wrapped in plastic wrap. In the center of the van was a metal rack that ran from floor to ceiling. The rack had been welded to the van. Stacked on the rack were two dozen cardboard boxes. One box had a black plastic device attached to it.

"Stand by," Staub ordered as he picked up a hand-held radio from the passenger seat. He checked his right-side mirror. A long stream of cars was behind him. Looking to his left he saw the concrete barricade called "the zipper" by locals. A large machine traveled along the zipper each day, moving it from one lane to another, to direct the traffic according to the flow, giving an extra lane for outbound traffic in evening and for inbound traffic in the mornings. It was a unique and useful design. It also played an important role in their plan.

Staub keyed the microphone and began a countdown. "Ten, nine, eight . . ." He checked his mirrors again. Behind him he heard "Ready" and knew that the two men had donned their ski masks. He heard metallic clicking sounds as banana clips holding rounds of ammunition were inserted into the weapons. "Seven, six, five." He tossed the radio on the passenger seat and grabbed a black ski mask which he deftly slipped over his face. "Brace yourselves," he ordered.

One second later, Staub slammed his foot on the brakes. The truck's tires protested loudly. Staub struggled to keep the van straight for another moment, then abruptly turned right. Cars behind him hit their brakes and sounded their horns. Yanking the wheel to the left, Staub steered across the lanes, then came to a stop. The vehicle was parked across two lanes of traffic. Passenger cars, delivery trucks, and buses squealed to a stop.

"Now!" Staub shouted as he drew a nine-millimeter pistol from its holster. He heard the back doors open. As he exited the truck, he was greeted by the vicious ranting of irate drivers. The slurs and accusations converted into screams as he unloaded fifteen rounds from his weapon into the radiators and engines of the cars closest to him. In a highly practiced move, he ejected the clip and inserted another in less than a second. The screams died down in time for him to hear the sound of screeching tires and metallic crunching as cars slammed into each other on the Coronado side. The other team was right on time and just a hundred yards away. Staub knew that two other vans were doing a similar maneuver at the bridge's two entry points. If the calculations were correct, they had just trapped 250 or more cars on the two-mile long structure.

Slowly, with his gun still leveled at the scores of cars that were amassed a few feet away, Staub worked his way to the back of the van. He glanced at the other two men. One stood with his automatic rifle pointed at the cars.

"Go," Staub ordered. Both men sprang into action. One man moved from the tangled mass of cars to one of the many light standards that projected up from the bridge's concrete perimeter barrier like tall, metal palm trees. He secured a half inch climber's rope to the metal cylinder of the light standard and threw the loose end over the concrete barrier.

The second man gathered the small bricks of plastic explosive and began placing them along the roadway. After he had placed six, he ran back to the van. "We're set," he said.

Staub nodded. "Take your position." The man raised his AK–47 and pointed it at the frightened crowd, cowering in their cars. Staub stepped into the van. A tote bag with the words "San Diego Chargers" rested behind the front seat. Deftly, he opened it and removed a nylon harness which he quickly donned. He then stepped to the pile of cardboard boxes that were situated in the center of the van. He removed a key from his pocket, inserted it into a black box that was situated in the middle, and turned the key. A small red light came on. He removed the key, stepped from the van, and threw it over the side of the bridge.

Reaching back in the van, Staub found and removed a megaphone. He walked to the front line of cars, raised the device to his lips, and spoke: "Ladies and gentlemen. Sorry to disrupt your day, but it was necessary. The van you see behind me is loaded with explosives. A similar vehicle is behind you and there are two more on the other side of the bridge. All of these can be activated by remote control. Do not meddle with the van. If you do, you will die. Do not attempt to leave the bridge, or you will die. Sit still and wait, and you might live. Might live." He knew an identical message was being delivered by his counterparts in the other vans.

Staub turned to the side of the bridge again and tossed the megaphone over the edge. "Shall we, gentlemen?" he said as he walked to the rope that dangled from the bridge to the water two hundred feet below. Crawling over the edge, he hooked his harness onto the rope. He stepped away and began a slow rappel toward the water. As he drew close to the surface, he heard the sound of a speedboat. *Right on time*, he thought. A few moments later he was standing safe on the deck of the high performance craft. Two minutes after that, his two men had descended to join him.

A hundred yards away, a similar boat was picking up three men who had also rappelled down. The teams that had blocked off both entry points had made their escape in cars parked nearby. The bridge was secured. Because of excellent planning and ample funding, they had taken captive at least five hundred men, women, and children. Now only one thing remained. Reaching into his pocket, Staub removed a small transmitter. "Let's go," he said, and the boat charged forward. As the craft pulled away, he pressed the button. Twelve plastic explosive charges erupted simultaneously. Because of their placement, they would not bring down the bridge, but it would garner the necessary attention. Chunks of concrete flew into the air and rained down into the bay. Other pieces fell on the crowd of cars.

N
↑

Barry Ludlow was furious. He had finally gotten permission to talk to someone in public relations at NAB. That had put him in a good mood. It wasn't anyone in charge, but at least it was an official interview. He was supposed to be there in thirty minutes, but now he was caught in traffic a quarter mile up the bridge. He pounded his fist on the steering wheel.

"Think that will help?" George Abbey asked.

"It helps me," Barry snapped.

Abbey shrugged. "If you say so. What do you think the problem is?"

"Probably some tourist taking pictures."

Abbey laughed. "You may be—hey, where are you going?"

"To see what's happening." Barry exited the news station's van and took a few steps forward. He could see a panel truck turned sideways on the bridge. "Great," he said. "Just great. That's all I need. An accident—"

The concussion from the explosion knocked Barry from his feet. One moment he was standing, the next he was lying on his back between two cars. The explosion was followed by the screams and wails of hundreds of frightened people.

Chapter 14

S tanton watched as Hancock dropped to one knee and took hold of the wheel that would unlock the hatch. Hancock strained as he attempted to twist the wheel. At first, it resisted, showing no sign of budging. Then it gave an inch, then another. Soon it was spinning freely.

"She's free, Captain," Hancock said. "Shall I open her up?"

"That's why we're here, son. Let's see what the old girl has been holding for us."

Thumpa, thumpa, thumpa.

Hancock swore. "There it is again."

No one moved.

"What now?" Donna asked uneasily.

"We carry on," Stanton replied immediately. "Pop the hatch, Mr. Hancock."

"Aye, sir."

There was another noise, but not from the submarine. Instinctively Stanton and the others spun in the direction of the sound. It had come from across the bay.

"The bridge!" Stewart shouted.

Smoke and dust rose from the bridge in dark, thick columns.

"Eastman," Stanton snapped. "Get me a pair of binoculars. On the double."

"Aye, sir." Eastman ran from the sub and down the pier. He reappeared less than two minutes later breathing hard. He handed them to Stanton, who snatched them and immediately sighted on the distant bridge.

"Traffic is not moving," Stanton said coolly. "It's stopped in both directions. I don't see any flame. The smoke must be from the blast, whatever caused that."

"A tanker truck?" Stewart suggested.

"I don't think so. There would be burning fuel."

"Maybe an airplane crashed," Donna offered.

"Perhaps, but I don't see wreckage." He handed the binoculars to Stewart, who took them and raised them to his eyes.

"Shouldn't we do something?" Donna asked.

Stanton turned to one of the marine guards stationed by the *Triggerfish*. "Corporal. Call 911. Make sure they're aware of the situation."

"Yes, sir."

"You know," Stewart said still gazing through the binoculars. "With traffic blocked both directions, the emergency personnel are going to have a difficult time getting to the problem."

"Look there." Donna pointed. "Those boats are sure in a hurry."

Stewart turned the glasses on the boats. "They're wearing masks," he said with surprise. "There are no identification numbers on the hulls either."

"I don't get it," Stanton said. "They're headed south toward Imperial Beach. There's no outlet from the bay there."

"No," Stewart said, "but there are a dozen areas to ditch the boats and escape by car."

"This ain't good," Hancock said. "This ain't good at all."

"An understatement," Stanton said. "We had—"

A roaring sound caught everyone's attention. A white pickup truck driven by a marine rumbled down the wood dock and came to an abrupt halt. The marine exited and jogged up the gangplank to Stanton. He snapped a sharp salute which Stanton returned. "What is it, Sergeant?"

"The base has been placed on alert, sir. I've been ordered to escort you directly to the admiral."

"We were just about to enter the sub," Stanton said.

"Begging the captain's pardon," the marine said. "The admiral wants to see you, yesterday."

"Understood, Sergeant." Stanton turned to Hancock. "Secure that hatch, mister. Then clear the deck. Lieutenant Wilcox, once the boat is secured, you join me in the admiral's office."

"Aye, sir," Donna replied sharply.

"You're with me, Commander. Maybe your Coast Guard buddies know something we don't." Stanton returned his attention to the marine. "Let's do it, Sergeant."

N
ʌ

Barry Ludlow sat up and shook his head. Things were spinning, his ears ringing, and his eyes were flooded with water. He furrowed his brow as he tried to remember where he was and why he was seated on the pavement between two lanes of traffic. Slowly the buzzing in his ears gave way to the wail of children, and the shouts of men and women.

"You okay, man?"

Barry looked up at the man standing over him. "Huh?"

"You okay? I thought that blast might have killed you." Barry recognized his cameraman, George Abbey.

Blast? The blast. The explosion. His memory returned like a flash flood. "Yeah, I'm okay. I think." Abbey helped Barry to his feet. "Where's your camera?"

"What?"

"Your camera, man. Where is it? You should be shooting this."

"Unbelievable," Abbey spat. "I thought we might see who was hurt—"

"Get your camera and set up the microwave dish," Barry ordered. He swayed and placed a hand on the hood of a car for support. "We gotta get this on the air."

"But—"

"Right now, George!" Barry shouted. "Don't waste another second. Go, go, go."

Abbey swore and headed back to the van.

Barry glanced around him. People were exiting their cars. Mothers held their children close. Men looked at each other in confusion. Barry staggered forward toward the source of the blasts. As he neared the front line of cars, he saw that many vehicles had broken windshields. Chunks of concrete and asphalt had been blown from the bridge deck and sailed through the air with meteoric speed striking cars, piercing their metal skins, puncturing radiators and wheel wells, and flattening tires. Tentatively, Barry looked in the cars. Most were empty, their occupants not wanting to be any closer to the vans than they had to. In one car was a woman. Her face was covered with blood that oozed from tiny cuts that came from shards of windshield glass.

Pity, Barry thought. *She used to be beautiful.*

N
Λ

Admiral Jasper Robbins was standing next to his desk with the handset of the telephone pressed to his ear. His salt-and-pepper hair lay in perfect order and his dark eyes blazed. Even from the doorway, Stanton could see that the admiral was tense. His jaw was firm and the muscles in his neck bulged. Stanton was glad that it was the phone and not he in the grasp of the admiral's hand. With the thrust of a finger, Robbins motioned Stanton in the direction of a chair. Stanton took a seat.

"Understood," Robbins said firmly. "I want updates every thirty minutes. Sooner if you have anything. Got that?" There was a short pause while the admiral listened. "Good. You call the police, fire, and Coast Guard and let them know that they have the full support of the navy." He slammed the phone down with enough force to shake the large oak desk. He then began to swear. Obscenities and curses flowed like water from a fire hydrant.

Had the situation not been so serious, Stanton would have smiled. He and Admiral Robbins had served together over many years. Robbins was Stanton's senior by five years. They had met when Stanton was a green ensign fresh out of the Academy, and Robbins was a lieutenant. Stanton had served under Robbins on several occasions and always found him to be an excellent leader with a keen intellect. He also had the worst temper in the navy. Watching the admiral's short tirade made Stanton feel glad that there was not a dog in the room, for it surely would have been kicked.

Robbins took a deep breath and stared at Stanton for a moment. "The base is on its highest alert," he said gruffly. "The same is true of North Island and every other base within twenty-five miles. We've got a situation here, Captain. A big and bad situation. And it has to do with you."

"With me?" Stanton said with surprise. "I don't understand."

"You're aware of what happened on the Coronado Bridge?"

"Only from what I saw while on the *Triggerfish*," Stanton answered quickly. "I know there was an explosion of some sort."

"I got a call three minutes before it happened," Robbins spat. "The conversation lasted one minute, which gave me two minutes to respond. There wasn't enough time."

"A call, sir?" Stanton asked. He could see the concern percolate up through the admiral's anger.

"Yes." Robbins began to pace behind his desk. "The phone rings and it's some nut who says that he's going to blow up the Coronado Bridge if I didn't follow through with his demand. Then he said I should take a look at the bridge. He hung up and I made it outside just in time to see the explosions."

"But the bridge is still there," Stanton said. "Surely—"

"You're missing the point, Captain," the admiral interjected. "That wasn't the explosion the terrorist was talking about. Those blasts did two things. First, they proved that this wasn't a hoax. Second, it helped trap a few hundred men, women, and children on the bridge."

"Are there demands?"

"Yes, he wants the *Triggerfish*. He assures me that he has explosives far more powerful than the ones we saw on the bridge. In fact, his exact words were, 'Think Oklahoma Federal Building.' That conjures up a picture, doesn't it?"

Images of the destruction caused by a truck full of homemade explosives flooded Stanton's mind. The blast in front of the Oklahoma Federal Building had literally ripped the face off the multistory building, killing and wounding scores. "What does he want with the *Triggerfish*?"

"He didn't stay on the line long enough to explain. He did say that he'd blow the bridge if any police or fire units show up on the scene."

"How can he expect you to control that? They must be flooded with reports."

"I made calls immediately. They're checking things out. We called the Coast Guard too."

Stanton nodded. "Commander Stewart from the Coast Guard is in the next room getting an update." Stanton fell silent for a moment then said, "I don't get it, Admiral. Why the *Triggerfish*? What does he know that we don't?"

"I was hoping you could tell me, Captain. Did you and your team make entry?"

"No, sir. We just cracked the forward hatch when we heard the explosions. Shortly after that I was told to report to you."

"I had to pull you away, Captain. If this involves that sub then it involves you."

Stanton shook his head. "A couple of days ago I was retired and playing golf."

"And you were probably bored to tears, too," Robbins said. He started to speak again but was cut off by the ringing of the phone. Snapping up the handset, he said, "Yes? Put him through." There was a brief pause as Robbins pressed a button that activated the speakerphone. "This is Admiral Robbins. Who is this?"

"Your new best friend, Admiral," the caller said over the speaker. "I'm going to keep this short, so please don't interrupt me."

"I'm listening," the admiral said.

"You saw the explosions, so you know I mean business. Now let me tell you how this is going to work."

Stanton saw Robbins's jaw tighten and his eyes narrow. He was not used to taking orders from anyone.

"There are four vans on the bridge," the man continued. "One at each access point and two near the middle. Each one carries enough explosives to make Oklahoma City look amateurish. The explosives are designed to blow down into the bridge. Trust me, we know what we are doing. If I give the word, those vans will explode and a huge hunk of the bridge will be on the bottom of the bay, as will a great many people."

"What do you want?" Robbins asked.

"I said don't interrupt!" the terrorist shouted into the phone. "Never interrupt me!" There was a lingering pause. "Where was I? Oh, yes. The bridge will go down if you don't cooperate. As to what I want: I want full and unrestricted access to the *Triggerfish*. I and my partner will drive on base, get what we need, and drive off. If we are followed: boom. If we are interfered with: boom. Oh, just so that you know. I've built in a few redundant systems and fail-safes. The explosions can be detonated at a distance by several different people. Capture one, and the others will set off the explosions. Is this clear so far, Admiral?"

"It's clear," Robbins replied.

"Oh, I almost forgot," the voice went on. "There is some urgency. There are also timers. If you take too long to make things happen, the vans will explode all by themselves." He laughed. "I'll call back to tell you when to expect me. There's no need to trace this call, Admiral. I'm coming to you soon enough."

There was a click. The man had hung up.

The admiral began to swear again. "I am going to throttle that man personally. There isn't a jury in the world that would convict me." He began pacing again.

Stanton said, "I'll bet this month's wages that he's nearby."

"A lot of good that does us, Captain. If everything he says is true, then our hands are tied. What I can't figure is why he wants the *Triggerfish*."

"I don't know, sir. I wish I had gone in sooner."

"Nonsense," Robbins said. "The situation calls for caution. That's why you're here, Captain. You do things in their proper order and time. A lesser leader would have charged in."

"Still, it would be good to know what the man is after." Stanton stood to his feet. "Okay, let's run down the numbers. He has hostages, but the hostages are distant. They're on the bridge, but he's someplace else. Most likely he's nearby. I bet he watched the explosions. By holding the hostages with explosives, he can walk on base unmolested. If we grab him, then people die. If it's true about the redundant players, seizing him or even killing him does no good."

"So we have to find the other players," Robbins said.

"But how many? Are there five? Ten? There must be a thousand places on Coronado to hide and still see the bridge."

"So this man is going to drive on my base—a secured base—and there's nothing I can do about it?" More swearing. "We're not going to roll over on this, Captain Stanton. We are going to do everything possible to save those lives and put this man in jail if not the grave. Is that clear?"

"Yes, sir. I'm with you. But we're going to need help."

"Such as?"

"I see several needs. We have a rescue to conduct, bombs to disarm, and very little information to go on. I'd like to suggest that we get the FBI over here as soon as possible to help identify the man. If we know who he is, then we might gain some advantage. I think we should call the SEALs in. Since they train here, they're close. Maybe they can figure out what to do about the people on the bridge."

"I'm way ahead of you on that part, Captain. I'm expecting the SEAL commander any moment."

"I'll take charge of the *Triggerfish* ... with your permission, sir."

"I disagree. We can put a substitute in. The man may be dangerous, and I don't want to put you at risk."

"Begging the admiral's pardon," Stanton said. "But our bad guy has too much on the ball. He knows the name of the sub. The only way he could know that is from the news media. I was interviewed when the sub was aground in Torrey Pines. He'll know if we make a swap. In fact, I'll bet he's planned on it."

"You could be right," Robbins said. "Okay, we go with that. You just be careful. Understood? I don't want to be the one taking bad news to your wife."

"Understood, sir."

There was a knock at the office door. Stanton turned and saw Lieutenant Wilcox standing just outside the office. "Did I miss anything?" she asked.

Stanton looked at Admiral Robbins, then back to Donna. "You don't want to know, Lieutenant."

N
⋀

"What now?"

Hermann set the cell phone down on the seat next to him and turned to Max. "We move our location. Take a little drive around. Then we make another call and drive on base."

"Why wait? That gives them time to prepare."

"I want them to sweat a little bit. Besides, these cell phones are easy to trace. I can't stay on too long." He picked up the phone and flipped the power switch, turning the device off. "Did you know that they can trace a cell phone even if it's not in use? If the power is on, then there is a signal to follow. Once they have the code to the phone, they can track us anywhere."

"So we waste some time," Max said with frustration.

"Not long," Hermann said easily. "Ten minutes tops. But we do need to change location. You have the other phone?"

"Yes, in my pocket."

"Good. Keep it off until we need it." Hermann reached for the ignition key and turned it. "It's almost over, and we'll have what we want. You've done a fine job planning the bridge takeover. Genius. Sheer genius. Now it's my turn to prove my worth."

"There has never been any doubt about that," Max said. "You are the leader and I am ready to follow."

"You are a good soldier, Max. Now let's take the next step." Hermann dropped the car into gear and pulled away from the parking lot in front of the small park. "Destiny is waiting for us, and we should not keep it waiting."

Chapter 15

Consciousness returned slowly to Karl Kunzig. The Possession was gone—as gone as it ever was. The Possession was never far away. He could feel it in the back of his mind, hovering over his thoughts. His heart had slowed from its jackhammer pounding and his breathing had become the smooth pattern of sleep. He ached inside from the fear he had just experienced and from the abject hopelessness that he felt. He had struck a deal and had lost. Alone as he was at the moment, he was never truly alone, and never would be again.

Willing his eyes open, he struggled to make sense of his surroundings. The rocking of the sub brought reality back to his fragile consciousness. The dim light of the wardroom gave a twilight feeling to the room. He wished it were so. He wished it were twilight in his homeland. He wished to be somewhere else, to be someone else. Slowly his fear evaporated and the determination that had driven his life returned.

"You okay?"

Kunzig sat upright on the bed. He blinked hard. Captain Morrison was seated in a chair nearby. "What?" He was disoriented.

"I asked if you're all right?" Morrison said. His voice was stern and his face hard.

"Yes, thank you," Kunzig answered. "I was napping."

"Napping?" Morrison stood. "We've been trying to wake you."

"We?" Kunzig looked toward the door. Commander Sapolsky stood with his arms crossed. "I'm sorry. I tend to sleep soundly."

"You were mumbling and shaking," Morrison said. "That must have been some nightmare. I was getting ready to call a corpsman."

Kunzig lowered his head. They must have seen him while he was . . . while the Possession had him. He had no idea what happened to his body while he was wherever he was. "I have epilepsy," he lied. "My attacks come only occasionally."

"Uh, huh," Morrison said, his voice laced with annoyance. "What's that?" He pointed to Kunzig's hand.

Kunzig looked down at the metal object in his hand. "It is an artifact."

"An artifact, eh? Like the ones in your bag?"

"Yes."

"I looked through your bag and didn't see that." He turned to Sapolsky. "You said he showed you everything in the bag. Did you see that?"

"No, sir. It's new to me."

This was difficult. No lie would get him out of the situation. He had to tell the truth. "The bag has a secret compartment in its base; a false bottom. You have to understand, Captain, these artifacts are very valuable. I am forced to take certain precautions."

"I have to take precautions too, Mr. Kunzig," Morrison snapped. "What else do you have that I'm not aware of?"

Kunzig sighed. "Nothing. That's the truth."

Morrison walked to the bed. At the head, between the small flat pillow and the bulkhead, was the bag. He snatched it up and emptied the contents onto the mattress.

"Captain, please!" Kunzig shouted. "Those are precious items. Their value is beyond imagination."

"Shut up, Kunzig," Morrison snapped. "I don't like secrets." The German watched helplessly as the Captain rummaged through the bag. A moment later he ripped out the false bottom.

"Empty," he said.

Kunzig stood and gently took the bag from Morrison's hand. "As I said," he uttered softly, "there is nothing else hidden."

"So what makes that piece of metal so special?" Sapolsky asked.

Kunzig held up the item and then handed it to Morrison. "Please be careful with it."

Morrison took it and studied it for a moment. "It looks like a spearhead," he said. "An old spearhead."

"Very good, Captain," Kunzig intoned. "It is both a spearhead and very old. It's Roman. Two thousand years ago, a Roman guard, in an effort to prove Christ was dead when he hung on the cross, thrust that very spearhead through the side of Jesus. The Gospels tell us that blood and water issued forth."

"Water?" Sapolsky asked.

"Probably from the pericardium, the sac that surrounds the heart," Kunzig explained. "The guard's name was Longinus, or so tradition tells us. It is said that he had an infected eye and when he stabbed Jesus some blood splattered onto his face. His eye was instantly healed. The spear of Longinus has been coveted ever since. It has been sought after by kings and popes. Wars have been fought over what you hold. That's why I tried to keep it secret."

"That important, huh?" Sapolsky said sarcastically.

"More than you know, Commander. More than you can imagine. Charlemagne possessed the lance for many years. He believed, as did everyone who followed him, that the spear possessed a power that would make any army victorious. In fact, no army who has possessed the lance has lost a battle."

"You were taking this to Hitler?" Morrison asked.

"Not *to*, Captain, *from*. Hitler wants this. He believes it will make him invincible. I stole it from him."

"That's why you don't want us to take you to Scotland. It's too close for comfort." Morrison handed the spearhead back to Kunzig.

"Exactly. There may not be enough miles in the world to protect me as it is. Being that close to Hitler and his followers is . . . unnerving."

"Well, you can keep your little toys, Mr. Kunzig," Morrison said. "We're still going to Scotland. I have my orders and nothing is going to change that."

"Do you believe in God, Captain Morrison?" Kunzig asked suddenly.

"What?" The question caught the captain off guard.

"Do you believe in God?"

Morrison laughed. "I skipper a boat in the middle of a war, Mr. Kunzig. When you sail under the water, you have to believe in God."

"I am serious, Captain."

Kunzig watched as Morrison's face turned hard. His gaze seemed distant. He shrugged. "I don't know. I send ships to the bottom of the ocean and their crews with them. Some are manned by the enemy, some are merchant vessels and sailed by men who are simply doing their job. That's the way war is, Mr.

Kunzig. It's unfair and it doesn't care who gets killed. What could God do with a man like me?"

"What about you, Mr. Sapolsky?" Kunzig inquired. "Are you a man of faith?"

Sapolsky shook his head. "Never had much use for church stuff. My parents used to take me when I was little, but I quit going when I got old enough to make a stink about it. It used to bother them, but they let me make my own choice. Besides, I was a bit of a troublemaker in my youth. The way I see it, church is a crutch."

Kunzig nodded and looked at the spearhead in his hand, the tip of which was stained with brown. He wondered again, as he had a hundred times before, if this was the dried blood of Christ.

"What about you, Kunzig?" Morrison asked. "Has the war made you a believer?"

Kunzig sat in silence staring at the object in his hand. A sadness fell over him and his eyes began to burn. Finally he shook his head and said: "Science has always been my god. I have built my life around it. Facts and figures and artifacts. Books and articles and lectures. That was my life. Now . . . now . . ." His voice trailed off. "Now it is too late for me. Still, I wonder . . ." Again he trailed off.

"Wonder what?" Morrison asked.

"Do you read Shakespeare, Captain?"

"I read some in the Academy. Why?"

"Hamlet, act one, scene five: 'There are more things in heaven and earth, Horatio, than are dreamt of in your philosophy.'"

"So what's your point?" Sapolsky asked.

"No point, really, Commander," Kunzig said softly. "No point at all. Just the musings of a weary man."

It was starting again. He could feel it. The electricity, the disorientation. The Possession was returning. *Oh, not now,* he thought.

Not in front of the captain. This is wrong. No. No. Not now. Kunzig dropped the spearhead and raised his hands to his head. He felt as if his arms were weighted. *Resist. Resist,* he shouted in his mind. *Go away. Leave me alone.* Tears began to stream down his face.

"Hey, you all right?" Kunzig could hear Morrison's voice. It sounded distant and muted. "I think he's having another attack."

Kunzig dropped to the floor, his body seizing, shaking, convulsing.

$$\lambda$$

"I'll get Armstrong," Sapolsky shouted.

"What the—" Morrison said. Sapolsky stopped midturn. "Kunzig. You still with us?"

Morrison watched as Kunzig's body relaxed. He sat up on the floor, his head between his knees. Morrison could see that the man's breathing was hard and labored. Slowly, Kunzig raised his head.

Something was wrong. Morrison could not put his finger on it, but Kunzig was different. Something in the face, something indescribable had changed. There was a hardness in the eyes, a stare that did more than take in light; it radiated evil—baneful, amoral evil. Kunzig's jaw hung open and a sound, indistinct at first, rolled free from his throat.

Sapolsky swore.

Flies. The sound of flies swarming filled the small room. Morrison saw nothing. He looked at the walls and the ceiling but saw no insects. Still, he heard them.

A haze rose from the German. It was barely perceptible but Morrison could see it. It was a mist, off-white like dirty snow, and it rose ghostlike into the room. Flies. Mist. Odor. Morrison felt himself gag. He wanted to run, to be someplace other than where he was, but his body would not respond. His muscles were in revolt. Morrison turned to see Sapolsky frozen in the doorway, an expression of incredulity painted across his face.

"What is this?" Sapolsky asked with disgust.

"I . . . I don't know," Morrison answered unevenly. He told himself he should act, but no ideas came to mind, no orders. Instead, he stared, slack-jawed at the macabre sight. The mist rose in the air slowly. "Kunzig? What's going on?" He took a step back, putting distance between himself and the German.

A voice answered, but Morrison was certain it was not Kunzig speaking. Words were spoken, but the captain did not recognize the language. He was sure it was not English or German. He was uncertain if it was even human. The voice vibrated in discordant tones, underpinned by the buzzing of nonexistent flies. It sounded like sharps and flats being simultaneously played on a piano. There was no rhythm to the words. No meaning that he could discern.

"What . . . what are you saying, Kunzig?" Morrison said. "I don't understand."

Kunzig sprang vertically to his feet and stepped forward. He was now inches from Morrison and Sapolsky.

"Hey, stand back, buddy, or I'll—" Sapolsky began, but he was interrupted.

A pale light filled the room. The sound of the flies grew until Morrison's ears hurt. His heart pounded and his brain felt aflame. His skin crawled as if unseen ants had covered his flesh. "Kunzig—" Again, he tried to back away. What he was seeing and hearing was beyond his experience. He thought of fleeing, but where could he go? He was on a submarine in the middle of the Atlantic. Besides, this was his boat, his responsibility.

The light, which now seemed viscous, thick, surrounded them. The mist engulfed them.

Something was on Morrison. He swatted at the air. Something was in Morrison. He grabbed at his head and groaned. The mist was seeping in through his pores, through his eyes and ears. He couldn't stop it. Morrison was drowning, not in water, but in something vile and thick and pervasive and evil. Tentacles of influence clutched at his mind. Suddenly, Morrison was no longer on the *Triggerfish*. He was falling through the misty white fog. Tumbling, dropping, plummeting to an unknown place in an unknown world. He screamed, but there was no sound. He screamed again, commanding all his might to the act. Nothing.

"Who are you?" Morrison shouted. "WHO ARE YOU?"

"We are here," came the undulated, discordant reply. "We are Multitude. We are Many. We are Legion. We are Possession."

Morrison brought his hands to his face. He could see through them. Morrison offered one more futile scream.

The conquest was complete.

N
⋀

Morrison moved through the ship feeling disconnected from reality. Everything was familiar, yet different. The hum of the diesel engines was there, but it had been joined with sounds that he could not identify. The vibration of the engines seemed to have more and deeper levels than he had noticed before. The artificial lights glowed with a muted rainbow of colors. Crewmen he passed in the hall seemed translucent. The air was a bouquet of ill-defined odors, all strange.

As he walked through the heart of the submarine, his footfalls echoed more loudly than they should. His lungs drew in air noisily. His senses were heightened to a barely tolerable level. He wanted to ask Sapolsky if he were experiencing the same thing but he didn't. Instead he moved easily along the corridor, Sapolsky following behind. Crewmen acknowledged their passing, but Morrison did not respond; he continued aft from the officer's quarters to the control room. Once there, he climbed the ladder through the conning tower and onto the open air bridge.

The submarine rolled and pitched as it plowed liquid furrows in the ocean. Salt spray, borne by a stiff breeze, pelted him as he emerged from the hatch.

"Good afternoon, Captain," Chief Bud Hill said. He nodded forward. "Surface is getting a little rough."

Morrison said nothing as he stepped to the metal rail and gazed over the ocean. The sky was darkening with a shroud of bruised and swollen clouds. The sea was a dark green. Sapolsky took a place beside him.

"It looks like we're in for a storm, Skipper," Hill said. "Time for the new boys to earn their sea legs." He laughed at his little joke and reached for a cigarette.

"There's an unusual odor below, Chief," Morrison said softly. "It may be dangerous. Bring the crew up and put them on the deck."

"Sir?" the chief said with surprise. "You want me to take a look at it, sir. I could—"

"I told you what I want, Chief," Morrison said sternly. "Get the men topside. Now."

"But sir, the ocean is getting rough."

"It won't be for long. I just want to make sure that odor isn't a toxic gas."

"Does it smell like chlorine, sir?" Hill asked with concern. "If so, then I better get a crew down to the battery space. If ocean water has gotten in, then we have a real problem."

"It's not chlorine gas, Chief," Morrison uttered. "Get the men topside."

"Begging the captain's pardon, but—"

"Chief," Sapolsky said loudly. "You have been given a direct order. Unless you want to be charged with insubordination, I suggest you carry it out. Now! Is that understood?"

"Aye, sir," Hill answered quickly. "Understood." Hill lowered his thick body through the hatch and into the control room. Through the open hatch Morrison could hear the chief bark orders: "All ahead slow. Secure rudders amidships. Stand by to abandon ship." The Klaxon sounded. Moments later the hatch forward of the tower sprung open and men began to pour out. A second after that, the hatch aft of the tower opened and another stream of men emerged. Ninety seconds later, the entire crew of the *Triggerfish* stood in the wet wind. Bud Hill reemerged on the bridge.

"They're all on deck, sir," he said. "I hope this won't be long. I didn't notice any odor when I was—"

"Mr. Sapolsky," Morrison said, "please inspect all compartments aft of the control room. I'll inspect forward."

"Wouldn't you prefer that I do that, sir?" Hill's face was cloaked with confusion.

"No, I wouldn't, Chief. Secure the hatches. I don't want water pouring in through those openings."

"Aye, sir." Hill stepped to the rail and called down to the men on the deck. "Secure that hatch." He then gave the same order to the men aft of the control tower.

"I'll make this quick," Morrison said.

"Sir," the chief said. "Are you all right? You seem different."

"I'm fine, Chief," Morrison answered. "Now let me do my job."

"Aye, aye, sir." There was uncertainty in his voice.

Morrison descended the ladder into the control room. Sapolsky was already gone, and Morrison knew exactly where he was.

Reaching up, the captain grabbed the nylon cord attached to the bridge hatch and pulled the lid down. A quick spin of the wheel sealed it tight. With an emotionless cold, he stepped to the dive station, flooded the tanks, and set the dive planes fifteen degrees down. As if on cue, the diesel engines shut down and the electric motors kicked in. Sapolsky had done his job in the maneuvering room. The *Triggerfish* was now submerging. It was a crash dive. In less than sixty seconds the sub would be under fifty feet of water.

Screams of terror-stricken men melted through the thick hull and rebounded off the metal walls. A pounding could be heard as men struck the deck with their fists. Morrison knew that it would take a few moments for the men to realize what was happening, to understand that their own captain and executive officer had sentenced them to death in the sea. By that time it would be too late to open the hatches. They had no hope. They were too far from any Allied ships to be rescued. Some would last days, most only a few hours. Even in the summer, the open Atlantic was cold. Hypothermia would set in, and then his crew would begin to die, one by one.

One minute later, at precisely fifty-two feet, he trimmed the tanks and eased the dive planes to zero. Against his will, he raised the periscope and scanned the horizon. In the distance he could see the small dark figures of his crew floating in the ocean. In his mind he could hear them call for help and see their faces draped with despair. He could also see the faces of their families.

Gazing through the periscope, Morrison laughed. But it was not Morrison at all. It was the Possession. As he laughed, tears of remorse streamed down his cheeks. He wished for death.

$\overset{\text{N}}{\Lambda}$

Kunzig thrashed and struggled. He fought against the count-less bodies that pressed against him. He felt no ground beneath him; he could see no sky above him. Just the misty white. Voices were everywhere, all speaking simultaneously. His brain hurt, his mind raced, his heart pounded with the force of a cannon. He was in their world, and here there was no up and down. No yesterday or today or tomorrow. Things were inside out and outside in. All space seemed occupied. There was no room to breathe, but breathing wasn't necessary. The only thing this world possessed in common with his was pain—scorching, scalding pain.

He had seen it all, heard it all. No detail had been allowed to escape his notice. The men on the deck; the captain submerg-ing the ship; the crew clawing and fighting and pleading for help that would not come; it all had been force-fed to him. They could do that in this world. Make him see what he didn't want to see; feel what he didn't want to feel; say what he didn't want to say. They were the puppet masters and he the marionette.

Kunzig had always been self-centered and he had never been accused of being a choirboy. He had often lied to get his way and cheated when he could. But these Beings, these things, were evil personified. He had spent an eternity with them and knew that he would spend another eternity. He hated them.

Now he could see Captain Morrison gazing through the periscope, laughing like a madman on the outside, but internally rotting with remorse. The schism was maddening to see, even more maddening to experience. A man could not live like this, between worlds, not his own, but possessed by someone, some-thing else. Kunzig began to weep.

It had been his fault. He had been the one to seek them out. He had played the part of Canaanite priest to Baal, and found the real Baal, the real Beelzebub. He had come face-to-face with Asherah, Tanit, Moth, and Molech. At first it had been a thrill to know such

Beings existed, that they were not myths. They made him feel powerful and alive. He felt invincible. Then they came. The Possession. They came without his bidding; without his longing. They came because they wanted to come. They took him because they wanted to take him. It was that day that Karl Kunzig ceased to have free will, ceased to be purely human. It was that day that he had become the property of otherworlders. They were no gods. Only one word fit them, only one description applied: demons.

"Let me go," Kunzig cried, but he knew they wouldn't. They would hold him longer simply because it tormented him so. "You've made a mistake. Three men can't run a submarine by themselves."

Laughter. Thousands, tens of thousands of voices cackling, guffawing. All at his expense. "They won't have to," the Possession replied in unison. "They won't have to."

"But—"

"Enough," they cried.

Kunzig awoke on the floor. Alone. Thankfully, blissfully alone.

For the moment.

N
⋏

Morrison could hear water rush past the submerged sub, the fluid gently, gracefully caressing the craft as it sped along at nine knots. The same gentle fluid was killing his crew. He struggled to move, but his body would not respond. He was no longer under his own control. All that was left was a part of his mind, a part that had been pushed to the back and imprisoned by a force he could not comprehend.

That portion of his brain still worked, and he wished it didn't. The names of his crew floated by like driftwood on the swells of an angry ocean: Hill, Armstrong, Rudling, Henry, Sanchez, Morrow, Dixon, DeHann, and the others. One by one they floated by and with each name came a face; and with each face came the sickening knowledge that he had murdered all sixty-nine of his crew. And with that act, he had killed a large portion of life in their wives, mothers, fathers, and children. They would never forgive him. He would never forgive himself.

The image of his wife Sandi rose to the surface of his mind. He could see her fawn hair, smell her perfume, feel the cotton dress she wore. She was holding little Ronnie. He had his fingers in his mouth, just like the last time he saw the boy, that day when he walked out in a huff. Now he would never see—Morrison screamed in his mind.

Then he screamed again.

Then again, but this time there was sound. He heard himself. He could move. They were gone. Those things. Those nasty, evil, reprehensible things were gone. Slowly, Morrison stood to his feet. He took a tentative step, still uncertain that he was truly in control.

The intercom crackled to life. "Captain? Captain, are you there?"

It was Sapolsky. Morrison turned the knob on the intercom. "Get up here, Sapolsky! We have to surface!"

"On my way."

"Up," Morrison said to himself. "Up, up, up, up. Surface, surface." He was screaming at the empty control room. In an instant, he was at the dive board. He pulled the levers for an emergency blow of the tanks. He then raced to the dive plane controls and cranked them to surface position. Sapolsky burst into the room. Morrison glanced at him and saw the terror in his eyes and the tears on his face. "Take the steering stand," he ordered. "Hard about."

"Aye, sir," Sapolsky said. "I left the motors all ahead full."

"Good. As soon as we break surface, I want us back on diesel. We need all the power we can get."

"Understood," Sapolsky said. "Captain . . . uh . . . I . . . uh."

"Save it. I can't explain it either. Let's just get back there as fast as we can."

The *Triggerfish* breached the surface like an enraged whale. "Get on the bridge and get us a bearing," Morrison said aloud. *Please, God*, he said silently. *Let us be in time. Please, please, God. Don't let it be too late.*

Sapolsky raced up the ladder and opened the hatch to the bridge. Morrison took the steering stand and centered the rudder to straighten their course, then followed his officer to the deck.

"See anything?" Morrison asked as soon as his head cleared the hatch.

"No, sir. Nothing," Sapolsky answered. There was panic in his voice. "What have we done? What have we done?"

Morrison didn't answer. Wanting the highest possible viewpoint, he climbed up the tower to the lookout station and raised the binoculars he brought with him to his eyes. He scanned the churning sea. Emotions boiled in him. His mind raged with anger and fear. "Are we on a good course?" he shouted down to Sapolsky.

"I don't know. Something's wrong with my brain. I can't remember our course. It's gone."

"I can't remember either." Morrison forced himself to think, to reason, to call up what logic remained in his head. "You cranked the wheel hard starboard, right?"

"Right."

"Okay, okay. Think, think. We were at periscope depth. I remember looking out the scope right after we submerged. That means that we were less than fifty-five feet below the surface. I did an emergency blow, so we came to the surface in just a couple of minutes." His mind started to fog. Morrison struck his forehead with the heal of his fist. "Think," he shouted at himself. He hit himself again, trying to use the pain to focus his unresponsive mind. "That means we couldn't have come full about. We're still heading in the wrong direction."

"We need to come to starboard more," Sapolsky agreed. "But by how much?"

Morrison felt sick. The Atlantic was huge. Finding men floating on the surface with rising swells was an impossible task without some idea of where they were. "How long were we submerged?"

"I don't know." Sapolsky looked at his watch. "An hour? I can't think. I don't remember."

Neither did Morrison. "Okay. Bring us starboard another ..." He thought for a moment. At best he was guessing. "Bring us starboard another eighty degrees. Then get back up here. We're the only hope those men have."

Sapolsky scampered down the hatch. Morrison could feel the sub turn in the water. He could also see the swells rising, breaking into whitecaps. The clouds overhead had turned dark. The sun was close to the horizon. The last observation made him sick. He had a vague recollection that the sun was close to its zenith when he and Sapolsky shut the hatch and—"Nooo!" he shouted into the wind. They had been submerged for hours. But he couldn't be sure. There was one way to find out.

As Sapolsky climbed back on the bridge, Morrison shouted. "Steve, check the charge on the batteries. That'll give some idea how long we were submerged."

"I already did, Cap. It's not good. Batteries are at twenty-five percent."

Morrison swore loudly. They had used seventy-five percent of the batteries. That meant they had been underwater for several hours. At maximum speed of nine knots underwater, they could be fifty or more miles away. The sub could travel at twenty-one knots on the surface, but even at that speed it would take at least two hours to make up the distance, assuming they were on the right course. It would be dark by then. Since he could not account for the hours, he could not account for his actions, and he could not be certain that they had traveled in a straight course. In short, he was lost.

Morrison sank in a sea of hopelessness.

N

The canopy of clouds hung overhead like the vaulted ceiling of a tomb blocking all light from the moon and stars. Waves, now four feet high, crashed over the deck in an explosion of angry foam. The *Triggerfish* rocked hard side to side and up and down through the ever-growing waves. Morrison stood his position on the lookout station. The gyrations of the submarine threw him into the guardrails, bruising his hips. Still he gazed through the binoculars into the blackness of the night. He saw nothing. If terror had a color, this black was it. There was insufficient light to even see the waves, but Morrison continued to scan the area. It was a futile, useless act, but he had to do something.

"You murdered your crew," a voice said in his head. "They trusted you. They followed your orders without question, and you let them drown." Morrison willed the now-familiar voice away, but it refused to leave. "They're floating facedown in the cold water, and it's all because of you." *Shut up*, he thought to himself. "You were their captain. You were their leader and you pulled the sub right out from under them." *Shut up!* "What kind of man are you?" the voice asked. Tears rolled down Morrison's checks.

Below, on the bridge deck, Sapolsky used a handheld lantern to shine a light on the ocean. "Ahoy. Anyone. Ahoy." He repeated the words, then repeated them again. His voice was rough and weak. Soon it would fail, but he continued to cry out. "Ahoy. Anyone. Ahoy."

Two hours after they had changed course to search for their lost crew, Morrison had gone below, cranked the rudders twenty degrees, and started a spiral search. They had found nothing, and Morrison knew they would not. They could be miles off course, and men would not last long in this weather.

It began to rain. Drops, large as peas, began to fall. Morrison did not care. He would not leave his post. He was determined to stay the night and the next day and the next until the fuel tanks of the *Triggerfish* had run dry. Then, when the last hint of hope was gone, he would submerge her with all hatches open and try to explain to God why he had killed his crew.

There was a new sound. Not a hopeful one, but new. It came from below him; it came from Sapolsky. He was weeping. Sobs that originated from a ripped and tattered soul poured out in great gushes of sorrow. It was the saddest, most pitiful thing Morrison had ever heard. He understood the pain. Looking down, Morrison saw Commander Sapolsky on his hands and knees, weeping loud enough to pierce the rising wind. Morrison wanted to say something, but no words came to mind. What could he say to comfort his comrade, his fellow officer, his friend? There was nothing in any language sufficient to quell the fire of guilt that consumed them both. It was just a matter of time before regret turned to self-loathing. They were no longer men, but shattered pieces of humanity held together by the weakest of glue.

Sapolsky fell silent. He coughed, then coughed again. Morrison watched as the man rose and wiped at his eyes. "I'm sorry, Captain." Sapolsky walked to the side of the conning tower and down the external ladder.

"Where you going, Mr. Sapolsky?" Morrison shouted through the wind. Sapolsky walked along the deck in front of the tower. "Mr. Sapolsky, I asked you a question." The commander was just a gray shape in the darkness, but Morrison could see him clear enough to witness what he feared. "Steve! Wait! Don't!"

Commander Steve Sapolsky staggered along the rolling deck until he came to the cable guardrail that ran around the perimeter of the submarine. He threw one leg over the rail, then the other, and stepped into the sea. He disappeared immediately.

"Sapolsky!" Morrison shouted as he turned to look over the stern of the boat. Morrison saw nothing. A half-second later a thud sounded from the stern. Captain Morrison closed his eyes. He had hoped that the water which was passing by them at twenty knots would carry Sapolsky past the propellers. It hadn't.

The binoculars slipped from his hands and crashed to the bridge deck. Morrison began to weep. He was dying from the inside out. Remorse, like a gangrenous infection, spread through him, threatening to suffocate him in his own emotions.

It was hopeless. Saving Sapolsky was hopeless. Finding his crew, which he knew must be dead, was hopeless. Forgiving himself was hopeless. Forgetting was hopeless. Life was now impossible.

Like a zombie, Morrison descended from the pitching lookout station to the bridge and then down into the conning tower. He closed the hatch behind him.

Chapter 16

It felt heavy and awkward in his hand. The smell of gun oil filled his tiny cabin. Captain Richard Morrison sat on his bed and stared unblinkingly at the .45 caliber pistol he held. He had cleaned it, checked that the clip was full, and pulled the slide to put a round in the chamber. The safety was off. He thought about many things: Sapolsky, his crew, his career, but most of all he thought about Sandi and Ronnie. What were they doing right now? He had lost all sense of time and place. It could be day or night back in the States. He no longer knew. It didn't matter. Maybe they were having dinner. Hot dogs. Ronnie loved hot dogs. Morrison was eagerly waiting until his son was old enough to appreciate a trip to a baseball game. He would introduce his little buddy to ice cream, peanuts, and ballpark hot dogs. Hot dogs always tasted better when accompanied by sunshine and the smell of a freshly mowed infield.

A tear dripped from his eye and landed on the metal pistol. Morrison gently wiped it away with the cleaning cloth that he still held in one hand. He thought of the tears his wife had shed when he had left. If possible, he would part the heavens, drain the seas, and change the course of the earth just to hold her one last time, to smell her hair one last time.

"Oh, God," he sobbed. "Oh, dear, dear God."

Closing his eyes he saw their small home, the living room with its plastic-covered furniture and twelve-inch black-and-white television. In his mind, he saw her giggling at Milton Berle doing a skit dressed as a woman. Her laughter was contagious and sounded sweeter than any symphony. He knew he would hear it no more.

Setting the gun down, Morrison reached to the small desk near his bed and removed the letter he had started several weeks ago after they had survived the depth charge attack. He had added just a few words: "My love for you will never die." He folded the paper, placed it in his desk, and picked up the pistol again.

"It won't help."

Morrison jumped at the voice. He looked up to see Kunzig standing in the doorway. The German looked drawn and worn, as if he were ill.

"The gun," Kunzig said. "It won't help."

"I killed my crew," Morrison said flatly. "I deserve worse than this." He held the gun up.

"You did not kill your crew," Kunzig answered. "They did."

"Who?"

Whispers filled the room.

"They did." Kunzig nodded in the direction of the sound. "You could never murder your crew, but they could. Or I should say, they could do it through you. It really is not your fault."

"Then whose fault is it?"

"The Many. The Possession. The Multitude. They use different names."

"I don't get it."

"They're creatures, like us, yet very different."

Morrison shook his head. "Creatures. Like from another planet or something?"

"No, something different. It's more like they're from a different place or a different space."

"What have you brought aboard my boat?" Morrison demanded. "Maybe I should use this on you first." He raised the gun and pointed it at Kunzig's head.

"It still wouldn't help," Kunzig said calmly. "Oh, and technically, I did not bring this on your boat. You did when you rescued me."

"Nothing makes sense anymore," Morrison said. The gun shook in his hand. "I don't know why I did what I did. I couldn't help myself."

"That is what I am trying to tell you, Captain. You could not help yourself. There was nothing anyone could do. They had you, took you. It is like driving an automobile, except now you are the auto."

"What do they want? Why me? Why my crew?"

Kunzig shook his head slowly. "I cannot answer that. They do not think like we do. Their motivation is their own. It appears that they need no motivation. They are evil, Captain. You just had a taste of it. I've been where they live. It's indescribable. It is like swimming in the sewer of hell. They take whatever or whoever they want."

"So they did come aboard with you?" Morrison raised a hand to steady the pistol.

"In a manner of speaking, Captain. Put the gun down and I will tell you what I know."

"I ought to kill you right here and now," Morrison spat.

"Then do it. Kill me or put the gun down, Captain. I am much too exhausted to care."

Morrison lowered the gun. "Tell me. Tell me the truth."

If Kunzig was relieved, he did not show it. He spoke like a professor. "They're otherworldly," he began. "I'm not sure how else to describe them. The best I can determine is that they live in a dimension higher than ours."

"Higher?"

"In number," Kunzig answered. "We have three dimensions of space. They seem to have more. Somehow, they can move between their dimension and ours. I don't know how, but they do. Of course that's not a new idea."

"What do you mean?"

"Ancient cultures are filled with stories of angels and demons who appear suddenly, can change shape, know things that it would be impossible for mortals to know, and even take over bodies."

"Is that what these things are? Demons?"

"That's as good a term as any," Kunzig acknowledged. "I know you said you were not a believer, but maybe you remember hearing a Bible story or two. The New Testament contains many accounts of demon possession. The creatures take control of a body and then seem to enjoy harming their host. The point here is that they seem compelled to occupy a body. In the gospel of Mark, a gathering of demons that called themselves Legion were cast out of a single man. They begged to be cast into a herd of swine rather than be sent away. Apparently their present place is rather unpleasant for them."

"It can't be bad enough," Morrison growled.

"What was it about those demons that made inhabiting a pig better than returning to their own abode?" Kunzig shook his head. "I don't know. I know the Bible in 2 Peter and in Jude speaks of angels who kept not their first estate. The things that inhabited you, me, and Mr. Sapolsky may have been similar. It appears that some are bound and others are not. I can't tell you why."

"So you don't know all that much after all."

"No, not much. They don't feel obligated to tell me anything. Scholars and tradition teach that demons are fallen angels. That makes them spiritual beings, at least by our definition. That also makes them more powerful than us."

"The navy didn't teach me how to fight demons. I can't shoot them; I can't even see them. How am I supposed to fight them?"

"You cannot. They win every time."

"So what do they want with me and my submarine?" Morrison asked.

"I have no idea, Captain. They may want it simply because they can have it."

"I thought they wanted bodies. Why kill my crew?"

"It is not a one-to-one ratio, Captain. That Bible account I shared with you is the story of one man filled with multiple demons. They called themselves Legion. A Roman legion consisted of three thousand to six thousand soldiers. They were all in one man. When Jesus cast them into the swine they all went. The Bible says there were about two thousand pigs. In short, there are a lot of them, and they can occupy one person."

"Is that what they did with you?"

Kunzig nodded and sighed. "I hate them, but I need them."

"Need them? How?"

"Power, Captain. Pure power. I've been trying to control them, use them. The creatures seem bound to the Canaanite artifacts. At least, that is, when I first encountered them."

"How are you going to control them?" Morrison asked with disgust. "They seem to be controlling you."

"The spear, Captain. That is why the spear of Longinus is so important. The spear that pierced Christ at his crucifixion—there must be power in it. That one artifact has changed history. The spear has protected kings and given them victory in battle. If I can learn to control it, use it, then I can master the creatures—"

"And control the world," Morrison interrupted.

"Is that so wrong, Captain?" Kunzig asked firmly. "Look at our world. Look at its leaders. Our world has produced Hitler and Mussolini. Think of Stalin. He is your ally now, but I know things about him that would shock your president. He will turn on you. History is filled with examples of despotic men who have crushed the populace under their feet."

"And you want to be like them. What makes you so different?"

"Nothing, Captain. Why should I lie to you? But I'd much rather rule than be ruled."

Morrison laughed.

"What's so funny, Herr Captain?" There was anger in Kunzig's voice, but Morrison did not care.

"Let's see, Kunzig," Morrison replied, chuckling between words. "You play with the devil in hopes of being a king. Now you're trapped with me on a submarine in the Atlantic. Just the two of us, Mr. Kunzig. And I'm the only one who knows how to make this sub work, and I don't plan on helping you."

"They will make you help," Kunzig said forcefully.

"Will they? Why? Because you'll command them to take me over again. It appears to me that you have yet to face reality. They control you; you don't control them."

Kunzig stiffened and his face flushed. "Listen, I can make you rich. I can make you powerful. There is room at the top for both of us. I will make it worth your while."

Morrison laughed explosively.

"What is it you want?" Kunzig shouted. "Money? Position? Women? Is that it? Women? Someone to make you forget your little wife Sandi back home? You can have all the women—"

Morrison charged Kunzig, gun in hand. He crossed the tiny cabin in one step and slammed the barrel of the .45 into the German's forehead. Kunzig staggered back into the walkway until his back was pressed against a partition.

"SHUT UP!" Morrison's heart pounded violently; his blood raced through his veins. "Never talk about my wife that way! I'll kill you for just uttering her name. I should kill you now!"

Kunzig stared past the gun and into Morrison's eyes. Neither spoke. Morrison was drawing deep, ragged breaths. He leaned his weight on the gun and watched Kunzig wince in pain.

"My wife is the most noble person to walk the face of this earth. My boy is the best son a man could have. I love them. Do you understand that? Can you understand love and commitment? You want power. All I want is to hold my family."

Kunzig said nothing.

"It appears, Mr. Kunzig, that neither one of us will get what we want."

"I need you to run the submarine, Captain. If I get what I want, I'll help you get what you want."

Morrison let the gun drop, but an instant later he brought his left fist up in a crashing blow to the side of Kunzig's head. Kunzig grunted, staggered, and fell to the deck. "You are crazy, Kunzig," Morrison shouted, his voice ricocheting through the *Triggerfish*. "I mean that literally. I don't know if those things rewired your brain, or if you're just nuts, but you don't get it."

"What don't I get, Captain?" Kunzig asked weakly as he rubbed the side of his jaw.

"You are a victim. You'll never control those creatures. You are their slave, not their master."

"I'll find a way. I have no choice. I am the victim of my own plan."

"No, you won't. They own you lock, stock, and barrel. And there isn't a thing you can do about it." He paused and lowered his head. Morrison's tone changed from anger to hopelessness. "There . . . there isn't a thing anyone can do about it." Morrison turned on his heels and stepped back into his cabin. "Nothing . . . nothing . . . nothing."

The sound of a gunshot echoed through the submarine.

N

The sun rose with agonizing slowness, brushing away the last remnants of night. A gentle breeze that belied the squall that had passed during the evening blew from the west. Karl Kunzig sat on the wet deck of the bridge, his knees drawn up to his chest, and watched the ocean spray cascade over the bow of the submarine.

He was alone. As alone as he had been for months. Even the creatures seemed to have abandoned him. After he had gathered enough courage to look in the captain's cabin and see the lifeless body, Kunzig had struggled to formulate a plan of survival. He was in danger. At any moment he could encounter an Axis warship that would unleash its arsenal to sink the *Triggerfish*. Or the sub could continue on until it ran aground somewhere, but he had no idea where that might be. For that matter, he had no idea where he was or where he was headed.

None of that really mattered. He knew that he could not run the ship by himself. He would have plenty of food and water, but sooner or later he would run out of fuel. His only hope was to use the radio. Of course that would give his position away, and the wrong ship might get there first. And even if he did raise a British or American vessel, what would he tell them happened to the crew? How could he explain that he, a German officer, was the only survivor of an American submarine? Worse than that, he would run the risk of losing his artifacts. He could not allow that to happen.

"Is this how it ends?" he said into the cool morning air. The creatures didn't answer. "Is this the best *you* can do? What happens if I die out here? Then what? Whose body will you occupy next? You'll be alone and sooner or later this submarine will sink." Still nothing. "Maybe I should just sink it myself." His voice was mocking. "Leave the hatches open and pull whatever levers will make this thing sink. Where would you be then?"

Nothing.

Kunzig began to weep. Nothing was working out right. He had believed that he could make the creatures obey him. After all, he had the spear of Longinus. But he had failed.

They were tormenting him, he knew that. There were many ways to make a man suffer. They could occupy him, drag him into their nonsensical world, or they could abandon him alone on this metal coffin until he slowly went mad. If there was anything he had learned about the creatures, it was that they possessed an insatiable thirst for evil; they desired to see others suffer. Now he was the only one left, and that thought terrified him. He was now the only target.

"You should have listened to me," he yelled into the wind. "We could have ruled the world." He heard laughter. "You think that is funny? I had a plan." More laughter. Kunzig jumped to his feet. "Why settle for just me, when I could have delivered countries to you? People for the taking. But what are you going to do now? Nothing. You stupid creatures. You threw it all away."

Something caught his eye. In the distance was movement. A ship? Kunzig scrambled down the ladder into the control room, found a pair of binoculars, and scampered back up. It was still there. A dark object on the water. He raised the glasses to his eyes and scanned the area until he found it. He focused.

In the pale gold light of sunrise was a bluish-black ball. It was the size of a battleship and coming his way. A ball? Not a ship, not an island, but a ball. And it seemed to skip along the ocean. Kunzig watched intently as the ball became oblong, then egg shaped, then square-like, then back to a ball again. It changed shape at an unbelievable rate. Only the blue-black color remained the same. As it approached, Kunzig could see a silver glow around the perimeter. The glow pulsated rhythmically.

Bounding and skipping, the ball closed the distance between it and the submarine.

"What is this?" Kunzig shouted into the air. "What are you doing?"

Closer and closer it came until he no longer needed binoculars. Closer. It seemed to suck in light around its edges, as if it were gulping it in. "Answer me! What are you doing?"

It was huge, towering into the sky, and expanding meters to each side of the sub. And it stood directly in the path of the *Triggerfish*. Kunzig thought of trying to steer around the obstacle, but knew it was futile. The thing moved on its own and could easily counter any evasive maneuver he could manage.

What the German saw next made his heart seize. He took a step back. "No," he said softly to himself. Then louder: "No. No, no, no. NO!"

The object became a ball again and began to sink in front of the moving submarine. As it did, ocean water poured into the blackness and out of sight. Kunzig could hear the flow of water. It sounded like a massive waterfall, roaring, falling. The ball continued to gulp the ocean as the *Triggerfish* approached.

They were taking him and the submarine. Taking him to wherever they lived. A portal had opened between their world and his reality. That was all he could surmise, but one thing he did know: Life as he had known it ended in that hole.

Scrambling for the hatch, Kunzig glanced over his shoulder one more time. The terror was still there, looming large and black and empty, a ravenous mouth. He dove headfirst down the hatch with a scream.

The submarine sailed forward, teetered on the ocean's edge, and fell into the black nothingness.

Chapter 17

Police, fire, and other military have been brought up-to-date," Admiral Robbins said as he hung up the phone. "I just hope they can keep everyone reined in. I'd hate to see those people on the bridge die because some hot dog can't control himself or his people."

Stanton nodded. He was standing in front of the admiral's desk, too agitated to sit. This was a tough situation and he had no real ideas how to alleviate it. "I'm afraid the ball is in their court, Admiral. I don't like having someone else calling the shots like this."

"I don't like it either, but we have no choice. Not yet anyway. If a ship or helicopter gets close, then they can blow up the bridge and with it, a few hundred people."

"If there are really bombs there," Donna said. She was seated opposite the admiral's desk.

"We have no choice but to believe them," Stanton said. "There are a lot of lives at risk here. Did the fire department or police have an estimate of how many people are stranded up there?"

"Close to six hundred people," Robbins replied. "That's just an estimate based on sightings they've taken from the air. The police helicopter had to stay out of the area, but they were able to get a good look through high-powered binoculars."

"Six hundred people." Stanton shook his head. "And all of them at the mercy of some crazed terrorist."

"I don't get it," Donna said. "What could possibly be on the *Triggerfish* that would drive someone to this extreme?"

Neither Stanton nor the admiral answered.

The phone rang. Robbins picked it up immediately. "Yes." He listened for a moment, mouthed the words "It's them," then punched the speakerphone button. "Okay, you have our attention. What's next?"

"You have ten minutes to clear the front gate," the voice on the phone said. "No cars, no guards. I see a man with a weapon and the bridge goes tumbling down. Understood?"

"Understood."

"This is no joke, Admiral," the caller continued. "I'm serious—deadly serious. If so much as a blade of grass looks out of place to me, I'll drop those people two hundred feet into the bay."

"You've made your point," Robbins said sternly. Stanton could see the admiral's neck stiffen. "Just tell us what you want."

"Okay, Admiral, here it is. I'm going to drive through the gate in ten minutes. As soon as I do, I want the gate secured behind me. I will then drive to the pier at which you have the *Triggerfish* moored. I want you and Stanton and the lady officer there. No one else. I'll be looking on rooftops and in windows. If I see a gun, the people die. If I see your Navy SEALs anywhere around, then boom. People will be watching me. If any attempt is made to detain me, then the bombs go off. My plan is foolproof, Admiral. You had better believe that. Foolproof."

"Understood," Robbins said through clenched teeth. "Why do you want the woman officer?"

"I don't really need a reason, now do I, Admiral? Let's just say, I like pretty things. Ten minutes, Admiral Robbins. That's all you have to clear the gate. Ten minutes. I suggest you get busy."

The line went dead.

"Cocky little worm, isn't he?" Robbins said.

"Yes," Stanton answered. "Except this worm has teeth." He turned to Donna. "Think you can handle this, Lieutenant?"

"You ask that as if I had a choice, sir," she answered. "I can handle it. I have to handle it. I wonder how they know about me?"

"I assume they've had the submarine under surveillance," Stanton said. "They probably saw you when we first tried to make entrance."

Admiral Robbins picked up the phone and dialed.

"Calling base police, sir?" Stanton asked.

"Affirmative." Robbins paused while he waited for the line to be picked up. When security answered, the admiral spoke crisply, not wasting words. "Captain, this is Admiral Robbins. I want the front gate cleared of all personnel. You have less than ten minutes. You get your people out of the way and out of sight. No questions, Captain. This is an order. Understood? Good. Now make it happen."

Robbins hung up and looked at Stanton. "I have a bad feeling about this."

N
⋏

The dark green Ford Explorer came to an abrupt halt, its tires screeching on the pavement in protest. Stanton stood at the juncture where pier met pavement. He watched through angry eyes as two men stepped from the vehicle. Immediately, he noticed three things: Each carried a side arm that Stanton judged to be Beretta M9s—the same side arm carried by U.S. military; one man carried a backpack; and the men wore ski masks. Neither man looked around as he exited the vehicle. *Cocky*, Stanton thought. *They're so confident that they don't care who sees them, or even if a gun is trained on them.*

The men marched toward the small gathering in which Stanton stood. With him was Admiral Robbins, Lieutenant Wilcox, and Commander Stewart. Stewart had joined them at the last minute and insisted on remaining with the group.

"How do we explain your presence?" Stanton had asked.

"I'll think of something," Stewart answered. "I feel like I should be there."

There was no denying the man's courage, Stanton had thought. He hoped they had not made a mistake in allowing him to come along.

Stanton studied his adversaries as they crossed the short distance from the car to the pier. The dock itself was capable of supporting the weight of the car, but since it could block the line of sight of the dozen SEALs hidden around the base, Stanton didn't want it next to the *Triggerfish*. By standing on the pier, he had hoped that the two men would exit the vehicle and walk the short distance to the sub. That would allow a few minutes for the SEALs and Stanton to study the terrorists.

"Who is he?" the first man asked, pointing a finger at Stewart. Despite the ski mask, Stanton could discern a few things about the man. He was Stanton's height, stoutly built, and had blue eyes. Not much information in a crisis situation, but Stanton was desperate for anything that might prove useful. The other man was the same size and build, but had brown eyes and the skin around the eyes was a shade darker. "I asked you a question," the first man said harshly. "Who is he?"

"I'm Commander Ira Stewart of the U.S. Coast Guard," Stewart said before Stanton could speak.

"Coast Guard," the man said with a laugh. "Afraid that you might miss something?"

Stewart did not answer. Stanton glanced at his new friend. He stood as straight as a steel pole, every muscle tensed, and his eyes burned with a barely controlled fury.

Blue Eyes saw it too. "Well, Commander," he said, "you are an uninvited guest, but I can use you anyway." He turned to the admiral. "Admiral Robbins, thank you for being so cooperative. I'm sorry to say that I must inconvenience you some more." He laughed. "Here's what we are going to do, boys and girls. The admiral is going to have a seat in my car. Once he does, my friend here," he motioned toward the other masked man, "is going to push a little button on his remote control device which will arm the bomb we have in the back of the car." As if to highlight the point, the other man removed from his pocket a small plastic box the size of a garage door remote and held it out for others to see. It had four buttons on it, each a different color. "Should one of you, or the Navy SEALs you have stationed around here, decide to play the hero, then he or one of my other operatives will activate the car bomb first, then the bombs on the bridge." He nodded to his partner who promptly pushed one of the four buttons on the remote. One second later an explosion occurred on the bridge three-quarters of a mile across the bay. Stanton snapped his head around in time to see smoke rising and concrete raining down on the bridge and into the water below. "That was just a little C4 plastic explosive. Consider it a free sample. Now each of you is going to do exactly as I say. Is that clear?"

"It's clear," Robbins said sternly. "You've made your point."

"Good. As for you, Mr. Stewart, you will remain where you are. Once my friend and I are in the submarine, your SEALs may feel like searching my car. I suggest you advise them otherwise. Should anyone approach that vehicle, my operatives will push the button and the admiral here will decorate his base with little bits of his body. That, of course, might damage his career." The man laughed.

"I'd rather accompany you on the sub," Stewart said.

The man took two brisk steps forward and then brought a crashing blow to the side of the commander's head. Stewart dropped to his knees. Instinctively, Stanton stepped in front of his friend and was greeted by the barrel of the Beretta pointed at his head.

"Easy, Captain," the man said. "I don't need you in order to finish my work here. If you would like to be the first casualty, I can arrange it." Stanton's heart was pounding with rage, but he could not allow himself to lose control. One wrong action, one wrong word, and hundreds would die.

Stewart staggered to his feet, wavered for a moment as he searched for balance, then raised his head high. "I'm all right, Captain," he said. "He didn't hurt me."

Stanton turned and looked at Stewart. The lie was evident. A fist-sized bruise was spreading across his face, and blood trickled from his mouth. Despite the unexpected blow, Stanton had the feeling that the Coast Guard man had enough rage left in him to handle a boatload of terrorists.

"Do you understand your role now, Commander?" the man asked. Stewart nodded stiffly. "Good. Admiral, get in the car."

Robbins sighed, turned to Stanton, and said, "Be careful, Captain." Then, without hesitation, he turned and walked to the Explorer and took a seat behind the steering wheel.

"I will kill him, you know."

You had better kill me first, Stanton thought. Inside him raged a concoction of apprehension and wrath. His tormentor was arrogant and that meant he was vulnerable. The moment would come when he would drop his guard and when he did, Stanton would be ready.

Then realization fell on him like a collapsing roof. So what if he did manage to overcome the two men? That was only part of the problem. There were others involved; at least the gunman said there were. It could be a lie. It could also be true and too much was at stake to take any chances. Stanton would have to wait for the right opportunity, if such an opportunity existed. He began to pray that there was and that he would be wise enough to recognize it.

The gunman stepped back and then to the side until he was standing in front of Donna. "You are lovely close up. Binoculars don't do you justice." He reached up and touched her hair with a gloved hand. She stiffened, then set her jaw tight. "It's good that you're feeling better. You looked quite ill earlier. Not something you ate, I hope."

The comment puzzled Stanton. What had the man meant by that?

"I'm fine, not that it's any business of yours."

"So you are in a bad mood too?" The man turned to his partner. "A few threats, a little danger, and they all become antisocial. What is this world coming to?" His partner laughed in reply. "Enough pleasantries. I came here for something and it is time that I got it. Captain, you'll lead the way. Your pretty friend will follow you. We will be close behind." He turned to Stewart. "You, Commander, will do well to remember my warning. Anyone, such as your SEAL team, approaches that car and the admiral is dead. Understood?"

"I got it."

"Let's go."

Stanton took the lead, with Donna behind him and the two men behind her. His mind raced. He hated being without options. He especially hated being the marionette to the madman in the mask. But at the moment, he was powerless. Anything he did could lead to the death of one or more people—perhaps hundreds. As he walked, he looked to the west and caught sight of the three fifteen-story towers that housed expensive condominiums. A terrorist could easily watch them from any of those buildings. There were also cars parked all along the Silver Strand, and any one of them could shelter a terrorist. Behind him, to the northwest, was the Coronado Yacht Club. Nearly a hundred boats were moored there. It was just one more place where a coconspirator could hide.

N
Λ

"We're just about ready," Abbey said as he shouldered the video camera. "Microwave dish is up, and the studio has been contacted. We have a feed and will go live in five minutes."

"It's about time," Barry said.

Abbey looked at the newsman, took the camera from his shoulder, and set it on the pavement. He crossed the distance between them in three quick, short strides and grabbed Barry by the shirt. Barry's heart began to race.

"What are you doing?" Barry shouted.

"Listen, you prissy little prima donna," Abbey shouted. "I've had enough of you. In case it hasn't occurred to you, my life is in as much danger as yours. And unlike you, I have a family to go home to. I may never see them again. That's what's on my mind, and it's a heavy burden. So the last thing I need is some mewling little runt like you who is so filled with his own importance that he thinks he can walk all over everyone."

"Hey, let me go," Barry said fearfully. "I'll have your job!"

"Oh, will you?" Abbey said with a laugh. He released Barry. "Okay then, I'll just go tell the studio you think I should be fired. Then you can file this report all by yourself."

"Okay, George," Barry said as he straightened his shirt. "I get the point. I'm scared just like you, and I'm handling it badly. I'm sorry. Now can we shoot this thing?"

Barry watched as Abbey stared angrily at him. Barry's stomach was twisted into a knot. He was stranded on a bridge with several hundred frightened people and George had to go ballistic. "Well?" Barry asked.

"Yeah, yeah. Okay. I'm a little over the top. Sorry."

"Don't sweat it. Let's just do the piece." Barry straightened his shirt. "How much time?"

"About a minute or so. Where do you want to stand?"

"With the van behind me. I'll do about twenty or thirty seconds, then begin to move to my right. You pan with me. I'll stop when the crowd is behind me."

"You know, Barry. I think you're an arrogant little worm, but you do know how to set up a story."

"Thanks," Barry replied. "I think."

"Okay," Abbey said as he picked up the camera again and shouldered it. "I'll start with a close-up and push to a wide shot. When you start walking, I'll close to a medium and then—"

"No," Barry interrupted. "Beginning with the close is good, but just push to the medium and stay there. We need to get these people in the shot."

"Got it," Abbey replied. "I wonder which is better. Seeing your loved one alive but on the bridge, or not seeing them at all and wondering where they are?"

"Neither one sounds very good to me."

"Stand by, they're doing the intro now."

Barry looked down at a monitor that Abbey had placed on the pavement. He could see the coanchors of his station seated, looking grave and speaking into the camera. Barry turned from the monitor and looked into the lens of the camera as if he were staring into the eyes of a friend. Out of the corner of his eye, he saw his image replace that of the studio anchors.

"Good afternoon," he began. "I'm standing on the roadway of the Coronado-San Diego Bay Bridge. A short time ago, several explosions rocked this landmark as armed terrorists, using vans like the one behind me, stopped the flow of traffic. I understand that the traffic outbound from Coronado has also been trapped on the bridge. Before the terrorists rappelled—yes, rappelled—over the bridge, they announced that the van behind me was filled with explosives. They also said that similar vans had been placed at the two entrances to the bridge."

Barry began to walk in a slow arch. Abbey followed with the camera.

"In short, we are being held hostage by an unknown group and for unknown reasons. As you can see, several explosions have already taken place, but each of these were small compared to that which the van is capable of doing—assuming it is filled with explosives. The most recent explosion occurred a few moments ago, sending chunks of asphalt and concrete high overhead. Fortunately, there were no additional injuries."

Barry stopped his movement when the crowd was behind him. "Unfortunately, there are injuries from the auto accidents that occurred when traffic came to an abrupt halt. Many injuries occurred when the first set of explosions went off.

"To their credit, these citizens trapped here on the bridge with me have not panicked. Instead, they have pulled together to help each other and to pray. I think I speak for the hundreds of people on this bridge when I say, pray for us.

"This is Barry Ludlow reporting live from the Coronado Bridge, high over the San Diego Bay."

There was a short pause, then Abbey said, "And you're clear."

"How was it?"

"Great."

"There is an award in this story," Barry said.

"Yeah, well you can have it. I'll be happy just to live. There's more to life than—"

"What's that?"

"—reporting the news. There's family. Man, I wish I was home with them now. I'd—"

"Shut up, George, and bring the camera here. I think that something is going on at the sub."

"You and that sub. We've got more important things to be concerned about."

Barry stepped quickly to Abbey's side and seized the camera. He then walked to the concrete rail at the side of the bridge. Aiming the camera across the bay, he pushed the zoom button.

"What do you think you're doing?" Abbey protested.

"Look at the monitor."

"What?"

"Look at the monitor!" Barry shouted. Abbey did. "What do you make of that?"

"It looks like two men in masks holding guns on two navy officers."

"Now we know what they want. They want the sub."

"Why?" Abbey asked. "What could anyone want with that dinosaur?"

"I don't know, but whatever the reason, it's important enough for them to trap us up here."

"Hopefully, being trapped is the end of it," Abbey said softly. He paused as he gazed across the bay. "How are they going to get us off of here?" he asked morosely. "I doubt the bad guys are going to come back to get their ... things. Even if they get everything they want."

Barry shook his head. The same thought had crossed his mind. No matter how successful the terrorists were, they would not be back to remove the bombs. "I guess we'll have to wish them success," Barry said.

"What? Are you serious?"

"As serious as I can be," Barry replied. "If the terrorists are successful, they'll make their escape. That means they'll be a long way from here. Hopefully far enough away that they can't activate the explosives. Odd as it sounds, George, we're forced to root for the bad guys."

Chapter 18

Donna felt sick, ill with fear and uncertainty, and that apprehension grew with each step she took along the pier. Everything around her seemed amplified. The sun shone down with blinding light, as if a cosmic magnifying glass had been interposed between it and earth. The normally beautiful cry of seagulls sounded like shrieks of an ancient banshee. The smell of salt from the bay was nauseating. The sound of footfalls, hers, Stanton's, and those of the two armed men behind her, rumbled off the rough wood planks.

Inside she felt a shambles. Her heart pounded wildly and forced blood, chilled by terror, through her veins. Air came to her lungs only after conscious effort. She was sure that if she stopped concentrating, her lungs would simply cease to draw a breath and she would suffocate from the horror of what was happening. She struggled for comfort, searched for some sign of peace, but the world, the universe was empty of anything that would make her feel better.

Donna believed beyond all uncertainty that she would die. And the death would be horrible.

A battle raged in her mind. A war between compulsion and abject fear. They had traveled a third of the distance to the submarine. Donna had taken each step with her head down, her eyes fixed on the timbers of the dock. She struggled to focus on each spike, each gap between slats, preferring to look at anything other than the *Triggerfish*.

It called to her. It beckoned her. It mocked her. Soon she would be in its grasp and although she had no idea of what would happen, she knew it would be terrible.

Don't look, she told herself. *Keep your head down. Say nothing. Do nothing. Just don't look.* She raised her head as if some invisible hand had taken her under the chin. Her eyes fell on the *Triggerfish*. Acid filled her stomach, which constricted into a tight knot the size of a fist. Involuntarily, she inhaled, making an asthmatic wheeze as she sucked in the thick air.

The submarine loomed before her, but not as she saw it last. It was no longer the sleek gray hull she had come to recognize as the *Triggerfish*. In its place was a pulsating hull the color of a deep bruise. A fog, bluish gray, like a viscous smoke, surrounded the craft. The surreal picture did not end there, for the submarine was not afloat in the waters of the bay, but instead hung suspended over an endless pit of nothing.

Then the sounds came. Dark tones. Evil emanations. A pernicious chorus of unworldly chant. Tone upon grotesque tone, note upon black note. And in the midst of it all was a one-word song sung by a chorus of the unseen. A single word lyric: "Donna."

Things began to spin. Up no longer seemed to be above her; down was somewhere to the side. Churning and turning. Spinning and swaying. Modulation. Shuddering and shaking.

"Are you all right, Lieutenant?" a familiar voice asked. A friendly voice.

"I . . . I feel sick, Captain," Donna stammered.

"Too bad, lady," the masked man said. "I don't have time for this."

"I can't help it," Donna pleaded. "Something . . . something is not right."

"What's not right?" Stanton asked.

"I . . . I . . ." Donna began.

"Shut up!" the gunman shouted.

"Back off!" Stanton demanded loudly. "You've got me. Just leave her behind."

"How chivalrous, Captain," the man shouted back. "That's one option. The other option is that I put a bullet in your brain and move on without you."

"No," Donna exclaimed. "I'll be fine. Let's just keep going."

"Are you sure?" Stanton asked.

"You heard the woman, Captain. Now get moving."

Donna took a deep breath hoping that the pure air would help her maintain her composure, but the air was rancid. There was no relief in anything she did. And she had no choice but to press on.

Donna. Donna. DONNA. The voices sang.

A tear ran down her face and fell to her uniform.

Three steps later, Donna made a decision. If this was to be her last day alive, then she would meet it with dignity and authority. She raised her head and faced the apparition of the *Triggerfish* as it floated in its ocean of nothingness. *You want me,* she thought, *then here I come.*

N
Λ

Stanton was more worried than ever. Donna Wilcox was terrified to the point of physical incapacity. The situation was fragile enough as it was. If she were to lose control, things could quickly go from horrible to disastrous and possibly cause the loss of a great many lives. But there was nothing he could do about it. He had seen the fear on her face, and he knew it was more than the fear of death at the hands of terrorists. Something had reached deep into her mind and planted a kind of terror that was beyond his understanding. He also knew the source of that fear: the *Triggerfish*.

Images and words from his conversation with her the day before welled up in his mind. He recalled the sincerity of her words as she described the impossible to him: a face appearing on the deck of the submarine. There had been nothing in word or manner to indicate that she was lying, and he could think of no reason for her to do so. As it was, she had entrusted her career to him. The story she told was beyond belief and would be just cause to doubt her sanity. Stanton, however, did not doubt her sanity. Not now. He had not seen what she had seen, not heard what she had heard, but he had had persistent concerns and unsettled feelings about the sub from the beginning. The feelings had been pressed to the back of his mind as he focused on the duty he had been called to perform. Indeed, he had been filled with excitement and admiration for the aging vessel. Still, it troubled him.

There were also oddities that remained to be reconciled with logic: the unusual sound they heard when the boat was under tow; the thumping noise just as they were about to open a hatch; the nonsensical appearance of ice around the hull; the fears and visions of Donna Wilcox; and, of course, the inexplicable death of the sailor drawn into the propellers.

Those mysteries were enough for one mission, but to now have two gunmen strolling along the pier behind them, intent on entering the sub for a reason still unknown to him, was beyond belief. A helpless feeling ate away at Stanton.

Then there were the words of Hawking Striber. Those words came back to him freely. He had spoken of demons. Stanton had wanted to get up and walk out of the room, and would have done so had not his brother-in-law been there to vouch for Hawking's sanity. Demons? Stanton's mind refused to accept it. Still, it would answer a great many questions.

Stanton turned to Donna. "You're seeing them again, aren't you? The images?"

Donna nodded. "Yes." She spoke only the one word, but a larger message was conveyed by her pale skin and watery eyes. Stanton recognized horror when he saw it.

"Seeing what again?" the blue-eyed man demanded.

"Ghosts," Stanton answered. "Didn't you know? The *Triggerfish* is haunted."

"I hope so. The paranormal doesn't frighten me, Captain. Who knows, maybe I can make use of ghosts."

"These ghosts may be different," Stanton replied as he started up the gangplank. "Maybe they'll make use of you."

The wooden plank gave slightly under the weight of Stanton and those who followed. Six steps later they stood on the deck. There was a pause as the four stood forward of the conning tower. Stanton turned to his abductor and saw him smile through the mouth opening in the mask. He was clearly pleased with himself. *This isn't over yet, bud*, Stanton said to himself. It was a brave thought that bolstered his courage, but it also seemed foolish. If it were just him against the two terrorists it would be different, almost hopeful. Stanton was a resourceful man; he could find a way to change the tide, to seize the advantage. But it wasn't just him against the other two.

"Okay," Stanton said. "We're here and you have the gun. What next?"

"We go in," the man said frankly.

"Fine," Stanton replied. "Any place special? You have a few choices."

"Like what?"

Stanton pointed to the deck. "There's a companionway there. Just in front of that is the escape hatch. Aft of the conning tower is another access hatch. Farther aft is another hatch. Then on the bridge—"

"The escape hatch will do. We can work our way back from there."

Stanton stepped to the hatch, squatted, and turned the wheel that would unlock the hatch and allow it to swing open. As he did a sound rumbled from within: *thumpa, thumpa, thumpa.*

"What was that?" the leader asked.

"We don't know yet," Stanton answered. He turned and looked at Donna. She was stiff with fear. "I guess you'll get to find out along with us."

"Don't get cute with me, Captain," the man said arrogantly. "I have no reservation about shooting you right here."

Stanton shrugged. "That might be preferable to what awaits us inside."

"What do you mean?"

"I told you. The *Triggerfish* may be haunted. I've had several people tell me that it is. More or less."

"More or less?"

"Ghosts, demons, spirits, devils. It's all just semantics at this point, isn't it?"

"I told you, those things don't frighten me. In fact, I find the thought exhilarating."

"So you've said." Stanton offered a small smile. He was still afraid as any man would be, but something had been added. He felt a presence, a beneficent, spiritual presence that reminded him of his childhood in church. It was welcome and familiar.

Stanton had no idea if this was the last day of his life, and at the moment it did not matter. Suddenly, death did not seem so fearsome. "Let me ask you something. You seem to have thought this little operation through, but I'll bet my dollars to your doughnuts that you haven't thought about what may be inside here. Am I right?"

"Don't be a fool, Captain. That's why I'm here. I've come to retrieve something."

"I guessed as much, but that isn't my point." Stanton stood slowly. "I'm talking about the crew. It could be quite a mess down there. Just think of the bodies, or what's left of them. Are you prepared to hike through ankle-deep corpses?"

"You don't frighten me, Captain. I have never known fear and never shall."

"Never been afraid, huh? Well, just remember, this boat has already killed one man. Who knows, you might be next."

"You'll go first."

"I'm ready. I made peace with my God a long time ago."

"I don't believe in God."

"I'm not surprised," Stanton said. Then in a gesture that was as surprising to him as it must have been to the others, he walked to Donna and took her in his arms, hugging her like a father hugs a daughter. "This isn't regulation, Lieutenant ... Donna, but this whole operation has been out in left field. I want you to know that I believe every word you've told me."

"Thank you, Captain," she answered weakly.

"I also want you to know that there is a greater power involved here. Greater than any of the horror you've seen. I can feel it. When I was a kid, I learned a Bible verse that has stuck with me: 'You, dear children, are from God and have overcome them, because the one who is in you is greater than the one who is in the world.' You need that verse right now. You need to believe that verse right now. 'Greater is he that is in you, than he that is in the world.' Got that?"

Tears streamed down Donna's face. She nodded. "I believe."

"Isn't this sweet," the gunman said sarcastically. Quickly, he stepped forward and placed the gun to Stanton's temple.

Stanton sighed and smiled at Donna, conveying a stream of strength and confidence. Then he slowly turned his head toward his abductor. The smile evaporated from Stanton's face. The barrel of the gun rested between his eyes but he stared past it, and past the hand that held it. He gazed firmly, resolutely, into the eyes of the gunman. He was about to comment when the other gunman strode forward and placed his gun in the ear of Donna. He pushed hard enough to press her head to the side. "No heroics, Captain," the man said, speaking for the first time since exiting the car. "I know that look, and I know that it will get your friend killed in an instant. So stand down."

Stand down? Stanton thought. *A military term. This man is military or ex-military. Which makes him an even more formidable opponent.* Stanton took a step away from the gun and walked to the hatch. Without hesitation, he reached down and threw it open. "Well, gentlemen. Who wants to be first?"

N
⋏

The Chart Club Restaurant was a two-story white building with a red tile roof that sat near the Coronado Yacht Club. Atop its pagoda-style roof was a windowed cupola with a short deck around its circumference that allowed a 360-degree view of the area. Dormers projected through the roof at the second floor. Built in the early 1950s, the structure had become a landmark in the community. The restaurant itself served lunch and dinner to a consistent and appreciative patronage. But there would be no meals served this day. A sign hung at its entrance: CLOSED FOR REPAIRS.

Inside the building, three cooks, four waitresses, and one manager huddled together in the kitchen, their hands, feet, and mouths bound with duct tape. In the cupola-like view room, Helen Muir watched through binoculars as the navy man crouched down on the submarine and opened the forward hatch. All that remained was for Hermann and Max Rohl to enter the sub with their hostages. At this distance, Helen could not make out which masked man was Hermann and which was Max. But that did not matter. All that concerned her at the moment was staying alert, watching for any sign that would prompt her to push the button of the black electronic box that sat on the old table next to her. She knew that another pair of eyes watched the events on the submarine, a pair of eyes stationed across the street from the base in a top-floor condominium. Even if she did not press the button, then Hermann's other flunky would.

Flunky? She chortled at the term. Is that what she had become? A flunky? Just another peon in the growing ranks of Hermann's New Reich? *No*, she told herself. *I do this because I believe in the cause and because I believe that Hermann will be the world's greatest leader. I do this for love.* It was a lie and she knew it. And the lie had grown.

Helen lowered the binoculars and wiped away the moisture from her eyes. How did she descend so far so fast? She looked at the electronic device that could send a signal that would destroy a bridge. If he were here, if he were angry enough, he could tell her to push that button and she would. With her eyes closed, Helen could imagine the titanic explosion and see the debris of steel, concrete, and bodies tumbling toward the water. Men, women, children, all falling, falling, falling.

A small battery-powered television sat on the floor near her feet. Hermann had insisted that it be left on. Once the first blasts erupted, the news media would be all over the place. They would become a source of information for her and the others. Barry Ludlow had just completed his report. The images from the bridge ate at her. She had watched as the camera panned from the explosive-laden vans to the crowd of frightened people. Terror was etched on their faces. The children were the worst. Their tear-streaked faces bore into her soul with a burning intensity.

The image of one of the children began to play across her mind. A little girl, thin blond hair blowing in the wind. Helen could almost hear her asking, "Mommy, why are you crying? Are you sick?" Innocence. Children were so innocent. They believed their mothers and fathers could protect them from anything and anyone. Nothing bad could happen as long as their parents were near. Their young minds could not see, could not comprehend the truth that mother and father were helpless and that they stood a good chance of dying.

The image of the little girl grew in her mind. She saw and felt the sadness and fear in her eyes. Then Helen saw the explosion as if she had pushed the button. The bridge beneath the little girl falling away, her screams being drowned out by the cries of the others. The image of the child reaching up helplessly toward parents who could not grab her and being forced to watch as their child plummeted two hundred feet to the water below. The vision struck her hard like a fist. An emotional knife cut through her as real as if the cold steel of a sword had been thrust into her belly.

Tears were streaming down her face and her breathing had become ragged. Helen died inside. Nothing of what had been her remained. She was a corpse who still could breathe and move, but there was no life in her. The degree to which she had allowed herself to sink had finally become known to her. There were no self-delusional words that could mask the monster she had become.

On the table, next to the transmitter was a gun. She was to use it if one of the workers broke free. The man with the other transmitter had helped her subdue the crew and bind them. Once she was ensconced in her lookout post, the man left to take up his own position. She had never met him before and guessed that Hermann had brought him in from outside the area. He had a hard look about him and seemed to enjoy the terror his gun and presence had brought the others. They had forced their way in an hour before opening time. It had been easy work to subdue the workers, and easier still to erect the signs that told the others the restaurant was closed.

Although the plan called for Hermann to claim a half-dozen people ready to push the button, only three people could set off the bomb: she, Hermann, and the unknown man in the condo. The metal hull of the *Triggerfish* would render Hermann's transmitter useless once he was inside the submarine. That left only two transmitters to do the job. That was enough. She picked up the small plastic device and held it in her hand. It had only one function: to kill innocents. And all it would take was the touch of her finger.

Thoughts percolated in her mind. She was a living human sacrifice, but unlike the ancient cultures where pagan priests cut out the heart of the one being sacrificed, she had done it to herself. First, she sacrificed her principles, then her freedom, then her will. No, she was the puppet at the end of Hermann's strings. She responded to his every twitch. When had it happened? When was the single definitive moment that she handed her mind and will over to the one who saw himself as the new Führer?

Another thought came tumbling forward: What would life be like after this? She might escape capture by the police, but she would never escape the prison of her mind. She was part of a horrible crime and she didn't even know why. Hermann wanted something from the old submarine, but he had told no one what it was. It was his secret, and all his followers were willing to accept that. Lives hung in the balance over items known only to one man. And she was part of it.

But she had no choice.

Or did she?

Helen knew why Hermann had insisted that she participate in the plan. His sole reason was to make her culpable. Her very silence made her an accessory; her participation raised her risk. Once again, he was controlling her. Just like he always did. And she was letting him. She would always let him do what he wanted, no matter who it hurt. Courage was a quality that she did not possess, and never would. If he were here, she would do as she was commanded, and she would do it without question. But he wasn't here. He was in the submarine, or soon would be.

Stepping back to the window, Helen raised the binoculars to her eyes just in time to see Hermann or Max descend down the hatch. She set the binoculars aside, picked up the transmitter and the gun, and started down the narrow, curved stairway. A few moments later she was standing in the kitchen. The bound workers stared at her through wide eyes. Tears ran down the cheeks of one waitress. Helen felt sorry for her but did not speak. Instead she picked up the phone that was mounted to a wall in the kitchen and dialed 911.

Maybe she could do one last noble thing. One last human thing. If not for herself, then for the little blond girl on the bridge.

Chapter 19

The hatch swung open easily, surprising Stanton. Even though the *Triggerfish* showed no sign of being better than a half century old, he had expected some resistance, or at least, a loud creaking sound when the heavy metal hatch moved on its hinge. It provided neither. Stanton stood erect and studied the dark hole at his feet. Hawking's words of demons raced into his mind as if they had floated from the hatch and wafted their way into his brain. Everything within him began to shout a warning. There was nothing good down that hatch, and if Donna's behavior were any indication, everything evil.

"Who goes first?" Stanton asked again.

"My partner goes first," Blue Eyes answered. "Then the woman, then you. I'll go down last."

"Figures," Stanton whispered a little too loudly.

"You are starting to irritate me, Captain. That could be dangerous." He motioned to his partner who quickly stepped to the hatch. "Move away," he said to Stanton. Stanton took three steps back. The terrorist holstered his weapon, checked his backpack, and then climbed down the ladder.

"Clear!" the man called from inside the sub. "Send them down."

The gunman motioned to Donna, who walked with halting steps to the open maw. She peered down the dark hole. Her face told of the terror that swirled within her. A fear that had its source, not in the gunman on the deck or the one below, but in a world seen only through her eyes.

"Down," the man said. "I'm tired of waiting."

Donna hesitated.

"NOW!" the man screamed. He raised the gun and pointed it at her head.

Donna turned and looked at him. It was as if she were deciding which was worse, being shot or descending into the bowels of the ship.

"Come on, come on, lady," the man at the foot of the ladder called out. "On the double, Lieutenant."

Taking a deep breath, Donna leaned forward, braced herself on the hatch lid, and started down the ladder. She paused when her chin reached deck level and turned her face toward Stanton. Her eyes projected reluctance and surrender.

"Remember what I told you," Stanton said firmly. "Greater is he—"

"Greater is he," she repeated, closed her eyes, and then disappeared down the hatch.

"You're next, Captain. Get going."

Stanton complied. At first he was tempted to quickly shut the hatch behind him, drop to the interior deck, and attack the gunman inside. Down there in the dark, one on one, he had a chance of subduing the man before he could react. It would take several seconds for the leader to reopen the lid from outside. But the image of the people on the bridge and the admiral in the car came to his mind.

Darkness engulfed Stanton as he descended the steel ladder. Fifteen steps later, he felt the solid deck below his feet. Light cascaded down the open hatch and pooled around him. He slowly turned to take in his surroundings. Except for the column of light in which he stood, the submarine was as black as a sealed tomb. The air was heavy with the smell of oil and diesel and cold. He felt as if he had walked into an industrial freezer. Thankfully, it did not reek with decaying flesh, battery acid, or chlorine gas. He could not see Donna or the other gunman.

"Lieutenant?" Stanton called out softly.

"Over here," she replied softly. "To your left about six paces."

Stanton turned and peered into the darkness. A bright light struck him in the eyes. The backpack the gunman was carrying must have held a flashlight. Probably more than one.

"Step to the other side of the ladder," the gunman said. "I want you out of the way of—" He stopped. Stanton reasoned that the man was about to use his cohort's name and then caught himself. "I want you where I can see you. Stay in the light, but walk to the other side of the ladder." Stanton did so.

The light from above dimmed as the other gunman started down. A few moments later, he too stood on the deck. The man paused and looked around. From deep inside Stanton a violent urge bubbled up. At that moment he wanted nothing more than to reach through the ladder, grab the jerk with the gun, and yank him through the rungs. But it was a foolish thought. He knew that he would be shot the second he laid a hand on the man.

"Is there a way to turn on the lights?" Blue Eyes asked calmly. The confidence in his voice irritated Stanton. This man held all the cards and he knew it.

"I doubt the batteries still hold a charge," Stanton answered.

"There was enough juice to run that sailor through a Cuisinart. It takes some juice to turn those props enough to chew up a man."

The disrespect stretched Stanton's composure. The urge to lash out was nearly unbearable. But he was still helpless. He reminded himself that victory went to those who chose their battles, who made their move at the right time and in the right place.

"Where are we?" the man asked.

"Forward torpedo room."

"I have another question. Where would the captain of a tub like this put a guest?"

"A guest?" Stanton asked, puzzled.

"Yes, a guest. Didn't craft like this pick up downed pilots and the like?"

"Yes, submarines were often assigned lifeguard duty. So what?"

"So if they picked up someone afloat in the sea, where would that person stay?"

The man knew of the German found in the raft. How could he know that? "Hard to tell. The crew berthing areas were always full, including those in the torpedo rooms. My guess is that they would put a wounded pilot in one of the two officers' wardrooms."

"Where are those? Are they close?"

Stanton chuckled mirthlessly. "A Gato class submarine is just over three hundred feet long and less than thirty feet wide. Everything is close." A second later, Stanton found himself sitting on the deck, pain racing along head and neck. Blood trickled down his cheek. He touched the spot where he had been pistol whipped. There was more fury than pain. Every muscle in his body was spring tight, his jaw set like a vise. He felt his fist clench.

"Captain!" Donna shouted.

"At ease, Lieutenant," Stanton said quickly, fearing that she may try to intervene. "I'm all right."

"Next time I ask you a question, you will answer it plainly and simply," the man said. "No smart remarks. No jokes. Just a simple answer."

Stanton said nothing. He was exercising every fiber of control he had to remain calm. "Yes, the wardroom is close."

"Take me there. Now."

"What about lights?" the man's partner asked. "He didn't tell us about the lights. Is there a way to turn them on or not?"

Stanton shrugged. "If there's sufficient charge on the batteries, then yes. But I don't know how to turn the lights on."

"Don't know how, or won't say?" the man challenged.

"I don't know," Stanton answered firmly. "I've studied submarine warfare and even written books on it, but how one turns on the lights never came up."

"Guess," the leader demanded.

"I assume that various compartments have light switches. Probably near entrance points. Try there." Stanton nodded to a passageway behind them.

"Do it," the leader said. His cohort turned his flashlight beam toward the bulkhead. A switch was mounted on the metal partition. He turned the switch and the overhead incandescent bulbs came dimly to life. "It's not much, but it will do. Let's go. You first, Captain. Give us the tour and turn on the lights as you go."

Without comment, Stanton rose to his feet, turned, and walked toward the passageway aft of the forward torpedo room. He stepped through, crossing into a narrow corridor. Searching the walls, he found another switch. Again, dim lights came on.

"Pantry to your right," Stanton said, pointing with his finger. "Wardrooms one and two are back-to-back. Chief petty officers' quarters down and to the left."

The leader charged forward, pushing Donna and Stanton to the side. "Keep an eye on them," he commanded. Stanton followed him in. The man was frantically searching the area with his flashlight. Stanton watched as he opened the metal cabinets and rifled through papers and personal possessions, grabbing what he could and throwing it to the floor. "Nothing," he said with anger. "Where is that other wardroom?"

Stanton stepped back into the hall and pointed. "Right there."

Again, the gunman ransacked the room, but came out empty-handed. "You said there were chief's quarters? I want to search it."

"Be my guest," Stanton said. "It's across the companionway. Five steps and you're there." The man made it in three steps. He emerged a moment later swearing loudly.

"It must be here," he said. "I know it's here. I can feel it."

"What are you looking for?" Stanton asked.

"That's none of your business," the man snapped.

"Okay," Stanton said calmly. "There are a lot of places to hide things down here. If you want to search each one by yourself, that's fine with me."

The man swore again, his voice rebounding off the steel hull. "I'm looking for a container, a bag or box or something like that. It has artifacts in it. I want those artifacts."

"Artifacts?" Stanton said.

"That's all you need to know. You'll recognize it if you see it." The man turned to his partner. "Max—" the man stopped abruptly. Stanton could see him cringe at using the name. Then, as if it didn't matter, he continued, "You take the woman and search the pantry and other rooms. I'll take Stanton and search the captain's quarters. Call me if you find anything."

"Yes, Max," Stanton said letting his captors know that he had not missed the name. "You do that."

"Still being cute, Captain? I took you to be a smart man, but it seems I was wrong. Yes, his name is Max. Mine is Hermann. Now what are you going to do with that information? Radio it to headquarters? How many people named Max and Hermann are there in the world? More than you can check out in several lifetimes. Especially if that lifetime is as short as yours may be. Now move. I don't want to spend any longer in this can than I have to."

Stanton led the way to the captain's quarters. Hermann was in it in an instant and turned on the lights. He froze midstep. "What the—"

Peering in, Stanton saw what had brought Hermann up short. On the floor lay a man, a portion of his skull missing.

"Who is . . . was this?" Hermann asked with disgust.

"My guess is Captain Morrison," Stanton answered softly, unable to believe his eyes. "He was the captain of the *Triggerfish*."

"It appears he wasn't too happy about it," Hermann said, looking around the tiny room. "He blew his brains out. Literally."

"He was a good officer," Stanton said. "What could have driven him to this?"

"I don't know and I don't care," Hermann said. "I just want the artifacts and we had better find them, or I'm not going to be happy."

"Perhaps you should care," Stanton said evenly. His stomach turned at the sight of the gore before him, but he kept the persona of composure intact. "You're missing something."

"What? A dead man. I've seen dead men before."

Stanton shook his head. "Captain Morrison was the skipper of the *Triggerfish*. Don't you get it?"

"What?"

"The *Triggerfish* disappeared over fifty years ago. Does this corpse look like it's been here fifty years? Look at him. It looks like he could have done this yesterday."

Hermann looked down at the body. "Maybe it's not Morrison. Maybe it's someone else."

Stanton, fighting the gorge in his stomach, leaned over the body and reached forward.

"What are you doing?"

"Proving my point." Stanton reached under the man's bloodstained shirt and pulled out his dog tags. As he did, something caught his eye. Under the body lay a Colt .45. It must have been the gun Morrison had used to kill himself. His first instinct was to grab it, but the other gunman had Donna.

"I said, what are you doing?" Hermann started toward him. Quickly, Stanton stood and pointed at a pair of dog tags hanging from the dead man's neck. "It's Morrison."

"Back away," Hermann commanded. Stanton did. Showing no sign of revulsion at the gore or respect for the man, Hermann grabbed the dog tags and jerked hard. The neck chain broke easily. He held the identification tags up to the weak light. He then dropped them on the body. "So what?"

"So how do you account for this? How can he still be here? If he were alive, the man would be in his eighties now. If he had been dead for half a century, then he should be a hollow corpse or pile of bones. And what about the blood? Does it look to you like it's been here five decades?"

"I don't care. It's not important. You are trying to distract me from my destiny."

"You can't be that blind."

The shot from Hermann's gun whizzed by Stanton's ear. Instinctively, he ducked and raised his hands in futile effort to ward off an attack that had already occurred.

"I told you," Hermann screamed maniacally. "No more smart remarks. The next bullet will hit you between the eyes. Then you and Morrison can spend the next fifty years together—DEAD!"

The sound of hurried footfalls filled the companionway. Stanton turned to see Donna running his direction. No, not running, but being pushed along by Max. He had his gun pointed at the back of her head with one hand, and was holding her by the collar of her uniform with the other. Donna was struggling to stay on her feet. As they approached, Max shoved her hard. She fell to the deck, sliding on its rough surface. Before Stanton could react, the gunman brought the Beretta to bear on him. Even in the dim light, Stanton could see the frenetic anger in the man's eyes. The same panicked anger rang in his voice.

"On the deck, now. ON THE DECK!" Stanton dropped to his knees, then his face. His head was inches from Donna's. "What's going on?" the man demanded as he looked in the captain's cabin. "What? Are you all right? I heard a shot."

"I'm fine, Max. That was me. I was making a point with Stanton."

"Did you . . . did you do that?" Stanton knew that Max was referring to the body.

"No. We found him like this," Hermann replied calmly. "It looks like he wanted an early discharge." Hermann laughed at his own joke. He laughed alone.

Max sighed noisily. "I thought that Stanton may have attacked you."

"He'd be dead, like his coworker here, if he had."

"Who is he?" Max asked.

"Captain Stanton believes that this was the original commander of the submarine. His dog tags show the name of Morrison."

"That can't be," Max said.

"It doesn't matter," Hermann said firmly. "Get up. You too, woman."

Both officers stood. Stanton studied Donna for a moment. "You okay?"

"Bruised a little," she replied. "Is that really Morrison?" she asked.

"Yes," Stanton answered. "Maybe you were right. This *is* a ghost ship."

"It's worse," she whispered. "Much worse."

"Enough talk," Hermann shouted. "It's not here. Where else could a package or bag be hidden on this tub?"

"Anywhere," Stanton answered. "Let's see, we could search the forward torpedo room, the control room, the pump room, the forward engine room, the afterward engine room, the motor room, the after torpedo room. Oh, and there's the crew's mess, berthing area, magazine room. And we don't want to forget the conning tower, battery space, and radio room. Of course, this boat has two hulls, so it could even be stored somewhere between. Then after that—"

Hermann screamed at the top of his lungs. Even Max took a step back. "I want those artifacts and I want them now!"

No one spoke. Stanton wanted to push Hermann as much as he could without sending him over the top. Hopefully, he would make a mistake and if he did, Stanton would be there to seize the opportunity. He also wanted to slow the search, hoping that someone topside could figure a way to save the people on the bridge.

"All right, all right," Hermann said, calming himself. "We will continue our search by working our way to the back of the boat. We will check every locker and storage area. If we don't find the items that way, we'll start looking deeper."

Thumpa, thumpa, thumpa.

The two terrorists tensed. "What was that?" Hermann asked.

"I don't know," Max responded. "Troops on the deck?"

"No," Stanton said. "Those weren't footsteps."

"Then what were they?" Hermann demanded.

"I don't know," Stanton said. "We heard it before. When we were topside."

"It's them," Donna said emotionlessly. To Stanton, she seemed dazed. "It's them."

"Them who?" Hermann demanded.

Donna shook her head slowly, as if she were in a trance. "Them."

"What do we do now?" Max asked coolly.

"We finish our search. The authorities would not risk blowing up the bridge and killing all those people. Besides, we have hostages in here."

"Maybe they found a way to rescue the bridge people," Stanton suggested.

"Impossible. My plan is foolproof."

"No plan is foolproof," Stanton said. "Just ask Stalin, Mussolini, or Hitler."

"Hitler made his mistakes," Hermann said. "I've learned from them. Now move. We have work to do."

The search continued for two hours. Every cabinet, locker, and cubbyhole was examined. Nothing was found. But what Stanton saw shook him to the core. The food in the pantry and galley were fresh, and date stamped 1943. Ashtrays were filled with the butts of cigarettes that looked as if they had been snuffed out only hours before. Through the diesel-tinged air, he could smell the scent of men. Playing cards and a game of checkers sat undisturbed on a table in the crew's mess. On two bunks in the berthing area were letters left unfinished, pencils resting by lined paper. Magazines and paperback novels lay on mattresses.

And then there was Donna. She walked zombie-like through the enigma, not speaking and gazing through unblinking eyes that darted back and forth. Stanton wondered what she was seeing that he was not.

N
人

Donna was cold, chilled deeper than anything she had experienced before. Worse than the cold was the loneliness. Stanton was there. The two gunmen were there. But she was alone. She knew that they did not see what she saw; they did not hear what she heard.

Something to her left moved. She cut her eyes to see what it was, but it was gone. This did not surprise her; she had been catching glimpses of undefined movement since she stepped foot off the ladder in the forward torpedo room. Flashes, glimmers, smears of white, danced just out of sight, just beyond her vision.

She moved slowly although her heart beat wildly.

There was a buzzing, like a million flies huddled together on fresh carrion. A fog, white and diaphanous, floated through the submarine, oozing in through the hull. She started to ask Captain Stanton if he saw it too, but didn't. If he had, he would have commented.

The fog thickened. It possessed no odor, no dampness. It just . . . was. Donna could not say why, but she felt the fog was alive, that it had intelligence. There was no doubt in her mind that it possessed a will.

It was as she and the others passed through crew's quarters that she first saw them. In the beginning they were indistinct and few, but their numbers began to grow and they became more substantial. They sat on the beds, hung from the walls and ceilings like insects, and even hovered in midair. Several clung to the gunman named Hermann's back. He did not seem to notice.

She had lost her mind. That was the only solution she could believe. Somewhere in the stress of the last few hours, she had rounded the bend of insanity. Nothing else would explain these child-sized creatures with the large heads and bulbous eyes.

The milk-white mist thickened.

An old saying floated to the forefront of her consciousness: "If you are rational enough to question your sanity, then you are sane." It brought her little comfort as she watched the creatures move about. Their movement was funny, unusual in degree and manner. They did not scamper or crawl or walk. They just traveled the distance from where they were to where they wanted to be, moving through all three dimensions.

They were intelligent, Donna had decided. They seemed to act with purpose and even communicate with each other. She noted something else unusual about them. They were interested in just two people, Hermann and her. They followed Hermann like hyenas waiting for just the right moment to attack. The creatures ignored the other masked man. As he walked through the sub, they paid him no attention, not moving out of his way, allowing him to walk through them. Somehow this seemed normal to Donna. Nothing was surprising any longer—except one thing: Captain Stanton. The creatures, whose numbers kept swelling until every foot of the submarine was occupied, filling the boat like bees fill a hive, avoided Stanton. Wherever he walked, they backed away. It was as if his touch was poisonous to them. Their faces, which showed little emotion, seemed to twist into expressions of revulsion. Or was it fear?

Those around her were more aggressive. The beings on the floor reached up to her. Those who clung to the ceiling stretched out thin willowy arms at her head, grasping, clawing. She felt nothing of their touch, but she could hear them. The buzzing she heard before had grown, adding incessant whispering. Buzzing. Whispering.

They called out to her: "Donna. Donna. Donna." She raised her hands to her ears but the sounds did not diminish. Instead they broadened like a symphony crescendo. To the buzzing and whispering was added clicking and chirping. Clicking and buzzing and whispering and chirping. It was a discordant chorus, a symphony of evil.

"Lieutenant?"

Now ringing. Buzzing. Whispering. Clicking. Chirping. Thick white mist. Creatures crawling, mewling, filling, occupying, grasping, clawing. Thousands upon thousands. Choking. Gasping. Suffocating.

"Lieutenant? Are you okay?"

Donna looked up into the worried face of Captain Stanton, who had taken her by the arms. "No. No, I'm not. We are all going to die."

Chapter 20

Tears raced down Donna's cheeks. Her eyes were vacant and seemed to stare at things that were not there. Stanton felt her shudder. Her skin was moist and clammy. He feared that she was plummeting into shock.

"Look at me, Lieutenant." Stanton shook her. "Look at me. That's an order."

"What's going on?" Hermann demanded. "This had better not be a trick."

Stanton ignored him. "I said look at me, Lieutenant Wilcox. You will look at me right now!" Slowly Donna turned her head and looked into Stanton's eyes. "Are you with me, Lieutenant?" No answer. "I asked you a direct question, sailor. I want an answer." *Come on*, Stanton thought. *Stay with me.*

"I'm . . . I'm here." Her voice was weak. Stanton expected her to pass out any moment.

"Greater is he that is in you, than he that is in the world." Stanton's voice was firm, loud.

"They're everywhere, Captain. Everywhere."

"Say it," Stanton commanded. "Greater is he that is in me, than he that is in the world."

"The mist. The sounds." She tried to raise her hands to her ears again, but Stanton stopped her.

Stanton shook her violently. "Look at me, Lieutenant." *Hawking was right*, Stanton said to himself. *There is evil here. This ship is demonic.* With that realization came the understanding that the greatest danger was not the gunmen, but the unseen. The preparation for this battle had not been in the training he received from the navy, but that which he received through faith. He understood now; he appreciated the complexity of the problem. There were great gaps in his understanding, but he knew that Hawking had been right all along and that meant that his only hope was found in God. It was also the only hope Donna had of surviving. Stanton sensed that the stress from seeing what they could not could kill her.

"I don't have time for this," Hermann said and started toward them.

Stanton spun on his heels, holding Donna with a vise-like grip with one hand and pointing a finger at Hermann with the other. "One more step and I'll feed that gun to you piece by piece. Do you get me, Mister?"

To Stanton's surprise, Hermann took a step back. Not even the mask he wore could hide the shock he felt. Stanton turned back to Donna. He pulled her close, wrapping his arms around her, and placed his mouth close to her ear. "Help her, Jesus. Help her," he prayed softly. Then to Donna he whispered in her ear, "Greater is he . . . say it, Donna. Greater is he that is in me, than he that is in the world. Pray it, Donna, pray it. Jesus can and will help. Pray it."

Her body was melting in his arms. She was losing consciousness.

"Say it with me," he pleaded. "Greater is he—"

"Greater . . ."

"Yes, yes. Say it. Greater is he that is in me—"

"Greater is he that is in me," she whispered, "than he who is in the world."

"Yes, that's it. Believe it, Donna. Believe it."

"They don't like you," she said absently. "They want me; they want him." She weakly raised a hand toward Hermann. "But they don't like you. You scare them."

"Not me, Donna," Stanton whispered in her ear. "Not me, but Jesus. Jesus frightens them. He is greater than them. He is in me, and he can be in you. Pray it, Donna. Pray it now. Believe it."

"Greater . . . is . . . he . . . that . . . is in me." Donna blinked. Then blinked again. For Stanton it was if he had seen the dead come back to life or glimpsed the first moment of creation. He felt her flaccid muscles tighten. She gulped in air.

N
Λ

They surrounded her, clung to her. She could feel the creatures slowly entering her mind. But a voice kept calling to her: "Greater is he. . ."

Her eyes were closed, but she could still see them. She could see everything: the sub, the people on the bridge, Stanton, the gunmen, the creatures. Strong arms wrapped around her, a voice whispered in her ear demanding attention, demanding words from her: "Say it, Donna. Pray it, Donna. Jesus can help."

The voice was right. She could see that now. This was beyond her, beyond anyone's ability to help. This required someone special.

"They don't like you," she heard herself say. "You scare them."

"Not me, Donna," the familiar voice said. "Not me, but Jesus. Jesus frightens them. He is greater than them. He is in me, and he can be in you. Pray it, Donna. Pray it now. Believe it."

Yes. That made sense; perfect sense. That was what she needed. All her life, something had been missing. A void, deeper than what she saw the frightening moment she looked over the side of the submarine and viewed the strange abyss, was in her life. Nothing had filled it. Not the navy, not friends, not even family.

"Pray it, Donna. Believe it."

Greater is he that is in me, she said silently, *than he who is in the world*. Things began to change. The creatures were backing away. *Jesus is greater*. They backed further away. *Jesus is greater*. *I believe that*, she thought. *I truly believe that*.

N
Λ

"Say it again, Donna. Say it again," Stanton urged.

"Greater is he that is in me, than he that is in the world." Immediately Donna began to snap her head around. Looking, searching for the invisible. "They're gone. They're gone." Tears brimmed in her eyes like water cresting a dam. "Thank God, they're gone."

Something cold touched the back of Stanton's ear. "If you are quite done with this Kodak moment, I would like to press on."

"Where?" Stanton asked. "We've searched everywhere."

"We still have the back part of the sub to search," Hermann said loudly. "The rooms with the engines."

"The conning tower," Donna said.

"What?" Stanton asked.

"It's in the conning tower."

"How do you know that?" Hermann demanded harshly.

"I heard it. In the buzzing and whispering. I heard it."

Hermann shot a glance at Max, who shrugged. "I didn't hear any whispering."

"The conn," Donna insisted. Stanton looked at her puzzled. "Trust me."

"What's it going to hurt, Hermann?" Stanton said. "You'll probably have to look there anyway. Why not now?" Stanton could see Hermann's eyes narrow.

"Which way?" Hermann asked.

"Forward again, into the control room and up the ladder. There's a small area up there. It's from there the captain would direct his attack."

"What else is up there?" Max asked.

"Periscopes, chart table, things like that."

"All right, let's go. But if it's not there, I am going to put a bullet in her knee. Have *you* got *that*, Mister."

"I hear you," Stanton responded.

Stanton directed Donna in front of him to interpose himself between her and the gunmen. It was a useless heroic. If they shot him in the back, it would take less than a second to take new aim and kill her. No matter how fast she ran, she could not get far enough away to save her life. Which meant that to survive, they would have to find a way to overcome their abductors. But even if they did, that wouldn't help those on the bridge. *One problem at a time*, he told himself. *One problem at a time.*

As they left the crew's quarters and walked past the galley and radio room into the control room, Stanton wished he could take just a few more steps to the captain's cabin. As horrible as it was to see the remains of Captain Morrison, the sight had given him a shred of hope. Lying just under the man's body was a Colt .45 pistol. It was standard issue in the forties. It must be in good shape. Everything else on the sub looked as it must have over fifty years ago. The gun would work. Stanton knew it. And it was powerful enough to shoot through one man and kill the guy behind him. It would be perfect—if only he could reach it.

He thought of sprinting for it. Maybe he could surprise them long enough that they would fail to shoot, or miss him if they did. No, he decided, the idea was ridiculous. He would have to wait. But wait for what?

"We'll have to climb the ladder," Stanton said as the four gathered in the control room. He turned to Hermann. "After you."

"Hardly, Captain," Hermann responded bitterly holding the gun on Stanton. "We will do this the same as before. Max goes first, then the woman, then you, then me. If you so much as twitch in a way I don't like, you die. Or maybe the beautiful lieutenant dies." He nodded at Max, who holstered his gun and sprinted up the ladder. "Now you," Hermann said to Donna. She licked her lips nervously and began the climb. Soon she was out of sight.

"What are you going to do if you find what you're looking for up there?" Stanton asked.

"That's the wrong question, Captain. You should be worried about what I'm going to do if I don't find it up there. Get going. We're wasting time."

Stanton turned, took the cold, smooth steel rails of the ladder in his hands, and started up.

The conning tower was dark. A flashlight beam cut through the black until it fell on Stanton.

"Take two steps to the side," Max said. "And put your hands on top of your head. Both of you."

"What?" Stanton said loudly. "You didn't care where our hands were before."

"Do as I say," Max commanded. "There's not much room in here. I want to see your hands at all times." Stanton and Donna did as ordered. Stanton guessed that Max was getting nervous. Maybe he sensed that Stanton would make a move soon. And he would, if he could think of a move to make.

"What about the lights?" Hermann asked as he climbed into the small room.

"Haven't looked yet," Max said. "I was watching our helpers."

"I have them covered," said Hermann. "See if you can find a way to turn on the lights."

Max's light beam moved off Stanton and was immediately replaced by one from Hermann's flashlight. Stanton watched as Max's light splashed on the surrounding walls and equipment. Over each switch was a small sign that listed its function. He flipped one of the switches. Dull red light filled the command center.

"Red light?" Hermann asked aloud.

"It was used during night attacks," Stanton explained. "It made seeing out the periscope easier. Going from a bright light in the conning tower to peering through a periscope into a dark night required the captain's eyes to adjust. That took precious seconds."

"Is there another switch—" Hermann began. He was interrupted by a gasp from Donna. She dropped her hands from her head and covered her mouth. She stared at a distant corner, behind Max.

"What is it?" Stanton asked. Donna pointed with a quivering hand. Stanton took a step forward.

"Stay where you are," Hermann ordered.

Max turned in the direction of Donna's gaze and suddenly jumped back. He swore loudly. Slowly, keeping his gun leveled at Stanton's chest, Hermann stepped around the shiny metal chart table that was bolted to the deck near the hatchway. He stopped abruptly.

"What is it?" Stanton asked.

"A man," Donna answered softly. "An old, old man."

Stanton shifted his position to see around the chart table. He too lowered his hands.

"I told you to stay where you are," Hermann snapped.

Stanton took another two steps in defiance. Crumpled in the corner was an elderly man dressed in standard issue navy khakis. His hair was dull platinum, his skin thin, parchment brown and deeply wrinkled. He didn't move. Resting on his lap was a doctor's medical bag.

"That's it!" Hermann shouted. "Cover them," he said to Max. Hermann holstered his weapon and stepped to the old man. Kneeling next to the ancient human, Hermann studied his face. A small groan dribbled from the man's lips. "He's alive," Hermann said with disbelief. "How can he be alive?"

"That's not possible," Stanton objected. "We did extensive acoustic tests on this vessel. If anyone had been alive, we would have heard it."

"Even an unconscious, unmoving man? A comatose man?" Hermann said. "Your equipment may be good, but I doubt it is that good."

"Who is he?" Max asked.

Hermann took the bag and looked inside. He chortled, then he laughed loudly.

"What's so funny?" Max asked.

"He is my granduncle," Hermann said. "Brother of my grandfather. He was picked up by the *Triggerfish* half a century ago." He rose and walked to the chart table and set the bag down. Slowly he began to remove objects. A gold statuette, a stone icon, and then finally a spearhead. Hermann held it up to eye level and studied it. Then he kissed it. "This is what we came for," he announced.

"A spearhead and a few trinkets," Max said with disbelief. "All of this for those old things?"

"Not just any spearhead, my friend," Hermann said with a grin. "*The* spearhead."

"I don't get it," Max said.

"That makes two of us," said Stanton.

"Of course you don't," Hermann said. "Very few people would. This is the spear of Longinus. The very spear that pierced Christ's side as he hung on the cross." He brought the iron artifact to his lips and kissed it. "Wars have been fought over this. It has been owned by rulers from Charlemagne to Hitler. Now it is mine."

"You're holding hundreds of people hostage on a bridge for an ancient spearhead?" Stanton said angrily.

"I've told you, it is the spear of Longinus. It holds unique powers. For example, Captain, did you know that no army that has possessed this spearhead has ever lost a battle?"

"If memory serves me correctly," Stanton answered, "Hitler lost his war."

"That he did, Captain, but he was no longer in possession of the spear. It had been stolen from him. Stolen by dear old granduncle. Word has come down through our family about the theft, but no one knew if it was true. This man just dropped off the face of the earth. Last word anyone had was that he had been picked up by the *Triggerfish* and was headed to Scotland. It appears that he didn't make it."

"How could you know that?" Stanton asked.

"Your Captain Morrison transmitted a message relaying the details about my granduncle's rescue in the Atlantic. That message was intercepted. Despite Allied coding, the German navy was able to decipher part of the message. Unfortunately, they learned such things too late."

"I don't consider it unfortunate," Stanton said.

"Of course you wouldn't," Hermann said. "Not that it matters. With this the New Reich will soon be in place again. We will be unstoppable."

"New Reich?" Stanton said the words as if they had soured in his mouth. "Is that what all this is about? You think that you can raise a New Reich?"

"You had better get used to the idea. You will be living under our rule someday."

"All of this so you could get your dirty little paws on a pseudo-occult object which you think will make you the most powerful man in the world." Stanton shook his head in disbelief.

"I will finish my mission and the world will be changed for it. You, of course, will be dead."

"What about him?" Max asked, motioning to the old man on the deck.

"There's nothing we can do for him," Hermann asked. "We can't carry him out of here."

"He's moving!" Donna said with alarm.

Stanton watched as the old man blinked slowly and turned his head. His motions were painful to see. It was clear that he was in his last days, perhaps even his last minutes.

Hermann walked to the man and bent over. "Can you hear me, Uncle Karl?" The man said nothing at first, but turned his head to face the sound of Hermann's voice. Watching the old man struggle to twist his neck just a little filled Stanton with a deep sadness. The old man squinted, a look of puzzlement draped across his face.

"You," he said. His voice was dry and painful to hear, like a gate turning on a rusty hinge. "It's you."

"Me. You couldn't possibly know me," Hermann said. "We have never met."

"They want you," the old man croaked. "They will have you."

"What?" Hermann stood erect. "Who wants me?"

"The spear." The old man raised an enfeebled hand. "The artifacts. Leave them."

"Sorry, old man," Hermann said, clutching the iron head in his hands. "You don't know what I've gone through to get it, or how much it cost me."

"No ... no. You don't understand. They ... they want you."

"Well here I am, old man. Let them come and get me." Hermann laughed.

The old man's arm dropped and his head tilted to the side. A gurgling issued from his mouth. Even across the room, Stanton could see the elderly man had breathed his last. It was as if he had been waiting for Hermann to arrive.

Buzzing. *Thumpa, thumpa, thumpa.* Whispers. Clicking. Clacking. Chirping.

"What the—" Hermann batted at the air as if he were suddenly in the midst of a swarm of biting insects. "Hey. Get ... get off me."

"What are you doing?" Max called out. "What's the matter with you?"

"No, no. Who are you? Get away. Get away." Hermann was waving his arms wildly. He aimed his pistol in front of him and pulled the trigger. The report was deafening as the concussive force rebounded off the hard steel surroundings. Stanton grabbed Donna and forced her to the deck, throwing his body over hers. Another shot. And then another. Bullets pierced sheet metal and pipes.

Stanton's biggest fear was that he would continue shooting blindly until a round found Donna or himself. The Beretta held fifteen rounds. The odds were bad. He had to do something.

"Hey, stop it," Max cried. "You're gonna kill us."

"Get them off of me. They're everywhere. No. No. NO!"

Another shot. This time the bullet hit the hull and ricocheted around the room. *That's it,* Stanton thought. Quickly he moved to his knees, grabbed Donna by the collar of her uniform, and unceremoniously dragged her to the hatchway. "Down the ladder," he whispered. "Now. Don't look back. Just go."

A half second later, Donna's legs were dangling through the opening in the deck. Stanton was still holding her by the collar.

"I can't reach the ladder—"

Stanton dropped her. He heard her hit the steel floor in the control room with a thud. He also heard a small scream of pain.

"Hey," Max shouted, pointing his gun at Stanton. Stanton rolled over on his back and stared down the barrel of the pistol. He wondered if his next sight would be heaven.

"Get them off of me," Hermann screamed. He fired another shot. Stanton covered his head, and Max flinched.

"Hermann, get hold of yourself. You're going to get us killed."

Another shot. This one hit the steel hull and bounced back and struck Max in the forehead. He stiffened, convulsed, and fell backward. His head bounced on the steel deck. Suddenly, Hermann stopped his manic waving. He dropped his arms to his side, gun in one hand, spearhead in the other.

Stanton wasted no time. He rolled over onto his stomach, grabbed the edge of the hatchway, and pulled with all his might. His body slid easily along the floor and, like a diver off a springboard, Stanton went headfirst through the hole, twisting as he fell. Extending an arm to help break his fall, he crashed in a heap, landing hard on his shoulder. Pain, hot and electric, seared through his body. The fall forced the air from his lungs. He rolled on his back. He saw Donna leaning against a bulkhead, holding her ankle.

"Run," he yelled, but with little air in his lungs his scream came out a whisper.

Instead of fleeing, she hobbled toward him, took his arm, and helped him to his feet. She winced in pain as she placed weight on her ankle.

"Stanton!" It was Hermann's voice, or rather something like Hermann's voice. "You are a dead man. We want you. Bring us the girl."

"Run," Stanton croaked. He grabbed Donna by the collar again and pushed her forward through the companionway. One moment Hermann was insanely frenetic, consumed by unseen things; an instant later he was focused and angry.

"Ahh," she cried. "My ankle."

"Run now, feel pain later." A shot flew through the hatch opening barely missing Donna. The two stumbled down the passageway. Behind them Stanton could hear Hermann's boots on the ladder.

"Faster." Stanton was regaining his breath, but his right shoulder felt immersed in flame. It throbbed and it felt as if loose ends of bone were rubbing together. He had broken something, but he had no time to think about it. It was only a few strides to the captain's cabin. It was his only hope. If he had another thirty seconds, he could reach the forward torpedo room and slam the heavy hatchway door sealing Hermann behind them. But thirty seconds was an eternity here. In a moment, Hermann would have a clear shot down the corridor.

"No need to run," Hermann called out. "You can't get away from us. We are Multitude. We are Many. We are Legion. We are Possession."

"We are nuts," Stanton whispered to himself. Two steps more and they would be in Morrison's cabin. As Stanton started to shove Donna into the cabin a bullet struck the corridor wall and bounded down the hall. Hermann was right behind them.

It was then that Stanton passed the point of thinking and began reacting. Without thought he pulled Donna as hard as he could to the right. She stumbled into the captain's cabin and fell on the floor, cushioned by Morrison's lifeless body. She screamed.

Stanton, in a move that surprised him and Hermann, spun and charged the gunman. Seeing Stanton change direction caused him to hesitate. It was enough. Stanton launched himself forward like a tackle on a football team. He struck Hermann hard in the midsection. The man stumbled back but did not fall. The force, however, was sufficient to dislodge the gun from Hermann's hand. Stanton dropped to his knees. The hard impact twisted his broken shoulder. His head was spinning and he felt nauseous. Darkness began to swallow him. He shook his head, valiantly trying to remain conscious.

A boot caught him on the side of head. Stanton fell in a heap. Hermann reached down with one hand and, with superhuman strength, lifted the semiconscious Stanton to his feet.

"We like this game," Hermann said as he brought a vicious knee to Stanton's ribs. The pain was beyond anything Stanton had ever experienced. One good thought fleeted through his dimming mind. At least he no longer had the gun. The next knee to the ribs made the thought seem inconsequential.

Stanton looked up into Hermann's face. It was a twisted sneer of all that was evil, all that was hateful.

Do something, Stanton thought. *Do something or you will black out.*

He watched as Hermann drew his fist back, ready to release it like a battering ram. In his hand was the iron spearhead, its point aimed at Stanton's face. Instinctively, Stanton reached forward with his good arm and seized the front of Hermann's shirt and pulled down. The action jerked Hermann forward and off balance. Stanton pulled his throbbing head back and then brought it forward as hard as he could. His forehead impacted solidly on the bridge of Hermann's nose.

Hermann dropped his hands for a moment, stunned by the unexpected blow. Stanton rocked back on one foot and kicked with the other. His foot landed squarely on Hermann's kneecap. The leg bent backward with a loud snap that sounded like a tree limb breaking. Stanton staggered back two paces. His mind cleared just in time for him to see the unbelievable: Hermann took a step forward, unhindered by the broken leg. The leg provided little support, causing Hermann to waver. No man could stand like that. But Stanton fully understood that Hermann was no longer just a man.

With startling speed, Hermann sprang forward and clamped a hand on Stanton's neck. He began to squeeze. Stanton could feel everything compress. His trachea was being pinched shut. In a moment he would be unconscious; a few moments after that he would be dead.

"We are the Multitude," Hermann said through his sneer.

Stanton brought the palm of his hand up, striking Hermann's elbow, hoping to force him to release his grip. It didn't work.

"We are the Many."

He clutched at Hermann's thumb and tried to pull it back, to break it and thereby break the grip. Nothing.

"We are Legion."

Stanton kicked at Hermann's other knee, but he was too weak, too close to unconsciousness to cause any damage. Blackness, swirling, flickers of light flashing at the edges of his vision. No longer able to support him, Stanton's legs gave way and he slumped to his knees, Kunzig's grip still tight on his neck.

Hermann let go and Stanton fell to the floor. There had been a sound. A harsh, loud sound. A gunshot. Stanton blinked back the darkness. Hermann stumbled back again as another round hit him. Blood spread from his shoulder and cheek. His face turned dark. He started forward again. Another shot, this time in the center of the chest. Hermann was knocked from his legs and crashed to the deck on his back.

Turning, Stanton saw Donna standing in the doorway to Morrison's cabin. Her arms were extended, the .45 in her hand. Tears streamed down her face, but her eyes were fixed with determination, the gun held rock solid on the unmoving Hermann.

"Very timely," Stanton said hoarsely as he stood.

Donna said nothing. She was as still as a statue in the park.

"Thank you, Lieutenant," Stanton said. He could barely stand. One arm hung limply at his side, the other was wrapped around ribs broken by Hermann's merciless kicking. "You can put the gun down now."

Nothing. She was in shock, and as far as Stanton was concerned, she had a right to be.

"Lieutenant, give me the gun." Stanton held out his hand. "Now, Lieutenant." She cut her eyes to him, but still held tightly to the Colt. "Please, Donna. It's over. Let me have the gun."

With the slowest of movements, she lowered her arm. Stanton reached down and took the gun from her hand. Donna leaned forward and rested her head on his chest. Soft sobs filled the room. Stanton leaned back against the corridor partition and let out a deep sigh.

A small metallic rattle echoed down the passageway. Stanton shifted his vision just in time to see Hermann reach for his gun which rested on the deck. With unbelievable speed Hermann brought the weapon to bear and pulled the trigger. Stunned by the sight of Hermann's movement, Stanton raised his pistol a half second later and squeezed off a shot.

Hermann's shot struck Donna with such force that it spun her around. She fell face first to the deck, blood gushing from her shoulder. Stanton's shot hit Hermann just above the left eyebrow. He crumbled into a lifeless heap.

A mist swirled above Hermann's body. Buzzing. Whispering. Clicking. Clacking. Then nothing. The air seemed suddenly warmer.

Stanton turned to Donna. "Nooo!" he cried. Despite his own pain, he dropped to his knees next to Donna. Blood poured from the exit wound at the back of her right shoulder. Stanton, ignoring the roaring heat of pain in his ribs and shoulders, turned Donna over on her back. Her eyes were closed. The bullet had struck her just below the left shoulder and exited below her right shoulder blade. He grabbed the front of her uniform shirt and pulled, ripping it open. A hole, the size of a dime, secreted a steady flow of blood. Next he pulled at his own shirt, popping buttons and tearing material. An avalanche of pain rumbled through him as he pulled the shirt from his broken shoulder. Tears of pain and fear poured from his eyes. Then, holding a portion of the uniform in his teeth, he began to tear with his good hand until he had ripped the shirt in half.

Wadding the material into a ball, he lifted Donna's right shoulder and placed the makeshift compress on the exit wound, then let her roll onto her back. He then pressed the remaining half of the shirt on the entrance wound.

He needed help. But how? He didn't want to leave her. "Oh, dear God," he prayed. "We need you now more than ever."

Thoughts swirled in his mind. Should he run topside and call for help? But what about the people on the bridge? If he popped up suddenly and others raced to the sub, then Hermann's accomplices could blow the bridge. Hundreds would die.

Donna choked. Blood trickled from her mouth. "Greater . . . is . . . he—"

"Don't try to talk. Just lay still."

Metal sounds, loud and harsh, came from the forward torpedo room. A second later the same sounds came from behind him, from the aft portions of the ship. Quickly Stanton looked for the gun and found it next to Donna's leg. He grabbed it.

The pounding of boots thundered through the *Triggerfish*.

"Clear," came an unknown voice.

"Clear," came another.

Stanton looked down the passageway and saw helmeted SEALs with automatic weapons at the ready. They wore flak jackets and night-vision goggles. To Stanton they looked like monsters from a science fiction movie.

The lead SEAL ignored Stanton, stepped over Donna, and charged into Morrison's cabin, gun ready to fire. He stepped back out. "Clear." He then moved on. Several others followed. One remained behind.

"Captain Stanton," he said. "I'm Commander Villa of the SEALs, sir. The bridge has been secured. The sub has been secured and the admiral is safe."

"I need a medic, now," Stanton demanded. "That's an order. I want a medic."

"Yes, sir, one is standing by. We need to get you out of here—"

"No, I want that corpsman here on the double."

"Yes, sir. We will take care of the lieutenant, sir." Villa squatted down to Stanton. "I have orders from the admiral to evacuate whomever we can as fast as we can."

Stanton grabbed the front of Villa's flak jacket. "Listen, Commander," he said loudly. "I will not leave this boat without my crew. Is that clear?"

Villa gave a knowing smile. "Yes, sir. Crystal clear." Putting the microphone of his portable radio to his mouth, he said. "The *Triggerfish* is secure. I need medics on the double."

"Thank you, Commander," Stanton said.

"Don't worry, Skipper. No one dies on my watch."

Epilogue

The salt air swirled around the bridge. Overhead, hungry gulls and terns cried out against a topaz sky. Blue-green water became a froth of white as it passed under the elevated dive planes of the *Triggerfish*. Sailboats, their multicolored sails full of San Diego wind, kept the submarine company as she sailed under her own power around the bay. On the bridge, a small gathering of people soaked in the experience.

"What do you think of her now, Lieutenant?" Stanton asked with a broad smile.

Donna Wilcox returned the smile. "She's a fine boat, Skipper. I'm glad to be aboard. I'd salute if I could." She looked down at the slings that supported her arms.

"You will soon enough, Lieutenant," Stanton said. "You will."

At five knots, the *Triggerfish* made her way toward the Coronado Bridge. "It's hard to believe that just a month ago this bridge held so many people captive," Commander Stewart said. "What a tragedy that would have been."

"I don't know how we would have solved that problem," Stanton agreed. "Kunzig and his gang had our backs to the wall all the way. If his girlfriend hadn't surrendered to her conscience, a lot of people would have died. Once she told the police there was only one other person with a radio detonator, and where he was, then they were able to shut things down. The San Diego police bomb squad was able to disarm the bombs on the bridge and the one in the car with Admiral Robbins. Kunzig wasn't kidding. The bridge would have really come down."

"They captured the drivers of the vans quickly enough," Jim Walsh said.

"Yes, again because Kunzig's girlfriend gave names. They were rounded up in less than a day."

"What will happen to her?" Donna asked.

"She's in jail and will remain there for a very long time," Stanton answered. "But not as long as she would have if she hadn't decided to help the prosecution. They closed down the largest neo-Nazi organization in the country."

"Something good did come out of all of this," Walsh said. "The part I like best is that I get to go along for the ride, and I didn't do any of the work."

"You did more than you know, Jim," Stanton said. "I was so stuck in my logic and navy ways that I would never have considered that all this had a spiritual aspect to it. I should have known better. Bringing Hawking into the picture was a stroke of genius."

"You'll make me blush, Captain," Hawking said. "How did you get permission to have me on board today?"

"I just asked the admiral for a favor. He felt like he owed me one. Besides, there is no technology on the *Triggerfish* that could be remotely considered classified. You earned it, Hawking. I owe you a lot. Without your insights I wouldn't have known what to make of the things I saw."

"God gives us all different gifts," Hawking replied. "I could never do what you do. God had you in this place for this time. Who knows how different the future would be if you had not risen to the task?"

"You helped restore my faith," Stanton said sincerely.

Hawking shook his head. "Nonsense. Your faith was present all along. You admitted that to me that day in the conference room. You had done what many Christians have: compartmentalized your faith, leaving it to holidays and Sundays, when in fact it touches on everything we do and everything we are."

Stanton nodded his agreement. "I don't think I'll make that mistake again."

"It looks like the admiral is enjoying the ride," Stewart said, nodding down to the lower deck. Barry Ludlow was holding a microphone to Admiral Robbins. A cameraman stood ten feet away recording the event. "This will make a good story."

"It will at that," Stanton replied. Turning back to Hawking, he asked, "You know, I have a lot of questions for you, Hawking. Since you were out of town, I haven't been able to ask them."

"I do travel quite a bit," Hawking said. "What did you have on your mind?"

"The demons for one," Stanton began. "Why did they suddenly leave? The spear of Longinus was still aboard, as were the other artifacts."

"First, let me reiterate my disclaimer," Hawking said. "We have more questions about the spiritual world than we have answers. Fortunately, the Bible tells us a great deal, but not everything. For example, the Bible gives many accounts of possessions but never tells us how those possessions came about. There has been much speculation and some erroneous conclusions."

"Such as?" Walsh prompted.

"That all demons wish to occupy a body. Do we know that? No. We know that some do, but we can't extrapolate further. It is my belief that Christians cannot be possessed by demons. There are some that will argue that point, but I can't get it to work biblically or theologically. That's why Donna could see the demons recoil from you, Captain. You, like all believers, have the indwelling Christ."

"That's why they left me so suddenly," Donna said. "When I realized my only hope was Christ, they fled."

"They fled because you let Christ in," Hawking agreed. "All through the New Testament, demons found the presence of Christ frightening. They would call out in fear as he dealt with a demon-possessed person."

"That explains why they suddenly left Lieutenant Wilcox," Walsh said, "but not why they left the submarine."

"That's a tough one," Hawking admitted. "It seems that the demons were not attracted to the objects, but to the people the objects attract. They weren't interested in the Canaanite figurines or the spear of Longinus, if it truly is the spear that pierced Christ's side. The demons were attracted to Karl Kunzig. I did some research on him while I was away. The information you provided was exceptionally helpful. I contacted a colleague at the University of Berlin. He teaches history there and is quite knowledgeable about the Nazi fascination with the occult. It turns out that Kunzig left behind some very interesting records. He was setting himself up to be a modern-day Canaanite priest. My guess is, that is when he encountered the demons. He may have assumed that he had successfully contacted the ancient gods."

"Boy, was he wrong," Walsh said.

"Something he found out," Hawking continued. "Anyway, it appears that the demons were attracted to Kunzig, but he could not live forever. That's when they took a liking to his grandson, Hermann. Once both of them were dead they left. That and the obvious reason."

"Which is?" Stanton asked.

"You and Donna," Hawking said. "Christ was working through you. The more dependent you became on Jesus, the more uncomfortable they became. You were not alone down there, Captain. Jesus was with you each step of the way."

"So," Donna said, "it wasn't so much the spear that mattered as it was Karl and Hermann Kunzig. Their hunger for power cost them everything. Even their souls." She paused and looked out over the water. "I almost lost mine."

The crew fell silent for a moment.

"But you didn't, Donna. You didn't," Stanton said softly.

"It was more than a hunger for power; it was an obsession," Hawking answered. "But remember, we don't even know if the spearhead brought on board by Kunzig is the genuine article, and even if it is, we have no reason to believe that it has any mystical powers. I for one doubt it. But Hitler believed it, as did many of his leaders."

"Why take the submarine?" Stanton asked. "And how did they do it?"

"The first question is easy. They took the *Triggerfish* because Kunzig was on it. How they took it, I can't say. Remember my saying that modern physicists speak of multiple dimensions?"

"You said that ten universes have been shown mathematically," Stanton replied.

"Ten or more. The problem is that we can't conceive of them. The human brain can't picture a five-dimensional triangle. We have the same problem that a two-dimensional person would have trying to conceive of a world with three dimensions. There would be nothing in his experience to describe it. The Bible has many examples of the sudden appearance of angels. Often they have a physical form similar to ours, but they seem unconfined by time and space. It appears that they can move physical objects too."

"Like the *Triggerfish*," Donna said.

"Yes, like the *Triggerfish*." Hawking paused, then continued, "It opens up a whole lot of possibilities, doesn't it?"

"And questions," Stanton said. "But I don't suppose you have all the answers."

Hawking laughed. "Not even close. Every answer brings more questions with it."

Stanton directed his attention to the bow and watched the water race by. He had many questions, unanswerable questions. One thing was sure. He would never again take his faith so lightly.

"So," Stewart said, breaking the quiet. "They're turning this old tub into a museum, huh? I think she's going to look grand next to the Star of India. An old ironclad sailing ship and an old World War II submarine."

"She's not so old," Stanton said.

"Did the navy buy all of this?" Stewart asked.

"Would the Coast Guard?" Stanton countered.

"Not for a second."

"The navy's no different," Stanton said. "As far as they're concerned, it was a simple act of terrorism and extortion."

"But they didn't ask for anything," Walsh said. "What do they think they were extorting?"

"The artifacts," Stanton said. "They have some monetary value. In fact, they are being shipped off to a museum in Germany. Technically, that was the spear of Longinus's previous resting place. There will be some lawsuits over that, but they'll retain possession for now."

"That brings up even more questions," Walsh said. "I don't think there will ever be an end to them. There is so much we don't know."

"There is one thing I know," Donna said. "Greater is he that is in me, than he that is in the world."

"Amen to that," Stanton said.

"So this will be your last official duty regarding the *Triggerfish*," Stewart said to Stanton. "Sail her in, give a speech, then back to golf, huh?"

"Nope," Stanton answered. "I have one more job to do."

They looked at him in disbelief. "What job is that?" Stewart asked.

"We found a letter in Captain Morrison's cabin. It was addressed to his wife. According to it, they had had an argument right before he shipped out. He was apologizing in the letter. She's a spry ninety-something still living in Connecticut. She never remarried. His boy is now a businessman in the same state. I'm going to present the letter to them after my speech. I'm glad the navy invited them to this function. They deserve to be a part of all this."

"Will she know about the suicide?" Walsh asked.

"No," Stanton answered. "I'm under orders not to discuss that or what happened to the crew. It's been given a Top Secret classification. The navy has sealed Captain Morrison's log. He made a full account of his actions. We are among the few who know."

"It must have been horrible for Morrison," Donna said.

"I'm sure it was," Stanton said. "Despite the return of the *Triggerfish*, her crew will still be listed as forever on eternal patrol."

From a bustling town to a wasteland, what has happened to the citizens of Roanoke II?

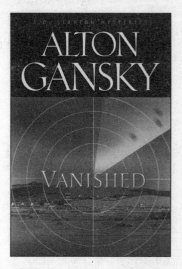

Vanished

Another J. D. Stanton mystery
by Alton Gansky

What sinister secret lies hidden in the town of Roanoke II? How did the entire population of this desert military instillation simply disappear? High-level Pentagon orders call J. D. Stanton, retired navy captain, back to active duty to investigate. Heading a crack team of military, government, and scientific experts, Stanton faces a bewildering scenario. Food still on dinner plates, gas nozzles still in the fuel ports of cars at the filling station . . . Whatever happened took the people of Roanoke II completely by surprise. But took them where?

The answer—far beyond what Stanton could conceive in his wildest dreams— carries a steep price. For forces higher than the Pentagon are invested in the top-secret research of Roanoke II. And they'll protect it ruthlessly. Caught with his team between trained paramilitary killers and an unearthly and deadly enigma, Stanton faces a choice that will stretch his Christian faith to the limits. It could supply answers to the mystery of Roanoke II . . . or unfathomable and irrevocable horrors.

Softcover: 0-310-22003-3

Pick up a copy today at your favorite bookstore!

ZONDERVAN™

GRAND RAPIDS, MICHIGAN 49530 USA

WWW.ZONDERVAN.COM

An exciting suspense story
about a mysterious red stain
spreading over the face of
the Moon

Dark Moon

by Alton Gansky

Astronomy professor Marcus
Stiller discovers a strange lunar phenomenon: a small red stain has
appeared on the surface of the Moon. Though visible only with the aid
of a telescope, the stain is unmistakable. Stiller reports his discovery to
the scientific community and suddenly he is the center of the world's
attention. The puzzle becomes even more amazing when Stiller discovers the enigma is growing at an alarming rate. It spreads across the
face of the Moon, soon becoming visible to the naked eye. Worldwide
alarm follows. Fringe groups spout theories about alien invasions, while
religious figures interpret the event to support their own agendas.

Confusion reigns as more of the Moon's gray surface is covered by
the red stain. A mysterious woman plagued with horrific visions may
hold the key—Julie Waal, who has recently escaped a mental hospital.
Unknown to them, the lives of Marcus Stiller and Julie Waal are irrev-
ocably connected. Marcus Stiller's life plummets deeper into chaos
when an unbalanced man, believing Marcus to be the cause of the
Moon's change, attacks his home and family. Questions abound and
danger grows as the stain covers more and more of the lunar surface.

Is it the end of the world?

Softcover: 0-310-23558-8

Pick up a copy today at your favorite bookstore!